CHRISTANNA

Life among the tribes, slaves, and settlers of North
Carolina and Virginia and their quest
for land, liberty, and for many,
peaceful coexistence.

1713 to 1718

Mac Laird

To Charles Crone,
For the good times,
achievements and stumbles
turned into achievements,
great leadership,
Best wishes,
Your friend
Mac Laird
Dec 2013

i

This historical novel is a work of fiction. References to real names of actual people are explained in the Author's Note. Except as noted in the Author's Note, all other names, characters, places, dialogue, and incidents portrayed in this book are the product of the author's imagination.

Library of Congress Control Number: 20139384754

Cover design by Quail High Books

Published by Quail High Books

www.quailhigh.com

ISBN **978-0-9825443-4-1**

To the memory of colonial Virginians and their
lifelong struggle against encroachment, disease, and
distant government from which evolved the
rugged American individual, the thirteen
united colonies, and finally, the
United States of America.

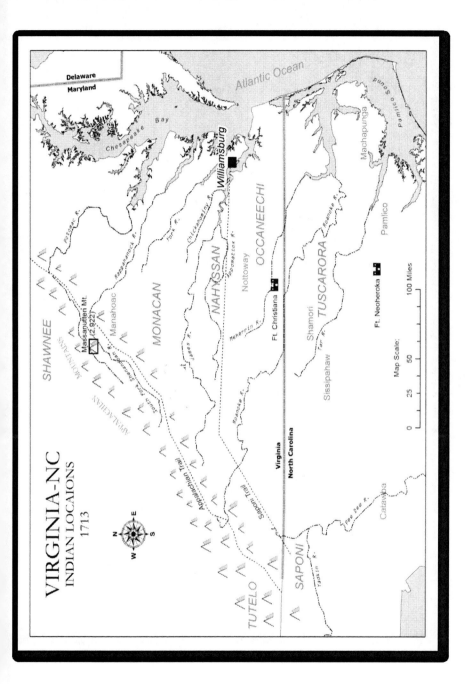

VIRGINIA-NC
INDIAN LOCAIONS
1713

SHAWNEE

TUTELO

SAPONI

MONACAN

NAHYSSAN

OCCANEECHI

TUSCARORA

Manahoac

Massanutten Mt
(2,922')

Nottoway

Shamori

Sissipahaw

Catawba

Machapunga

Pamlico

Williamsburg

Ft. Christiana

Ft. Neoheroka

Delaware
Maryland

Atlantic Ocean

Chesapeake Bay

APPALACHIAN MOUNTAINS

Appalachian Trail

Sodoni Trail

Virginia
North Carolina

Potomac R.

Rappahannock R.

York R.

James R.

Chickahominy R.

Appomattox R.

Meherrin R.

Roanoke R.

Roanoke R.

Tar R.

Pee Dee R.

Yadkin R.

Shenandoah R.

Map Scale:

0   25   50   100 Miles

N
E
W
S

v

FORT CHRISTANNA

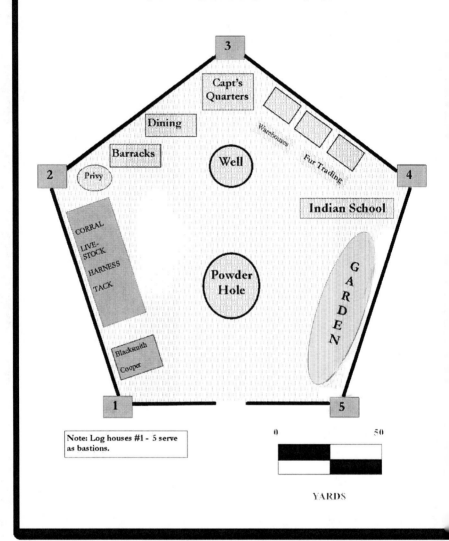

Note: Log houses #1 - 5 serve as bastions.

0   50

YARDS

FOREWORD

In the first quarter of the eighteenth century, settlers, slaves, and the Indian tribes of Virginia struggled against each other for survival at a time when they were threatened by the most powerful nations on Earth: France in the north, Spain in the south, and the British Empire under which they were governed.

Despicable as it was, slavery was well past its infancy in Virginia by 1713 and growing rapidly not only from imported slaves but by the births among existing slaves in the colonies. Plantation owners abhorred and encouraged slavery and lived in constant fear of insurrection. Still, slaves were the chosen source of labor to keep tobacco flowing and settler purses bulging. Under Virginia law, the slave was "property". The slave had no hope, nor was there reason to give him hope. His future was simply to avoid the overseer's whip, and he learned to do that and still resist. Slaves survived beatings, starvation, and ruthless separation from their families in the slave markets, but their *will to be free* could not be enslaved.

Settlers suffered falling tobacco prices and taxation without representation in the parliament of people who lived a seven-week sea-voyage east. English law forbade colonists to trade with anyone but England. They had barely survived two major massacres (1622 and 1644) and Bacon's rebellion (1676), and they were still under constant Indian attack on their southern and western borders. Instead of guns and soldiers to protect their frontiers, the British Crown just sent more and more shiploads of unfortunate citizenry hoping for a better life than the jails, prisons, and hospitals of overcrowded England.

The Indian tribes, already decimated by the European diseases for which they had no immunity and the powerful guns against which they had little defense, had been pushed by the relentless wave of settlers into the foothills of the Alleghenies. They saw their life-sustaining hunting grounds occupied by strangers in overwhelming numbers. In many cases, the chiefs of their tribes bargained away the lands of the people and pocketed the price.

And yet, the individual found ways to survive, even prosper, but the price came high. This book is about that individual and the price: the slave by which Virginia became prosperous; the land-hungry settler; and the proud Indian. You will meet the two young slaves, Zack and Ella, the educated Indian, Kadomico, and a capable young Scot street fighter from Newgate Prison named Seth about to complete his indentured servant contract. Charles Griffin, an extraordinary teacher at the Fort Christanna Indian school, will win your confidence in the ability of one man to make a difference in the face of staggering odds. According to one visitor from France, the Indians loved this Englishman so that they would have made him their king if he had permitted it.

Christanna is the story of six of these individuals and their extraordinary achievements and devastating failures. It was a time when these six and many more like them began to embrace liberty, free enterprise, and self-sufficiency from which eventually emerged the bedrock of the American individual.They were willing to account for themselves and unwilling to yield one iota of freedom and liberty while they were about it. It took time, but these settlers, slaves, and Indians began to define what they would later document as *unalienable rights. . . life, liberty and the pursuit of happiness.* The legislators, patriots, and politicians who signed the *Declaration of Independence* are well known. Now meet the kind of people who made such extraordinary human endeavors possible and forever enduring.

1

The first lash of the whip drew a sliver of dark skin from Zack's right shoulder diagonally down almost to the waist. Pain burned through his back and into his chest; his body shook as though struck by lightning. Summoned by the terror of lashes yet to come, sweat formed and trickled across his face and neck. Zack Hunter tightened his lips over clenched teeth and choked back the scream. He took that first lash in silence and waited for the whistling arrival of the next one and the other twenty-seven to follow. When they cut him down from the whipping post, he was still conscious, still silent.

Albert Ripken placed his whip in the holder under the shed roof and growled as he pointed to the closest group of slaves. "He's working new ground tomorrow. See he's ready at sunup."

Master of the cart-whip and the top overseer at Green Spring plantation near Williamsburg, Virginia in the spring of 1713, Ripken had many years of slave management experience. He could open a line of flesh to the bone or let only the braided popper at the end of the whip make contact in some tiny untouched area. Sometimes he made the whip crack so loud the sound would make a bystander tremble.

Wisely, Ripken had spared Zack a whipping that would render him useless. After all, Zack was the best slave driver on the plantation, and Al himself had taught him how to use the lash to hurt, take skin, or frighten. He was not about to render Zack useless, not even for a day. Slaves were difficult to train as slave drivers; they were never to be trusted, but without good ones, crops failed, plows broke mysteriously, harvests suffered, and the overseers were held accountable.

Now the thing was done, the lesson delivered, the slaves would stay in line, and Zack would recover. Ripken wiped the sweat from his face, reached in his pocket for the little container of rum, and headed for the cool water of the spring.

The slaves swarmed over Zack and placed their hands under him from head to toe, lifted him gently, and carried him across the whipping-post yard. No one spoke. They walked silent, heads down. They'd made this trip often, and although blood oozed from massive welts on Zack's back, twenty-nine lashes was light punishment—twenty and nine, the slaves called it, that was the usual whipping for small offenses; a hundred, sometimes more, for the more serious offenses: runaway, disrespect, and outright disobedience.

Zack felt the cool surface of the pine-board table against his bare chest and stomach as they eased him down. He turned his head, let his cheek rest on the boards, and tried to ignore the pain tearing at his back. It would heal, he thought. Something was different though, a realization, a surety not yet identified, but nevertheless a cool reality— and then, he knew.

Troubled for many months by thoughts of running away, he had always believed he could succeed where others had failed although he did not know of a single runaway who had escaped. Worse yet, he had no place to go, no one to help him. The colonies, north and south, shared the commitment to capture and punish runaway slaves. To the east lay the ocean, to the west lay an unknown wilderness. He often thought of the wilderness and the Indians out there. Maybe they would help him, maybe not. But this whipping convinced him—he had to run away, and he began to plan.

Gladys, dry-eyed in a face frozen with hatred of the man who did this, silently smoothed a salve of animal fat and medicinal herbs over the whip wounds. She had grown to love Zack as much as a mother would love a son.

Born a slave here at Green Spring twenty years ago in 1693, Zack had never known his father, and the owner had sold his mother when he was seven years old—just before he was old enough to work in the fields. Gladys was twenty-seven at the time. She had made a place for him to sleep in her quarters and shared her food with him. It was Gladys who had added Hunter to Zack's name. Gladys knew his parents well.

"Zack Hunter," she'd said. "Now you named proper." Although she reminded Zack from time to time, the name was not recorded until many years later when she told Hannah Ludwell, mistress of Green Spring plantation, hoping that she would correct the records. At the time, few slaves had registered surnames, but Mistress Ludwell had seen to it that Green Spring records were changed.

As he grew older, Zack began to enjoy special treatment by the owner's son, 41- year-old Philip Ludwell II. Philip's aging father now looked to his son for management of the estate. Zack often accompanied Ludwell II on hunts through the fields and forest, carried the powder and ball, and retrieved the birds that fell to Philip's fowling piece; he also gathered the downed squirrels and rabbits, and afterwards, he skinned the game and dressed it for the kitchen. On these trips, Zack learned many things about the forest and streams, things that few others knew, and *no* other slaves knew: the richest berry patches, nut trees, medicinal plants, highly coveted straight-grained trees, and how to find and follow the animal trails.

The two Green Spring overseers were white men. During planting, hoeing, and harvesting, they selected and trained slave men to see that the large groups of slaves worked in unison at peak performance—no lagging, resting, or other interruption to the rhythm of their work—no wasted motion. The lead worker set the pace. The others followed faithfully or endured the slave driver's scolding voice and the crack of his whip. The work of good slave drivers was the key to successful farming. Unlike the white indentured servants who were working out their contracts before their eventual release, most slaves who worked the fields had no contracts, no hope of release, and thus, no reason to work except to avoid the whip.

As Zack grew and matured, the overseers gave him special attention because he learned quickly, was respectful, helpful, obedient, and stayed "in his place." Eventually, he came to know the overseers so well that he could anticipate what they wanted—this team of horses, that ox cart, how much water, which tools. He rarely spoke or needed to beyond, "Yassuh, Massa." Therefore, it was natural that the overseers chose him to carry messages, fetch their food at noontime, and handle livestock. Slowly they turned him into a slave driver with a sound understanding of working slaves, farming, and the skills of the whip.

Zack had a natural curiosity that extended beyond the labor of a task to the "why" of it and to the results of it. Consequently, he learned more, dangerously more, than slaves who were allowed to learn only enough reading and writing to serve some special purposes on the plantation, like keeping inventories and marketing records. He soon found that the less he spoke, the more eager the white people were to teach him to do their work: gathering, cleaning, clearing new ground, planting, tilling; and later, mending harness, weighing and packing tobacco hogsheads, and working the horse and ox teams. Lately, he had begun to admire the knife work of the coopers, carpenters, and cabinetmakers. How he would love to know how they fitted and fastened barrel staves, framed a wall, or built a cabinet of shelves. He saw these things and found excuses to visit the makers hoping to learn. But they seemed to guard the secrets of their trade. Occasionally, however, the artisans sent him for working stock with instructions on how to choose it. Thus, Zack learned a little each day and began to apply his knowledge to simple things like making hooks and pegs from green wood limbs and twigs. Because he often used his knowledge to help his fellow slaves, they generally accepted Zack and his special position.

Gladys was the invisible counselor and leader of the slave population. The news of a change of any sort seemed to reach her first. Better than any other slave, she seemed to know and understand plantation matters. The Green Spring slaves looked to her, though they were careful not to expose her as a leader among them, careful not to expose her as a threat to the owners. Because the owners lived with the ever-present danger of uprisings, slaves were denied regular assemblies of any kind. They could not own or carry knives, guns, clubs, or any kind of weapon. They could not marry, assemble, vote, testify in court, or use the courts and the law against a white person. Gladys had a sixth sense about these matters, and Zack Hunter owed much of his success on the plantation to her counsel. Thus, he walked a fine line between the sanctions of the plantation management and acceptance by his fellow slaves.

This morning he had crossed the line. Virginia law was clear: twenty and nine lashes on the bare back, . . . *if any slave shall presume to lift up his hand in opposition against any Christian.* Zack broke the law when he came between an overseer and a slave who was about to be punished. He knew better, but he had not had time to think. He knew he could explain the slave's innocence, so he had stepped between them and raised his hand a little to be heard. Both overseers and many slaves were present. The whipping demonstrated the penalty of opposing an overseer, and although only the courts could sentence a white person to be whipped, a slave owner had the legal right to punish slaves as he saw fit without interference of colony or British law.

2

Kadomico, a twenty-seven year old Saponi warrior from the Yadkin River country of North Carolina, stood well concealed behind the upright roots of a huge fallen white oak as he checked the area where his party of nine warriors rested. There was little evidence of their presence—no barricades, no campfire, no hastily assembled shelters. Thanks to the storm winds of many years ago, they used the gigantic limbs of the old blow-down white oak for a natural barricade and the forest undergrowth to conceal them. Nearby, a tiny stream spilled over limestone, past clumps of plump cressie greens growing profusely along the bank. Their tiny pale green leaves had grown fat with juice and now dipped into the cold water. Kadomico thought how excited the Saponi women would be to find such an abundance of these fine greens.

Satisfied with the security of their campsite, Kadomico eased his slender, six-foot, body down to a sitting position with his back against a young beech tree. His jet-black hair, tightly banded at his neck, fell in two parts upon broad, naked shoulders that had recently been relieved of a quiver of many war arrows. The quiver now rested by his side with a powerful bow of Osage orange. Before him, a chest-high tangle of blackberry and honeysuckle released unmistakable sweet scents, and made a perfect blind. Tomorrow they would join the North Carolina militia, commanded by Colonel James Moore, in the fight against the enemy Tuscaroras at Fort Neoheroka.

North Carolina had been at war against the Tuscarora since September of 1711 when the Tuscarora captured, tortured, and then executed John Lawson, a North Carolina surveyor and historian. While that event provided the spark, the actual cause was much more complex, long standing, and centered around the endless waves of Europeans encroaching on Tuscarora hunting grounds.

Kadomico sat still, his knees drawn up close against the barely moving, cool, March night air. Sleepless, he pondered the task before him. The nine warriors with him came from a mixture of tribes: Tutelo, Occaneechi, and Saponi. Last year, he had visited the Trading Ford, a place in North Carolina where several Indian trails crossed and trading flourished among the Indians. There he had learned that the Yamasee and several other tribes had allied with North Carolina in their war against the Tuscarora and that they were looking for more warriors. He also learned that once the Tuscarora fell, their territory would be re-opened to white settlers. He then reasoned that to join North Carolina in the fight against the Tuscarora would likely be beneficial to Kadomico's people, especially if they could share in the redistribution of hunting rights to the land along Virginia's south border.

The forces of Colonel James Moore, just under a thousand South and North Carolina Indians and thirty-three militiamen, spent the night about two miles south of Fort Neoheroka. Their mission was to rid the settlers of the Tuscarora threat. For nearly three years, terrified settlers had crammed themselves into the town of Bath for protection, not daring to venture back to their farms while the war raged on. Now the Tuscarora, having been defeated in other parts of North Carolina, had spent a full year preparing Fort Neoheroka for this final stand.

Kadomico and his band hoped to return to their people victorious, with the promise of new hunting grounds and the friendship of North Carolina magistrates. A large part of that land was on the Virginia-North Carolina border not far from the site of a fort planned by Governor Spotswood of Virginia. It would be named Fort Christanna after Christ and the popular Queen Anne. Indian raids on Virginia's southern frontier had successfully blocked further settlement there, but Fort Christanna would make it safe again. The fall of Fort Neoheroka would provide additional assurance. Several allied tribes had agreed to participate in the construction of Fort Christanna and hoped to supply guards for the project when it was completed. Kadomico saw that as an opportunity to strengthen his people's position with the English and to work toward alliances with neighboring tribes. Therefore, it was not surprising that he had emerged the leader of the Saponi, Virginia's point of contact for matters involving native tribes.

Now after several years of off-and-on attendance at the College of William and Mary, Kadomico spoke flawless English. He had been encouraged to take classes there in the years preceding the formal establishment of the Brafferton Indian school. He was well known and had many friends in Williamsburg, the Virginia colony capital. Governor Spotswood was delighted that he would have Kadomico's support at Fort Christanna. Approval by the Burgesses was almost certain, and construction would begin in the spring of next year, 1714. The news of the Tuscarora war and the beginning of Fort Christanna gave Kadomico hope for a better future for his people who, like the Tuscarora, had lost most of their lands and hunting grounds to the Europeans.

His thoughts turned back to the present. He reckoned they were less than a half-day's trek to Fort Neoheroka, where they would meet the Moore army and join the siege. Even with overwhelming numbers, Moore would have a tough fight on his hands. In addition to being among the most ferocious of Indian warriors, this time the Tuscarora would be fighting for their very existence. There would be no surrender and few if any prisoners. They will fight to the death, he thought, all of them, women and children as well. Nevertheless, the English will not be defeated, and even if they are defeated, they would come again in even greater numbers and with bigger guns. It was a lesson Kadomico had learned well over the years on his visits to Williamsburg and during his studies at the college.

In desperation for a way to coexist peacefully with the settlers, his Saponi people had sent him to Williamsburg when he was fourteen to learn about the talking papers, to learn to read and write, and to see the way of the English. Several other tribes had participated at the Virginia governor's invitation, but only Kadomico returned to the college after the first term. Once he'd learned how reading worked, how he could see marks on paper and know what they referred to, he became a serious, dedicated student with an insatiable appetite to understand and to learn more. Now, thirteen years later, he was still welcome at the college, and he visited as often as he could for short courses and when summoned by the college to assist in matters concerning the management and teaching of Indian students. On these visits he wore English clothing and behaved differently, smiling, shaking hands, using traditional English greetings and table manners. In Williamsburg, he always considered himself a guest and politely tolerated the inevitable insult from those occasional citizens who harbored hatred and contempt for Indians. Even now, he switched back to his native garb and manner as soon as he could. All that he learned from the white man simply reinforced his pride in his people and their way of life and his commitment to lead them through the coming threats to their town and hunting grounds.

3

Colonel James Moore, Commander of the Carolina Militia, had distributed his forces around Fort Neoheroka keeping it in view to prevent escapes. On arrival yesterday, he had offered old Chief Hencock safe passage to a fair trial for unconditional surrender. His answer had been a strong volley of musket fire. After that, it was a quiet night.

It was still dark outside when Moore opened his eyes and stretched his full length to awaken the long muscles in his legs and shoulders. He shook the heavy blanket aside, sat up, and shivered against the cool March 1713 morning. Camped in the wilderness these days, his long woolen shirt and knee-length stockings doubled for sleeping and daywear, especially in cold weather. They do, however, have their drawbacks, he thought, as he stretched again to scratch an unreachable shoulder blade and finally settled for twisting back and forth against his shirt. His belly signaled hunger, but there would be little time for food this first day of the siege of Fort Neoheroka, the last days of the Tuscarora war.

In the pitch-black darkness, he drew on knee-length breeches, tightened the waist lacing in the back, and reached into a riding boot for his spurs. Knowing that this would be a day of riding the battle line, he buckled the spurs snug before he stood and reached for his waistcoat. He was not up to fumbling with the twelve-button "weskit." Instead, he stepped toward the tent flap where he could see a bit of light from the tiny flames of a dwindling campfire in a circle of cleared ground—his makeshift headquarters for the time being. He ignored the folded greatcoat that had served as a pillow and picked up his sword belt. There would be time enough later for helmet and breastplate if needed, though he rarely used such cumbersome, heavy, and constraining armor anymore.

His waistcoat flapped open against a sudden draft of air as he shouldered a bandolier and stepped outside. He walked past the campfire toward the smoldering coals of a tiny cooking fire and a kettle of hot tea.

"Mornin', Colonel. 'S mighty early, sir." The night orderly spoke softly as he filled a tin cup with tea for Moore.

"It's all of that, Calvin and, yet, maybe not early enough. Get Captains Burns and Rivers over here. I'm going to the woods and have a wash-up in that spring you mentioned yesterday." He accepted the steaming tin cup and turned toward the spring and the barely perceptible first light of day. As he made his way among the arousing men and their tents, he felt renewed confidence that his army of over nine hundred Indians and thirty-three militiamen would destroy the fort. He was less certain about how much time it would take and how many lives would be lost.

He had been with Colonel John Barnwell, also of South Carolina, during the last two years on a campaign to free the territory of Indian raids on the frontier settler farms. In the last three years, the Tuscarora had set out to reclaim all their hunting territory along the Pamlico and Trent Rivers, and to drive the white man away—they hoped forever. They used every means available to send terror through the settler communities; they tortured, mutilated, dismembered; and spared no one, not women, children, or the infirm, and not the aged. The news of these horrors had spread so far that even settlers on the western frontier and other places far from the fighting fled their homes. No North Carolina frontier family was safe, and they knew it. Nor did they

11

believe that the current peace was any indicator of future safety. On the other hand, the Tuscarora were badly outnumbered and outgunned, and they did *not* know it until it was too late. The Carolina militia, augmented by allied Indians, just kept coming. Indian fort after Indian fort fell to the Barnwell campaign until now—Fort Neoheroka, standing strong and silent in the first light of day.

Moore also knew from trader reports over the last few months that this fort was a masterpiece of defense architecture. It incorporated design similar to pre-historic fortress construction but also some surprising features of colonial and European fortresses: semi-subterranean hardened houses, two-tiered fighting positions at the palisade walls, and support platforms made of earth and logs layered horizontally to raise the fighters to the firing slits.

Yesterday he had seen that the ground on which it was constructed rose much higher than imagined at the briefings last year. The enemy's high ground advantage was going to be troublesome. In addition, the bastions at the four corners of the fort rose above and protruded beyond the wall line all along the palisade walls. Walls stood twelve-feet above ground anchored three feet in a trench. Where knots, warps, or curves caused gaps between the pales, they had lashed smaller pales to close the openings.

Captains Burns and Rivers were working on hot tea and yesterday's biscuits. They rose to acknowledge Moore when he stepped into the firelight.

"Planning a siege in the comfort of the headquarters building back in Fort Barnwell is one thing. Facing it on the battleground is another. What think 'e, gentlemen, now ye've seen it?" Moore asked. He sipped the last of his tea and spit a stubborn tealeaf as he sat down and motioned his subordinates back to their seats.

Flickering firelight exposed the wrinkles in Burns' forehead as he pondered Moore's question. Since the beginning of the war in 1711, he had been with Barnwell and Moore as they destroyed one Tuscarora fort after another. Barnwell had returned to South Carolina. Moore took command along with a promotion and stayed. Good man, Colonel Moore, smart Indian fighter, wilderness wise, good soldier, Burns thought.

"Well one thing's certain, Colonel. That clearing 'round the wall in front 'o them firing slits makes an attack on foot today too costly. We'd pay a heavy price 'f we try it before we soften it up with cannon and sharpshooting like we figured back at Fort Barnwell. I think the plan is still good, but it's sure to take more time than we thought."

Rivers nodded agreement.

Cooking fires began to show throughout the visible woods. A fierce looking young warrior wearing Yamasee war paint trotted toward their sentry. Captain Rivers rose and walked toward them, spoke with the sentry a moment, and returned.

"He's a messenger from the Yamasee Chief Black Hawk. He says ten more warriors have joined him. One of them is a Saponi war chief named Kadomico. Speaks English and has been inside this fort. The messenger waits in case y' have a reply, sir."

"Rivers, better send one of your lieutenants back with the messenger. Thank Chief Black Hawk and tell him we welcome the warriors, then see what this Kadomico has to say."

"Aye, Colonel." Rivers summoned an orderly and made the necessary arrangements.

Moore turned his attention to the fort. A large expanse of cleared land protected the fort on three sides from surprise attack. On the backside lay a swampy area where a man would bog to his knees before he could reach the fort—a virtual killing field. On that same side, a branch of the parent creek ran close to the palisade wall so that water remained available during a siege. Inside, just over a thousand armed, barricaded, and battle-ready Tuscarora waited for the inevitable cannon fire.

Moore said, "Burns, have two of your cannon target the gate. As soon as you have an opening in the wall, have another work the interior with grape. Begin firing when you can see the targets. After a few cannon shot we'll give them one final chance to surrender. Watch for my cease-fire order and for motions to surrender or talk. If that gate falls, and I doubt it will any time soon, saturate the inside with cannon fire and prepare to hit with every man we have. In the meantime, keep the sharp shooters and the other cannon trained on the bastions. We want those firing positions destroyed before we storm the fort."

Burns acknowledged the order and left as the commander turned back to the battlefield before him. Under the cover of darkness, the sharpshooters, bowmen, and cannon teams had set up barricades and trenches within killing range of the fort. Deployed in a semi-circle to face three sides of the fort, they also kept the swamp side under close watch. The four cannon that he had managed to bring, sometimes in litters slung between two horses through sloughs, ravines, and over shallow creeks, were key weapons. The fort would fall, but whatever was to be done, it must be done quickly. There were over a thousand men to feed and keep supplied with weapons and ammunition.

The resounding booms of the cannons and muskets shattered the morning silence, and the rising white smoke plumes exposed their location to clouds of arrows and murderous musket balls from the fort. The shooting slits and bastion positions of the fort had the protection of thick logs and barricades. The firing from the fort could be furiously fast if they chose. A musket man fired at the enemy smoke plumes, stepped aside for the next musket man and reloaded, ready for his turn at the firing slit, little more than a second between shots. The men behind the smoke had to move fast.

As long as their ammunition held out, the advantage was clearly with the fort, but they had no way to resupply. Moore, however, remembered one siege that had lasted ten days before a burning fort surrendered. Too long, he thought.

Not far behind his battle line Moore noticed some tall trees on a hill, out of firing range of the fort and decided to have a look. Responding to Moore's motion, a young soldier led his horse forward. Moore pulled on gloves, gathered the reins, swung into the saddle, and steadied his mount. Fresh from a full night's rest and a belly full of fresh spring grass shoots, the horse was eager to move and resisted Moore's reins with a slightly bowed back and two stiff legged half-jumps before he settled down.

"Rivers, follow me, and bring someone to climb and have a look at the inside over there."

While he spoke, two Indians appeared. Moore cursed. After all these years of fighting Indians in the wilderness, he still did not understand how they could move in full sight and not be seen.

"Thunderation! Where on God's green earth are the bloody sentries?" Moore exclaimed. Still, he knew that it was not a matter of sentry carelessness. He'd once lost a bet to an Indian when he boasted that his sentry line could not be penetrated. The next morning the Indian had handed him the musket of one of Moore's sentries and asked him to check the soles of the boots of others. Sure enough, unknown to three of the sentries, their boots had been marked with a white X. Moore never forgot the lesson.

Rivers was already on his feet with his pistol pointed across the campfire at the nearest intruder who had raised his open hands in peace.

Moore sighed in defeat. "Ease up, Rivers. If they wanted to kill us we'd already be dead."

Kadomico spoke in perfect English, "The white commander of this army speaks the truth. Your sentry refused to admit us to your presence. We simply went away and returned from a different direction—in peace. I am Kadomico, War Chief of the Saponi and Assistant to Governor Spotswood of Virginia. This is Tree Son, Senior Warrior of the Saponi. We fight with our friend Chief Black Hawk of the Yamasee who sends us to you."

"Well that's just plain dandy of you," Moore replied, still mounted. "And maybe ye'd explain what happened to the soldier I sent to talk with you and Black Hawk?"

"Apparently, we left before he arrived. For certain, we have not seen him."

Moore dismounted and turned to Captain Rivers. "Send someone into the highest tree over there on that rise. Have a look and get back to us. Let's hear more from this Saponi." Moore had heard of Kadomico. If this paint-smeared savage was the same man, he could be trusted, but that did not explain the proper English flowing from the naked warrior before him.

Tree Son stepped forward and spoke in broken English. "I go. I know the trees."

"It is true," Kadomico said. "Tree Son moves among the trees like a squirrel: unseen, silent, and fast. In addition, he has been with me inside this fort. He will know what to look for."

Moore and Rivers looked at each other for reassurance. Rivers spoke first. "I can send two men with him while we speak with Kadomico."

Moore nodded agreement. "Give them that spyglass out of my pack."

Moore passed the reins of the disappointed mount to the orderly, dismissed him, and motioned Kadomico forward. Tree Son joined the soldiers and trotted toward the higher ground.

The cool sunlight of early spring bathed the scene with the promise of dry weather and, therefore, dry powder for the weapons. Musket fire from both sides had eased.

Ammunition was precious and not to be wasted. Still, every attacker's smoke plume drew three or four musket balls and a flight of arrows from the fort.

Moore ordered food for the three of them and motioned toward a huge fallen white oak tree on the backside of the perimeter. It made good protection against the odd musket ball. Some of its old weather-worn branches, thick as a hog's belly, offered seats. He and Rivers sat down. Kadomico followed their example.

"Kadomico, I know this name as an Indian who speaks among Indian and English parties to settle disputes and make treaties. Are you the same?" Moore asked.

"I am."

"You said Assistant to Governor Spotswood?"

"Yes."

"Well, maybe you can tell us why the good governor refused to send reinforcements to his neighboring North Carolina friends in the time of need and on their mutual borders."

"The governor walks a fine line as he strives to maintain peace on Virginia frontiers among the Indians and the settlers."

"Well, it looks to us like he's content to let us fight his battle on our common frontier border without risking a single Virginian."

"Did he not send generous supplies of powder and ball?"

"True and we appreciate it, but that's not the same as men and guns," Moore said. "Be that as it may, let's get on to your visit here. Do you know this fort?"

"I was in the fort last fall on a trading trip. Previously I interpreted for a Siouan-speaking tribe in an exchange of prisoners with the Tuscarora. I speak their language and they know me, but we are enemies from long ago."

"So tell us what you know of the fort's defenses."

Johnnycakes and honey arrived, and while these flat cakes of fried cornmeal were passed round, Kadomico described the interior structures. He confirmed the use of logs and earth against fire and cannon, and estimated the population at one thousand men, women, and children, perhaps six or seven hundred of them well-armed warriors.

"And the gate?" Moore asked.

"Double walled with logs lying across the entrance, I expect. I did not see this but I did see the frame built to lay the logs in. It would double the strength of the gate, and I saw a great quantity of what looked like reserve logs stacked alongside the frame."

Moore sighed at the waste of ammunition. "Rivers, have Burns cease firing on the gate and join us here," Moore said.

"We'll come back to the cannon fire when my artillery commander, Captain Burns, gets here. How is it that a North Carolina Saponi is Assistant to the Governor of Virginia?"

"I began attending the College of William and Mary in 1700 at Governor Nicholson's invitation and became friends with the widely known Sam Layton, a Shawnee white Indian who worked closely with Governor Nicholson. Eventually, I worked alongside Layton and learned other languages and became a standing member of the governor's staff as an interpreter."

"And why are you here?"

"Not far north, almost on the North Carolina border, Virginia's Governor Spotswood will build a large fort to be militia-manned and with warriors from my tribe as needed. We will move close to the fort on Virginia land that has been marked for us by the governor. All the North Carolina land and the Virginia land near the fort are excellent hunting grounds. We hope to find favor with North Carolina and to share the hunting grounds along the North Carolina border with Virginia."

Moore was having a hard time accepting Kadomico's flawless English. Better than mine, he thought, and wondered for a moment just how much education this savage had. He shifted his position and checked the area for signs of Burns. He saw that the men were improving their barricades and shooting positions, while the fort resumed a withering but futile musket fire at the heavily protected cannon positions. Satisfied for the moment, Moore turned back to Kadomico.

"When Burns gets here, give us the best account you can about those palisades, weakest points in the wall, and so forth. In the meantime, let's see what your friend has to say. Looks like that might be him now."

Tree Son hailed the sentry and went directly to Moore and Kadomico in the safety of the white oak blow-down. "Captives at burning stakes. Maybe three. All women. Not much movement because of the cannon grape. Seventeen houses. All covered in bark. Easy to burn."

"The captives appear alive?" Moore asked, knowing full well that under those "easy to burn" roundhouses probably lay subterranean houses covered with log and earth, not so easy to burn.

"Alive. Yes."

"Colonel, there is a chance we can exchange prisoners. I speak the language of the Tuscarora. If you will stop firing, I will see what can be done," Kadomico said.

"We'll come back to that," Moore replied, then turning back to Tree Son, he said, "And the bastions? How are they built inside?"

"Logs inside and out. Packed with earth and logs. Ramps for climbing to the shooting places. Many warriors," Tree Son replied.

Burns joined them and Moore repeated what he had learned from Kadomico and Tree Son.

Moore instructed Burns to redirect the grape cannon fire to the firing positions of the two nearest bastions.

19

"Train the rest of your cannon fire on the base line of the bastions," he said. "Start firing flaming arrows as soon as the pales show enough splintering to burn. Keep firing and burning until the bastions are disabled and make every shot count."

Burns acknowledged his orders and left to change tactics.

"Kadomico, you are likely to be cut to pieces with musket fire if you show yourself, white flag or not. I have already made Chief Hencock a generous offer if he will surrender. He not only refused that offer, he refused to discuss releasing the captives, and he knows we can't attack the fort without harming our own."

"Now that Hencock has seen your strength and determination, Colonel, he is likely to be more amenable to talk. Suppose I tell him that you will personally guarantee his safety and continued leadership of the Tuscarora people, if he will surrender?"

"Not possible. Hencock has committed so many atrocities against the settlers that the people of North Carolina see him and his warriors as criminals. They are murdering savages who have committed the most heinous of crimes against settler families—women and children included. Unconditional surrender is his only alternative."

"And as you know," Kadomico said, "they see us as invaders. Their hate for us reaches the core of their being. They will die before they surrender. They welcome death and a new life beyond, and their last act will be to take as many of us as they can, but if we offer two or three of them safe passage to their friends the Iroquois, there is a chance you can save the captives."

Tree Son said, "Two captives are young women, white, one is a man, white too. Maybe more, I cannot see. I go with Kadomico, carry white flag, and we will give this message to Chief Hencock."

"And if you don't come back?"

"It is possible but a risk I am glad to take," Kadomico said.

Moore glanced at the sun and sighed. The first day of the siege was well past noon. What they were proposing might work, but work or not it would take more time, a lot more time, and he meant to get this over with quickly. He stood, retrieved the long glass, and climbed a barricaded observation post. The cannon fire was tearing wood to splinters at the base of the two nearest bastions. One was beginning to burn from the onslaught of flaming arrows. It would take some time, but the bastions could not last much longer. Even the repairs that the daring defenders made were not going to make much difference. He estimated it would be late the next day before he could be ready to storm the fort, maybe the day after. He started climbing down.

Tree Son spat at the ground and spoke in Siouan. "Kadomico, you make no sense. I wonder you can speak your own language let alone reason in the white man's. I think that that devil schoolmaster back in Williamsburg has cursed you with no brains instead of giving you more."

"I have brains enough not to be pestered while I am doing important business. I do believe I can manage the weight of a flag attached to a stick. You are needed here, so stay where you are needed." Kadomico tossed his head and rose as Colonel Moore stepped back into the protection of the great white oak.

"Here are your instructions, Kadomico. Take Tree Son. If they have counter offers, they'll hold you while Tree Son brings the message. Offer Hencock ten women and children for each captive, no warriors. Deal only with Hencock. I will resume firing at sundown and continue until every splinter of that fort is ashes with or without your return. Therefore, it is in everyone's best interest for somebody to show up before sundown. I hope it is you and Tree Son, but if not, you are on your own."

Tree Son saw Kadomico nodding agreement.

"There is one condition," Kadomico said. "I want a paper signed by you that guarantees my right to the body of Chief Hencock and for its safe passage to the Iroquois."

"That sounds mighty close to sympathy for this renegade," Moore replied.

"First of all, he is doomed, and I no longer consider him an enemy. Secondly, you are right. I have great sympathy for him and his people. Thirdly, I demand this as a condition for saving the white captives because it is the only way that Tree Son and I will be spared once we enter that fort."

"Done," Moore said. "What they say about you is true. May God be with you."

The noise dwindled to silence as both sides ceased firing. Shadows grew long in the mid-afternoon sun. Gun smoke drifted and thinned in the west wind under a clear sky. Despite the splinter damage to the base of the two nearest bastions, the wall showed no serious destruction and the fires died.

Kadomico and Tree Son, clad only in breechclouts and having removed their war paint, stepped out of the forest with the white flag, walked a few paces into the open space, stopped, removed all their weapons, and placed them on the ground. There was a flurry of activity visible on the bastions where men repaired the damage from cannon fire. In two other places, logs slid over the tops of the pales and slipped into place over spots weakened by fire, cannon ball, and grape shot.

Facing a gentle rise and a field of early spring switch grass reaching halfway to their knees, Kadomico and Tree Son breathed relief. Easy targets for desperate shooters, yet not even a warning shot had been fired at them. On the other hand, why would they waste the ammunition?.

Whether they would be shot down outside, tomahawked as they entered, or allowed to have their say just remained to be seen. They moved forward. Halfway there a crude ladder of vine and hide-lashed footholds came over the wall—an invitation. But to what?

4

Gladys was tending a pot of collard greens and a Dutch oven of corn bread cooking in the fireplace of the one-room log cabin when she heard the creak and rumble of the field wagon. She knew the sounds of that old wagon as well as she knew the low of each milk cow coming in to feed. She reloaded the lid of the oven with fresh coals from the oak fire, walked to the door and watched as Zack slid off the back of the slow moving flatbed wagon. She felt relief to see Zack back from the new-ground work where he'd been since sunup—hard work for any man, let alone one with twenty-nine fresh lash wounds on his back.

Her relief quickly changed to curiosity, then worry. Something was different. Bare back and shoeless were usual enough, but Zack got off and stood staring off down the road as though he was expecting somebody or something. She couldn't see what it was, though she stepped out a bit and looked, looked carefully. Then he was walking toward her slowly, head down. Normally he would be striding toward her cupboard for pone and pot likker, head up, alert. She frowned and went inside. Maybe it was the whippin'.

The front door of her cabin opened on a single room that served as bedroom and kitchen. Gladys did a lot of cooking there for the mansion, which accounted for having that rare Dutch oven and a big fireplace, features normally not found in slave quarters. On the opposite side of the room, two beds with cornshuck mattresses stood in the corners. Gladys' was on a rope bed raised above the hard packed dirt floor. Zack's mattress lay on the floor snug against the corner.

Zack walked around the house to the back door and began to wash at the little bench with bucket, basin, and gourd dipper sitting alongside the house.

Gladys leaned out the back door. It was not like him to come home without speakin'. "Zack, maybe I ought to salve that back before supper."

"No m'. It don't hurt no more 'n proper for the lickin' it took."

Although disappointed that breaking the silence did not lead to more words from him, Gladys decided to wait a bit longer.

"Supper 's ready."

"Yessum."

Zack ate in silence, head mostly down. She kept her back to him to give him the space she thought he needed. Whatever was troublin' him was troublin' him bad. Best let him be 'til he's ready, she thought.

Zack finished the collards, salt pork, sweet milk, and cornbread, but he neither spoke nor moved more than necessary to eat. Afterwards, he just sat there absorbed in his thoughts. Gladys had had enough. She wiped her hands on her apron, untied it, and hung it on a wall peg. She stood for a moment looking at Zack, shook her head in resignation, and started to walk out.

"I gonna run away," he said quietly.

Gladys went cold all over. It was as bad as a death sentence.

"Best you let that back heal first. It's bound to git infected, you runnin' from them dogs, sweat pourin' all over, no healin' salve. Infection follows such as that. It happens, you better off if the dogs getcha. Come on in here now. I'll give them welts a extra helpin' t'night."

"I didn't 'spect to go jus' yet."

Praise God. Time, just a little time, and we can fix that kind of crazy thinkin', Gladys thought, as she collected her medications and sorted them out alongside the bed. Zack came to her walking hesitantly but feeling better. When it comes to stomachs, full beats empty every time. He stretched out face down on Gladys' bed. Gladys pulled the milk stool close and prepared to treat the wounds

"I know a white Shawnee Indian who lives way over yonder in the wes'. He come here a long time ago. Come to git two horses. I brought 'em up for 'im. We talked some and he tole me he hoped t' see me agin someday. Mebbe I could find that man or someone like 'im 'f I go wes' where the Indians are."

"That young Ella gal over on Middle Plantation you been talkin' bout, she'll be heart broke," Gladys mused aloud as she smoothed on the salve and noticed the beginning of scabs on the wounds. Good, she thought, healin' good.

"Mebbe I come back for her." Zack spoke without conviction. Impossible as it was to imagine there could be a future for him and Ella if he left, it was just as impossible to think of life without her. For sure, there would be no life together if he stayed.

So that's it. Not surprised, Gladys thought. If Colonel Ludwell would buy that gal and marry them up, that'd be the end of Zack's runnin' away. It was as simple as that, but not a chance Colonel Ludwell, or any other slave owner, would make such a move for the sake of a slave. Let this set for a while, she concluded. There's time yet.

The next Sunday, Zack and Gladys got permission and walked the five miles to Middle Plantation where the slaves had been allowed to assemble to hear a preacher. They set out early for the two-hour walk. Although unspoken, they both knew the purpose of this trip was so Zack could see, maybe even talk to Ella, and that is what troubled Gladys. It's one thing to think about runnin' away, somethin' different to talk about it. Zack could be whipped to death for just sayin' it, never mind doin' it. It is why Gladys was making this walk. The subject had not come up again, but she could tell that it was still heavy on his mind.

The old horse path to Middle Plantation was easy walking that cool March morning, plants budding, skies clear, and the air scented with new growth. The trail was wide enough for a wagon or sled but such conveyances were seldom on the trail after the first mile beyond the fields of the plantations, so the way for them was packed smooth ground mostly—easy walking.They had been talking about it being almost planting time.

"When hickory buds are big as a squirrel's ear is when old folks say t' plant—there's some time left yet," Zack said. "But the plowin', now it starts soon's th' ground's dry enough, 'n 'at could be t'morra." Green Spring grew both tobacco and corn, but the money crop was tobacco.

"Well, there be plenty to do now it's warmin'. You think they'll put you back to drivin'?"

"If I'm here, they will—for sure, they will."

Gladys flinched and looked over her shoulder. Lawd God, in the ear of a white man such words meant serious trouble. She whispered the words.

"Anybody hear you say that, 'n I means Ella too, you be back on that whippin' post or worse. In case you fergit, they took off Mean Willie's foot."

"Well, I ain't no fool, but I'm goin'. I got t'try."

"Jus' don't speak it, Zack. Jus' don't say it out loud. We talk some more soon."

Gladys knew time was running out. The past few days she had hopes that the passage of time would take care of it, but no, Zack was goin' and that was that—not a thing she could do about it.

They walked in silence until the buildings of Middle Plantation appeared beyond vistas of rolling, cleared land, fenced pastures, and acres of hilled tobacco. The rutted wagon road skirted one cleared section, turned alongside another, and wound its way onward toward the outbuildings of the farm. They followed the strong scent of cooking meat and smoke rising in the distance until they could see slaves moving about near one of the buildings, probably the one for the preaching. A mounted overseer stopped them to check the note from Master Philip Ludwell II. The overseer had no idea what the writing meant, but he knew the Green Spring seal and waved them on toward the church. They passed the cooking pits and spits of meat roasting over coals.

"Looks like somebody's been coon huntin'," Zack said, as they made their way to the door of the makeshift church. It was not unusual for the slaves to have game they could snare from the local woods and creeks, but it was unusual to allow this kind of gathering. White people who owned dozens, often hundreds of slaves, worried constantly about uprisings. Slaves had no hope of reward, relief, or freedom. In other words, they had little to lose if they rebelled, and they appeared to grow bolder in gatherings. Consequently, if allowed at all, slave owners watched carefully such gatherings as weddings, funerals, and churches, and so far, there had never been a slave uprising in Virginia.

When services were over, the congregation gathered around the spit-roasted coon, possum, and pork and the food from the winter kitchen gardens next to their quarters: collards, turnips, and dried fruit. There was molasses candy as well for the children. Gladys glanced at the sun and shadows and motioned to Zack, who stood talking to Ella. The two of them joined her and they set out on the path home. Gladys slowed to give them some privacy. There goes my best hope for somethin' to make him change his mind, she thought, then prayed that he would not say the runaway word. Ella would turn back at the far fence. Gladys and Zack would be home by dark.

That night Zack tossed and turned in fitful sleep thinking about Ella. After a while, his eyes flashed open. Somethin' was not right. He listened, but the normal night silences did not give him ease. He rose up on one elbow and saw that Gladys' bed was empty. Maybe she was sick from all that rich food. He lay back down and waited, unable to sleep, but she did not return. Just before dawn, he watched her ease down on her shuck mattress.

Zack didn't mention it the next day, but Gladys did it again that night and the next four nights. Zack finally concluded that she must have been meeting one of the field hands. Had to be the only thing, but on the third day, he lifted the lid on a cooking pot and slammed it back over what looked like roots simmering in entrails. That was not the only thing. Gladys' eyes seemed locked in a partial stare and she nearly quit talking. Each night she left the little log cabin. No dog barked and no sound came from the woods. Even the crickets hushed when Gladys walked away into the night with Zack peering after her through a small crack in the door.

Things normally went well on Green Spring plantation but recently there had been a series of mishaps. Al Ripken broke his shoulder, the right one, his whipping shoulder, when he fell off the big riding horse while out checking field work. It was a strange thing, he said. The horse hadn't shied or bucked and he couldn't account for falling off. Shortly after that, varmints got into the seed corn and ruined most of it. Then, one of the plantation springs went dry. That had never happened before either.

Ripken walked from his quarters to the kitchen in the early morning chill and found a seat near the warm fireplace, and sat shivering with the shoulder pain. The March wind blowing across the muddy landscape groaned aloud and did nothing but deepen his mood as he sat contemplating the mishaps and the misery from his useless shoulder. He was wondering what else could go wrong when a young slave named Jason came into the kitchen, slowly approached the table where Riken was sitting, and stopped, head bowed.

"Speak, boy, and it better be good. This here kitchen ain't no place for the likes of you."

Jason's eyes opened wide in fear, but he managed the words that he had to say. "Massa, he say you come, and I couldn't find you 'til I come here, suh."

"Git out, then. I'll deal with you later. No tellin' when he sent you."

Jason swallowed his answer, grateful for the dismissal.

"Mr. Ripken," Philip said, "the Governor's man was here this morning. Wanted to let me know that money for the new fort they have been discussing for years in Williamsburg is about to be approved by the burgesses. He said that Governor Spotswood is looking for labor to get the land cleared and ready for building next spring. He says it will be up to us planters to do our share, it being a huge protection for the general population."

"Sounds like he wants oxen, ax men, and sawyers," Al said. "Did he say when?"

"He thinks after the crops are laid by this summer and maybe again after the harvest, but he sounded mighty anxious. Wouldn't be surprised if we hear from him earlier. With all that has been happening here lately, Green Spring can't spare overseers for such as that, but keep it in mind, be thinking about it. When the time comes, be ready to loan out some labor and some work animals, oxen, horses, supplies—whatever they need. Seth Jackson will be keeping a detailed account of what Green Spring furnishes."

Ludwell understood the governor's early alert to Green Spring, a richly endowed plantation with an extraordinary record of production and successful experimentation in horticultural pursuits. Fully recovered from the devastation during Bacon's Rebellion back in the seventies, Green Spring was a shining example of what Virginia had to offer to those of good management skills and colony loyalty. Green Spring owners, Philip Ludwell II and his father before him, were good examples of that.

"I see, sir," Al Ripken replied. "Whatever we give up durin' those times will only slow the new-ground clearin' we're doin' over by the creek. We'll be ready, sir."

That night Gladys stayed in the woods until almost daylight. Zack was up when she came in without speakin' and walked over to her bed, placed something in the corn shuck mattress, and carefully restored the mattress to its place under the blanket. Across the room, Zack continued fueling the fire with splinters and small pieces of firewood, but in the semi-darkness, he could not help seeing Gladys linger over the mattress. It troubled him that, trance-like, she had ignored him. He felt better when she finally turned, smiled, and walked over to him.

"Mornin', Miz Gladys."

"Morning, Zack. I 'spec you wonderin' some bout my comin's and goin's lately."

"No 'm, not me. I jus' hope you ain sick."

"I'm not sick." Gladys spoke emphatically as she sat down on the milking stool by Zack and waited while he slowly raised his eyes to hers. The kindling caught and flames leaped through the dry feeders and on through the three oak logs. Zack felt suddenly helpless in the gaze of

31

Gladys' penetrating stare. He could not avert his eyes, nor could he close them and block out the streaming consciousness of her strength. It was like one of those spells he had heard talk about among the old slaves. He wasn't afraid, but he wished she would not look like that.

"Now you lissen, Zack. Times goin' to change. Somethin' good goin' to happen to you, but it gonna take some time, maybe until after harvest, and it can't happen 'les you put that runaway notion outta y' head quick, like right now."

"It don' seem natural, somethin' gonna change."

"Did I ever lie to you?"

"No 'm, I jus'. . . "

"Then do it. Put runaway outta y' mind. Hear me good, Zack."

"Yes 'm." Zack would obey and not ask questions. Just the thought of questioning Gladys made him ill, like it was a black, unseen, but real danger.

Al Ripken rose at dawn, pulled on his knee-length trousers, and laced them tight on his waist. While he finished dressing, he pondered Master Ludwell's words. Sure enough, there were strange happenin's at Green Spring, but he brushed it aside, big plantation, lots of slaves and indentured servants, plenty of things to fall to misfortune. He doubted any of it was mischief . . . still, it all seemed to come at the same time, or nearly so, and why would a spring dry up in the middle of the wet season? He'd keep an eye out and see if the other overseer had noticed anythin'.

Ripken shifted his thoughts to giving up slaves to Governor Spotswood this summer. He could do with a lot less of the governor's interference, though he would not argue that with Col. Ludwell. Well, he would just make up a group of the worst workers he had among the slaves, probably no more than ten would suffice, and there were close to two hundred to choose from at Green Spring. There were seventy-eight slaves, counting men, women, and children, quartered near the mansion—twenty or more quartered on each of the outlying farms: Archer's Hope, Hot Water Land, Scotland, Cloverton and other locations on the vast estate—plenty to choose from.

For early spring, the day was clearing fast. Only the cold wind reminded him that warm weather was not here yet. Still there was the hint of spring in the rising temperature, and that caused Ripken to think of planting—time to get tools, seed, and people ready. Zack could make the rounds and check on what each farm needed. There was some plowing to be done, but a great deal was still planted in hills in open fields of stumps and therefore more dependent on hand work with hoes and shovels than on weather and plowing. As Ripken neared the kitchen, set apart from the mansion for fire safety, he stopped a young slave boy, arms around a load of kitchen firewood.

"Billy! Find Zack. Tell him to come to the barn. Be quick!" Billy put his firewood down carefully and left at a run.

Ripken gave Zack his orders and told him to get started at once. It would take Zack the rest of the day, maybe more, but he could straddle Ole Sue and get the word out to the outlying field bosses, check the status of things, and bring back a list of tools and supplies needed.

Ripken took a bench seat at the kitchen table and signaled the cook for breakfast.

Zack was glad to have the job of visiting all the outlying Green Spring planter locations. The ride on Ole Sue would give him time to think. He had no idea what Gladys meant this morning except he knew he was not to think about running away. He could not imagine anything happening that would be good enough to replace his resolve to run-away.

Hoping that he might see Ella, he started toward Middle Plantation and Williamsburg. The Hot Water slave quarters area lay in almost the same direction. He knew that seeing Ella was not part of his assignment, but once out of sight of the Green Spring overseers, he chose the route that best suited him. Besides, this horse path was much easier on his mare, than the newer, more direct trails over in the forest. Middle Plantation lay dead ahead and he was moving away from the James River and Powhatan swamp land that was also on his list of visits.

He was well known in the area, and word would spread fast once Zack was seen riding alone. While those thoughts summoned visions of Ella learning that he was near, a fine, mud-splashed roan, pranced out of a side animal trail quite a distance forward of him. The rider was richly dressed in white and black riding clothes, black boots, and a conventional three-cornered hat. He either did not see Zack or ignored him as he turned away and cantered forward to join two other mounted men farther along where the trail met the first of Middle Plantation garden fences. It was enough to stop Zack's daydreaming as his survival skills kicked in and he turned into the cover of the animal trail. It led directly to Hot Springs.

Just before Ole Sue reached the top of the hill where Hot Springs slave quarters were located, she topped a little rise, and like a vision from heaven, there stood Ella smiling alongside the trail. Zack blinked hard. Tall by any measure, she was a striking, fine featured, black woman dressed in the dullest of slave clothes that hung to her small waist before falling over her hips and parting to expose long perfectly formed legs in glancing sunlight. Zack swallowed, but it did no good. He could not get a single word out. His head spun with surprise. All he could do was lean back without taking his eyes off Ella, get one leg over Ole Sue's back, and slide slowly onto the ground, one hand resting on the mare's side to steady himself, as well as to let her know where he was.

"How'd you know?" he almost whispered, still using the mare's convenient side.

"Someone heard this mornin' that you'd be ridin' this way." Ella moved slowly toward him.

"But *I* didn't know m'self 'til jus' a little while back." Conflicting emotion swept over Zack the strongest of which was seeing Ella, but also the inexplicable fact that she somehow knew he was coming.

"Is it so important?" Ella whispered.

Zack pulled Ole Sue around to shield them from the sight of anyone beyond. When he turned back, Ella melted into his embrace and they stood so for a long while, neither speaking nor needing to.

"Zack, tether your animal over there and follow me. I know a place."

They circled the small one room wooden buildings until Ella motioned Zack to stop. She was gone only a few minutes before she reappeared and motioned him to follow. They entered the back door of one of the houses into a dimly lit room. Ella led the way to a shuck mattress on the floor in the corner.

"Speak softly and no one will know except my friend," Ella said.

"Ella, Gladys says somethin good's goin 't happen. Maybe this is it, I dunno, I jus' know I want us to marry."

"I know. I do too but I don't know if our Massa'll let us"

"It don't make no difference. You my wife now, right now, and I promise to protect you with my life. Now that's it. We married. You say, you too."

"Me too, Zack. Lord have mercy on us, me too. Soon's we can, we goin' to marry proper." Ella slipped the knot in the waist rope of Zack's trousers and pushed them away as she pulled him to her and gave herself up to the passion that would live in her memory for evermore.

5

Kadomico said, "Stay close to my back, Tree Son. We'll use the rope ladder."

"Your back is as good a place to die as any, my friend. I'll be there."

"No more talk of death, Tree Son. Just stay close." Kadomico spoke as he took the first step onto the ladder hanging from the pales of the fort.

At the top of the palisade, two warriors seized him, ready to take his life if he resisted. Instead, Kadomico surrendered to their grasp, but spoke quietly in the dialect of the Iroquoian Tuscarora language. "Does it take two Tuscarora to handle the son of a Saponi chief who speaks for the Governor of Virginia and the Chief Warrior of the white man's army that surrounds you?"

Then without waiting for an answer, Kadomico commanded, "Take me to Chief Hencock, but first tell him that Kadomico, War Chief of the Saponi, comes."

Two young Tuscarora warriors waiting nearby left trotting, probably to deliver the message.

Surprised and impressed by Kadomico's ability to take the offensive, Tree Son spoke in Siouan, well aware that his captors would not understand. "Do you think that these squaw warriors are so afraid of us that they shake in their moccasins? I don't think so, and I wonder why we are not dead yet. I hope you still have some of whatever is keeping us alive left for Chief Hencock."

"It all depends on him. We'll see," Kadomico said as they passed three semiconscious prisoners hanging from posts over layers of dry wood waiting for a flame. Two were white women, the other, a white man, perhaps a farmer.

Their captors led them into a large roundhouse. Inside, a huge mound of earth sloped toward the hide-covered doorway almost blocking it. They stepped inside and walked around the mound toward the opposite end of the long room where the Tuscarora council sat before a small fire. Wisps of smoke rose toward an opening in the ceiling and dispersed quickly in the light breezes of the afternoon. Chief Hencock sat at the head of a circle of war chiefs, medicine men, and an old woman in a scarlet robe. Their captors pushed Kadomico and Tree Son forward.

"Speak," Hencock said.

Kadomico shook off the hands of his guard, stood straight, and in the language of the Tuscarora, spoke to Chief Hencock as though he were the only person in the room.

"I return, Mighty Chief of the brave Tuscarora. Four moons past, I came here and we traded. You drove a hard but fair trade. I come now with a message from the Governor of Virginia and a message from Colonel James Moore who leads this army against you."

"Like our trade, your messages may be fair, Kadomico, Son of Chief Custoga of the Saponi. I remember you well, but I have no interest in anything the devil James Moore has to say. He lies. As for the Governor of Virginia, he is also a white man and far away. So why should I hear these messages you seem to think are worth your life?"

"I speak for the captives you hold."

"Why? They die when the first fire arrow strikes the fire pit beneath them."

"Moore knows this, but it will not delay the fire arrows. To him, your prisoners are already dead. The only reason the fire arrows have not started is that he has agreed to give me time to speak for the captives. We have until the sun touches the western hills. "

"And then?"

"And then the cannon will splinter the walls of the bastions. Flaming arrows, as thick as clouds of passenger pigeons, will fire the roundhouses. Within these walls, thousands of bits of flying steel from the cannons will deliver certain death. With the first light of the next sun the splintered walls will burn. By the time the long shadows fall on the scorched earth of this fort, all the people here will be captured or dead. It need not be. . . ."

Kadomico did not see the war club of solid seasoned locust burl coming. Hastily delivered in a spontaneous rage, the guard struck a glancing blow that brought Kadomico to his knees. The guard's momentum carried him around almost face-to-face with Tree Son who responded so fast that he seemed to be waiting for his enemy to reach a conveniently open position. Tree Son struck the Tuscarora's neck just below the ear. The shock of the blow sent the nerve bundles asunder and the man fell unconscious, near death. Chief Hencock raised his hand to stop the other guard whose tomahawk had targeted the back of Tree Son's neck.

Kadomico closed his eyes and struggled to stop the spinning room. Slowly he regained his balance and rose facing Hencock. Somehow he managed to mask his blurred vision and keep his balance. The council members had called for removal of the injured warrior and restored silence waiting for Hencock to speak. Kadomico locked his eyes on the chief's but he refused to look at Kadomico. What had happened was a forbidden move by a careless warrior. The chief chose to ignore the transgression, at least for the time being. He turned to Kadomico as though nothing had happened.

"The council has heard you speak of Tuscarora defeat as though the big musket you call cannon will destroy us. No. It can destroy the walls and the roundhouses but not the Tuscarora. To do that Moore and his warriors must come here and fight us face-to-face."

Still struggling to retain his balance, Kadomico measured his words and spoke slowly. "Still, there is no need for Tuscarora women and children to die when they could be the means of survival of the Tuscarora people. Your women and children could join your friends the Iroquois or other tribes of Tuscarora alliance."

Hencock was about to dismiss the proposal as preposterous when Rain Cloud, the woman in the scarlet coat, stared into the tiny fire and addressed the council.

"It is possible," she said without looking up.

Hencock shifted his position. Obviously, the words of this woman carried great weight. The other council members were quiet, waiting for Hencock to respond. Kadomico recognized the change and continued.

"For each captive you have here, Moore is willing to let three of your women leave with their children. There is no cost to you for that, and it is a guarantee that the Tuscarora will live on."

"If they wish to go, it is good for our women to go to our friends that they may carry on after us or return unharmed to us to begin again," she said. "The choice must be theirs."

The men in the council shifted nervously. How would Hencock take this interjection? Would the women even go? Hencock let the silence continue long enough for each of the council members to ponder the idea of releasing some of their people. There was bound to be dissension, argument in families, trouble if the women had to deal with such a decision. Besides, there was little time remaining. The sun was over half way to the treetops. What guarantee did they have that Moore would keep his word?

Hencock said, "Rain Cloud speaks true." He motioned for the council to speak, but before any could answer, Rain Cloud said, "We must send all women who wish to go. They alone will decide what children will go with them. There is no other way."

The council members struggled with this thought. This was sensible, but this was not the offer from Moore. Kadomico had said three for one. There could be two or three hundred women and children.

The council seemed to agree with Rain Cloud. Hencock turned to Kadomico, and this time he looked him straight in the eye.

"You will remain here. Your friend will return to Moore. Our women and their children will leave from that wall before the sun touches the trees. They will not be counted. Moore may have them pass through his sentries to be sure they are what they appear to be. They will return to our friends, the Coree and the Machapunga. There will be ten groups. After each group passes one of our captives will appear alone. When our captive is with Moore, another group will appear. You, Kadomico, War Chief of the Saponi, will be the last to leave. Moore's agreement will be spoken when one of his militia and one of the Yamasee set up a station of two white flags. Our women will pass between them."

"And if Moore will not agree?" Kadomico asked.

"He has said that the guns will begin again at sundown. When the first shot is fired, you will be staked out and turned over to the women here to begin dying slowly."

"Fair enough," Kadomico said as he turned to Tree Son. "Tree Son, here are the conditions."

Kadomico then gave Tree Son instructions in Siouan. "Moore must understand that he is in the position of saving ten captives, most of whom were sure to be white people and that the number will be uncounted. His agreement will be confirmed by placing two white flags in the ground through which the women and children will pass. You will lead them through the army lines. Moore must make sure those lines are open to your free passage. Go with the

41

women to the Coree and the Machapunga. When we see the two white flags, the women and children will follow. See them safely on and meet me at the great bend of the Roanoke River."

Tree Son swallowed his anger at Kadomico's agreement to this separation and replied in Siouan. "I will do as you say. I go. You will have it no other way, but I promise you that when that first shot is fired, if you are not back with me, Moore will die."

He turned away then, unable to meet Kadomico's eyes, and left, followed by the guard. Kadomico turned his back to the council and watched Tree Son pass through the skin-covered doorway. The council, led by Rain Cloud, filed out. The hide covering closed as Kadomico stood transfixed on the scene where Tree Son had angrily marched away.

Encouraged by the eerie silence after the ear-piercing sounds and the whistling projectiles of gunfire had ceased, women and children began to emerge from the round-houses. Now they were curious about the two men who had climbed over the walls to certain death. As they milled about murmuring to each other, Rain Cloud called out to them:

"You are free to go with your children to our friends, the Coree. If you must speak to your husbands or sons, do so quickly else, you miss the chance to leave. Once the procession stops, it will not begin again. You will start leaving as soon we make an opening in that wall. I will lead the first group of ten. A captive will follow, then another group, then a captive and so on until all captives are released and all of you who wish to go have gone."

Colonel James Moore saw Tree Son running alone coming straight from the fort. Just as he had thought, some sort of counter offer. He sent word to his officers to remain alert but to continue to hold fire until he gave the orders. Tree Son leaped the first obstruction in his way and swept into the headquarters area.

Moore listened closely before deciding he had nothing to lose by agreeing; it was certainly worth it if he could save the white captives. He ordered the two white flags into position and asked for volunteers to man the screening post. He also sent word to the Yamasee to open up passage to Tree Son and the refugees from the fort. When he turned back, Tree Son was nowhere to be seen.

Scanning the walls of the fort, Moore saw a small section open up. A woman in a scarlet cloak emerged. She used a huge staff to signal the others to follow her as she began striding away from the fort. She stood straight, head high, the red cloak billowing in her wake as she marched directly toward the sentries and the white flags. Moore watched, suspicious of every move in the group.

Suddenly a white woman stepped through the opening in the wall and began to run toward the white flags. A second group of women and children followed her, then another captive, then a third group, and so on until twelve captives and many Tuscarora women and children had left the fort. Then, no more came, no Tuscarora women, no captives, and no Kadomico.

Moore glanced at the sun and dispatched a messenger to alert the army to prepare to resume firing.

Kadomico saw the last captive released and turned to a warrior standing behind him with blackened face marked with three fingers of white paint smeared across the cheeks. Suddenly he recognized an old friend.

"Hawk! You are a member of this Tuscarora council! I did not know."

"I fight with my Tuscarora brothers against the white devils. I saw you and Tree Son as you came over the wall. You have not changed since we were in Williamsburg together many winters ago. You continue to be with the white man."

"It is so, Hawk. It is the only way for my people. Now we are so few that we need the protection of the Virginia guns and forts to survive. I work with Governor Spotswood. You can join us. We will build a fort near the Meherrin River."

Kadomico's mind was spinning. Here was Hawk! Thirteen years ago, their tribal chief fathers had sent them to the grammar school at the College of William and Mary to learn the way of the English. Kadomico tried hard to understand the lessons and eventually became a trusted interpreter and go-between for the settlers and the tribes. Hawk refused to have any part of anything associated with the white strangers except to fight them. Finally, Hawk escaped from the school and disappeared. Now here he stood, still fighting the white man. His tribe, the Occaneechi, had lost many of its people by defending their little group against raids from hostile Indians and from the devastating European diseases. They were about to join the tributary tribes who paid an annual tribute to Virginia's governor for protection. But not Hawk.

Kadomico glanced at the sun nearing the western horizon. Before Hawk could reply, he grasped his forearm in a gesture of reunion. "Hawk, there is no time to talk. I must follow the women. Can you speak to Chief Hencock for me? Tell him that if he does not survive, his body will be given to me and I will deliver it to the Tuscarora women in their new quarters where he may have a proper Tuscarora burial and cross to the other side as a great leader of his people. Tell him I promise to do this, and I have Moore's talking paper to prove it. Tell him I must be released and that you will escort me to see that I do as I have said."

"Come. I will do this. Stay close to me. The brothers of the warrior that Tree Son struck down seek revenge. They will try to kill you on sight but not in the presence of Chief Hencock or me."

Hencock heard them out and agreed. Kadomico and Hawk left the fort, together again after thirteen years, now at war on opposing sides but bound tightly to each other, each ready to defend the other at the risk of his own life. They made their way to the sentry station of the white flags where Tree Son was preparing to join the last of the Tuscarora women and children and escort them to the safety of their allied tribes. Tree Son signed to Kadomico, nodded his relief, and disappeared with the women.

At the fort, men scrambled to re-enforce weakened places in the wall and the bastions. The sun touched the western ridge and a musket fired. Its white plume of smoke drifted above one of the bastions and was answered by cannon fire from the siege army.

Two of Moore's militiamen escorted Kadomico and Hawk to the place behind the lines where Kadomico had met previously with Moore. The militiamen told them to wait there for Colonel Moore. It looked to them as though they were under guard because their escorts settled down near them.

"I go now." Hawk spoke in Siouan.

"What good will it do? You can see that the fort walls will fall tonight when the fire arrows strike the splintered walls. Only death or captivity waits there. Stay with me and we leave together."

"Nothing has changed, Kadomico. I go to fight the white strangers. For me, captivity waits here also."

"No. This army will not touch you as long as you are with me."

Hawk ignored the remark. "When you enter the fort," he said "go back to the council room and through the door in the earth mound. I will stay with Hencock until the end, then meet you there."

A hail of fire arrows soaked in oil or animal fat and carrying bits of gunpowder, lit up the sky then splashed into the flames of the two nearest bastion walls. The guards were fascinated with the fire-lighted night. They moved closer and stared at the cannon fire smashing the base of the bastion walls. When they turned back to their charges, only Kadomico was there.

Much later, Colonel Moore rode in from the front lines, his uniform and face covered with dust. He held the reins in his left hand. The sleeve of his right arm was blood soaked from a musket ball. The arm hung motionless at his side. Two mounted aides came with him. One of them rode forward to take his reins while he dismounted. An orderly arrived with a box of medical supplies. Moore found comfortable seating in the protection of the old white oak as the orderly began bandaging the torn muscle.

The din of gunfire, smoke, and blazing firelight coming from the fort made an eerie scene there in the late night of Moore's makeshift headquarters. He filled his lungs with the fresh night air from the forest and stretched out his legs. It felt good to lean back into the old, blow-down white oak, weathered clean and bark-free smooth after years of seasoning. They had rescued twelve captives, and except for this arm, without a single casualty. Now destruction of the fort was proceeding according to plan. With any luck, he could be back in South Carolina this time next week. He looked over at Kadomico, who was under close guard and dozing beyond the smoldering coals of the campfire.

"Wake the Indian and bring some of that coffee I smell," he said to Kadomico's guard.

The guard turned to nudge Kadomico with his musket, but found him standing.

Moore motioned Kadomico to come closer. "That was a good piece of work, Kadomico, getting those captives out alive. I'll not question the differences between the numbers I gave you to work with and the number of Tuscarora women released. It just turned out that they had more captives than I expected. Wise decision, well done. Take a seat."

"There was no time for bargaining," Kadomico replied. "The woman in red simply announced that the women were to be given the choice and that all captives would follow. No one argued. She was the first to leave."

Moore smiled, and then said, "Neither did anyone here argue with her as she continued to manage the processing at the white flags. It was clear that she would lead them away safely or else we had to kill them all—not much of a choice. The first captive released from the fort was a woman. She ran toward the white flags where the sentries were inspecting for weapons and such, pointed toward the woman in red, and told the sentries that we must do whatever that woman said because there were many more captives and she knew who was to pass and who not if there was a problem.

"She thinks straight and acts fast. Her name is Rain Cloud," Kadomico said.

"Probably a good thing we don't have to face her in combat." Moore smiled respectfully. "Now it looks as though you also released the enemy among us, and even as we speak, he could have us in his sights."

"He is my friend, Hawk, Senior Warrior of the Occaneechi. He has returned to the fort where he will guard Hencock or his body until this is over."

Moore could not mask his admiration for Kadomico as he leaned forward and looked him straight in the eye. "You have done well. This army is grateful. North and South Carolina are grateful. Go back to the Yamasee and join your men. I will let Governor Spotswood know what you have done."

"I go," Kadomico said. "I will need one of the horses if Hencock is killed."

Moore understood. "Take this to the corral, your choice of mounts. See that you don't take mine." He signed a paper, and handed it to Kadomico. "When you're done, turn the horse over to the militia commander at Bath."

Kadomico rejoined his band of warriors. The cannon fire lasted all night. By sunup, several places along the pine walls of the fort were in flames. By dark, they were ashes. The two front bastions lay smoking under a maze of pales. Musket fire from the fort had weakened. Many of the fort population had slipped away during the night.

Kadomico saw that the end was near. He spoke to his band of warriors. "Moore will take the fort tomorrow. Go now. Find Tree Son and meet me at the great bend of the Roanoke River. I will bring Chief Hencock and be there within two suns."

By mid-morning the next day, March 23, 1713, Moore led his army through the burned-out walls into the fort and reduced it to ashes. The remaining warriors huddled behind makeshift barricades at the back of the fort now visible to the siege army.

Kadomico walked to the edge of the forest leading a brownish-red Spanish mustang stallion named Red. A white blaze stretched from between his eyes almost to his nose. The flowing black mane, rich black tail, and four black stockings, marked his Spanish breeding and spirit.

Kadomico checked his weapons: two knives, a tomahawk, a bow, and a quiver of arrows. Looking through the burned-out walls he could see that the fighting had moved inward toward the back of the fort where it became hand-to-hand with pistols, swords, and bayonets against knives, clubs, and tomahawks.

Yamasee Indians milled around in the cleared field with captives and loot from the fort. It was no time to visit with them, not with such a valuable prize as the horse beneath him. He gathered the reins, swung onto the bare back, and let his weight shift with the stallion's quick steps until he settled. Kadomico eased the tension in the reins and touched the sides with his heels. The stallion moved into the open. Kadomico scanned the scene before him once more, then gave a battle yell, dug his heels in, and braced for the lunge. Red stretched out in a hard run alongside the forest until he reached the point opposite the entrance Kadomico had chosen. Kadomico leaned further and reined Red into a sharp turn.

The mustang entered the turn low to the ground, feet dislodging clods of earth amid clouds of dust. A few warriors gathered in their path and signaled them to stop. In the absence of a whip, Kadomico used his heels and the extra length of the reins to signal the mustang for more speed. The Indians barely escaped collision as they dived away on both sides of the red horse and his rider. Kadomico leaned into Red's neck and shoulders so close that he was barely visible. By the time the Indians recovered and reclaimed their weapons, it was too late. Horse and rider easily cleared the fallen timbers of the wall and disappeared.

Kadomico left the mustang's back as they slid through ashes and dust at the remains of the council longhouse. Yamasee Indians and militia ran past him toward the back of the fort and the two bastions there. They seemed not to notice him in the excitement. The council longhouse had burned, leaving the mound of earth and the pole door untouched. Kadomico tethered Red to the door and quickly disappeared into the mound of earth. Within, there was a large underground room comfortably furnished with beds, water, food, and clothing, nothing else.

While Kadomico gazed at the dim candle-lit scene, Hawk entered. He pointed to a blanket-covered body on one of the beds and said, "I saw you come in. Chief Hencock is dead, cut down by musket fire. He lies there."

"Then we guard his body here until the fighting is over."

"The fighting is nearly over. The militia is firing muskets or using their swords on the few who continue to fight. The Yamasee Indians have already gathered many captives among the Tuscarora, and will be leaving immediately for the slave market in Charlestown, leaving Moore to finish with less than half his army. He will not be pleased with his Indian allies."

"We go, then," Kadomico said. "I have a horse to carry the body, but we may have to fight our way back through the Yamasee out there with their captives and loot."

"We will tie the body on the horse in front of you. Leave the way you came. When you are outside, turn that way, toward the river." Hawk pointed north. "I'll cover your back and join you later. Go fast."

Sure enough, that part of the open field was less populated. Still, Kadomico ran the mustang into the forest before he reined him in to wait for Hawk. Although he waited a long time, Hawk did not come. Kadomico dismounted and began walking. He estimated it was about a day's walk to the bend of the river where he was to meet Tree Son.

Four days later, Moore wrote to North Carolina President Pollock that he had burned the fort to the ground on the third day of the siege. His army had rescued eight white captives and four allied Indian captives. They had taken 392 prisoners, 192 scalps, killed 366. He wrote that some setters had joined him and he had lost a total of 22 white men killed, 36 wounded, 35 Indians killed and 58 wounded.

Tuscarora resistance and threats ceased with the fall of Fort Neoheroka, and the settlers returned to their Carolina farms. The surviving Tuscaroras drifted north and joined their friends, the Iroquois. Moore returned to South Carolina.

6

When Kadomico realized that Hawk was not going to meet him, he made haste to get clear of the fort area, then set a course just north of northeast toward the Roanoke River. When he came to an open place like a meadow or savanna, the early afternoon sun warmed his naked shoulders, but most of the time he was in forest. Sometimes the undergrowth of briar, honeysuckle, and young saplings were too dense for the horse, and he would have to change course. Guided by the north-facing moss on trees, he managed to make good progress even without a visible sun and shadows.

By nightfall, he came to an open area rich in new grass, good grazing for the horse. He had no rations of any kind, but the activities of the day had left him no appetite, and he felt neither hunger nor weakness. But the horse needed rest and food.

Kadomico loosened the lines holding the heavy, blanketed body of Chief Hencock and used one to tether the horse to a young sycamore sapling near the edge of the little meadow. He had needed Hawk to help lift the heavily wrapped body onto the horse. It was not likely that he could repeat that alone—best leave it strapped on the horse. He adjusted the load to give the animal as much comfort as possible and left it to graze while he moved back into the concealing shrubbery. Kadomico dozed in a sitting position on the trunk of a huge blow-down beech. After awhile a half-moon came up and flooded the scene with a soft light. Kadomico saw that the horse had stopped grazing and was

51

at rest on three legs, the fourth one relaxed in its turn. His mind turned to his people, the Saponi.

His tribe must move again, and soon. They could no longer use the hunting grounds to the east of their village located on the Yadkin River near the North Carolina Blue Ridge Mountains. White families had already established a few farms on the choice savanna near the streams draining that part of western North Carolina. What he had told Colonel Moore was true. He hoped to gain the favor of the North Carolina magistrates and have permission to hunt the area near the North Carolina and Virginia border, formerly Tuscarora trading, trapping, and hunting grounds. The most pressing problem now was where to settle his people. No longer could a tribe settle on unused land. The white man surrounded the land and streams with fences and other marks of possession denying even their own neighbors permission to use or hunt in places where they held patents, talking papers. The Saponi elders were eager to hear from him and his band of warriors.

When the moon reached its zenith, Kadomico broke camp and proceeded in the half-light, walking and leading the horse. By daybreak, they could feel the dampness from the waters of the Roanoke River. Encouraged, they moved on. After a short time, Kadomico stopped. He placed a reassuring hand on Red's thick neck to keep him quiet and listened carefully. The call of the cuckoo followed by two chirps came again, faint, but clear. He smiled. He and Tree Son had used that call since their boyhood.

"Kadomico, you are here." The words came from one of his young warriors, now striding toward him. "Tree Son gave us the call. We are along the river waiting for you. Tree Son is there." He pointed east.

"Two Deer! You have done well. We will go on to the river, and wait. Let Tree Son and the others know." Kadomico released Two Deer's forearm. His praise brought a wide grin of surprise and pleasure to the young warrior's face.

"I go." Two Deer beamed respectfully before turning downstream at a fast trot. Tree Son would be pleased when he came in view with the other warriors he collected along the way.

The riverbank sloped gently toward the stream where several flat boulders rose just clear of the shallow backwater. Red followed Kadomico toward the water, then rushed past him and began drinking deeply. Kadomico splashed his face and drank lightly from cupped hands before picking up the reins. Red shook his head and resisted until Kadomico spoke softly.

"Go easy, my friend; too much, too quick will bloat your belly." They took a long time refreshing themselves, then, Kadomico found a place near the river where spring grass made excellent grazing. He led Red alongside a large flat outcropping of limestone in the shade of three great pines and eased the Chief's body to the ground. Red stepped away, shook his head enjoying relief from the weight and began grazing while Kadomico set up a small ring of stones, gathered a little pine straw, and struck a flint to start a fast-burning, dry, hardwood fire.

With Tree Son close by and his promise to Chief Hencock about to be kept, Kadomico let himself relax. Only then did he know hunger. He had been almost two days without substantial food. He glanced at the young stallion grazing contentedly and considered his options: food from the woods or the water. The water could be faster, this being the nesting season for fish. He climbed onto a great stone and scanned the banks looking for the telltale fish fin working the surface over a nest. He did not have to look far.

Kadomico nocked an arrow and moved slowly toward the fins. Although the light reflections obscured his vision of the fish, the fins told him about where his target was. He stopped well short of the nest and fired his arrow into the midsection of the fish. He waded out to the thrashing water and brought the big bass out, slit him evenly into two sides, and cut two arrow-straight stems from a nearby storm-damaged hickory's second growth. He shoved the sharpened ends of each hickory skewer securely into the sides he had prepared, leaned the skewers over the hot coals, and left them to cook.

Kadomico sat down on a huge stone partially immersed in the river, confident that Tree Son would try to surprise him. He wondered how many times he had tried, often succeeding, to make a mock attack. It had been going on since they were small boys barely able to walk. An idea began to form bringing a smile to Kadomico's face.

There were three young sycamore saplings growing together between the cook fire and the horse. He fastened his group of three trophy feathers to them on the upstream side and then walked downstream to see how they looked. A slight adjustment and he was satisfied they were what he wanted.

Kadomico returned to the great limestone outcropping that extended into the river. The fish would not be ready for a while yet. He sat down out of view, and was about to relax when a noisy splash of water splattered him. He knew the game was over. Knowing that Kadomico expected him to arrive from downstream, Tree Son had traveled around the camp, entered the river upstream, and floated back down, and there he stood, waist deep in water, smiling.

"The great Tree Son has again taught the master of all things English a lesson in sneak attack." Tree Son never masked his chagrin with Kadomico's education. He just could not get over how much stock Kadomico put into languages, reading, writing, and ciphering.

"You have won this one, Tree Son, but there will be another day, and you don't know when or where."

"True, but surely I have earned a fair share of that fish you are cooking."

"You have. Follow me."

They retrieved Kadomico's feathers without ceremony except Tree Son did turn away once to hide his smile. The fish had broiled tender and filling.

The rest of the Saponi band drifted in with their own provisions of wild duck and turkey and joined Tree Son and Kadomico in a circle around the fire. Before eating, Kadomico produced a small quantity of tobacco and sprinkled it on the fire as a sacrifice. Some of the others followed his example and dropped some small possession on the fire.

Under a clear sky except for an occasional drifting cloud, the river made a reverent sound circling boulders and moving on, leaving tiny pebbles and sand in small crannies near the shore.

Kadomico glanced at Red, still grazing nearby, oblivious to the sudden appearance of the young men jostling and greeting each other. Kadomico stripped a piece of the white meat from the skin of the fish, and they all began to eat. When they were finished, Kadomico bridled Red, led him alongside the body of Chief Hencock, and motioned to Tree Son for help to lift the body into position.

After breaking camp, they fell in single file behind Tree Son. With Kadomico leading Red in the center of the line, they moved forward at a brisk walk. They were still in enemy territory and they were definitely the enemy of that enemy. For that reason, Tree Son deployed scouts ahead and on their flank far enough out to give them plenty of notice if there was trouble. They kept the river close on their left. After a while, Two Deer intercepted them. Rain Cloud was not far behind.

Two Deer had been unable to refuse Rain Cloud's insistence on returning with him. He approached Tree Son, hesitated, and began, "I . . . I . . . the woman . . . ."

Rain Cloud clutched her red coat tighter and interrupted softly. "Two Deer, a brave warrior is our enemy. Yet, he walked alone into the Machapunga town to give us your message. We are grateful that you have come. Stop here."

Hearing the words, Two Deer straightened and backed away. This was high praise from one who would be remembered at the ceremonial fires of many tribes for years to come. He beamed at the words said in his favor.

Kadomico stood nearby with Red. Sunlight flashed off the jet-black mane and tail of the young stallion. Kadomico let go of the reins and whispered something to Red. Without moving his head, Red stepped slowly forward and stopped when he reached Rain Cloud.

Rain Cloud caught Kadomico's eye. He nodded in recognition. She raised her hand, palm outward, then placed it over her heart. A single tear escaped and traveled over the deep wrinkles of her cheek. Kadomico returned her hand gesture and motioned his two strongest warriors forward to remove the remains of Chief Hencock. They placed the body on a flat shelf of limestone by the river. Rain Cloud took a position close by. Tree Son and the band turned away upstream. Kadomico mounted Red and followed. It was clear that the women of Fort Neoheroka would arrive soon. Rain Cloud had averted a confrontation between the Machapunga warriors and the Saponi band of Kadomico's warriors.

When they reached the great bend of the Roanoke River, Kadomico rode forward and spoke to Tree Son. "I go. I will return the horse to the militia commander at the English town, Bath. Moore expects it. When you arrive, tell my father and the council that I go to Williamsburg to speak for land for the Saponi on the Meherrin."

Tree Son shook his head. "Any warrior here can say those words to our council. Out there, some are the enemy, some not, but all will take your life for that horse. I will lead the way to Bath. Try to keep up."

7

Green Spring was now a plantation of more than four thousand acres of forest, swamp, savanna, and croplands of tobacco, wheat, and corn. To simplify management of such a vast property, Col. Philip Ludwell II had followed his father's example and continued to divide the property into small farms. Zack took the path leading along the southeast boundary to the Hot Water farm. He had found the slave overseer there, delivered Ripken's message, then moved on toward the Governor's Land boundary to Cloverton and New Quarter farms.

Thoughts of Ella dominated Zack's mind while Ole Sue plodded on over the bare, earth-packed trail, occasionally sidestepping the blackberry briars reaching into their path for sunlight. The woods were awakening in a sea of the faint, transparent hues of unfolding fernlike shrubs and fresh new fronds of the sumac, walnut, butternut, and locust leaves. The sturdy dark green of the wild bulb plants and grasses were already approaching their maturity and settling down for the summer. Fortunately, Ole Sue needed very little of Zack's attention and seemed to know where she was going..

He remembered when Ella gently touched the back of his neck and pressed lightly to bring him back to consciousness. He moved his hand there now as though to recreate the warm pleasure of that touch. Ella and him— that's it—the way it is. He straightened with the thought, filled his lungs to near bursting, and kicked Ole Sue to make her go faster, but the mare seemed to know that the kick was out of place and character. She ignored him, as aged animals often do when they sense risk, threat, or foolishness.

Zack visited each of the seven Green Spring farms where small groups of slave field hands lived. They farmed the crops and worked to claim more farmland. They girdled trees and cleared brush to make room for more hilling and planting. At each stop, Zack checked the seed, tools, and provisions and made marks on a paper he carried to indicate shortages. It was late the second day when he finished his visits and headed home.

He found Al Ripken talking to one of the few remaining indentured servants at Green Spring, a carpenter who was busy fashioning a plow frame from a piece of well-seasoned white oak. Al motioned Zack aside and continued. "Beats me how they figure—gov'mt people. Bad as we need roads and docks right here, they want to send every penny they can raise into a wilderness of nothin'."

"No doubt you 'ave a point, Mr. Ripken. No doubt." The carpenter pulled his curved drawknife along the oak grain, leaving a smooth surface. "I m'self wouldn't mind seein' one our warships here in our waters. The pirates are havin' it far too easy out there," he said, gesturing toward the mouth of the York River. "Just a matter of time before they start comin' ashore. Then what?"

Zack picked a spot out of the way but still in hearing distance and listened.

"And it's not just that. 'S bad enough we been told to send a lot of labor south, we got strange trouble right here."

"And how's that, Mr. Ripken?"

"Spring's dryin' up, seed corn rotted, somethin' killed two heifers, sheep are actin' nervous, even Zack here got out of line last week, and I had to whip him, and this mornin' the breakfast milk was bitter. I say it ain't normal. Know what I mean?"

"Well, yes, I do. Maybe there's somethin' to what they're sayin'."

"And what would that be?"

"Luci Mingo, that high-yeller slave who makes trouble just by showin' up, told me Gladys has been workin' voodoo. I just considered where it came from and forgot it, but maybe there's somethin' to it."

"Well, of course there is!" Al Ripken said. "That's probably it." Then turning to Zack he said, "Zack, get over here. You know anything about Gladys usin' voodoo? Rag or cornshuck dolls, pins, night fires, strange potions? You know anything about that? Don't lie, boy. There's plenty more lashes left in that whip."

Zack's wide-open eyes were a dead give-away but his answer was strong. "No, sir, Massa Al. No, sir. I don know nothin' 'bout no voodoo. And Miz Gladys, she don either. I know cuz I see her jus' bout all the time, day and night. Miz Gladys don know no voodoo. No sir, I know she don."

Al decided that was all he was going to get out of Zack and let it be for the time being. He shifted subjects. "How come it took you two days to do a one day job?"

"It's Ole Sue, Massa Al. She jus' go slow. Same pace alla time."

"Well, next time you ride the farms, see that you take one of the mounts that can move. It ain't like there's nothing to do around here but go visitin'. Now, what you got for me?"

Zack gave Ripken the list of materials and the conditions of the outlying farms, and as he turned to walk away, Ripken grabbed him by the shoulder and spun him around. "Find that yeller woman and send her to me. Be quick. And, Zack, I'll see you at the whippin' post if you're lyin' to me."

Zack remained silent until Al released him, then walked away slowly, cautiously, to conceal a smoldering rage gathering inside him, fed by his conviction that Gladys was about to fall victim to Ripken's death-dealing whip. He had never known such a blinding all-consuming fury.

He found Luci Mingo struggling uphill from the spring with two large buckets of water suspended from a wooden yoke resting across her back and shoulders.

Zack grasped Luci's clothing near her throat, yanked her free of the yoke, and threw her into a tangle of young pines and wild grape vines. She fell through the first of the young trees, her buckets flying away in different directions, then tumbled onto her back and watched wide-eyed in terror as she saw Zack's rage concentrated in his blazing eyes and snarling lips. There would be no talk. Zack was going to kill her. If she screamed, he would just kill her sooner and leave.

"No, Zack. Ella!"

The name stopped him. "Ella will know," she said.

Zack reached for Luci's clothing again, gathered a fistful at her chest, and lifted her clear of the ground, then slammed her back jarring the breath from her. Luci's face turned red as she struggled to recover. The terrifying loss of breath now overcame her fear of Zack. She teetered on the edge of panic, then as air returned to her lungs she drew deeply and sensed a moment of enormous relief before certain death again loomed before her. Zack saw the recovery, closed his hands around her throat, and pressed until Luci's eyes began to bulge. He eased the pressure, raised Luci's ear nearly to his lips, and half-whispered the words, "If Miz Gladys has to answer for voodoo, I will finish killin' you. Go now 'n speak to the carpenter and Massa Ripken. If he comes for Miz Gladys, I come for you."

He released Luci Mingo and walked away. She scrambled to collect her buckets and went directly to the carpenter, then Al Ripken. Her story resulted in twenty lashes laid on by Ripken, but Luci's tearful story about her consuming hatred of Gladys, great regrets, and plea for forgiveness convinced him.

"Twenty and nine lashes, you trouble-making whore and a hundred more if I find you have lied to me. Be at the whipping post at sunup."

Zack found Gladys busy preparing cornbread and collards. She barely noticed him when he entered the little room. He took his place at the split log table and waited for her to serve the food. Outside the shadows had disappeared, the light was failing, chickens were already on the roost, and silence had claimed the day. Zack listened but the crickets had not begun nor did he hear the usual call of the owl. He moved the unlit candle forward but Gladys ignored it. The only light in the room came from the fire, but it was enough, no need to waste a candle. Gladys served the food and Zack poured pot liquor from the bowl of collards over a thick piece of cornbread. He spooned up some of the hot liquid and sipped it. It was one of his favorite foods but he couldn't enjoy it. His stomach churned, reacting to the realization that this woman who was the closest thing to a mother he had ever known, was a witch and sure to be hanged if found out.

"Zack, that little bit you think you learned don't change nuthin'. You needn't talk to me 'bout it, 'n you don't have to b'lieve it or not b'lieve it. Jus' you go on like always. Best you don't think 'bout it no more 'n sure you don't speak on it, ever! You hear me good. Now eat."

Zack tried to get it all out in one breath. "You wuz right bout sumpin' good happenin' to me. I saw Ella yesterday. We goin' to marry, me'n Ella. Now Massa. Ripken is talkin' bout strange things happenin'. Luci Mingo tole that white man carpenter, and he tole Massa. Ripken you doin' voodoo. She tryin' to fix that now, but I don know if she can. I sure don want nuthin' bad to happen to you."

"Slow down, Zack. Nuthin' bad will happen to me. Now that's the end of it. Eat."

The next day Zack took a few men and worked all day girdling trees and clearing brush on the southern part of Green Spring property near Governor's Land. When he came home late that evening one of the children told him Overseer Ripken wanted to see him. The news sent chills up his spine. It was sure to be bad but he had to go. He found Ripken at the barn, smoking a pipe.

"Soon's the plantin's done, you're gonna take five men, this cart, and go with the governor's men down south to clear land for a new fort, maybe two days' travel. You'll be fellin', barkin', snakin' up, and sawin' to length." Ripken propped a foot up on an ox cart at rest near the entrance to the barn and drew on his pipe. "You'll see that our animals and equipment gets back here in good shape and in time to lay the crops by 'til harvest."

"Five men ain much to clear land for a whole fort, Massa Al."

"There'll be others from other plantations. Can't say how many but there'll be enough. Gov'nor himself is seein' to it."

Zack's mind swirled among the prospects of traveling south into Indian territory, not seeing Ella for a long time, Gladys' safety, and his own ability to manage troublesome slaves and take care of equipment among strangers.

"How much gets done 'pends a lot on who's doin' it, Massa Al."

"How much gets done is the governor's problem. You just see to the care of our equipment and animals. We can decide who goes later. They'll be slaves from the outlyin' farms."

Zack knew that this meant he would get the laziest, weakest, and the most likely troublemakers. On the other hand, it might offer a better chance to run away. He might even find the Indian that had befriended him long ago. The more he thought of it the better he felt about it.

That night Gladys sat up until past midnight. She did not go to the woods. She just sat at the little table by the fireplace, her back to Zack, her hands busy with something on the table. Zack wondered. But when two people live in a small room, they learn to grant each other privacy even when they are just a few feet apart. When Zack woke just before dawn, he could hear Gladys' gentle snore.

Early April often did magical things to the Virginia and North Carolina forestland and savannas. Tree Son and Kadomico travelled north from Bath, North Carolina to Williamsburg in three warm spring days over a forest floor heavily spotted with brilliant red bud trees in full bloom. Occasionally, the fading blossoms of the shadbush signaled the end of the beginning of spring only to give way to young Virginia blue bells, trumpet vine, and Carolina Jessamine still enjoying the limited sunlight finding its way through the young leaves and buds of the forest ceiling.

Kadomico and Tree Son ran when the animal trails permitted, passing the western edge of Albemarle Sound, turning upstream at the mouth of the Roanoke River to a place of easier crossing where they swam the river and moved on north to the Meherrin River. There they rested and dined on roasted duck from the Meherrin.

"Not far from here, I don't yet know where, will be the Governor's fort," Kadomico said, as he reached for another piece of the roasting bird.

"And not far from here, I don't know where, is a war-party that could be be angry Tuscarora survivors," Tree Son replied. "We cut their trail after the sun passed noon, six maybe eight men, no women, no children. You didn't see that at the big creek we crossed?" Tree Son sat cross-legged, elbows on knees, smiling at his news.

"Yes, I also saw the tracks of the same group turning south soon afterwards. We're alone for the time being." Kadomico didn't press the point. He'd said enough to remind his friend that he could read trail sign as well as he could speak several languages. Darkness closed in and the cook fire was turning to coals. Kadomico rose and pointed upstream. "I'll go there and see if there have been others here recently."

Tree Son shrugged his shoulders indifferently and took the soft tops from three pine saplings to fashion a pallet in a place among the young pines away from the campfire. He then cut three more and left them nearby for Kadomico before stretching out in the swirl of fresh pine scent and instantly falling asleep.

The next day they swam the Meherrin and Kadomico detoured upstream about a mile. Tree Son followed without questioning. When they turned north again, Kadomico stopped and took a long look. "Not far from here, Tree Son, not far from here. We are on Virginia land now, no settlers, no Indians. The Occaneechi are the nearest, not far ahead. This is good land, good hunting grounds, a good place for our Saponi town."

"Yes, but what about the Occaneechi and settlers?"

"I think the Tuscarora and Iroquois raids are why there are no settlers."

"And the Occaneechi?"

"Like us Saponi, they are so few now that they can barely defend their town and impossible for them to patrol this huge hunting ground."

"So?" Tree Son said.

"So it is why we go to Williamsburg. We will talk with our friend Jock Adams about this. First, we meet with the Chickahominy and visit Tom Singleton. Perhaps he will go with us to Williamsburg. "

The Singleton plantation joined the Chickahominy tribe lands at the mouth of the Chickahominy River, about a

65

half-day's walk from Williamsburg. Tom Singleton had hosted Kadomico and Tree Son on many occasions in the past. An escort would be insurance against a possible confrontation with strangers if they attempted to approach Williamsburg alone, fully armed, and dressed only in breechclouts.

They arrived on the evening of the third day on the south bank of the James opposite the Chickahominy River and signaled one of several fishermen in Chickahominy canoes preparing for night fishing. Fires on scaffolds attached to canoe bows cast their light over the water in the fading twilight. It was a good way to attract fish. One of the fishermen recognized Tree Son, paddled over, and ferried them across. Tree Son remained with him to join in the fishing. With darkness descending, Kadomico accepted the offer of a young boy who escorted him to the Chickahominy camp. Although they retained fishing privileges on the Chickahominy and James Rivers, their town was now located near the York River.

8

It was Friday, March 31. Philip Ludwell had sent the coach for Ray Stilson to discuss the best way to decorate the porches and gates of Green Spring with wrought-iron filigree. Ray's daughter Ann had been included and invited to a small party given by Philip's wife, Hannah, for young people. In the late evening when the coach returned for them, Ann Stilson ignored the arm of the liveryman, missed the step-up, and fell into the arms of the coach driver, an indentured servant named Seth Jackson, who had stepped down to inspect a noisy brake. The fall left her confused between clinging to Seth for support and pushing him away to regain her independence.

"Miss Stilson," Seth said as he steadied her.

He knew she was the young daughter of Williamsburg's highly respected and prosperous blacksmith, Ray Stilson. And he knew that indentured servants and the daughters of respected citizens of the colony rarely mixed, at least not casually and never without formal introductions. Seth knew his place. He would be careful to keep it because, by the end of summer, his seven years of indentured service would be over and he would be a free man.

He did not resent the seven years he had spent under contract to Philip Ludwell. On the contrary, that contract had abruptly ended his confinement in Newgate prison in London where he had spent almost a year awaiting trial in leg irons on bare, dirty floors eating weevil-infested bread and sipping water that smelled of rotting fish. Better conditions were available at Newgate for a price, but he had no money. During the first few weeks in that prison, he had nearly died from exposure to filth, disease, and starvation.

Somehow, his body had adjusted, and he had begun to plan his escape when Old Morgan, the jailor, peering through the bars of the tiny cell, had tempted him.

"Laddie, I know this 'as been tough on you," Old Morgan had said to him, "Aye, tough like Satan's hell itself, I say. What would ye say to end it all with a voyage to America?"

Although Seth's health had suffered, he retained enough strength to reason and act. Now he reasoned that things were about to get even worse. He was about to be thrown into the bilges of one of Her Majesty's ships.

As miserable as he was, he'd peered back at Morgan through blond strands of matted hair hanging over the filth-encrusted skin of a near-wasted body. "I'd be no use there, sir. Makes me deathly ill to think on't."

"Well, listen close, laddie. A fine English gentleman in Virginia has papers from the court authorizin' your release and is willin' to pay your way, not as a prisoner but as a passenger, good as any man aboard, you'd be. Ye can be sure of that, if you'd help him with his great plantation of rich tobacco crops and grand timbers. It's a fresh new world for a strong young lad like yer ownself. "

"I may have only a little while left before my trial, and I could be a free Englishman. Free to do as I am able."

"Not likely, laddie. Ye'd not be here if there was doubt of your guilt, and surely ye can see that no man is likely to survive these cells for very long. Them as has are so demented they're *afraid* to go back to life in London. This gentleman will release you from his service after seven years and will help you get started on yer own."

"I've no wish to leave my homeland, sir, but I will think on it." Seth's reply was timorous. Lies and treachery at

Newgate were well known, but Morgan's remark about survival in Newgate, especially without money to buy favors, rang true.

"No, laddie, the gentleman's men are waitin' at the gate. You go with me now, sign the contract, and leave Newgate, or I find another man for them."

Seth had relented and it had all turned out well. Finally, it was about to end. Come September, his seven years would be up, and he would be a free man. His health had returned quickly, and now at age twenty-two with seven years at Green Spring, he made a striking figure. He was tall and fully muscled with eyes the color of a summer sky and a smile that put people in his presence at ease. He kept his thick blond hair trimmed to shoulder length, combed, and tied back from his face.

He had saved all he could. With his savings and the fifty acres the colony would offer him, it seemed the opportunities were endless. He could even return to Scotland or England. He had the passage, but the frontier, especially the southern frontier, offered vast opportunity. There were furs to harvest, fertile unclaimed land, endless timber. Seth had no formal education, but he had learned to swing an axe, square a timber, split rails and rive shingles. The blacksmith at Green Spring had shown him the way of heating and shaping iron. Nor did he have a serious challenger in musket marksmanship. His seven years of indentured service had yielded just the kind of education a man needed to meet the challenges of the Eastern Woodlands. His mind turned back to Ray Stilson's daughter, and he was uneasy. Nothing must interfere with the end of his indentured service in September.

Ann regained her footing and twisted around to face Seth, so close they almost touched cheeks. Their hats collided, hers held by a chinstrap, fell askew; his conventional three-cornered uniform hat went flying. It would have been just part of her recovery had their eyes not met. The contact was fleeting but unsettling, as though something unsaid had passed between them. Ann pushed once more to free her waist from Seth's supporting arm.

She mumbled a thank you as she straightened her hat over her auburn curls and smoothed her slightly disheveled clothing, found firm footing on the step-up, and boarded the carriage unassisted. Nevertheless, she was keenly aware and irritated that he remained so close behind her. "The imp! What is he thinking! I am not an infant," she muttered, as she slammed the door and took her seat next to her father. Ray Stilson had missed nothing of what had just happened, including the momentary eye contact.

Seth retrieved his hat, swung nimbly up onto the driver's bench, and gathered the reins. The matched pair of horses sensed the movement and stepped forward.

Something in the slam of the coach door gave him pause. He was sure he had not offended her, so why slam the door? Please, God, don't let this hinder my freedom, Seth prayed in earnest. Ray Stilson was no man to cross. One word from him and Seth would be in court explaining some kind of misconduct.

Seth became anxious to deliver his passengers to their home in Williamsburg and get back to Green Spring.

"Are you all right, Ann?" Stilson asked his daughter.

"Of course, father. I simply missed the step-up."

"You seemed troubled when you entered. Did that coach driver behave properly when he stopped your fall?"

"Father! Please!"

"Well, sometimes such things get out of hand. You must never allow forward behavior to go unnoticed. Best to face it and let your objections be clear immediately."

"No forward or any other kind of behavior," Ann said with hopeful finality, but to tell the truth, she *was* inexplicably disturbed. In any case, it was nothing to concern her over-protective father.

The next day was the first Saturday of April and Williamsburg turned out for one of the governor's sponsored gatherings of the colony's finest horses, a pre-racing season event where citizens in all walks of life got to see the year's best horses. In anticipation of the opening season, spirits were always high on this day. There would be much speculation about winners of the opening races the first Saturday in June. Spotswood loved competitions and made sure that games and races were frequently a part of the Williamsburg summer entertainment: men wagering, young people partying, evening dances, and a great deal of feasting and drinking.

Seth was there with the entry from Green Spring plantation. His horse was a dark bay named Chance, stepping sideways and tossing his head enough to shake the rich black mane and tail against the glancing sunlight but calm enough to convince Seth that he knew why they were there. Chance was the favorite. Horse and rider were a good match, and both responded to the excitement of the crowd. They had won the modest purse last year, and while there were some new entries this year shipped in from Canada and brought in from England, both expected to win again. The track was a straight quarter mile marked at the end with upright stakes. Judges positioned themselves at the stakes and decided the winners. In the actual races, it was rough-and-tumble. Riders tried to unseat their opponents, men wagered large sums, and horses gave their all at the finish line, but this was a pre-racing show. Each horse ran alone, the crowd watched, and the judges, standing at the finish line, simply recorded the time.

A small crowd pressed against the fence set up to protect the track. Seth led his horse past the crowd, answered questions, and let Chance show his sleek lines and spirit. Before mounting up and heading for a demonstration run on the track, Seth talked easily with the crowd, turned

Chance when asked, answered questions politely, and confirmed that he would be riding him again this year.

Seth mounted and walked Chance to the gate to wait for the gate master to signal them onto the track for a trial run. Chance settled as soon as he saw the gate open to the track. He walked to the starting line and stopped, spectators opened their pocket watches, the crowd pushed closer to the rope fence, and the starter official raised his pistol. Chance heard the shot, summoned the powerful muscles of his hind quarters, dug into the soft turf, and was running full out before the sound died away.

Ann Stilson watched unseen. It had been a troublesome night for her. She could not get the young coach driver out of her mind. He was so devilishly quiet and maddeningly casual holding her there in his arms . . . in his arms. Yes, in his arms, that was part of it. She felt his presence then, much more so than his touch and movements. She remembered his warmth and strength and it was reassuring, not at all like that of a stranger, not at all as it should have been. For an instant, it was a sensation of safety, comfort, and well-being, something like an old friend. But, he wasn't an old friend, not even a known person. He was a servant, a total stranger. No wonder she was disturbed. After all, he seemed to think that it was all right for her to be there in his arms. What impudence! Certainly, he was at fault for her confusion. He ought to have acted like the stranger he was. Who was he anyway? Well, what does it matter, she thought . . . it doesn't . . . not to her. Still . . . .

After the trial run, Col. Philip Ludwell stood tall among several well-dressed men of the colony answering questions about Chance and his future as a sire or in additional races. Seth dismounted and led Chance toward Ludwell and the crowd. There he pulled the saddle and began to sponge Chance's sweat covered neck and shoulders while the crowd admired the beautiful horse. Ann, standing with her mother well back in the crowd unobserved—observed silently.

"Mother, let's congratulate Colonel Ludwell on such a fine horse," Ann said and stepped forward, making her way to the rope fence. Mary Stilson chose to let her go alone into the dense crowd but was not surprised to see people greet and open the way for her. At the fence, Ann exchanged greetings with Ludwell, acknowledged the success of the party she had attended in his home, and congratulated him. Not once did she let her eyes rest on Seth before turning and melting back into the crowd.

Seth saw Ann making her way to the fence and stopped his work on the sweating horse and stepped up to his nose, stroking the mane and ears. He was close enough to hear the exchange between Ann and Colonel Ludwell, but although he glanced frequently at Ann, she did not once look his way, and then she was gone.

"Wasn't that the carriage fellow that you and your father encountered at Ludwell's last evening?" Mary asked.

"What fellow, Mother?"

"The one with the horse. Your father told me about the carriage driver catching you in a fall. Could this be the same fellow?"

"Mother, as you know, father exaggerates any attention any man shows me. I can imagine what he might have told you, but I simply slipped and brushed the driver accidently. I then entered the carriage unassisted. That jockey with Chance today might very well have been the same. Why on earth would you ask about him?"

"Oh, nothing at all, dear. Nothing at all," Mary said. Her interest, however, did not escape Ann, who was already looking forward to opening day of the race season, the first Saturday in June.

That night Seth thought again about Ann, surprised that he had hoped for her acknowledgment and relieved that there had been no such confirmation of her interest.

The daughter of Ray Stilson could be trouble. He felt much better.

Showing Chance had brought several words of praise from Colonel Philip. In fact, before they parted Ludwell had ordered Chance saddled and ready for a trip to Williamsburg early Monday, then said, "You bring him to me. Your indentured service will be over the first of September, and we need to have some words."

Seth was wary. Virginia, although not so severe but still very like England, was definitely a class-structured colony, so much so that there were laws defining the social classes' privileges and the common man's place. Even at the races, only gentlemen could enter their horses—not the common folk. Unless there was some profit in it for them, it was not likely that the middle or upper class would care much about an indentured servant seeking a living in Virginia. And yet, Colonel Philip had spoken to him in a friendly, personal manner—unusual but sincere. He took comfort in remembering that the laws of Virginia protected the rights of the indentured and all free colony citizens, and he would be free in September. His thoughts turned back to Ann. Her auburn tresses and green eyes—they were really something. The vision lingered.

Monday morning, fresh from a day's ration of oats and coming off a day of rest, Chance's coat glistened under the polished saddle and silver studded bridle. Seth stood close to his head, barely touching the leather just below Chance's ear when Ludwell appeared elaborately dressed in caramel breeches, glistening black riding boots, a black waistcoat, and a white cravat. He held his gold trimmed, three-cornered hat under his left arm as he stepped down to the hitching rail and rested against it.

"It appears we are ready, Seth. Chance looks fresh and eager. That was a fast quarter-mile he ran Saturday."

"A strong horse, Colonel, as good as they come."

"Yes, right you are," returned Ludwell, then, "Virginia is securing the southern border with North Carolina. There will be great opportunities. If you would like to join me in some land holdings there, we both might very well prosper. The time to prepare is now although final approval is at least a few months off. I will send Zack and some field hands down there soon. You could go along, have a look at what is going on and see what opportunities may be there. I am interested in the fur trade, timber, water transportation to the sea, cropland, and travel between here and there. As an indentured servant of completed service, you are qualified to receive fifty acres of land. We can work out the details for an agreement between us once we know more about our common business opportunities. You can be sure there will be others speculating with the same interests, and that will be important to us. If you are interested, be ready to leave as soon as the planting is done—maybe even before."

Seth was overwhelmed. Ludwell was talking to him, if not like an equal, certainly as some higher station than servant—unheard of. He was surprised that Ludwell even spoke to him. Here he was talking about a business agreement. He decided not to get his hopes up until he knew more. He wondered what Zack might know.

"I am definitely interested, sir, and I thank you for your confidence. I will do the best I can."

"Keep in mind, Seth, it is business we are talking about. I'll know more about this when I return later today."

Ludwell gathered the reins and mounted. Horse and rider made a splendid sight indeed. Seth tried to gather his thoughts but it was just more than he could handle. He went back to the wood yard, picked up an ax and started splitting kitchen wood. It felt good to swing his blade and watch the straight grain wood fall apart in colors of white and heart red as it released the cleansing fragrance of new wood. This, he understood. This he could count on. There were no uncertainties, no questions, no surprises, just deep satisfaction with that useful work. Wouldn't Ann Stilson be surprised to learn that he had such a future: landowner, wilderness adventure, a new frontier fort. Seth drew his ax with renewed strength and laughed at the flying pieces of firewood.

Two days later, Seth found Zack at the barn cleaning the earth floor of the cooper's shed. Arby, the cooper, sat straddling a workbench that clamped cedar staves under pressure from a foot pedal while he drew a double-handled knife across the fine cedar heartwood.

Seth greeted the cooper and leaned against one of the shed roof posts. "Beats me how you get those angled cuts just right to make a round bucket, Arby. It's near magic."

"Well, truth be told, I don't get 'em just right. I just get 'em close enough that they can seal themselves when the bucket is filled with water. I hear tell you're getting' close, Seth."

"So I am. Come September, my time's up. You'd know about that. You've been a free man for years even though you're still here in the same place." Seth said it like maybe there wasn't much difference.

"True enough. Difference is I speak my piece now, just like a man ought to. Things don't seem right, we talk—works both ways. The overseer and Col. Ludwell have their say. After a while there's not much to be said. The whole business leaves me feelin' more like a cooper than a servant. It's a livin'. More to the point, it's the way it is." Arby spoke these last words with a tone of finality. Seth acknowledged Arby silently as he pulled at his floppy hat brim and ducked under the low overhang of the shed; time to see to the livestock, some of them were onery enough without making them wait past their feeding time.

They discussed the lot of the indentured servant and Seth's forthcoming freedom. Zack listened and thought how it made sense—seven years work for passage from England and keep. Why couldn't slave people have somethin' like that, he wondered.

Zack finished his sweeping with an old yard broom made of tightly bound dogwood branches and hung it on a wooden peg, just as Seth called out to him. "Whoa there, Zack," Seth called. "Looks like you and me will be traveling."

"Yes sir, Mr. Seth, I know. You tole me we be travellin' soon but not when."

"Monday, eighth day of May. The colonel sent me word this morning. Colonel figures the plantin'll be done by then. We'll be joining a few other men that the governor is sending to the fort site down south on the Meherrin River. No work. Just a look-see to get some idea of the size of the work we're to do later and be sure we have the right equipment. Come that Monday daylight, I'll have Molly saddled and ready for you. Everyone will be mounted."

"I'll be ready. Looks like we won't be carryin' much."

"Just us and the horses. They figure two days of travel to get there and not much more than that on site. Figure on a week barring mishaps."

9

Jock Adams stepped through the front doorway of his two-story brick home located on the center lot of three adjacent lots he had bought just off Duke of Gloucester Street. He had been quick to take the town's offer with the condition that he build with brick or wood forty-feet long by twenty-feet wide. Now his brick house with two chimneys and a full basement was a prominent addition to Williamsburg, the young capital of Virginia.

"Do my eyes deceive me?" he said aloud. "Is that Kadomico and Tom Singleton?"

"It is for a fact," Tom replied as he dismounted and threw the reins over the hitching rail next to Jock's mount that stood saddled and waiting. He extended his hand to Jock. Kadomico followed Tom's example and turned to face Jock.

"Jock Adams, I come," Kadomico said, as he spoke the traditional Saponi Indian greeting. He knew that Jock would not miss the implication toward his own Iroquois boyhood. Like Sam Layton, Jock's family had been massacred and the infant Jock taken captive by the Iroquois. At the age of eight, Virginia militia found and recaptured him, and the Adams family adopted him. Unlike Sam, Jock had eventually become a cherished member of the Adams family, educated in grammar schools in the colony, then sent to England for a higher education in business.

"Kadomico caught me by surprise last night, Mr. Adams, else I would have given you some notice," Tom said.

"Don't give it a thought. Come inside. Mrs. Adams will . . . ." but Rebecca Adams had heard the greetings and was walking toward them.

"Oh, my goodness, it *is* Kadomico. I thought so." Rebecca gathered her long skirt, took Kadomico's hand, and nodded her greeting to Tom. "Yes, do come inside. It has been such a long time." she said. "Your and Tree Son's room and clothing are just as you left them. We often hear of your work as an interpreter, of course. You are well known, respected, and admired. Jock and I are so proud of you." She held Kadomico by the arm and walked briskly toward the house.

"Tom, you and I might as well not exist," Jock said, nodding toward Rebecca. "You may recall that Kadomico lived with us while he studied at William and Mary. He became much like a member of our family back then. We see him from time to time but not so much recently. To Rebecca this is like having one of her sons return. The three of them, Matthew, Mark, and Luke, have been away now for several weeks. She won't be noticing anyone else until she has every bit of news there is to have from Kadomico."

"I won't be staying long, Mr. Adams," Tom replied. "Seems a lot to do back at our place, and I need to be there soon as I can. I wanted to be with Kadomico until he changed clothes. There aren't that many breech-clouted Indians about any more, and one armed with bow, arrows, tomahawk, and knives might be more than some citizens could stand."

"Well," Jock said, "Come on in. The breakfast fire is still hot, and I expect we can find a cup of tea or coffee and some of Rebecca's fresh bread. Let's sit in here and see if something can't be done about that. You can bring me up to date on things up your way." Jock led Tom toward a sitting room, but before they settled, Rebecca appeared with a pot of tea and a tray of biscuits, butter, and jam.

"Kadomico is changing clothes. How he makes the shift so quickly is a wonder," Rebecca said. Flushed with excitement, she swept into the room talking and bustling about with the food.

"When I first saw him talking to you there by the gate I was startled," Rebecca continued. "He looked so wild, so fierce. He has grown taller, stronger, and he looks warlike, more serious than when we saw him last. It is strange to hear perfect English spoken so clearly by one who is fresh from the frontier. He is married now, you know. Sayen is her name. They have a boy named Keme."

"See? What did I tell you, Tom. Rebecca has already started collecting the news," Jock said.

Rebecca was pouring tea for Tom when Kadomico appeared. On entering, he had not spoken, and they did not notice his arrival, but there he stood dressed in a fringed buckskin shirt and trousers and wearing beaded moccasins. He smiled at Rebecca and accepted a cup of tea.

Jock noticed the silent arrival of this young man and shook his head knowingly. His mind flashed back to his own boyhood days of captivity among the Seneca people of the Iroquois nation. He remembered the serious training to move without sound. He had lost that skill almost immediately after the English militia found him and returned him to Virginia.

"Sit down, Kadomico. We are glad to have you here and we hope you can stay a while. There is much to catch up on," Jock said.

These days when settlers were dying on the frontier at the hands of hostile Indians, a stranger would be confused and suspicious of the contrast between Kadomico's natural charm, carefully learned parlor manner, softly spoken English, and his buckskins, moccasins, black eyes and hair, and chestnut brown coloring. But here in Rebecca's parlor, his friends knew him to be an educated linguist of the Saponi Siouan-speaking people and dedicated to the search for understanding and peaceful coexistence between the English and the sovereign tribes of Virginia. They welcomed and applauded him for that and supported him in every way they could.

They talked for a time about their personal lives. Rebecca gave Kadomico a thorough update. Matthew and Mark were on the western frontier serving in the Virginia militia. Young Luke, Tree Son's favorite, was in London in a special school of commerce and trade preparing to work with Jock on his return. Yes, the Stilsons were still prominent blacksmiths in Williamsburg, their iron products always in high demand. Their daughter, Ann, had just returned from a school for young women in London. The Indian school at William and Mary was still active but struggled to produce good readers, writers, or Christians. Reverend Blair continued relentless in his determination, but there had been no more Kadomico-like students. Kadomico said, "I am glad to know about Matthew, Mark, and Luke. Tree Son often speaks of young Luke. He will be pleased to know that he will join his father when he returns."

Jock spoke of Governor Spotswood: an able, energetic, forward thinking man of the people—fair, productive, effective, well liked by the crown, "But he struggles for support from the planters and the burgesses for the arms and ammunition needed to make our frontiers safe for expanded settlement."

"And what about Tree Son?" Rebecca asked. "Is he well?"

"He is totally unchanged except now he is a skilled warrior, but still full of joy, mischief, and adventure. He waits for me at Tom's home to avoid returning to Williamsburg. He is more like Hawk than I."

"I will write to Luke tonight and tell him this news. Rarely do I hear from him that he does not mention his friend Tree Son. And what of Hawk? Do you see him?"

"Part of the reason for my visit this time has to do with Hawk. Tree Son and I met him in battle two weeks ago at Fort Neoheroka in North Carolina."

Jock and Tom straightened and leaned toward Kadomico. "You were at Neoheroka? We know only that there was a great fight going on there. We know nothing else. What of the fort and the Tuscaroras?" Jock asked.

"The fort fell after a siege of three days. I led a small band of warriors to assist the North Carolina army under Colonel Moore. They sent Tree Son and me into the fort to bargain for some kind of surrender. There we met Hawk, a prominent chief among the defenders. A striking warrior, he is. Hawk is now a full head taller than I. Just the appearance of his massive chest and muscular shoulders and arms will stop most would-be attackers. If anything, his dedication to the expulsion of the white man is redoubled since you knew him. However, it was only with his help that Tree Son and I were able to return from the fort with our lives. I left the fort under his direction hoping that he would follow me, and waited a long time for him to come, but he did not. I cannot imagine that he fell with the fort, but I do not know."

"Kadomico, this news is powerfully important. I doubt that Governor Spotswood knows these details. Can you meet with him?" Jock said.

"Yes, it is why I am here. I was about to ask you to help arrange a meeting."

"I will go directly and let his aide know. My guess is he will want to meet with you immediately and later with the council and the burgesses as well. Are you up to that?"

Kadomico stood to thank Jock but instead raised his hand for silence and listened. The familiar call of the black-billed cuckoo, rapid, repetitive *coocoocoo*, followed by a single chirp came unmistakably clear.

"Tree Son comes," Kadomico said.

Rebecca rose, ran to the front door, and threw it open. Tree Son stood at the first step smiling, but she knew Tree Son well and she cringed as she realized that this unannounced visit meant that the news was indeed bad.

"Rebecca, I come," Tree Son said in broken English.

"Tree Son, you are here," Rebecca replied in broken Siouan and stepped forward to take his hand. It was a game they had played years ago to learn each other's language. She led him into the parlor. Jock and Tom stood up to greet Tree Son. Still standing, Kadomico turned to face him. He knew that Tree Son's presence meant trouble and it was not at the Singleton's plantation, else the messenger would have been from the family.

"You are here, Tree Son," Kadomico said without changing expressions. "Speak."

"While we fought the Tuscarora, our town was attacked. Many dead, many wounded. Some captured. Maybe Iroquois. I go," Tree Son said in his best English.

Kadomico left the room without comment. Rebecca fought back a tear and said, "He will leave now. He must— his wife and son."

"Tom, please go to the stables and bring three mounts. I will ride with them," Jock said as he reached for Rebecca's hand.

"And I," said Tom. "And you need only two mounts, one for you and one for Tree Son. Kadomico and I have horses at the hitching rail."

Jock turned to his wife. "Rebecca, let the governor know what we have heard. This is important to him and his plans for our southern frontier. With the horses, we will be in Saponi town and back in less than two weeks.

"Once we ferry across the James, we will pick up the Occaneechi trail and follow it to the Trading Ford in North

Carolina. Saponi town is nearby. We will return the same way.

"Also, you had better send a messenger to the Singleton plantation to let them know where Tom is and when to expect him back." Jock removed his waistcoat and kept talking as he started toward his bedroom.

"I will do that. I'll also load the saddle pouches with trail food while you change into riding clothes. They will be ready when Tom returns with the horses." Rebecca spoke as she turned toward the kitchen and swallowed to suppress the thoughts swirling in her mind: frontier travel is dangerous, all her men will be away, why must Jock go, and how bad was the raid on Saponi town? She must let Matthew and Mark know. These troubling thoughts did not distract her from packing the saddle pouches with bread and pantry leftovers. She added dried fruit and meat from the cellar.

Kadomico entered the kitchen in breach clout, armed, and ready to travel. They carried the pouches to the hitching rails at the front gate where Tom had just tethered two saddle horses for Tree Son and Jock. Within minutes, the four of them were mounted and riding southeast to the James River ferry.

10

The horses dug into loose shale and earth just before gaining the top of the steep slope. At the top, Jock and Tom reined back to give Kadomico and Tree Son the narrow view through the big oak and chestnut trees. They could see their small town about a quarter mile west near the Yadkin River. It looked uncommonly silent: no life, no cook fires, no people. Charred pole frames of round-houses stood over burned out bed frames, partially burned furs, and other furnishings. No one walked the paths leading to the maize fields and the little creek beyond. Curiously, two of bark roundhouses remained unscathed.

Kadomico sat the saddle straight, eyes locked on the Saponi town. He had seen the remains of raided towns before, but never a town of his people. The Saponi were a peaceful tribe. There were no vengeances to be settled, no continuing wars. With the exception of their children, they held no special treasures for raiding parties. Apparently, this raid had happened simply because the town was there, unprotected, and occupied mostly by women and children.

Kadomico yearned to be on the trail with the Saponi party tracking the raiders, but first came the care of the survivors. He turned his mount toward the trail and down the gentler slope on the west side of the hill.

They rode across the level valley through switch grass belly high to the horses and came to the field of small mounds of earth prepared for seeding with maize and beans. They crossed the field, dismounted at the edge of the town, then walked toward the surviving longhouse.

Kadomico's twenty-one-year- old sister, White Water, appeared first. She limped heavily. One bandaged arm hung loosely at her side. Overwhelmed with a mixture of rage and sorrow, Kadomico swallowed hard against the bile rising within him.

"I come," he whispered and reached for White Water's hand.

For a moment she stood silent, head bowed, then lifted her eyes searching for his; but he had turned his head away as though he could not bear to face his wounded young sister. Her greeting had always been to challenge him to a race. It had been her way since she was able to walk and even after she'd become a full grown woman.

Kadomico turned toward her. Their eyes locked and he saw a deep-seated strength in White Water that had been masked by the wounds and bandages. As damaged as her body was, her spirit had been untouched. This woman had lived through the crushing wounds of war clubs and tomahawks and witnessed the unbearable sight of the hideous deaths of her people, and yet she came offering him strength and support. Suddenly he knew why he was there and what he must do. The rage subsided.

"Mother died this morning. Keme is captured," White Water said.

"Sayen?"

"She sleeps, badly wounded."

They walked slowly back through the frames of roundhouses toward the longhouse. Tree Son, Jock, and Tom followed at a respectful distance. Others began to emerge from the longhouse and stood aside for White Water to lead Kadomico to Sayen. Inside, about fifty old men, women, and children milled about as they attended another fifty or more wounded souls as best they could. They found Sayen covered by a thin blanket lying on her back on bare ground, her hands at her side. Her head was swollen grotesquely from a war club wound, and there were other wounds in her body, hands, and arms. Tom, Jock, and Tree Son left the two of them alone.

Kadomico knelt beside his wife. Her breath, weak and shallow, barely moved her chest.

White Water touched Kadomico's shoulder and said, "She fled with Keme as soon as she knew we were attacked. Two warriors caught up to her before she reached the creek. She pushed Keme onward to cross the creek without her, then turned and threw a tomahawk into the chest of one enemy and drew a knife on the other, but they fired an arrow into her left shoulder, then beat her head with war clubs and left her for dead. Then they caught up to Keme and brought him back. Some of our survivors, hiding near the creek, saw the fight."

"Has she spoken?"

"No. But she has taken a little broth and water."

"What of the council?"

"Only three have survived, all seriously wounded," White Water said. She pointed toward the opposite end of the room. "Father lies there next to Tonawanda of the Nahyssans. Chief Three Bears of the Occaneechi lies near them, still unconscious."

Kadomico rose as he asked, "Have our friends the Occaneechi and Tutelo been told?"

"They have, and many are already nearby gathering materials to build houses for us. They are also bringing more furs, blankets, medicines, and food."

"Let us find father," Kadomico said, and started in the direction White Water had pointed.

They found Custoga barely conscious with his eyes half-closed. He had taken the first musket ball in the chest and been left for dead. During the chaos of looting and killing, he had dragged himself among shrubs and leaves.

"Someone, I do not know who, opened the wound and removed the lead ball. I covered the wound with those heavy poultices," White Water said.

Chief Custoga lay feverish and weak from loss of blood, but he recognized Kadomico.

"You're here," he whispered.

"Yes, Father. We will find and punish the enemy. Our friends the Occaneechi and Tutelo are with us. We will rebuild near a new English fort, three suns east," Kadomico said. "It is a good place for our people." Kadomico spoke with confidence, even though he knew that neither fort nor land for the Saponi had been approved.

Custoga lifted himself on one elbow and waited until the pain subsided a little before he raised his eyes to Kadomico and said, "The Saponi have never looked to others for protection, but now it is different. Perhaps what you say is possible. We are so few now."

Custoga closed his eyes and lay back beneath the fur covering.

White Water touched Kadomico's shoulder and whispered, "Sayen is awake."

They stepped carefully among the wounded back to Sayen's place on the longhouse floor. When she saw Kadomico, she tried to turn, to rise toward him but could not. Her eyes rested on him as he gently slipped his hand under hers and watched for a sign of consciousness. Although no muscle in her body could respond, something stirred within her at the sight of him; not strength or joy, but more an awareness that this nightmare was past. Kadomico was here.

He saw her effort to move fail, and leaned in close so that his ear came near her swollen, feverish lips. He heard two jumbled words; the first was only a faint rasping noise, the second was clearly "Keke." He knew she meant it to be Keme, but her lips could not form the *m*.

"Yes, I will find Keme and bring him home." Kadomico spoke softly into her ear.

Sayen's eyes closed and she was asleep again.

Suddenly, from outside came a great noise mixed with excited voices of men and women. Kadomico and White Water left the longhouse to find dozens of Indians from other tribes dragging young sapling poles for fashioning roundhouses. Women brought bands of bound bark on their heads or strapped to their backs. Some had harnessed themselves to two poles brought together in a V and loaded with other poles and bark. They dragged the load into the burned-out town and began assembling roundhouses. Across the field another large group of Indians came with more bundles.

Tom, Jock, and Tree Son set aside their feelings of helplessness in the midst of so much tragedy. Glad to have something to do, they joined a group of workers, muscling poles into position for the bark covering. Several youngsters set about clearing the frames and ashes for the new houses.

"Jock, can we talk?" Kadomico said, as he picked up the opposite end of a long pole that Jock was lifting.

"Of course, what is it?" Jock said, as they tossed the pole into place with others.

"You can help us best by reporting all this to Governor Spotswood as soon as possible."

"Tom and I can leave now. There is a good bit of the day left for travel. What shall I say to the Governor?"

"There is a good chance now that we Siouan people and at least five tribes, perhaps more, will come together as one people allied with Virginia. We are ready to make a new town near the fort on the Meherrin, provide warriors, hunters, builders, and trade with the English there. Governor Spotswood has only to mark the place and we will build there."

"What else?"

"You can see we need blankets, medicine, bandages, and a doctor. I know this is probably not possible but we need them. If you think there is a chance, Tree Son will return with you to bring us what the Virginia people can spare. Also, I wish to keep one of the horses until I return to Williamsburg to speak to the Governor—maybe one or two weeks."

"That is all possible. Tell Tree Son to meet Tom and me at the trailhead yonder in one hour. In the meantime, take all these travel pouches and blankets from the horses and do what you can for your people with the content. We'll expect you in a few days," Jock said, extending his hand to Kadomico.

Kadomico found Tree Son with his parents. Both had escaped into the woods and returned to help the next day. Tree Son spoke first, "I have heard, and I am sorry for your loss."

"Tree Son, I am glad you are here. Now I ask you to leave again," Kadomico said, and told Tree Son of his talk with Jock and plan for the people.

"I understand. I go," Tree Son said and grasped Kadomico's forearm in affection and devotion to his friend, something rare for the carefree Tree Son. But it was hard for him to see Kadomico so drawn, shaken, and suffering.

Kadomico joined the workers, by nightfall he had his father, Custoga, his wife, Sayen, and his sister, White Water moved into their own roundhouse with the added comfort of fur and blanket bedding.

The day was almost spent when Tom, Tree Son, and Jock arrived at the James River ferry near Hogg Island just before the owner shut down for the day. After their crossing, Tom headed straight up the riverbank to his home near the Chickahominy River. Tree Son and Jock rode back to the Adams' house just off Duke of Gloucester Street in

Williamsburg where a surprised Rebecca rushed out to greet them at the gate. Yes, she had told the governor herself of Kadomico's news. He had many questions she could not answer and looked forward to meeting with Jock. She was delighted to learn that Tree Son's parents had survived the attack and could not suppress her tears when she learned of the mindless slaughter of the Saponi people and Kadomico's tragic losses. Rebecca assured Tree Son that the people of Williamsburg would make many gifts to the Saponi, probably more than he could manage in a single trip. She would get started on it this night, she said, as soon as she had set out a supper for them.

"Trail-dust piles on heavy, Rebecca. The only things that need bathing more than me are these horses. They're trail weary and starving for some decent food. It will take me about an hour if the stable hands have shut down for the night," Jock said, and started to turn back toward the stables.

"Jock Adams, I will set the table and walk these horses over to the stable myself. There is plenty of wash water out back and you know where your clean clothes are. Tree Son, your room is just as you left it. You know what to do," Rebecca said. "I will see that the horses are fed, washed down, curried, and turned out to pasture. I need the walk back so that I can visit ladies who will help me raise relief packages for the Saponi. They will bring what they can here. Tree Son can bundle it and be ready to travel in no more than a day. Now come in, please."

After ten days in the saddle, Jock was not up to arguing with such determination. He looked at Tree Son, shrugged his shoulders, and bowed him on to follow Rebecca who, skirts raised to free up her quick-stepping feet, was half way to the front door.

When she returned from the stables and the visits two hours later, Jock was already in bed sound asleep. Tree Son's room was empty. She was not surprised. Tree Son favored open spaces to enclosed rooms and sure enough, from the back door, she could see him now clothed in his buckskins, asleep on the floor of a little well shed in the back yard—his usual place. Rebecca dismissed her plans for the next day as she slipped into bed alongside Jock.

Tree Son woke and stirred about before anyone in the house. No morning light yet, not even the first beams of a sun that would eventually rise into a cloudless sky. Tree Son drank deeply from the well and splashed himself liberally with the cold water, pouring generous buckets of the icy water over his head and naked shoulders. By the time he finished, dawn began to break. As he walked around the house toward the front gate, he heard the unmistakable sound of cartwheels.

The neat little green and white painted cart arrived behind an old mare called Annie. Once she had been called Ann and was worthy to wear that royal name. In those days, she wore a shining coat of deep red marked with coal black feet, mane, and tail and a white splash across her eyes and nose, strong evidence of her Canadian birth. Once she bore prize-winning racers and breeding mares. No more. Her coat showed the grey marks of age and she chose a slow, yet proud, gait. Nowadays only Miss Rebecca called on her. Annie didn't mind the cart harness or the cart. Loaded or empty, she could pull it all day if Miss Rebecca was driving.

Tree Son leaned against the fence post and admired the outfit. The driver wrapped the reins around the brake lever and hopped down.

"Be ye that Saponi that stays with the Adams sometime?" he asked Tree Son.

"I am."

"Well, Miz Adams ordered this rig last night. Said have it here early. I 'ave to be over on the James River by good sunrise so I figgered to just tie Annie to the hitchin' rail there and be off. She be gentle as the feather down of a gosling, that lassie. Just needs a bit of company, she does.

92

Now maybe you could be with 'er 'til Miz. Adams is ready. Early as 'tis, I wouldn't want to wake 'er," the driver said.

Tree Son missed most of the words because the Scottish Highland accent smothered them, but he did understand that he'd been asked to tend to the horse and rig.

"Yes, I stay," Tree Son replied.

As dawn gave way to the rising sun, Tree Son noticed movement at the windows and walked toward the house but kept Annie and the cart in view until Rebecca motioned him to come to breakfast.

Jock finished the meal quickly and departed for the capitol building.

Tree Son continued eating silently. Rebecca hustled through some of the kitchen chores and instructions to the maidservant, then approached Tree Son.

"Today I hope that many people will bring gifts for the Saponi. Mary and Ann Stilson will be here to receive them. You and I will visit Middle and Green Spring plantations and ask for supplies for your people. You will be able to leave tomorrow with at least one pack-horse fully loaded," Rebecca said.

Jock sipped a cup of tea sitting opposite Governor Spotswood as he finished his warm milk and fruit. The governor tore off a generous piece of breakfast bread, covered it with blackberry jam, and folded it into a roll slightly more than a comfortable mouthful.

"See here, Mr. Adams," he said as he eyed the size of the sweet roll, "make no mistake about it. We will build that fort, and our trade with the Indians will be centralized and controlled there, and there *will* be a place for the Saponi town." He hesitated, then decided he could handle the whole sweet roll and took it all in at once.

Jock took advantage of the pause to venture a doubt. "There is fierce opposition . . . ."

Between chewing and swallowing, Spotswood shook his head and managed to interrupt. "I know all about the opposition. It amounts to nothing. What counts is how right this is. It is for the crown, for the colony, and for the people. The opposition is primarily from the plantation owners who think it will cost them heavily in support to build and to maintain. It won't. I will show them. The other opposition is from William Byrd. He and his father before him have made several fortunes on the fur trade. This will convert such future profits to the colony. Byrd is just one man, an influential one, but just one.

"True, sir, but he is well known in London."

"Right, and that is a problem. I will prepare a letter to London and speak to the burgesses this day. These events you bring to me are good news indeed. It is time to act."

Jock knew that it was important to leave before this conversation slipped into a quagmire of minutia. There were still too many unanswered questions, but so far, so good. He had enough to satisfy Kadomico. He stirred in his chair in preparation to rise.

"Not so fast, Mr. Adams. I said act. We must get on with it. Send Kadomico word to see me as soon as he is able. I'll have the land for the Saponi town marked out for him. His people can start clearing immediately. For the time being, do this in secret. Word will get out soon enough."

"Yes, Governor, I will see that he gets this message soon. Tree Son, his partner, is leaving tomorrow with gifts from our Williamsburg citizens. My wife is coordinating it today."

"Splendid. I should have thought of that. See that powder and ball from our reserves are included in the gifts. And be sure Stilson, the blacksmith, knows. He will help. My compliments to Mrs. Adams. She is a treasure in our colony." Spotswood wiped away the crumbs from his lips as he rose from the table.

Jock stood respectfully as Spotswood reached for his three cornered hat and smacked his leg with it. He paused, caught Jock's eye, and smiled. "And Mr. Adams, see that the blacksmith gets a few axes and saws into that gift shipment to the Saponi."

11

The day had dawned clear over the Saponi town. Barely above the eastern ridge, the sun forced Kadomico to ease down the armload of bark covering and shade his eyes as he squinted east to confirm that it was one of his young scouts running towards him across the maize field. Kadomico set out at a trot to meet him. Someone was on the trail. Friend or enemy? If enemy, every second counted.

"Tree Son comes with two horses," the youngster said.

"How far?" Kadomico asked.

"He has just started to climb the hill. He rides a horse like a devil white man."

"You have done well. I will meet him. Tell Tree Son's father and Chief Custoga." Kadomico gave the boy a gentle push forward and then turned at a hard run toward the trailhead. He wanted some time with Tree Son before he arrived among the people.

Sitting astride a large black horse with supply packs strapped on in front and behind him, Tree Son led a smaller packhorse loaded with rolled bundles. Securely strapped to the horses and double fastened with extra lengths of line, the loads shifted and strained against their lines just as the horses lunged and strained against the steep slope. Once the little packhorse lost footing and went down on its knees, but the rider and the horses made it safely to the top.

On the western slope, Kadomico stopped half way up the trail winding through dense growths of hardwoods in full spring leaf. It would be unusual if Tree Son could be surprised, but it was worth a try just to keep him alert. He concealed himself and started to wait, but he had barely taken a position when he heard the familiar call of the cuckoo followed by two chirps. Tree Son was expecting him. Kadomico stepped out on the trail, returned the call, and walked forward toward the elbow of a switchback in the trail. Sure enough, there was Tree Son afoot, walking with two horses behind him, one after the other.

Kadomico and Tree Son met on a patch of level ground where the horses could rest and graze the new grass.

"You travel alone with valuable horses and big packs," Kadomico observed as they greeted each other with clasped forearms.

"Turned out to be seven suns with the horses loaded. Jock arranged for two men to ride with me. They turned back the other side of this hill."

They tethered the horses while Tree Son gave an account of Rebecca Adams' work to arrange for the gifts.

"We could only bring this much. There is more. I will leave again after these gifts are unloaded. I will need two warriors to go with me," Tree Son said. "The trip is about six suns, maybe less on horses without loads. We cleared most of the trail obstructions."

When Kadomico learned that the governor was eager to see him, his mind began to spin. Could the Saponi somehow begin to relocate to the Meherrin soon—maybe even in time for the winter hunts? Could they raise their winter food of maize, beans, and squash here this summer and move the harvest to the new location later?

This was good news, but it added to the tasks facing him. In addition, this required immediate attention at a time when Sayen and the Saponi needed him here for the rebuilding. Also heavy on Kadomico's mind was the pursuit of Keme's captors. Each day the trail grew colder. Six Saponi warriors were trying to recover Keme and the other captives and to wreak vengeance on the raiders. Yet, there was no word from them. He wanted to join that pursuit.

Still pressing as these needs were, Kadomico knew he must not chance the cooling of this issue in the governor's mind. The Saponi needed to seize this opportunity for settlement land, hunting rights, and affiliation with Virginia's militia. Here was a chance to become defenders of the fort and key participants in the Indian fur trade. Not the same life as before but a life, and Kadomico knew that with the changes would come the protection of the well armed militia, the medicine of the English, steel tools, guns, ammunition and many other benefits. He would leave for Williamsburg with Tree Son and two warrior escorts at first light of the next sun.

Seven days later Kadomico and Jock sat at a large table poring over a map of the area that Governor Spotswood had in mind for Fort Christanna. They had just come from the governor's office where they learned that he was sending a survey party soon to the site he planned for the new fort. The governor's marks for the fort and the Saponi town were about a musket shot apart. Both would be on high ground on the south side of the Meherrin River.

Jock pointed to the Saponi town mark and said, "Look, here are the six square miles marked for your people."

"Yes, and the site for town. We can start clearing now for the town. The governor wants the land cleared and the timber ready when construction starts with the first warm days of next year." Kadomico hesitated. There were not nearly enough strong men and women left in the Saponi tribe to undertake such a huge building task. If they united with other tribes, yes. But that would take leadership, organization, and agreements accomplished only once before among the tribes of Virginia. Some years ago, Chief

Powhatan managed it to some extent, but even he left each tribe its sovereignty, and they remained living apart, independently in their own territories until disease or war decimated most of them. The remainder settled on Virginia reservations and some migrated north.

"Why the silence, Kadomico? Is something wrong?"

While Kadomico explained, Jock began to smile. "You're right, of course. But there is one man that can bring the kind of leadership you need, a man known and trusted by all the tribes."

"Sam Layton!" Kadomico knew immediately whom Jock had in mind. Virginia officials and the governor himself knew Layton's go-between work. Most of the tribes north and south knew Sam or his work, and all who knew him trusted him.

Seneca Indians had destroyed Sam's family when he was an infant. They had carried him away to the Ohio Valley and traded him to the Shawnee. Eight years later the Virginia militia recaptured him and placed him with the Layton farm family in Virginia, but Sam never forgot his Indian mother and upbringing. He silently tolerated family meals, holidays, church, and all daily interaction with the family without show of affection. He rejected everything about life with the Laytons except the farm work and the school. In those activities, he excelled and became a valuable member of the Layton household.

During his time with the Laytons, Sam's only friend was a schoolmate; a white boy his own age adopted by the Adams family and named Jock. Like Sam's experience, the Iroquois captured the infant Jock, and years later the Virginia militia recaptured him. Sam and Jock often worked together on their family farms, especially during planting and harvest times. On days when they finished their school and farm work, they roamed the woods, hunted, and fished. They kept alive their Indian values and beliefs but Sam more so than Jock. Unlike Sam's experience with the

Laytons, Jock became a beloved son of the Adams and an average student. Like Sam, he became a good hand on the farm but went beyond farming, mixed with the men of the community, and when he was old enough he went to sea on one of the merchantmen. Fascinated with the brisk commerce and trade among the planters and ship owners, Jock learned how both functioned and what they wanted. Eventually, he became a successful businessman in the Virginia colony.

Not so with Sam. When he became fourteen, he walked away from the Laytons and his friend Jock and returned to the Shawnee. A voracious reader skilled in farming and livestock management, Sam also spoke Algonquian, Iroquoian, and English. Languages came easy to him. Because of those skills, the Shawnee took him to council meetings with other Indian nations, and eventually to meetings where English speakers and Indians discussed land transactions, trade, and court cases. Other tribes and colonies began calling on him and he soon became a well-known trusted interpreter, a "go-between." It was not of his choosing, but his command of the languages, life experience with the Laytons and the Shawnee, and knowledge of the rivers and land of the Eastern Woodlands qualified him to work with those struggling to possess those wilderness lands. It was these go-between experiences that awakened in Sam a keen awareness and understanding of the dangerous differences between settlers and the Indians. Sam could see firsthand the increasing numbers of Europeans and the gradual shift in control of the land. He knew it spelled certain trouble for his people, and for a long time now, he had known an abiding concern for them.

Still, Sam's world was among the limestone riffles of the Shenandoah River and the tree-covered ridges and mountains that define the Shenandoah Valley. There, he met Starlight when he walked into the Shawnee town twenty-five years ago. She was only twelve then, but she knew immediately that they would be together forever even though Sam saw and treated her as one of the children of tribe.

One summer morning two years later, while bending over his canoe packing for a trip north, Sam looked up and saw the girl Starlight standing above him on the riverbank, legs slightly apart. She stood outlined against the clear western sky watching him, a small basket in one hand by her side, the other hand rested on her hip as though she did not wholly approve of what she saw. She might have been three canoe lengths from him when Sam noticed the sun flashing white across places where her coal black hair fell past her shoulders, across her small breasts, and almost to her waist. Standing ankle deep in the clear inlet water of the river, he paused and stared, his task forgotten. That day something stirred within him and permanently realigned all his being with the realization that the woman, Starlight, was no longer a girl, and the image of her there high on the bank would be forever in his mind.

Starlight raised her hand in greeting and said, "Sam Layton, these tortoise shells hold bread soaked in honey and covered with walnuts. They will give you strength for this trip." She wanted to add 'if you must go' but knew better than to say something that suggested she had the right to question him. Besides, she knew instantly by his open-mouthed stare that he now saw her as a woman and she would not risk changing that. She had seen the same stare from many other men and boys these last few weeks as she herself became more aware of her appearance. She was not flirtatious but when she smiled, it was a freely given gift and men and women both enjoyed her friendship. She cared deeply and equally for all of her Shawnee people, except Sam. She had loved him for two years and now she wanted him to know and to love her. This day she had brushed her long eyelashes and perfect eyebrows emphasizing the black irises of her eyes and prepared this gift of honey bread for him. It is time, she reasoned.

Shortly after he returned from that trip, they married. Two years later, Starlight gave birth to their daughter, Kanti. When Kanti was six, Virginia Governor Nicholson called Sam Layton to Williamsburg to escort three young frontier Indian boys to the grammar school at the College of William and Mary. One of them was Kadomico. They became friends, and from that time, Kadomico measured every thought of the settler/Indian conflict against what he imagined Sam Layton would think.

Now facing Jock and the prospect of gaining land on the Meherrin for his people, Kadomico said, "I will go to Sam Layton, Jock, and invite him to lead us. Even if he refuses he will advise me."

"What about the governor's survey party? The governor invited you. They are staging now over at Hogg Island. Also, Rebecca and Mary Stilson have enough gifts collected to load two packhorses."

"Yes, we must go with the governor's men. They will place the first markers of the fort and the Saponi town. Will you go with the governor's party?"

"No, there are enough people under his instructions as it is, but your presence with that group is important. Your people are depending on you."

"Tree Son and I will go. We will see the place the surveyor marks for the Saponi, then we will go west to the mountains and find Sam Layton and my son Keme. We know that Layton's Shawnee town is near a river in a land the Indians call Shenandoah, meaning Daughter of the Stars."

"And the gifts for the Saponi?"

"We have two Saponi braves camped outside Williamsburg to take the packhorses. They will not need saddle horses. They prefer to walk, and they can leave immediately. They will return the horses to your stable here in Williamsburg. Tree Son and I will work with them to get them started today, escort them on the trail for the first two days or until they are comfortable working with the horses, and return here in plenty of time to join the governor's party.

"Good. I'll let the stable know that you will be taking two of my saddle horses and two of the pack animals. I am sure your men will be welcome to travel with the Fort Christanna party. They leave in a few days."

"Jock, I thank you, but the packhorses can gain a few important days by leaving immediately. As for the horses Tree Son and I use to travel with the governor's party, we will leave them with the governor's party. We will travel on foot from the Meherrin to the Shawnee town. "

"As you wish, Kadomico. Rebecca and I have a small gift for Sam. It is Robert Beverly's *The History and Present State of Virginia.* Beverly's treatment of Governor Nicholson has caused quite a disturbance here as well as in London. Sam will find it interesting. Perhaps you could deliver it?"

"I will," Kadomico said.

12

The May morning dawned on four men milling about in the courtyard of the capitol building staging their departure for the Meherrin River. They were Kadomico, Tree Son, the master overseer from Middle Plantation, Luther Kingston, and Paul Lambert, assistant to the surveyor—four riders in all. Seth, Zack, and John Allen, the Surry County land surveyor, would bring the party to seven when they met at the James River southside ferry landing on Hogg Island. With the exception of the slave Zack, the men would be armed.

When the last of the horses and men were unloaded at the Hogg Island dock, John Allen swung into the saddle and raised his voice so there would be no mistake about his leadership. "I'm John Allen, Surry County Surveyor. The governor sends us to locate a suitable site for a fort on the Meherrin River—maybe two days on the southwest wilderness trail. We will go there again as soon as the burgesses and the crown have approved the fort. Until then, we remain silent about this trip. Your job is to determine what men and materials you need to build it. My and Paul's work is to conduct the surveys when the land grants are approved. Hold your questions—time enough to talk when we get to the Nottoway River campsite tonight. That's the halfway point. We'll be on the trail two days there and two days back, so manage your water and provisions accordingly."

John Allen and Paul started their horses toward the trailhead. Paul led a packhorse loaded with surveyor equipment: a sturdy tripod, plane table, Gunter's chain, paper for maps and plats, a telescope, surveyor's compass, and a set of plotting instruments.

At the trailhead, John Allen turned and rode back about half way along the line of riders. "Each of you has your own tasks to perform on this trip, but you are all assigned to me by the governor to assist as needs be in the surveyor work and that means before your own work. Keep in mind that we leave as soon as we are done with the surveying, and I will keep in mind that you need some time for your own work.

"This trip will take us close to or through the territory of several different tribes. The governor has sent them word that we are coming in peace. Therefore, I don't expect trouble from them. I do expect trouble from renegade survivors of the recent Tuscarora war. Three weeks ago they intercepted a large caravan of traders, killed several, and got away with over a thousand pounds of trade goods. Paul, Seth, Luther, and I will take turns riding point. If there are any objections, I need to hear them now."

"No questions, sir, but when I ride point, Zack will ride with me," Seth said as respectfully as he could.

John bristled silently. He didn't like add-ons to his orders. He had spent many years as a county surveyor, fought off Indian raids, suffered hunger, loneliness, and sickness far from help. John knew how to survive. He also knew the risks of traveling the wilderness in the company of those who did not know. If they encountered trouble on this trip, however, these people must work together to survive. This was no time to argue, best to allow but ignore Seth's remark. He turned his mount and walked him onto the trail without comment.

Taking the first point position enabled John to demonstrate exactly how he expected them to ride point.

The trail ran south-southwest. Occasionally, fallen trees or wild vegetation blocked their passage. While he had no more use for slaves than he had for Indians, he soon developed a respect for Zack's ability to clear the trail. He and Seth had wisely brought an ax and frame saw. The saw assembled easily and fit neatly under saddlebag straps. Working together, they made short work of trail obstructions. Clearing land was an everyday task back at Green Spring. John finally decided they were good, valuable men. Still, this was no time to trust strangers.

As for those two Indians, neither had spoken a word. The governor had mentioned their unusual language abilities and friendly, helpful backgrounds, something he listened to cautiously, without comment: Indians that could or would help Englishmen? Not likely. John had barely suppressed a snort. Well, the governor must have his reasons, he thought, and after all, he *was* the governor. John left it at that, but he tried to keep an eye on the savages. Trouble was, riding point in strange territory kept him busier than expected. Sometimes the trail forked, sometimes it just disappeared, and although John's compass kept him going in the SW direction, there was little to confirm that he was following the trail.

Within an hour, the party was deep into the wilderness, surrounded by huge oak, beech, and hickory trees. The forest undergrowth of dogwood, sassafras, and young saplings of locust, maple, and sweet gum often grew among threaded tangles of briar and vine so dense the horses had to travel around them. During one of these swings off course, John came to a fork. Both trails were marked with ax blazes, one looking west, the other east-southeast but much clearer and well travelled. He chose the east-southeast trail even though he felt they might be going away from their destination. When he looked back, the two savages were missing. He motioned Paul forward.

"What happened to the Indians?" John asked as he steadied his horse.

"Don't know, Mr. Allen. They were there the last time I looked." Paul spoke hesitantly unsure of whether the surveyor held him responsible.

John did not like the looks of it. There wasn't much sun to be seen through the forest canopy but he figured it was near noon.

"All right, close up and we'll keep going. No stops until we reach the Nottoway River. I figure we're still three hours from it. Tell the others."

The party strung out a little closer together and followed John. They had traveled less than a mile when John saw Kadomico walking his horse toward the party.

"What is the meaning of this? Where is the other Indian?" John said, as he rode up alongside Kadomico and stopped.

"Mr. Allen, my friend's name is Tree Son. He knows these woodlands as well as the palm of his hand. From the time we entered the forest, a warrior trailed us. About two miles back, Tree Son watched the warrior break off and disappear. We split up, left the party, and intercepted him. He is Tuscarora. Although he denies it, there is not much doubt that he intended to alert one of the outlaw bands in these woodlands."

This plainspoken savage spoke English as well as any educated Englishman John knew. He took a moment to let it sink in. He had expected the English. Most Indians in the colony spoke English well enough to get by in day-to-day living, but this was clearly enunciated, pure English. Add to that the information that they were already in danger confounded him for a moment. His mind finally processed the news that he may owe his life to this savage, this Kado . . . how did the governor call his name?

John gathered his wits and faced the situation head on. "All right, go get the renegade. We'll show him how we deal with outlaws."

"If you like, you can question him," Kadomico said. "I will interpret for you if you do not know the Iroquoian language he speaks, but that is all."

The other riders were close enough to hear the exchanges. That they had been followed caused them serious concern. Killing the spy and leaving him for the forest to dispose of would make sense.

John spit the words at Kadomico, "What do you mean, that is all? Do as I say or you can leave this party, and without the prisoner."

"Mr. Allen, I am Kadomico, Senior War Chief of the Saponi nation, son of Custoga, Chief of the Saponi. The Tuscarora is not a prisoner, but he is in my custody, that is the custody of the Saponi, and so it shall remain. Nor should you dismiss Tree Son and me. You are on the wrong trail and about to add at least another two days of travel to your trip."

Murmurs among the riders caught John's notice. Everyone was showing nervousness. He shifted in his saddle, leaned over, and spat at the ground. He wore a great leather broad brim hat that completely hid his face. Slowly he lifted his head level with Kadomico's. From the deep shadows of the hat, the whites of his eyes blazed controlled anger. His choices were troublesome: dump the savages and risk getting lost and the breakup of this party, or admit defeat by a savage and go on. His job was to get the survey work done and bring these people back safely. As his mind worked, he began to cool. He had misjudged these men from the start. He faced his party.

"Gentlemen, the governor saw to it that we would have a reliable guide on this trip even though no one imagined that we would need one. He also saw to it that we have an interpreter. Kadomico and Tree Son of the Saponi have captured a renegade who would no doubt have pointed us out to the Carolina raiders. From here on they will guide us through to the work site."

The announcement stemmed all doubt. The riders were ready to go on.

John turned to Kadomico. "Your move, Kadomico. We'll follow."

"The Tuscarora is a young boy, dangerous but not yet a proven warrior. We disarmed him. He will remain with us until we return. He and Tree Son wait about a half mile this way." Kadomico pointed east. "Send someone to bring them. Tree Son knows the way."

By now, John had learned to rely on Seth. He stood up in his stirrups. "Seth, you'll find Tree Son and another Indian down this trail east a ways. Bring them with you. You'll be shy a horse, but I doubt that young renegade will notice. He'll keep up with the people who have his weapons. We're turning back. If you haven't caught up by the time we get to the next fork, we'll wait."

Kadomico dismounted, looked up at John, and smiled his approval as he handed him the reins. "We will reverse our direction here. There is another trail south about two miles west. It leads us to the ferry at the Nottoway River. It is marked. I will circle you on foot to be sure there are no others watching. You need not be concerned. I will have you in sight at all times, and I will rejoin you when you turn south."

They found the Nottoway River and ferried to the south side. John Allen figured they had made almost forty miles, probably half way and were in position for an early start the next morning. It had been a good day after all.

They found the Meherrin close to dark the next day. The river was hardly more than a stone's throw wide, but the dark water suggested a depth that could be troublesome to ford with horses. There was flat rich grassland on both sides but no high ground at this point. Thickets of young trees and vines shielded the view of what lay beyond, but there was less flat land here. After the Nottoway River the land began to roll gently with irregular hills.

"It looks like we'll have to swim the horses over," John said. "We'll camp here for the night and cross over early tomorrow. In case of mishaps we'll be better off with daylight ahead of us."

The men stripped the horses and staked them out on good grazing ground. Seth and Zack marked a spot for themselves by stacking their saddlebags and tack on a level spot of ground before they began gathering stone and wood for a cook fire.

Seth pulled a tuft of grass, pressed the root ball between his fingers, and handed it to Zack. "This is rich growing soil, Zack," he said. "And there seems to be no end to it, no sign of any previous use of it, not even old hunter campsites."

"It's bottom land, Mr. Seth. Best there is. A man could do all right 'f he could have a few acres of this. Have to watch that river during the spring runoff. See where it got out of its banks not so long ago?" Zack pointed to watermarks on one of the elms near the river's edge.

Seth looked around for higher ground. This side of the river was mostly low land with widely spaced young saplings growing in vast areas of grassland, and on the banks, many outbreaks of rushes. Could he possibly get a patent for land like this? His fifty-acre land allotment would be due along with his freedom in September. Of course, there would be a rush for every inch of the river land as soon as patents were ready—something Col. Ludwell would definitely be interested in. He hoped he could get a look at the maps and plats Mr. Allen would be working up.

Seth did more than make mental notes. He had blank paper and a graphite marker in his pocket, and although his spelling was cryptically inventive and heavily accompanied with small drawings and counting marks, he had been making notes since they started. Now he drew a small rectangle and with a crooked line for the river through the length. He made notes and small drawings of interest: navigable river, rafts, canoes, low, rich land, grass, flood levels, higher land.

"Zack, where are the Indians?" Seth asked.

"One upstream, t' other took 'at captured boy 'n went downstream. Checkin' for trouble, I 'spect. Dunno who they be, but it sure is good to have 'em along."

"There's a little daylight left," Seth said. "Let's have a walk back into the timber. Looks like pine breaks aplenty and any size you want. The land starts to rise above the river just a little ways, but trees of every size and many kinds, oak, sweet gum, maple, walnut, hickory, and many good straight pines."

"I see that," Zack said. "Some of the pines'll make three palings and they'll need palings for a palisade. That old wall 'round the Jamestown fort?" Zack took a deep breath remembering. "Mos'ly gone now, rot and broke up for firewood, but the palin's once stood ten or twelve feet high, and no tellin' how deep they set. Coulda been as much as three feet."

They walked among the pines on clear, straw-matted ground keeping the campsite in view. A good strong campfire was already blazing. Seth was excited. The timber all around him was perfect. There were many trees between eight or twelve inches in diameter standing forty feet tall, and more for some. Over two-thirds of that was clear of branches. It would just be a matter of felling, barking, and sawing to length.

The trees varied in size, some perfect for the fort palings but some of the largest were perfect for building. What a strong house they would make, and in his mind there stood Ann on the porch backed by log rooms made of gold-colored logs under a shake roof. Zack had to tap him on the shoulder to get his attention.

"Now's th' time to cut 'em, Mr. Seth. Now's th' time."

The sap was running so high that a man could make to girdles and run a cut long ways from one to the other and pull the bark away in one piece. Not so after mid-summer, and by winter every inch would have to be draw-knifed or chopped away from the white wood. Zack's right, now is the time, Seth thought.

"Zack, if we have to wait until Green Spring planting is done before we take these pines, the barking will double or triple the labor."

"Yes, sir, be a lot easier to start now, but there's still plantin' to be done at Green Spring. Hickory leaves are already the size of a squirrel's ear. Old folks say ats plantin' time, and we're nearly past it."

Seth ignored the reference to planting work at Green Spring. "And if this is an example of the forest along the river, we can raft the palings and building logs right down to Allen's building site." Visions of a fort with buildings, settlers clearing land, boats on the river, set Seth's mind spinning so that he almost missed the return of Tree Son and Kadomico. Some kind of carrying on and laughter was coming from the campsite. It looked like the Indians had brought in a turkey and a young deer. Zack and Seth started back.

Full darkness now slowed their approach to the camp. It was alive with men skinning and butchering, feeding the flames for light, and hustling their saddles and equipment into little pockets of sleeping arrangements. John and Paul made a crude but efficient raft of dry driftwood for their survey instruments and tools. Luther, the overseer from Middle Plantation who had remained silent the whole trip, stood naked before the roaring flames wringing out his breeches just as Seth walked up to the fire.

"Waded 'er clean across to the other side, I did. Never got more than chest deep," he said to Seth. "And the current's mild enough, horses won't have no trouble atall."

Luther spread his breeches on a huge driftwood log back from the fire and picked up his saddlebags for dry clothes.

"You reckon Mr. Allen already knows where the fort site will be?" Seth held Luther's saddlebags while he dressed.

Well covered now, Luther eased down alongside his wet clothes to rest. At age forty-five, two days on the trail and a blind river crossing twice in the cool night air took its toll. He shivered and drew his saddle blanket over his shoulders as he spoke. "You'd be Seth of Green Spring, I'd say." His sturdy hand reached out toward Seth.

Seth took his hand and said, "Pleased to meet you, but you have the better of me. I don't know your name."

"Luther Kingston, longtime overseer at Middle Plantation." Then returning to the subject, he said, "I doubt he knows yet. Sure didn't see any high ground over there, and I can't imagine a fort on low ground. But it looks like he is bound to build on the south side of this river."

They settled into a discussion of what to bring with them to clear the land and to harvest building and paling logs, the axe men they would need, barking and staging crews, oxen, and tools. Zack listened. The man Luther must know Ella, he thought, as he dragged a great lot of coals into a second cooking fire and surrounded it with green hickory skewers of turkey and venison. His cuts were small, thin, and ready to eat in minutes. As they simmered enough to suit him, he laid them on a large flat stone covered with green rushes from the riverbank. The skewers disappeared as fast as he could deliver them until he finally began to get ahead of the hungry men. When he had a large mound in reserve, Zack took a skewer and retired to where the horses were tethered. He made sure he was close enough that he could listen to Seth and Luther planning the next trip.

Tree Son stopped in the midst of taking a bite of venison and looked up at Kadomico who had also stopped to listen. He nodded to Tree Son. The crickets had gone silent, a sure sign that someone had touched the tree where the crickets gathered.

The next morning under a clear sky, instead of crossing the Meherrin, John led the party upstream until the river took a sharp curve south, ran for almost a mile before turning west for a short way, then back north to about even with where the curve south had begun. At the base of the U-bend, they found a passable ford and crossed to the south side where the land began to rise in a steep grade. It turned out to be about a quarter mile to a hilltop.

John Allen broke out of the undergrowth at the top of the hill and gazed south over the gently sloping land toward a pine forest in the far distance. Because there were no trees on this long slope in the tiny valley beyond, John concluded that it was probably burned annually to attract the larger animals to grazing there. The land to the north, all the way down to the river, consisted of mixed pine and hardwood in virtually every size.

John Allen stepped off distances in several directions and drove a stake that would mark the center of the fort. Paul set up the plane table, telescope, and compasses. He laid out the Gunters chain for measuring distances while the surveyor unrolled his maps on a flat rock outcropping and used small rock weights to hold them in place.

"Better than I expected," he said, and turned toward Luther and Seth. "The fort will be five sided, one hundred yards each side. Instead of bastions, they will build hewn log houses at the five wall junctions. I'm not a builder, but you can be sure we're looking at a few thousand logs to get the buildings and the fort walls up. That works well for the clear cutting needed from the fort to the river and a couple of hundred yards on all other sides. The governor and the burgesses will want your assessment of time and labor for that."

John glanced at Kadomico and Tree Son who were waiting quietly behind the others. He motioned them closer.

114

"You may have noticed that ground we passed on the south side of the river just before we arrived here is flat and high enough to make a good site for your town. The governor marked it and asked me to confirm it. It looks good to me. What do you say?"

"The Saponi will build there. Our people are eager to start," Kadomico said.

"Good. We will go there on the way back, and I will mark the Saponi town building site with a steel stake as the point of reference," John said.

Kadomico suppressed the excitement welling within him and nodded agreement. "We are being watched," he cautioned. "If we blaze trees, leave stakes, or other markers, the Indians of Carolina will know and prepare as much mischief as they can."

"You're sure?"

"Very sure. They were here last night. There isn't time for them to get a war party together before we leave. I released the young captive this morning. He will report us as a heavily armed hunting party."

John had not thought through it, but he knew that Kadomico was probably right. Releasing that savage boy might be the best move yet. He would let his people know that this was not a helpless group of women and children out foraging for food, and the Indians would think twice before attacking a band of armed and ready wilderness fighters.

Building would likely begin in the spring of next year, 1714, and would require a great number of men, arms, and tools to work the forest. It would also clearly announce the coming of a heavily armed and manned fort to settlers, traders, and roving bands of Indians between the Nottoway and Roanoke Rivers. A land rush was certain. The Saponi town and the fort practically guaranteed the safety of settling in these river rich savannas and adjacent forest.

Overwhelming numbers of Virginians and North Carolinians would seek patents.

John Allen and Paul Chandler would come with the first builders, survey the boundaries, and lay out the building lines. They would mark their maps where they drove steel stakes below the surface to make reference points for the fort and the Saponi town survey. They could be ready to start home tomorrow, and that would suit John. Beyond his work as the Surry county surveyor, he was also a planter and one of the few students studying mathematics of surveying at the college. This trip had interrupted those activities, and he was eager to get back to them.

The current North Carolina/Virginia boundary dispute could easily include the new fort site. If it came into question, John intended to be ready with the latest surveying procedure and equipment. For the time being, he was confident that the site was safely to the north of the disputed line and south of the Meherrin River. He faced Kadomico. "You make some good points. We'll leave no marks. The stake marking your town will be buried here." He pointed to the map and drew a quick sketch showing the locations of the fort and the town.

"I understand," Kadomico said. "We will leave now to make preparations with our people, the Saponi and other tribes. When that is done, probably about the time the leaves turn, I will join you in Williamsburg and let Governor Spotswood know when we are ready to furnish the men he needs to clear the land and prepare the logs. Tree Son goes with me. Will you return our horses to Jock Adams?"

"You can count on that," John said as he finished the sketch and handed it to Kadomico. "You are a remarkable man, Kadomico. I thank you for what you have done for us on this trip."

Kadomico took John Allen's hand and replied, "Because you are alert and moving fast, you will be safe to return the way you came. We go now."

13

Kadomico and Tree Son had been running the trail west when Tree Son yelped, abruptly left the trail, and disappeared. Kadomico took it as a sign of trouble and followed suit. Kadomico found cover in a thicket of honeysuckle vines and cedar saplings and stopped, listening. Nothing. He waited for Tree Son's call of the cuckoo. Only silence. After a long while, they reunited.

"Someone follows," Tree Son said.

"Whoever it was is no longer here. We go," Kadomico replied, and they resumed their run.

After less than half an hour on the trail, a tall warrior, fully armed and able, stepped from the cover of a gigantic old beech growing inside a sharp curve just ahead.

Kadomico and Tree Son froze, waiting for his next move, looking for signs of others. Then recognition and realization enveloped Kadomico like a warm coverlet. He whispered, "Hawk, you are here."

Hawk stepped toward them, smiling. Widely known for their wilderness skills, these two were not easily surprised. Hawk enjoyed the moment.

"It was you who watched us from the forest back on the Meherrin," Kadomico said, as he took Hawk's forearm with genuine respect and welcome relief.

"Don't you know better than to touch a tree of crickets, Hawk," Tree Son teased, remembering the dead give-away that they were being observed that last night on the trail.

"I do, but the youngster watching you is still learning. I will tell him. It is a mistake best learned when his life is not at stake. It is good to know that you have not yet grown lazy and careless among the whites."

"Careless!" Tree Son snorted. "Careless! You who just came crashing through trees after us like the great god Okeus' storm. Why not just call and speak?"

"That was not me, Tree Son. That was the little boy you so bravely captured back there on the trail to the Meherrin. He came to me as soon as you released him, and I sent him back to follow you. Just now, he quit the trail after you told him you knew he was there."

"We spoke no words to him," Tree son said.

"Same thing. You ran for cover when you could easily have taken him with just a little patience once you knew he was there."

Kadomico smiled at this exchange and felt young again with the memory of arriving in Williamsburg with Hawk, Tree Son, and a young Tutelo named Shanda. It was thirteen years ago. At that time, the four of them were all about the age of the boy sent by Hawk today.

None of these young men had changed. Hawk, true to his nature, was now a leader of Indian opposition to the white man. Kadomico was a trusted, competent linguist among Indian and white men alike. Tree Son continued to focus his life on hunting, fishing, warring, and parading his achievements among young women, none of whom he took seriously. Shanda had contracted a serious disease and returned to his tribe. The young men were older now and more accomplished, but their natures hadn't changed.

"Join us, Hawk. We seek my son, Keme. The Iroquois captured him when our town was attacked during the Fort Neoheroka siege," Kadomico said.

"I know. I also know the raiders of your Saponi town. When I heard what they had done, I followed them north.

Keme is in my house waiting for you. I have told him you are near."

Kadomico choked back the swelling in his throat. Joy and relief eased the burdens of his concern about Sayen and Keme as he realized that just knowing that Keme was safe would hasten Sayen's recovery.

"You came looking for me."

"Yes, and I found you working with white men to take more Indian land."

"Hawk, we are on opposite sides in this war with the whites."

"But Keme is not. Follow me," Hawk said.

There was no question that Hawk was an outlaw Indian wanted by both Virginia and North Carolina. Also, he was probably the leader of a band or bands of renegades. To go with him meant discovering his lair. Could he then just walk out with Keme? Not likely with anyone except Hawk, but he trusted Hawk implicitly. Somehow, Hawk would make it work. It meant postponing the search for Sam Layton, but there was time. He turned to Tree Son and said, "I go with Hawk. Tell Sayen Keme is safe. When I return with Keme, you and I will continue to the town of Sam Layton."

Tree Son was quick to respond. "No. Sayen can wait another day. I go with Hawk."

There was no point in arguing with Tree Son. Kadomico turned back to Hawk. "We go."

After a few miles, they came near to the headwaters of the Meherrin River, now a small stream.

"Wait here," Hawk said.

They waited all night. The next morning the sun was nearing its zenith when Hawk returned with Keme. The boy was ecstatic to see his father, hardly able to contain the excitement within him, but his new friend, Hawk, had schooled him in how to behave bravely and without show of emotion. He simply said, "Father, I come." Kadomico felt the surge of emotions again. Keme was strong and

119

healthy. Kneeling there with Keme, Kadomico looked up at Hawk and rose never letting his eyes leave Hawk's. "You saved my life at Neoheroka, a debt I hope to repay. Now you return my son. This debt I can never repay."

"It is not a debt. I am glad. Leave it there."

Kadomico knew he could not leave it there, but neither were there any words left that would help. He removed the necklace of bear claws given him by his grandfather, Choola. Generations of great Saponi hunters had worn the necklace. He placed it around Hawk's neck and said, "From the Saponi. Your welcome is forever."

"I will wear it so," Hawk replied without emotion.

A moment of silence passed between them, then Kadomico spoke. "Hawk, the raiders of the Saponi hold other Saponi captives. I am Senior Warrior of the Saponi, and I will find and kill those who destroyed our town and took our people captive."

"I understand," Hawk said.

Kadomico bowed his head in sadness, then looked up hopelessly and said, "We cannot defeat the white man, but there are ways we can work together with them if we ourselves work together. Join us."

"It is not possible. I have abandoned my own Occaneechi people who pay tribute to the white man. I will not join others who do the same."

"I know." Kadomico barely whispered the words, knowing that he may someday come face-to-face with Hawk in battle, and if it happened, he, Kadomico, would lay down his weapons. He turned away and took Keme by the hand. When he looked back, Hawk had disappeared.

Kadomico, Tree Son, and Keme spent four days in the wilderness, often without benefit of a trail. They traveled steadily west-southwest from the western most part of the

Meherrin River to their own Saponi town on the Yadkin River in the Piedmont country of North Carolina.

Custoga's wounds were responding to the poultices, and although unable to walk yet, he was taking food and sitting up. Sayen had battled a fever and the beginning of infection, which White Water had managed to control with medications, poultices, baths, and frequent sessions of spoon-fed broth.

With all her wit and skills and in spite of the wounded arm, White Water was able to keep her new lodge warm, tend her patients, cook, and forage for the medicinal roots and plants she needed. There were times when she had to leave her patients to console others, help remove the dead, and share what food she had. She knew that her condition was no worse than that of many of the other survivors, and Sayen and Custoga were responding to her skillful care, but it was the loss of her mother, Tanaka, that so drained her strength and drive. She mourned deeply as she went about the overwhelming housekeeping, nursing, and community work expected of her.

White Water felt alone and badly needed help. She had lost her young husband in a skirmish with the Northern tribes and had not remarried. Neighboring tribes continued to bring meat, firewood, and water to the little roundhouses they had quickly fashioned, but their numbers became less and less as the emergency shelters became available and medical treatments progressed. It was already past planting time and they must get their own fields prepared and seeded with the three sisters: maize, squash, and beans. When White Water thought of all these things going undone among her people, she was afraid. How could they possibly survive a winter without planting and preparing? The weak and ill would simply starve. The newborn would die at their mother's dry breasts. She had heard the stories many times at the ceremonies and harvest celebrations. She longed for her mother and constantly asked herself, what would mother do?

As White Water adjusted the sleeping Sayen's blanket, the skin-covered doorway suddenly admitted a flood of sunlight into the room. Startled, Custoga and White Water looked disapprovingly toward the intrusion. It was Wolf, the ten-year-old son of their neighbor. The council had assigned him to watch the trailhead daily for strangers and to alert the town. He performed that duty diligently and with great pride.

"Kadomico comes," he said.

White Water's heart surged, but she remained calm as she turned quietly to Custoga. "I go to meet him," she said. She went to Wolf with tears in her eyes, took his forearm, and said, "Come." They ran side-by-side under a cloudless morning sky of deep blue. They leaped the winter remains of the planting hills and felt the cool morning air splash their faces. The loose earth around the little hills gave gently under their bare feet as they ran. Grasshoppers and butterflies flushed ahead of them. As they approached the trailhead, White Water's tears gave way to joy at seeing Kadomico and Tree Son as they stepped out onto the flat grassland beyond the still unplanted maize and bean field, but she was unprepared for the third person with them. When she realized it was Keme, she stopped and fell to her knees weeping, shaken beyond control.

By the time Kadomico and Tree Son reached her, she had gathered herself and started to rise. "Keme is safe," she said, looking directly into Kadomico's eyes for confirmation.

Keme stepped forward to be alongside his father. Kadomico had spent many days away working with the Virginia and North Carolina tribes as an interpreter, a go-between as the Virginians called him. White Water had been Keme's refuge since his birth. She had worked with Keme during his father's absences racing him, shooting the bow and arrow, throwing the tomahawk, and making arrows the way their grandfather had taught them. With the loving care of Sayen and White Water, Keme had become a strong boy, already skilled in the ways of hunting and fishing, but he was too young for the big animals, cougar, bear, elk, and deer, or for the intense huskanaw training that would qualify him for warrior status. At the sight of his distraught and wounded aunt, Keme's eyes glistened, but he choked back the tears and said, "I thought you and mother had been killed. I was afraid."

White Water took Keme's hand and said, "We were hurt, but I am well enough, and your mother will recover fast now that you are here. Come with me." White Water and Kadomico both suddenly realized that until now Keme had not seen the devastation of their town, nor did he know of his grandmother's death and that of many of his friends. As they walked, White Water tried to soften the bad news and to prepare Keme for the scenes of destruction and the wounded, assuring him that they would overcome this and make a new life. She emphasized his important part in the reconstruction of their town. Keme shifted his eyes to Kadomico and Tree Son, resplendent in their feathered headdress, war weapons, and their greased bare muscular arms, shoulders, and glistening copper colored skin. Keme straightened and looked up at White Water just as she squeezed his hand. Reassured, he smiled and asked, "We go to mother now?"

White Water stood, drew in the cool spring air drifting over them from the waters of the Yadkin River, looked again at her brother, and let the mantle of relief wash away all her concerns. She shook her shoulders as though casting off invisible weights. A gentle breeze tossed her shining black hair softly over her shoulders. No more tears. There is work to be done.

"We go," White Water said. "Your mother and grandfather are waiting."

White Water stopped at the door, signaled them to wait, and stepped inside. She went to her father, Chief Custoga, first and gave him the news in a whisper. Only then did she approach and kneel by Sayen, who lay still beneath the furs on the little bed raised slightly above the floor.

She waited quietly until Sayen opened her eyes, confused, worried, and in pain. White Water took her hand, moved closer, and smiled. Sayen's worried look melted away when in the dim light of the little roundhouse she saw the smile. White Water was caring for her and needed assurance that she was healing. She ignored the pain and returned the smile. White Water moved closer and whispered, "Keme is safe." Tears formed in Sayen's eyes and flowed over her bruised smiling cheeks. Breathlessly, she squeezed the hand that held hers, eyes locked on White Water, as she waited.

"He and Kadomico are here now, waiting outside."

White Water pulled the white wolf fur up to Sayen's chin, freed her good right arm, and covered the rest of her. She straightened Sayen's waist-length black hair across her right shoulder and arranged it over the white fur across her chest.

"You are beautiful, Sayen. I go now," White Water said as she nodded to her father and left the roundhouse.

Outside she approached Keme and Kadomico standing in a circle of friends who retreated as soon as they saw the grim disapproval on White Water's face. Tree Son had moved on to his own family.

White Water knelt before Keme. "Keme, do you remember when the enemy chased you and your mother across the creek?"

"I remember," Keme replied.

"She pushed you on and turned and fought the enemy with her knife, tomahawk, and finally with her bare hands. They shot through her with an arrow, then beat her with war clubs, but she survived. Now when you see her, you will see only her face and one hand and she will whisper, so listen close. When she sees that you are well she will heal fast, and it will soon be as it was before. We will take good care of her, and now that you are here you can help."

As Keme listened to White Water, the suppressed memory of that morning surged forth mingled with fear and uncertainty. He had not run that day, and he had not obeyed his mother. Instead, he had stopped and turned to look back. He had seen his mother take a throwing position and send her tomahawk into the chest of one of the charging enemies just before the arrow took her to her knees.

Keme had run back toward her and had leaped onto the back of the warrior that was beating her. Infuriated with the grip Keme had on his neck, the warrior stopped beating Sayen and twisted to rid himself of Keme. The other enemy grabbed Keme by the hair of his head and pulled him away.

Just before Sayen fainted, she realized that Keme had disobeyed to save her life. It was her last thought before sprawling into the ankle-deep water of the sand-bottomed creek.

The enraged warrior grabbed Keme and threw him bodily into a huge boulder. The warriors shouldered the unconscious Keme and left Sayen for dead.

"Go in now," White Water said to Kadomico. "She is awake but weak. She cannot move her head and there is great pain on her left side where the arrow struck. Take her hand. She is much improved since you saw her but her speech is broken and mostly in whispers."

What Keme saw on the bed of furs in the darkness of the room was part of a bruised and broken face barely visible between the poultices and bandages.

"My mother, I come," Keme said as he placed his hand next to Sayen's hand. He was uncertain and confused. Only half of Sayen's face was free of bandages. The exposed half was so swollen and bruised that he could not recognize the person that had played games with him, taught him lessons of sky, earth, and streams, raced him to the creek, threw targets for him to shoot, and told him stories of his father and grandfather.

Sayen took his hand, summoned all her strength, and spoke faintly, "You are here, Keme. Soon I will be well again."

Confused and choking back tears he wanted to comfort his mother, make her be well, but he dared not touch her for fear of hurting her more. He turned away and took a step toward the door. Kadomico blocked his way and gently nudged him toward Custoga who was sitting up observing this reunion. "Go. Speak to your grandfather," he said.

Kadomico saw the stress of Keme's visit on Sayen's face. For all the joy and reassurance of his safety, the visit had sapped her strength. Now she was fighting pain and weariness. Kadomico moved to her bedside and lightly placed his hand in hers, but before he could speak, White Water came with pain-relieving drink made from the leaves of the willow tree.

"She must rest now," White Water said.

Kadomico gently pressed Sayen's open hand, backed away, and left the roundhouse without speaking. He made straight for the river, waded to the other side, and climbed the mountain to a thick outbreak of mountain laurel and wind-shaped pine, oak, and hickory. He broke through the thick foliage and made a few steps over a small clearing to the edge of a steep solid rock precipice facing east over the valley and river below. It was here many winters ago that he and Sayen had pledged their lives to one another. He built a small sacrificial fire, stood by the rising smoke, faced east, and prayed.

With the little fire between him and the eastward view, Kadomico sat down and began to think. Hours later as the long shadows of the mountain crept across the valley, he took one last look, and began his descent. When he reached his roundhouse, he sent Keme for Tree Son.

"We must plant the winter food, Tree Son. It is past time."

"I am a hunter, Kadomico, not a farmer. What of Sam Layton?"

"True. We are not farmers, but if not us, who will plant? You see the sick and wounded about us, and without the maize and squash, the winter will starve our people and the Saponi will be no more. Our work with Sam Layton can wait the few suns it will take us to do the planting. We can leave as soon as it is done."

Doing woman's work was not Tree Son's notion of what a senior warrior did, but these were special times and he knew the truth of Kadomico's words. If it had to be done, he would do it—all the more reason to find and punish the Iroquois that did this.

"After we find Sam Layton, we find the Iroquois who did this, and make sure that their death will be slow," Tree Son said.

"I feel the same, Tree Son, but once we have spoken with Sam Layton, we must prepare the land that will be ours on the Meherrin."

"When do we punish the ones who have killed our people?"

"When our people are safely in houses in the new town on the Meherrin, we will go together to punish the Iroquois. Hawk could help us. He knows the raiders."

"He knows the raiders, but he would never betray them, Kadomico. He may even have joined them by the time he sees us alongside the white men in a fort."

"We will find a way, Tree Son. Right now there is much to do here and not many to help."

14

The first Saturday in June, Seth and Chance won the opening race of the Williamsburg racing season just before a cloudburst drove them to the shelter of the stables. Ann made her way in a driving rain toward the stables looking for her seventeen-year-old brother Nathan. She found him talking to Seth, who was rubbing and drying the big black racehorse. Seth stopped when Ann stepped into his view next to her brother at the half-door of the stall. Nathan, annoyed to have his man-talk interrupted, hesitated to make the introduction, and Seth seized the opportunity. Without looking eager or slighting Nathan, he turned toward the stall door with a brush in one hand, a towel in the other, and said, "We met not long ago, Miss Stilson, at the wheel of my carriage. I'm Seth Jackson, Green Spring plantation."

"I do remember. It was one of my clumsier moments in more ways than one," Ann said, closing her umbrella. "I don't remember thanking you."

Still annoyed at the interruption, Nathan gently took Ann's arm and guided her aside from the path of a passing horse and rider. "The stable area is not the best place for ladies and even less so for girls without boots on such a day as this," he said. They stood in front of Chance's stall in the narrow space under the shed roof of the stables. The rain was letting up but the grounds were a sea of mud.

"Well, you disappeared, and it is time to go," Ann said briskly. Then dismissing Nathan altogether, she said to Seth, "I am glad to be able to correct my bad manners when we met before. Thank you for your help."

"My pleasure," Seth said over the back of Chance as he continued rubbing and drying.

"I know your reputation with horses, and I am considering buying a saddle mount. If you know of one that might be suitable, please let me know, "Ann said.

Nathan's mouth popped open involuntarily. That was not so. That wasn't even possible. Their father would never permit it, not for a girl, not before his father bought him his own horse. The subject had never come up. Or had it? Another hesitation and he again missed his chance.

"A pleasure to meet you, Mr. Jackson," Ann continued, as she turned and stepped out into the drizzle taking no notice of the mud closing around her high-top, buckled shoes. She held her skirts just above the ground and walked chin up, oblivious to her frustrated brother who was coming along behind still putting the whole scene together.

Following that encounter, Seth and Ann would meet often in the stables after the Saturday races. Seth would come to anticipate it, and both Stilson parents became concerned. So far as they knew, Ann had never shown that kind of attention to anyone. Mrs. Stilson knew as well as Ann, and better than Seth, what was going on. As the weeks wore on, she prayed that Ann would eventually realize the impossibility of a friendship with Seth, and that nothing more would come of these chats.

Ann, however, settled naturally and comfortably into visits with Seth at the stables after the races, and the friendship proceeded slowly. Indeed, it seemed to be moving toward something more than a casual friendship. If Ann was aware of the social class distinction, she ignored it.

Seth, on the other hand, was especially cautious of the strong, influential blacksmith who was openly protective of his only daughter. Stilson could wreck the plans of a simple indentured servant with a wave of his hand. To his credit, Seth had a winning way with people—landed gentry or slave, running thief or local preacher. People in general liked and trusted him, and that included the young women of the colony. Being unaware of this magical trait may have been one of the reasons for its unwavering success. For the time being, though, Seth would be especially careful not to give her father reason to dislike or suspect him.

If Ann refused to acknowledge this unspoken barrier to their friendship, she did seem to accept it. She never openly flirted, but her eyes and smiles betrayed her. When the desire to hold her possessed him, Seth looked away, but the act itself was a dead giveaway and Ann knew. She also knew with certainty that it would be different when Seth established himself as a free Virginian. And so, like moths to a flame, with each visit they drew closer.

15

Sunlight streamed through the window and across the paper under the goosequill pen held poised by Alexander Spotswood as he considered the next words of his letter to the Bishop of London. This letter would report the progress of the Indian schooling and the need for more funding and other resources. It was just one more letter in a stream of reports and appeals that he kept sending to appreciative authorities in London. Of many pressing matters before him, Spotswood placed two above all others: a secure southern and western frontier and the education and conversion of the Indians to Christianity. As to the latter, it was not surprising that the Bishop was funding and demanding conversion of the Indians in keeping with the holy obligations of the church. Spotswood's letter glowed with Indian school progress and made a powerful case for more resources. No wonder he enjoyed the trust and support of so many of those in authority in London after only three years in the Lieutenant Governor's job.

Alexander Spotswood was thirty-four years old and backed by an outstanding record of military service when he came to govern Virginia. At first, he worked to satisfy the authorities who sent him, but gradually he convinced himself that he could accomplish that best by focusing on the needs of Virginians and Virginia. Young and experienced in leadership under trying conditions, he set out to open the frontiers and work with the Indians. He was quick to step into a saddle and lead militia to solve a problem on the frontier, board a ship to investigate suspicion of piracy, and to personally deal with slave and fur trade matters.

The Virginia Council and Burgesses supported his proposal to build Fort Christanna in the south, and to finance the fort, he proposed the establishment of the Virginia Indian Company, a private enterprise to be owned by shareholders. The company, if approved by provincial statute, would fund the maintenance of fort operations and security in exchange for exclusive rights to Indian trade there.

As Spotswood sat writing to the Bishop of London at his tiny desk that morning in 1713, he paused to review his support and opposition. The Bishop and the Lords of Trade were listening to him with genuine interest in his promise of additional revenue-producing settlements and more taxpaying citizens.

The powerful and influential planters of the colony, however, were still cool to the expense of building and maintaining another fort. Some would align with him only when they knew how self-sufficient this fort would be under the management of a shareholder company authorized to control all south and southwest Indian trade. Others could see the lucrative advantages of settling yet another frontier. The fur and tobacco trade alone would easily support the fort and leave a tidy profit for the shareholders.

On the other hand, William Byrd II, his staunchest adversary, led a deliberate effort to defeat the notion of a Virginia Indian Company endowed with control of the fur trade—an outrageous monopoly, he called it, and attacked Spotswood as personally profiting by it. Byrd wielded an enormous influence in the colony as one of the largest landholders and as a member of the twelve-man Council that constituted the powerful upper house in the Virginia Assembly. Because he stood to lose his long-standing control of the fur trade on which the Byrd fortune had been made, he was overtly passionate in his opposition to the fort in general and realignment of the fur trade in particular, and the fight was on.

Responding to the recent surveyor's report, Spotswood's pen fell to its task and words flowed like soldiers passing in review, every line straight, every soldier the perfect height, every space the same. He wrote of the Saponi participation and pledge of labor for building and guarding the fort, of the surveyor's praise of the hilltop location over fertile lands, and of a river rich in fish and sweet water. In addition, he reminded the Bishop of those important personages that publicly supported the fort: Ludwell of Green Spring and Page of Middle Plantations. He smiled at his words as he folded the sheets and sealed them. It was definitely going to happen. The Assembly had authorized him to continue studying, exploring, and planning, and it was already working. Frontier hostilities had eased as Spotswood had personally led forays among the Carolina hostiles to set up trade and boundary agreements. Nor was it a secret in the colony. Rumors flashed among the speculators, opportunists, and new settlers.

Spotswood's next letter would be to the Board of Trade emphasizing the continuing waves of settlers arriving in Yorktown, Point Comfort, and Williamsburg and calling on Virginia for land. To meet these legitimate demands, Virginia must open and secure the territory on its western and southern frontiers by placing a fort in each area. He explained how to do it with a minimum of expense by establishing the Virginia Indian Company at the southern fort. The fort would be named Christanna after Christ and Queen Anne. All Indian trade would be controlled through that company, and the profits would be used to build and maintain the fort. Then, with the fur and other Indian trade under control, Virginia would make treaties with the Indians and turn Fort Christanna into a thriving community of Indian education, religious training, and commerce.

Pressure for land continued to build. The land office finally posted announcements on the door that patents for frontier land were pending completion of surveys. Ships continued to unload land-hungry Europeans, and each day a few more of them turned up in front of the land office building to petition for patents.

Spotswood finished his letter to the Bishop and began to sketch a five-sided fort with log houses to do double duty as quarters and bastions at the corners. His drawing skills matched his penmanship. The sketch soon rendered a gated fortress of palisades with large log houses instead of bastions. The houses were a hundred yards apart, and like a bastion, each was able to defend the other. The Indian town would be similar, with log houses instead of bark-covered roundhouses. English builders would train the Indians and see that they had the tools to get the job done. With this drawing and a few selected visits, he would soon have the shareholders he needed to establish the Virginia Indian Company.

The more Byrd II heard about Fort Christanna, the more incensed he became. Over many years his father, William Byrd I, had created a rich estate from the Indian fur trade—*and without interference from any governing body.* It was not surprising that his son, Byrd II, intended to keep that lucrative business under his control. His young bachelorhood had kept him in school in England for twelve years—in school and enjoying London's fine coffee shops and beautiful women, some of them rich and powerful. Back in Virginia since 1704, he was sole successor to the Byrd fortune, a well-known, well-liked, powerful planter and an influential Virginia official. He married Lady Lucy Parke, daughter of the Governor of the Leeward Islands and inheritor of considerable lands in her own right.

In spite of Byrd's popularity and vigorous opposition to the development of Fort Christanna, it continued to gain favor locally and in London. After all, the case for stopping the bloodshed on the frontier was a strong incentive, and certainly a fort would make a difference. He knew that Spotswood was summoning support from the Bishop, the Board of Trade, certain Earls, even the Crown, but Byrd, was no quitter and certainly no loser. This time the choice of weapons was logic, reason, oration, and persistence rather than steel, powder, ball, swords and patience. Fine. He was at home with either, and he picked up the pen to begin his own letters to London.

16

In the three weeks since their return to Saponi town in mid-May, Kadomico and Tree Son had managed to hill the soil and plant the maize crop for the coming winter. They were a little late with the planting, and it was not work they were accustomed to. Tree Son, however, had spent more time recruiting women to do the work than doing it himself. He laughed and joked with them and praised their skills at hilling and planting. Many of them came to the field just to escape the sorrowful scenes of their recovering village. Kadomico had to admit it was a time when Tree Son's charm and popularity did double duty. The women, old and young, loved being with him and the work in the field was finished in half the time they had expected.

Reduced to a few dozen families and less than thirty warriors, the Saponi people were eager to move to the place on the Meherrin near the future Fort Christanna. Kadomico had cautioned them that the fort must be finished before the land would be theirs. Although they could send in work parties to fell trees, cut logs for housing, and fashion the palings for the fort, they presently had neither the skills and tools nor the labor force needed. The problem was beyond Kadomico's knowledge, and his thoughts kept returning to Sam Layton.

Sam, a white Shawnee Indian was an experienced trapper, trader, interpreter, negotiator, and trusted go-between of Indians and settlers. He would know how to approach these problems and the tribal counsels would welcome him, listen to him, and above all, trust him. He badly needed Sam Layton's help. Kadomico called Tree Son, and they set the time to leave for Layton's Shenandoah Shawnee town.

Kadomico and Tree Son inhaled the fresh late spring mountain air as they ran northward in single file. They watched the trail for sign of travelers and kept glancing west for the beginning of the valley of switch grass, deer, and elk Sam had described to them. Eventually there was a break in the hills rolling west and a ten-mile-wide valley of tall grass came into view. Occasional clusters of shrubs and saplings peppered the flat land. It was clear to Kadomico that hunters burned it seasonally to keep it the perfect grazing ground. Sam had said it was called *Sherando* after a famous Iroquois Chief who often visited there. On the far side of the valley at the base of another ridge of mountains, a thin line of mature trees marked a serpentine river twisting north toward Layton's home.

They turned off the trail and descended, often with only vines to break their fall over precipitous terrain. As they leveled off and started their run again, grouse, quail, and other birds flushed ahead of them. It was obviously a rich hunting ground, but they saw no hunters. When they came to the edge of the trees bordering the river, they stopped in a concealment of honeysuckle and wild grape vines, branches, and small saplings. Tree Son was uneasy.

"It is not right that there is so much here and so few, if any, people," Tree Son whispered.

Kadomico tapped him on the shoulder, rose to full height, and raised his open hand in peace.

"We come for Sam Layton, Shawnee warrior and friend of the Saponi." Kadomico spoke in Algonquian.

Tree Son was about to question him when three tall warriors appeared more like a vision than a reality. They were armed with steel tomahawks and long bows nocked with steel-tipped arrows. Although their faces were not painted with war paint, their feathered warlocks and muscular torsos, strapped with knives and arrow quivers, made an imposing sight.

The front man of the trio stepped away to the north and said, "Come. Sam Layton."

It could be a trick, but the name seemed well known to them. With a Shawnee warrior in front and behind them, they walked single file toward two dugout canoes resting high on the riverbank.

Tree Son said, "How did you know? I did not see them."

"They were upwind and smelled of bear grease." Kadomico did not press the point as they often did when one excelled over the other. He was still uncertain about these warriors and their destination.

The spring run-off was barely over, giving the river many long stretches of smooth water. Still, now in canoes, they had to navigate around huge limestone boulders, fish traps of stacked stone, and twice they had to portage around small waterfalls. They paddled for half the afternoon before they came to the shaded mouth of a shallow creek flashing white before emptying into the river on the west bank. One side of the creek was deep enough to run the canoes upstream to a sandy beach bordering an area of quiet water where several canoes rested safely ashore or anchored in the inlet. The path beyond led to the Shawnee settlement.

The town had only a dozen bark roundhouses, each with a doorway of hanging skins. There were no palisades around this town but it was located in the center of a large open space where the grass and shrubbery had been burned away making a surprise attack unlikely. Each house had an area set up for working a variety of animal skins stretched on frames made of split tree limbs. In one area, Kadomico saw a tawny colored cougar skin of thick winter fur stretched inside a tall frame. Placed there among several muskrat, deer, and elk skins, it dominated the scene. These hunters must be good and the game plentiful, he thought, as he admired the quality of the fur and the work.

They stopped at the center of the town. One warrior remained with them. The other two left. Children and a few of the women had stopped working to stare at them when one of the warriors reappeared with a woman of slight build in a buckskin skirt, waist length black hair tied back with a band of leather decorated with dyed porcupine quills. She walked briskly, a little ahead of the warrior. He had interrupted her work just when the skin she was working on was beginning to harden and before she had finished tying the stretchers. She had doused the skin with water and left it. As she drew near the visitors, she stopped. The warrior stopped behind her, his tomahawk drawn. She stood legs slightly apart, arms folded over bare breasts. She must be the queen of these people, Kadomico thought. He and Tree Son stood.

"Who comes here?" she said.

"I am Kadomico and this is Tree Son. We are Senior Warriors of the Saponi, here to speak with Sam Layton, friend of our people. Would you be Starlight, mother of Kanti?"

Starlight's face changed from frown to surprise. She knew those names well. Her husband would be elated. She found Kadomico's eyes and smiled showing even rows of gleaming white teeth behind full lips in deeply tanned skin. But it was the dark eyes behind long black lashes under arched eyebrows that struck the visitors silent. Starlight's presence was more than beauty; it was commanding beauty. Well aware of how she sometimes affected men, she gave them a moment before speaking.

"Welcome, Kadomico and Tree Son. I am Starlight. Sam Layton is on the river." She spoke in Siouan. "He will return before sundown. We are a small hunting town. You will sleep in our house. Come." She dismissed the warrior with a word in Algonquian and a hand gesture.

She led her visitors to the worksite located alongside their roundhouse. There, with her back to them, a young woman was lacing a fox skin to a frame made of young sapling staves assembled with rawhide thongs.

"This is our daughter Kanti," Starlight said and turned toward Kanti. "These are friends of your father."

Kanti nodded to them and resumed her work. Tree Son stepped forward with a bone awl from his side pouch in one hand, took the edge of the skin she was working on in his other hand, and paused looking straight into Kanti's eyes. She released her hold on the skin to allow him to pierce a place for the next lacing. They found a working rhythm so quickly it was as though they had always worked together; Kanti pulling, smoothing wrinkles, choosing thongs, tying laces; Tree Son sorting thongs, helping with wrinkles, supporting the frame to stabilize it, and piercing the edges of the skin for her laces. They worked silently, as one, not at all like two people who had just met.

Starlight disappeared into the house and returned with a turtle shell of dried fruit, smoked fish, and parched maize. Kadomico took a small portion of fish and watched Tree Son curiously. Starlight placed the shell of food high on the stack of firewood and returned to her work near Kadomico. They talked of their families and Kadomico's time with her husband at the grammar school in Williamsburg. In a little while, Starlight went into the roundhouse.

Since it looked as though Tree Son and Kanti did not intend to stop their work, Kadomico walked away into the village looking for the warriors that had brought them there. He found them rubbing their bows and arrows with a grease of animal fat. He exchanged greetings with them and they fell to discussing their hunting and fishing grounds. After a while, Kadomico saw Sam Layton with three warriors striding across the open space surrounding the village.

"Sam Layton comes," he said, and made a motion of friendship and departure before walking away to meet Layton.

They met at the edge of the village. Only Sam's blue eyes and shoulder length brown hair, held in place with a headband, made him discernible from the Shawnee. He was not as tall as his companion warriors, but he was muscular, solid through the chest and shoulders with powerful arms and legs. In typical Shawnee fashion, Sam had continued to train for strength and endurance all his life. Now at the age of thirty-nine, clad in breechclout and a bright green cloth of silk binding around his hair, Sam made a striking figure. He reached out for Kadomico's forearm in the traditional greeting of friendship.

"You have come a long way," Sam said.

"But I come and Tree Son is with me. He has met Kanti and is acting strangely." Kadomico had to struggle to control his excitement at seeing his mentor of thirteen years ago.

"Yes. Men are apt to act differently when they meet Kanti or Starlight for the first time. Make no mistake. They are strong sensible women. Kanti is usually with me on these trips to hunt or fish. This time she wanted to prepare some hides for trade."

They reached the roundhouse and found Starlight preparing food for the celebration in honor of the visitors. There would be a fire at the center of the village, a steady beat of drums, and warriors would dance their hunting and warring feats. Some of them would be in feathered costumes and fierce animal masks. Others wore masks they had carved or assembled and colored. The village would assemble at sundown.

Kadomico and Sam found a place on the furs stationed near the smoldering cook fire in the center of the house, produced pipes, and began to tamp them with tobacco. As they sat down, Starlight moved toward the skin-covered doorway and said, "I will let Kanti and Tree Son know you are here."

"I did not see them when we came in," Kadomico said.

"They are not there," Sam added.

Starlight's eyes flashed at Sam as she turned back to them. "Not there?"

"Not there," said Sam, "Probably on the river. There is a finished fox skin leaning on the firewood."

Starlight held her anger, stepped through the doorway, and checked the work site for sign. The pair of footprints left in the dust of the worksite led unmistakably toward the river. Starlight saw that one pair was slightly larger than the other and closer to it than necessary and her heart stirred. She looked upward and whispered, "No, No. Please no."

Kadomico handed Beverly's *History and Present State of Virginia* to Sam. "Jock Adams wants you to know that you are welcome in his home. He sends you this gift."

Sam gasped to see the shiny new volume, an uncommon treasure in his house, a gift. He drew it carefully to his lap, laid a handful of dry twigs on the coals, and shifted to catch the firelight. He opened the cover. There in Jock's clear cursive were the words, *To my Shawnee brother, Sam Layton. Jock.*

"Jock Adams knows what this means to me but remind him anyhow. I will cherish it. Tell him that I will visit them before the leaves turn again."

"I will tell him. It is good to know that you will return to Williamsburg. I have much to tell you."

"I am sure there is, but first tell me of your family and the Saponi."

"It is why I am here, Sam." Kadomico drew lightly on his pipe and exhaled a wisp of silver smoke into the still air.

142

"Recently the Iroquois attacked our town. Our losses were heavy, houses , food destroyed, more than half our people dead or wounded. My mother died in battle, my wife Sayen barely lives, and my son Keme and other Saponi children, were captured."

Sam listened, staring at the smoldering coals of the cook fire. Now he stirred, his eyes slowly lifting from the coals to Kadomico's eyes where they locked. The veins of anger rose on Sam's forehead and neck, but he waited, anxious to know why Kadomico was here instead of there. Finally, he said, "Tuscarora."

"No, Iroquois," Kadomico said, and went on to explain that he had taken several Saponi warriors and fought with the Carolina militia to defeat the Tuscarora at Fort Neoheroka. "The Saponi town fell to Iroquois raiders during the time of the Neoheroka siege."

"And Hawk?"

"Tree Son and I met Hawk at Neoheroka when we climbed the fort walls with a white flag and an offer of terms if the Tuscarora would surrender. They refused and Hawk fought with them against a thousand Indians, who were mostly Yamassee from South Carolina, but thirty-three were seasoned Carolina English and Scot militia. They had six cannon. Although they refused to surrender, they did accept our offer to let the women and children pass free. Hawk saw to it that Tree Son and I safely followed the women out of the fort. Two more days of cannon fire and the fort fell."

"But not Hawk. Right?"

"Right. The day the fort fell, Tree Son and I started for Williamsburg to report to Governor Spotswood and to learn of new frontier lands he intends to open. While we were in Williamsburg, my eight Saponi warriors returned to Saponi town only to find it in ruins. They immediately picked up the Iroquois trail and followed but there has been no word from them."

Kadomico continued. "Hawk survived the Neoheroka siege and learned of the Iroquois attack on our town. He sent a young tracker to find me. He must know the raiders. He went straight to them, came away with my son Keme, intercepted us on our way home, and returned Keme to me. Now Hawk leads a band of remaining Tuscarora warriors against the settlers and white traders. He is a well-known and respected warrior among the Tuscarora and the Iroquois, but stays in hiding until he strikes. The English authorities have posted a reward for him at the trader trail crossings in Virginia and Carolina. Hawk is still as deeply committed to driving the white man away as ever."

Sam now understood why these visitors were not on the trail of the Iroquois. He also saw by Kadomico's tone and omission of details that there was more to come and decided to let him tell it in his own good time. He relaxed, drew deeply on the pipe, and settled back.

"Sam, the English settlements have reached our hunting grounds on the Yadkin River. They have cleared much of the forests, planted crops, and built fences. It becomes more and more difficult for the Saponi to find and store winter food. Although not yet announced, Governor Spotswood is determined to build a fort and trading post on the Meherrin River near Virginia's southern dividing line with North Carolina. He has set aside land marked for an Indian town close to the fort. He expects considerable Indian help, labor, fort defenders, and hunters—more than the Saponi can provide.

"We need to bring the Siouan-speakers together, the Occhaneechi, the Tutelo, Meherrin and others. They have suffered losses as severe as the Saponi and although they, like the Saponi, are reduced to a few families, they remain as determined as ever to hold on to their independence. Now they may see a 'coming together' as the best option we all have. Jock Adams is helping me. We believe that only you can unite these small tribes at the new fort. If you can and if we can work together, we will have a new combined strength, the protection of the fort, hunting grounds, and a trading post sanctioned and guarded by Virginia law."

"I see," said Sam. "Let's walk a little. My legs grumble at me when I force them to be still."

They stepped out into afternoon sunlight.

17

Seth and Zack led their horses off the James River ferry, mounted up, and took the horse path to Green Spring, quite a change after eight days of coping with the wilderness. Homeward bound now in mid-May, they relaxed in the safety and comfort of the cool, deeply shaded, and well-maintained path. The trip to the Fort Christanna building site on the Meherrin had been rewarding. Seth could envision his own farm back there, his own land under the protection of a fort, neighbors all around him but not too close, and in each scene there was Ann Stilson—quite a vision for one not yet free from his indentured servant contract.

Zack imagined working on the fort and being free of Green Spring plantation. Maybe he could show his timber skills: ax and saw work, riving and splitting, hewing and squaring—an array of skills rarely seen in one man among the slaves. He enjoyed fishing that Meherrin River and working with Seth. He saw himself working at the fort and when Mr. Luther came maybe he would bring Ella—woman like Ella could do a lot: skinnin', cookin', washin' clothes—free up the men to work the timber. Zack dozed in the saddle and let his mind run free in spite of the ever-present improbability of it all.

Seth glanced over his shoulder and saw Zack's bent head. He let his horse drift back alongside the dozing Zack. He was about to have a bit of fun. He raised his hand to smack Zack's horse on the rump.

"Oughtn't do that, Mr. Seth," Zack said without raising his head. "I was jus' havin' a little doze."

"Why, Zack. Surely, you don't think I'd spook your horse, you being such a good rider and all."

"Did enter ma mind, Mr. Seth. Shorely did. Shoulda known better. Long as I'm awake now, maybe I could ax you somethin'?"

"Depends, Zack. What's on your mind?"

The horses changed pace and jumped a tiny stream of black water and muddy banks. When they were side-by-side again, Zack straightened in the saddle and spoke as clearly as he could.

"You'll be free in a little while, Mr. Seth, and I 'spect you might go back down on the Meherrin River where we jus' been. Leastways, you talked about it some."

"It's possible, Zack, but a long ways off, even if my contract is up soon."

"Well, I wondered if you could speak to Colonel Ludwell to get me sent back to help build the fort. Maybe be with you, if you go back."

They turned into one of the fields belonging to Green Spring to take a shortcut to the plantation barn and stables. Now on familiar ground, the horses quickened their pace, knowing the next stop would be for good feed and water back in their stables.

Seth took up the slack in the reins and steadied his mount. "I'd like that, Zack, us workin' together, but it is not something I have much to say about. I sure don't have money to buy you. Truth is, I can't say yea or nay. Depends on too many things, but you can count on me to speak to Colonel Ludwell about it if I get the chance."

Zack was pleased. It was on Seth's mind now. There was plenty of time.

They gained the stables just before good dark. Seth turned the horses over to Zack and headed for the kitchen at the manor house. Zack led the animals over to the water trough and pulled the saddles and blankets while they drank. Back in the stables, he spoke to them. "Jus' ease your prancin' and head shakin', Jake. Your stalls gotta be fixed clean and some fresh hay put down in there. Feeds comin'. You too, Smoky. Feeds comin'. You actin' like we been starvin' you." Zack threw the latch on the half-door to Jake's stall. As he reached for Smoky's reins, Jake snorted his annoyance, shaking his head and bridle vigorously over the half-door. "I don need you tellin' me, horse. I know you ain been fed yet."

Zack kept up a running chatter with the horses until the feed troughs were full and both horses had settled into their portions of the fresh grain. His hand rested on Smoky's shoulder as he watched him filling up, breaking the silence only with the nuzzling of the trough to get into the corners for the last morsels. Suddenly a vision of Gladys' hot cornbread, greens, and fresh milk stirred his own appetite, but as eager as he was to see her, he took the time to rub down the saddle marks and clean the stalls. Finally, he inspected the saddles, bridles, and leather pack bands and decided that what patching and oiling they needed could wait. It was dark when he started toward the slave quarters.

Seth gave Jason, the house slave, a message for Philip Ludwell saying that he and Zack were back. He had not gone far toward his quarters when Jason caught up with him.

"Colonel Ludwell wants you to come back now."

Back in the parlor, Ludwell was waiting.

"Sit down, Seth. Tell me about the trip." Ludwell reached for a decanter and filled a small glass.

"It is two days' travel on a poorly marked trail but with some clearing, passable by horse or ox-drawn cart. All the land we saw between the James and the Meherrin is rich farm and timberland. After John Allen's place, a few miles south of the James River, we saw no settlers. Mr. Allen marked the fort and the Indian town on high ground near the Meherrin River." Seth paused, looking for some sign of interest, but Ludwell kept a straight face.

"Who was with you?" he asked.

"The surveyor and his assistant, an overseer from Middle Plantation, and two Saponi Indians, both interpreters, sir."

"Any idea of when the building will start?"

"We don't know, of course, but the talk among us was that building would probably begin in the spring of next year, and my thinking is that there will be felling and cutting much sooner. The land abounds in good straight pine and oak building material and the Indians are anxious to move in."

Ludwell stood and took the last of his drink. "You have done a good piece of work, Seth, and you could be right about activity down there sooner rather than later. What would you say to more trips there during the summer, maybe even spending a few weeks on site?"

"I think it is a good idea. I'm pretty sure the surveying will continue as soon as Mr. Allen makes his report. While we were there, I could see where he had marked up maps of the land starting with all the river-front land on both sides."

"Have Chance saddled and ready right after breakfast. I'll be meeting with the governor tomorrow."

"He'll be ready, sir. And, sir, Zack saved the day for us several times. His strength and knowledge of getting about in the brush and swamps of the wilderness came in mighty handy. Mr. Allen said so himself. If there's any way you could spare him to travel with me, we will be better equipped and manned to do just about anything that needs doin', sir."

Ludwell understood. The more people he had on site in the beginning, the better his chances of getting the choice patents. "We'll see," he said.

18

Hawk drew the fine edge of a tomahawk across a worn limestone rock and looked up at the approaching youngster. The boy was lean, naked to the breechclout, smeared with dust and sweat-caked mud—likely coming in off a long run. A rag headband kept his long black hair away from his face. His leggings had seen a lot of rough treatment from briars and vines, but they made good their job of protecting his legs and the tops of his moccasins. He stopped five paces short of Hawk and waited. Three of Hawk's warriors stood behind him.

Hawk returned to working the steel edge, but now he honed it against his leather leggings. "Why do you stand before me without your weapons, Chitto?"

Chitto dropped his head. "A Tuscarora band led by a warrior named Kajika captured me, stripped me of my weapons, and sent me here with a message, Great Chief."

"So you have led an enemy to the secret place of your brothers?" Hawk nodded to the three warriors who immediately disappeared.

"No, Great Chief, I would die first."

"But you are not dead."

"I am not dead because I refused to lead them here, but I did promise to return with you in two suns."

"And they believed you?"

"They kept my weapons and promised to return them."

Hawk summoned two more warriors, spoke softly to them, and faced Chitto again. "Why do you believe they did not follow you?"

"When I left them, I ran for a long time away from them and away from this place. Then, I came back to the river before dark, swam it, and took a position where I could see if they crossed. I waited all night, and at first light, I entered the river concealed by a floating tree and floated out of sight of that place and turned toward this secret place. When I cut the trail to this place, I kept going before turning back to it and coming here. They did not follow."

A returning warrior went directly to Hawk. "Nothing. Chitto speaks true."

Hawk said, "How far to this Kajika?"

"We can be there before the sun reaches the mountains," Chitto said.

"How many men does he have with him?"

"Five that I saw, but more, I think."

Hawk summoned a warrior. "Take three warriors and follow Chitto. I know of this Kajika. I thought he was dead. He was defeated in a knife fight with Tonawanda of the Nahyssans many years ago and left to die among his people the Tuscarora. He was my enemy then. Now we fight the same enemy. Blindfold him and bring him to the river when the next sun is highest. Let's see what he has to say."

The next day Hawk sat concealed and shaded from a strong spring sun that warmed the earth and rocks along the riverbank. After a winter of bare limbs and frozen ground, the leaves of trees and shrubs had appeared, turned a darker green, and now moved gently in the stirring air. The redbuds and dogwoods had lost their blossoms, as their leaves grew to provide welcome cover to birds and small animals on the move. At this point before the fall line, the water splashed white and danced around boulders of limestone in the shallows then ran deeper and formed occasional pools of quiet water before moving on to the next outcropping of limestone. Well shaded and concealed among huge riverside boulders, Hawk watched as two of his warriors led the blindfolded Kajika into the clearing and flicked a blade under the blindfold tie. Kajika blinked to adjust to the brightness and tugged at the rawhide thongs binding his hands to his waist belt.

Hawk, still unseen, almost gasped at this shadow of a man. Kajika wore long buckskins to conceal the grotesque damage on his left leg. A scar on his face ran from an empty socket behind a sagging left eyelid, across the cheek, and downward to the corner of his mouth extending it into a hideous grin. Matted black hair spilled over his face down to his chin so that his one good eye, now opened wide, glared through the wild strands.

Hawk moved into view and stopped near the trunk of a huge sycamore. Another flick of the warrior's knife and Kajika's hands fell free. In the same instant, Kajika produced and threw a knife into the trunk of the sycamore, head high to Hawk, then raised both hands in submission.

"Stop," Hawk commanded the two warriors, before they clubbed Kajika. "There is no danger. But take his buckskins and leggings." Hawk had not moved when the knife flew past him and plunged into the soft wood of the sycamore. Nor did his eyes shift away from Kajika, who remained in the delivery position leaning forward, grinning through matted hair.

The warriors stripped Kajika, found another knife in the seam of his buckskins, and shoved him roughly toward Hawk. His massive shoulders and arms stood in sharp contrast to the mangled leg and scars over much of his naked body.

"You did not miss," said Hawk. "Is there a message in that throw?"

"I did miss," Kajika said through a grin over missing teeth. "I aimed at the head of the butterfly but got only a piece of a back leg. I need practice. The message is, I let you live."

Hawk had not seen a butterfly, but it didn't matter. "Maybe," he said. "Why are you here?"

"You know of me from long ago."

"I know of your betrayals and attacks on your own people."

"I fight when necessary, no matter the tribe, but I *war* on the white man. It is the same with you. It is why you have not killed me. Let me have my buckskins. I have no more blades. "

Hawk measured the distance to this disfigured hulk with the lightning knife, a deadly snake of the worst kind. When Hawk was one of three young boys sent to Williamsburg by their chieftain fathers for schooling, Kajika and his band raided an unprotected Nahysson town, murdered an old man for no reason, and captured a boy and a girl of the tribe to ransom or trade. The Nahysson were friends of Hawk and his traveling companions. He tried to leave the school to pursue Kajika, rescue the children, and avenge the deaths of his friends, but he was stopped by his escort, a warrior who was assigned by his father, Chief of the Occaneechi, to watch over him.

At the time, so strong was Hawk's rebellion against the school and the white strangers that he struggled with the dilemma of fighting the white man or obeying his father and the senior warrior escort. He had finally managed to quit the school, denounced his own tribe, and joined a band of Tuscarora raiders. By the time he became a Senior Warrior of the Tuscarora, he had become well acquainted with the villainous work of the outcast Kajika.

Hawk nodded approval for the return of the buckskins, but watched as Kajika twisted and turned his mangled leg into the trousers, tied the waist band, and returned to the old blow-down and sat down.

"Now the Tuscarora make peace with the whites, but not you." Kajika thrust a crooked finger at Hawk, shook it, then paused, and grimaced, his good eye glaring contempt through the matted hair. "And not me." he continued barely above a whisper, spitting the words and shaking the crooked finger. "They hang talking papers on trees—outlaws, Kajika and Hawk for English silver, they speak." He shifted his weight toward his good knee and leg, stretched the wounded one, and eased the extended arm back to his side. "They *fear* Hawk and Kajika." His head slowly bowed and rested as though asleep.

Hawk was not impressed. His patience waned and the mention of his name in the same breath as Kajika's disgusted him. He turned his back and started to walk away. Kajika stood abruptly and shouted, "I have many steel tomahawks, knives, muskets, powder, and ball, and I know where the white man will build his fort. Join me and we will stop him—no fort, no settlers—and there are many in these hunting grounds to fight with us if we want them."

"You cannot defeat the white man," Hawk said.

"True and they cannot defeat me . . . or you. You have seen it. We can stop them when they come here and they cannot touch us. We strike and disappear. Listen, now."

Hawk returned and heard Kajika's plan and watched him draw in the bare earth to show the location of the fort on the Meherrin and the supply trails from Williamsburg. Kajika wanted two bands of carefully chosen warriors striking at different times and places, switching regularly and retreating to different hideouts, leaving no trace. To exchange information and plan alternate strikes and strategies, they would meet alone at one of five locations on the day following the full moon. Neither would disclose the content of their meeting to anyone, including their own warriors. So what was to keep one from betraying the other? The meetings would take place prior to moonrise in the darkness of night. They would announce their presence with prearranged animal calls. Each was free to scout the surrounding area for any suspicious activity, sounds, or evidence of prior movements.

It was brilliant. Two well-supplied, unidentified, independent bands striking and running at different times and locations could keep the enemy guessing, even destroy him if he chose to pursue, but there was no way to guarantee against betrayal. Hawk countered.

"I fight for my people, you fight for yourself. The time will come when we will turn on each other, but until then we both fight the white man. It is as you say. If we stagger our attacks, it will give us time between strikes to rest and prepare for the next strike. The enemy will be under constant attack, the fort will be stopped, the settlers will not come. When the moon is full, we change from one to the other: strike or rest. That is all we need do."

"Done," said Kajika. "I see that you do not trust me— not a good thing for us. Together we could be stronger, share weapons and war supplies, and exchange information on the white man's movements."

"It is true. I do not trust you. If we need to speak, it can be arranged by placing an arrow head under this stone." Hawk pointed to a large flat stone on which he stood. "Check the stone from time to time. If there is an arrowhead, it means we will meet here at the next full moon and if agreeable, place another arrowhead with it. If you suspect a trap, send a warrior in your place. I will do the same."

Kajika bowed his disheveled head and shook it. "Not good, but it is all that can be done for the time being. We will both set watches on the trail and at the site. I will watch the trails north of the Nottoway River. You take the trails south of the Nottoway. We can both station watchers at the site."

As much as Hawk disliked doing business with this snake, he knew that the two of them had no one to turn to since the fall of the Tuscarora. Just as the wanted posters said, they were outlaws, on their own in the wilderness, dependent on what they could extract from the forest and streams, attacks on settlers, and encounters with the white man's militia. At least, this was a way to continue the fight.

19

S am Layton and Kadomico made their way downward toward the river over a packed-earth trail wide enough for them to walk side-by-side. The air was cool there among the dense green foliage of the nearly expired spring. It filled the lungs easily and gave the body a lift. Both men were aware of the many things they had to discuss but neither was eager. They walked slowly without speaking, stopping occasionally to examine a branch, an insect, or the trail sign of some passing animal. Kadomico had not known such peace in many suns. Just being near Sam was reassuring that they could overcome the problems of settlement for his people.

Finally, as though awakening, Sam chuckled. "You know, there is nothing we can do about it, but I think Starlight and I may be on the verge of losing someone who is very close to us."

"You mean Tree Son and Kanti? But how can you be sure?" Kadomico replied. "It looks like Tree Son is smitten beyond his ability to reason, but Kanti seems level-headed, confident, and of good judgment."

"True, and that is why I am sure. Kanti married a young Shawnee warrior when she was fourteen. He was killed shortly afterwards in a battle with the Iroquois. She turned to her mother in her grief and they drew closer. Starlight is strong, and the people here grew to know and trust her. It became clear to me shortly after we married that Starlight was born to lead, and as she grew into that position among the people of this town, she kept Kanti by her side.

She guided Kanti through her grief and taught her the way of life. Now, she knows herself very well. She has never shown interest in another man until today. I expected it to happen eventually, but I did not dream it could happen so suddenly without some kind of sign."

"You don't seem worried about it."

"Whatever happens between those two, it will turn out well. But if Kanti leaves our house, it will be difficult for Starlight. If she leaves our town, it will be a tragic loss to her. We will have to find a way to deal with that."

Silence settled between them while they made their way to the canoe landing area. Kadomico shaded his eyes against the strong light of the afternoon sun and squinted downstream. Something was moving near the western shoreline.

"That will be them," Sam said. "Kanti loves that birch bark canoe like it is alive. She'll be showing it off to Tree Son."

"Well, I hope Tree Son doesn't ruin the moment by letting her know that he knows that canoe well enough from our times with you long ago in Williamsburg."

"They'll work it out. Let's get back to the relocation of your people and other tribes."

Unaware that Sam and Kadomico waited for them, Tree Son and Kanti returned upstream slowly and from time to time disappeared altogether. Where Sam and Kadomico sat, the sun-warmed day turned cooler as the mountain shadow moved silently over the valley. Across the river from them, a swarm of this year's hatch of little bronze-back bass flashed the white of their bellies as they leaped in a feeding frenzy in the rock strewn shallows making their splashes as big and noisy as possible, just as youngsters everywhere are apt to do.

Kadomico told Sam about the fort and the surviving Saponi. "Spotswood has set aside a section of land six miles by six miles along the Meherrin where he wants the

Occaneechi, Monacan, Eno, Tutelo, Saponi and others to settle. There is 23,040 acres in it. The town site is already marked close to the fort."

Sam looked longingly at the rippling water bounded by the rich foliage of sycamore, walnut, willow, and ash. The story he had just heard described yet another concession of the hunting grounds of the Indian people to the white settlers. He did not say so to Kadomico, but it was the same here in his own town. Already he and Starlight were preparing to move back west toward the homelands of the Shawnee in the Ohio valley. Although it would be another twenty years before the first families would appear at the northern end of the Shenandoah and start the surge of settlements, already the white man hunted, trapped, surveyed, and explored the valley. The buffalo had vanished. Beaver traps yielded less and less each winter. Fur traders moved freely among the valley Indians with English cloth, metal, and rum. From observation and from all the treaty negotiations he had attended, Sam knew what was happening to the tribes in Virginia and North Carolina.

In a gesture of finality, he thumbed a pebble into the shallows and stood up. "Kadomico, it is not a good thing, but it may be the only thing the tribes can do. We will begin by visiting the chiefs of the Virginia tribes. I will come to your town on the Yadkin River before the leaves turn and we will go together to the chiefs. You best let the governor know what we are doing. Tell him that we will come to Williamsburg when we have seen the tribes."

"We are grateful for your help, Sam." Kadomico stood with him and gripped his forearm in friendship.

"Well, there they are at last," Sam said, watching the now visible paddle strokes of Kanti and Tree Son. They hugged the quieter water near the western bank paddling smoothly, Kanti in the bow navigating around submerged rocks while Tree Son's strokes powered the streamlined birch bark craft forward over a thin draft of river water. It did not escape Sam that these two, sitting front-to-back, did not need to see or hear each other. They worked together, without straining, silently, rhythmically, and the canoe raced over the water with the grace of a beautiful bird, deftly dodging an occasional underwater rock or slowing to Tree Son's backstroke as he aligned their course with a V formed in a rock dam for trapping fish.

"Let's leave, Kadomico. It is best that whatever Kanti has to say to her mother, she say it to her first."

They returned to Sam's house where Starlight was busy making beds on the floor for Kadomico and Tree Son. "I hope your grumbling legs carried you to your daughter," Starlight said, as she added furs and a blanket to the bedding.

"No, but we did see her and Tree Son on the river. They will be here soon."

Kadomico sensed the intensity in the air and stood quietly by as Sam reached for the Beverly book of Virginia history and motioned Kadomico to the back of the room opposite the entrance. There they both sat down in the darkness of the room now lighted only by the small cooking fire in the center of the room.

The hide covering the entrance suddenly moved aside and there stood Tree Son and Kanti. Even in the dimly lit room they made a handsome pair. Tree Son moved toward Sam. Kanti moved with him and the two of them walked past Starlight without speaking to her.

Tree Son took Kanti's hand and faced her father. "Sam Layton, if you, Kanti's mother, and the Shawnee people permit, Kanti and I will be married tonight."

Sam was not prepared for this, but he was glad he had not waited for them at the canoe landing. He wanted to ask' and if the answer is no?', but he knew the answer, and it would just make this situation worse. Starlight moved to his side.

"Kadomico, please take Tree Son and Kanti to the work yard. I will come for you."

When they were alone, Sam sat down on the soft furs near the fire. Starlight knelt beside him and they faced each other in the flickering light of the flame. Starlight searched Sam's eyes, hoping for a sign that he would stop this intrusion into their lives, but there was none. A single tear welled and spilled softly onto her cheek.

Seeing the tear, Sam almost began to sympathize with her but realized that Kanti and Tree Son needed their support, not their interference. For a long time now, he and Starlight had discussed Kanti's rejection of the young warriors. Now that she had chosen, they must support her.

"It is not a bad thing," he said.

"I know," She replied, and wiped the tear away. "I am relieved that you seem to accept Tree Son."

"Yes, I know him to be a strong warrior, committed to his people, and his friend, Kadomico. He will be even more committed to Kanti. They make a fine pair."

"But do they have to leave? Could Tree Son not be with us here?"

"He is welcome, Starlight. We can ask, but if he chooses not to, he will go and Kanti will follow."

Kadomico followed Kanti and Tree Son into the work yard, gripped Tree Son's shoulder, and spun him around. To his surprise, Kanti turned also, but Tree Son's smile stopped him cold. It was simple, brimming with confidence as though he now had something new and wonderful. This was not one of his tricks. It was time for a Tree Son quip or a snappy put-down, but it did not come. Instead, Tree Son's eyes rested on him, gently. Tree Son had made it plain that he and Kanti would be together from now on. It was difficult to believe that he had undergone such a transformation, but it was so. Suddenly Kadomico felt like he was intruding. He released his grip and turned to Kanti.

"He is my friend."

162

"I know," she said. "You will be uncle to our children. You will be proud."

Kadomico practically gasped. How fast this one moves, he thought. Just then, the hide door covering opened and Starlight came out.

"You have not spoken," she said to Kanti.

"He will be my husband, my mother, but no one will ever replace you."

"You will go away?"

"Yes, I follow my husband."

Starlight nodded to Tree Son, and took Kanti by the arm.

"We will talk," she said, and they walked away.

The following day, the Shawnee shaman announced the marriage of Tree Son and Kanti and declared the traditional acknowledgement of the union and a feast that night to celebrate the event. By nightfall, the ceremonial fire was ready. Spectators and musicians with drums and rattles had taken seats on the ground around the fire. Young warriors, led by Tree Son and dressed in elaborate costumes of sun-bleached doeskin filed in walking to the rhythm of low drumbeats. After they had taken standing positions, Kanti appeared leading an equal number of young women in similar doeskin dress. Costumes were richly decorated with brightly colored porcupine quills, shells, and feathers and intricate designs formed with bits of brass and copper. Ankles were wrapped in brightly colored shells. Both men and women wore bracelets and armbands of beaten silver.

The warriors stood quietly without expression while each woman found her partner of choice, stood before him, and smiled. The beat of drums and rattles changed and the dancers began, moving and swaying with the beat. When they changed again to a slower and quieter beat, an elder of the tribe picked up the rhythm, walked to the end of the line, and began a chant. The dancers moved slowly, swaying, and turning with the moves of their partners who followed the drumbeats as they grew faster and louder.

Finally, Tree Son drew Kanti close and the beat changed again as he pressed her slender body to his broad chest and spoke to her beauty, her strength, and the warmth of her body.

"You are my wife," he said, drawing her closer.

Kanti eyes were moist and her voice low but crystal clear. "Your arms will hold me always, your words lift me up, and I am yours. You are my husband."

They continued embracing as the drum beats quickened and the others broke away from each other and began a wild dance of celebration. This was the signal for Kanti and Tree Son to leave when they wished and Kanti led him toward the river and the beautiful canoe in the first slivers of light from the rising moon.

The next morning, Tree Son, Kanti, and Kadomico said their good-byes to the Laytons, and set out across the valley. They carried only weapons and trail food. A light rain whipped by occasional gusts under stubborn grey clouds warned of serious weather in the offing. The temperature was mild, however, and the rain gentle, so they moved on. By noon, they were on the crest of the Blue Mountains traveling south.

Tree Son took the lead position, set a fast pace, and in stretches where favorable drainage promised sure footing they made good time. By early afternoon, the southwest sky had turned darker, the wind freshened, and the rain grew colder. Just before nightfall, they came to a huge chestnut tree lying across the trail. Located on a steep slope, it had been on the ground for several days. The upright root system formed a disk about ten feet in diameter. It faced east. Forty feet of the tree's big trunk blocked their way, but stout limbs in its crown held the trunk well above the trail.

Tree Son and Kanti slipped beneath it and waited on the other side.

Kadomico stopped, squinted west at the darkening sky and checked the underside of the trunk for dry wood—damp but not soaked—a source for splinters to start a fire if needed. The wind became gusty, forcing overhead leaves to give up tiny streams of water. Darkness was about to descend on the soaked land, and the storm was close. There was still time to rig a shelter. He pointed west at the darkening sky and motioned Tree Son and Kanti to come back. They would camp here.

Kanti fashioned a drainage ditch in the soft earth at the base of the upright roots. The steep slope below the roots made a natural drain leaving the root basin to drain of its own accord. She began to clear the floor area for their shelter while Kadomico and Tree Son gathered long slender poles and set them upright to form the skeleton of the walls. From a nearby outbreak of ash trees they gathered young saplings and wove them into a grid to complete the skeleton of the wall. Young vines and the inner bark of hickory provided the thongs they needed for fastening.

With sap running high this time of the year, bark was plentiful and easily taken from the trees. The big chestnut gave up huge slabs of bark from its trunk. By dark, they had a small half-roundhouse anchored in the soggy ground and fastened to the root-disk. Kanti gathered bark and boughs from the thick fo
rest of evergreens and soon had dry flooring and soft bedding.

The wind grew stronger and louder, and visibility faded with the oncoming darkness. Outside, Tree Son and Kadomico worked by feel rather than sight, ignoring the gathering rain and wind. They leaned on the structure for support while they went over the covering one last time, feeling for errant branches or bark. They fastened two large hemlock limbs thick with leaves to allow temporary movement for an entrance. Not a proper roundhouse, but what it lacked in appearance, size, and shape, it made up for in strength, comfort, and promise of a dry bed.

When Tree Son and Kadomico entered, Kanti stopped them at the doorway. "Strip and wring out everything you are wearing, then put it back on," she said. "Our bed is nearly dry. The wind strengthens, the air is cooling, and you will grow cold when you stop moving. We sleep together this night, draw warmth from each other, and by morning, we will be much drier. The bed is here. There is room on each side of me. Come."

Tree Son made the first move and started crawling through the damp darkness toward the sound of Kanti's voice. Kadomico took longer, found his way to the outside edge of the soft boughs, settled down, and stretched out, his back to Kanti. The wind howled, the rain came in noisy sheets. They adjusted their sleeping positions, Tree Son on his back, Kanti on her side, her head on Tree Son's arm and shoulder, but Kadomico, feeling awkward with this arrangement, hugged the far edge.

Kanti spoke softly, "Tell your foolish friend he must stay warm and dry." As she spoke, Kadomico felt an unmistakable tug on his wet buckskins.

The next morning he woke facing Kanti and Tree Son, his arm over Kanti. He slowly withdrew his arm and straightened on his back. The morning brought little relief. The wind howled, trees cracked, lost limbs, and sheets of wind-whipped rain showered the forest, but a sliver of welcome light reassured him that the sun had returned, almost totally obscured but there beyond the raging weather with no promise of overcoming the storm clouds any time soon. No need to wake Tree Son or Kanti, there was nothing left to do but wait it out. They would be here at least another day and night.

He eased himself to the entrance, found a stone he had placed there, and began sharpening and honing his tomahawk and knives in the dim light seeping through the entrance. His thoughts turned to Sayen and Keme.

20

Now back from his first trip to the Fort Christanna building site, Zack finished his work at the stables and walked over to the slave quarters in the darkening evening. He squinted through the trees to see if there was chimney smoke coming from Gladys's cabin, but he couldn't tell. If he could surprise her she would laugh and fuss and carry on about him being back. It was always a happy time to be coming home to Gladys. When he was with her, he felt different—useful, manly, and able. She made him feel that way even when he lay on his stomach while she salved the whiplash marks. Once he'd tried to tell her that—about how she made him feel. Instead, he'd hung his head and mumbled, unable to find the words. She'd told him to not feel bad about sayin' how he felt. Thing to remember, she'd said, was that the way you *feel* about y'self when you alone or with me, well, that's the way it *is. That's* the truth. And, the other way you feel—like when you're slavin' and bowin' to that devil overseer? That's just the way they *want* you to feel. But them wantin' it don't change what you are. You a man, Zack, a good man, remember that. And he had.

When he saw the smoke over Gladys's house, he thought, Lordy me, she's there! She gonna be some surprised to see me. But Gladys was not surprised. The door opened as he turned into the yard, and she met him halfway, took his hand, and led him inside. She motioned to the chair at the table and began to stir the fire.

"That Massa Ripken was here little while ago, wants you to be ready to go to the field at first light—that's how I know you home. He acted mad, 'n he got no call t' be mad—leastways, that I know of." Gladys set a cast iron skillet on the coals and drew a large pot of greens over the fire.

"Me neither. I ain' seen him since I come back. Mr. Seth wants me tomorrow, too." Zack leaned over to watch Gladys mix the corn meal, milk, egg, and salt.

"Don't surprise me none, and that could be the cause of him bein' mad, you off ridin' around with Mr. Seth with all the work here goin' wantin'." Gladys stirred the mixture to a good thickness and set it aside. She reached for the bowl and spooned a drop into the hot grease. The sizzle satisfied her that the skillet was ready for the pone.

"Well, Massa. Ripken, he the boss, the overseer. I'll be ready," Zack said as he watched Gladys grease the skillet again with a piece of pork fat. His hunger pangs were beginning to speak to him, and at the same time, he was near bursting inside to tell Gladys about the trip. To his delight, she poured the mix into the skillet and watched it sizzle and bubble around the edges before she placed the cast iron lid over it and set it cooking near the fire.

"Jus be careful around Massa Ripken 'til you know what he's stewin bout," Gladys said, returning to the table where she sat down. She leaned forward, elbows on the table and said, "Now tell me bout the trip. The bread'll be ready pretty quick."

Zack related the major parts of the trip, who they traveled with, what they did, and how well he and Mr. Seth got along. He was just getting to the part about Seth and the Indian traveling companions when Gladys set milk and butter on the table. He continued his description of the travelers and the trail until she returned with a huge pot from the fireplace. He watched her fork a large piece of pork hidden by a huge mound of steaming greens dripping pot liquor onto the chipped stoneware platter in front of him. The mouth-watering aroma forced him to swallow before he resumed his account of the trip, only to be interrupted again when Gladys returned with the skillet of hot brown corn pone.

Gladys touched him on the shoulder and bowed her head. "Lord, we thank thee for Zack's safe home-comin' and for this food. Amen."

Zack ate.

Satisfied, he returned to his account of the trip.

"Miz Gladys, all these riders, they be good men . . . hard workers and I 'spect hard fighters, though we didn't have no fights. Mr. Seth, he gonna ax Colonel Ludwell 'f I can go back with him on the next trip, maybe soon, June for sure. And, Mr. Kingston, he Massa Page's man over everything at Middle Plantation, he was there too. And he and Mr. Seth got to be close frens. When the buildin' starts and lots more men come there, maybe Ella might be one of the ones come down, specially 'f somebody was axin' about it."

"Chile, you just spoke more trouble in one breath than you can handle in a lifetime. Anybody find out 'bout you 'n Ella, Ella gonna suffer for sure, specially 'f you say it. Now best you keep quiet about it, leastways 'til you know more. T'other thing that worries me is this bizness 'tween you and Mr. Seth. Mr. Ripken's bound to take that as a loss of both of you. Best thing you can do is get up tomorrow mornin' and go to the fields like always, quiet. Do whatcha told. You understand?"

"Yes 'm, I'll do what you say, but I heard a lot on this trip I never knew."

"Go on, but I already heard more'n I *need* t' hear."

"The Indians I talked to tole me about capturin' people and sellin' 'em as slaves—even tole me where. And did y' know some bring sixty pound sterlin' silver, and some, more? They tole me that some slaves can buy their own-selves. It's like buyin' their freedom. Like if I have the money and the colonel is willin', I could buy my freedom. Some slaves already done that. It's true."

"I heard about that, but I never put no stock in it. In all my years, I never saw it happen. Ain't likely it will, either. You keep such thoughts to yourself. Nothin' but trouble down that road."

"I will, but out on the trail they talk about all the things we never talk about here on the plantation. The trail is a good place to be."

Gladys stared directly into Zack's eyes for a long time. He was gettin' dangerous notions on that trail. She held back further words of caution and gathered the empty dishes.

The next morning, the work wagon came creaking and bumping along the deep rutted road. Zack heard its unmistakable noises long before it arrived. When it did pull up in front of his house, Al Ripken rode in from the opposite direction trotting his horse straight at Zack. He stopped between Zack and the wagonload of field hands, unfurled his whip, and struck. The popper on the end of the six-foot whip flashed by Zack's head and unfolded in a deafening crack. Zack flinched involuntarily, stopped obediently, and took his hat off.

"Boy, it looks to me like you need refreshin' on how to live and work on this here plantation. Even that indentured trash, Seth Jackson, had the respect to check in with me when he got back."

"Time I finished with them horses, sir, I thought it 'uz too late, Massa Ripken, suh. I sho didn't mean no disrespect, suh."

"Yeah, well, it's more likely you just didn't want to getcha work orders for today. Now, git on that wagon. We'll see how long it takes you to make up the work you missed while you were off ridin' around." Ripken glared at Zack, spit at the ground, and re-coiled his whip.

"Yessuh, Yessuh," Zack murmured and stepped lively toward the wagon. As soon as he'd climbed onto the flat bed of the wagon, the driver shook the reins and the old mare shifted her weight to take the first step.

Arriving unseen and standing with the wagon between him and Ripken, Seth had heard it all. He pulled his hat down over his eyes and slipped onto the crowded, slow-moving flat bed wagon, his back to Ripken and Zack.

Ripken spurred his mount and was quickly out of sight. Gladys gathered her skirts and backed away from the tiny window. The wagon creaked and rumbled on into the brightening morning. It was going to be a hot day before it was over.

Seth leaned across the wagon and tapped Zack on the shoulder. "I heard it, Zack. This could mean trouble for both of us—probably not, but best stay away from me for a few days. Be ready to leave again in about three weeks. I'll let you know."

Zack leaned backward, closer to Seth, and nodded. Seth slipped off the slow-moving wagon. When Zack looked back, he had disappeared.

Philip Ludwell II held militia commissions in James City and Isle of Wight counties, giving him the power to call a small army of armed and mounted militia and Rangers. The magnitude of this responsibility was on his mind as he crossed the threshold of the capitol building to meet Governor Spotswood. There had been no call to assemble the militia, but the Governor's message was a request to meet *to discuss travel to and security of building Fort Christanna.* That would eventually involve the militia.

A clerk led him across the first floor entrance to a doorway at the right of the stair landing. Inside, a large room was furnished with a huge table. Several chairs had been removed to allow standing and working space along one side. At one end of the table, stacks of river and trail maps of the areas south of the James River had been arranged. At the other end, Governor Spotswood and the surveyor, John Allen, stood poring over a plot plan of the proposed fort and Indian town.

Spotswood removed his spectacles and greeted Ludwell. "Ahh. Come in, Colonel, and thank you for coming on such short notice. You know our surveyor, Mr. Allen, of course. Join us here, and maybe I can explain the short notice."

"Glad to, Sir. Good morning, Mr. Allen."

Allen nodded a greeting and stepped back for Ludwell to see the plot plan as Spotswood pointed to the pentagon of palisades with corners a hundred yards apart.

"This is it, Colonel. We can start gathering materials as soon as we can arrange the labor. The Council and Burgesses have given me assurances and encouraged us to proceed. We will be ready to build by spring."

"Patents, hostiles, and funds?" Ludwell posed the questions cautiously and with genuine respect as he inspected the content of the plan closely.

"I am taking a small Ranger party south next week to meet with the hostiles and make a treaty. The Saponi will get the tributary Indians together and send labor to start preparing the logs and palisades. The Burgesses have authorized funds for immediate building expense. It is not yet much but enough to hire the skills we need to get started, and there are plenty of settlers eager to work while they wait for land patents for that area."

"Green Spring will support you in every way it can. What will you have us do?"

"Splendid, splendid. Mr. Allen here is preparing to return to complete the marking of the parcel layout and boundaries. I want you to get enough of your militia together to escort him, and stay with him until he is done. Then organize a party of militia, say ten Rangers, the best of your riflemen, to set up a temporary fort configured to withstand siege and attack by large bands of Indians. You will supervise the defense of the site. There will be small work groups in and out of there throughout the winter. The first objective is to clear land for the fort, buck the trees into fifteen-foot pales for the walls of Fort Christanna and to survey the land for the fort, the Indian town and fifty-acre parcels for settlers. Plan on a month of work, then a second and third visit as needed to get the materials prepared for building next year."

Ludwell bowed to Allen. "At your service, sir. Just let me know when you will be ready to leave and where to meet you."

Allen smiled and returned the bow. He knew Philip Ludwell to be a strong leader and fair man. "Three weeks from today, Hogg Island ferry landing?"

"Done." Ludwell smiled back.

"We're fortunate to have Green Spring workmen. Your man, Seth Jackson, and the slave, Zack, proved themselves in many ways on our first trip," Allen said.

"They will be with me. Would you agree that twenty mounted militiamen will be enough to protect the working parties and surveyors?"

"Yes, I believe so."

"Good, and as soon as we have a temporary defense set up, I will release ten of them. Now in preparation for the trip, I will arrange for staging people, livestock, and supplies at the Hogg Island ferry the week before we leave. Seth Jackson will manage that and take good care of anything you wish to add. He will be ready to receive cargo and livestock a week from today. Give him two more weeks to collect cargo, tents and such and we could be ready to strike the trail to the site."

"Excellent, Colonel. There will be at least four of my surveyor assistants; two to remain on site after the preliminary boundaries are marked." Allen reached for his hat. "Governor, unless I can be of further service, I will take my leave. It is my pleasure to serve you."

"Gentlemen, that settles it for the time being. Fort Christanna is off to a good start." Spotswood beamed. He followed Allen to the door and shook hands. When he turned back, Ludwell was waiting, hat in hand.

"Governor, as a matter of security, I need your support to maintain control of people coming and going to the site."

"You have it. All Fort Christanna visits and workers will be regulated by the fort commander—whomever you designate, sir. I'll notify the Burgesses and the Council today. By the way, I am sending a builder on this trip. His name is Angus McHale; not just a Scot, an Ulster Scot, he'll quickly tell you. He has travelled extensively in Scandinavia and worked his building trade along the St. Lawrence River and in New Jersey and Pennsylvania. He is recently arrived with extraordinary recommendations, and he builds with timber. They say he swings his ax in a steady rhythm, never makes a quick move, seems never to tire, and he can fell and buck a tree before you can clear the underbrush for him at the next tree."

"That is a man I will be glad to meet," Ludwell said, as he chuckled and prepared himself for his personal issue. "As we discussed some time ago, Excellency, I have sent the patent office notice of my wish to buy riverfront land in the Fort Christanna area. I hope that I will be able to apply in time to assure approval when I am able to submit the official application."

"I understand and have discussed this with John Allen. He will mark a copy of the plot plan for my approval. You have only to let him know what your preference is, get the land identification codes representing the plot or plots that you prefer, and submit your application in the established procedure."

Ludwell was satisfied. Having those identification codes in advance and with the governor's cooperation, he felt sure he would get his choice of property. He bowed to the governor and stepped out into the mid-day sunlight of early June.

21

On a cool, June morning, White Water rose early and kindled a small fire in their roundhouse. Nearby, Sayen was stirring under a bed of furs. Custoga snored on in peaceful slumber. White Water stepped outside and splashed cold water on her face from a bench top basin before walking on toward the women's private section of the woods. As she walked, she bound her long black hair at her neck as best she could still favoring the wounded arm. She was grateful that Sayen and Custoga were mending, but caring for them left her little time for cooking, planting, mending, cleaning, and gathering, all badly needed work if they were to survive the winter. She longed for Kadomico and Tree Son.

When she returned she saw that Keme's bed was empty but took no particular notice. After all, it was time to start the day, even though Custoga continued sleeping. Sayen was awake and sitting up. The room was still dark, but morning sunlight splashed through the partially open doorway and painted a bright patch on the packed earth floor. Dim shapes of bedding and wall mounted hangers of weapons, tools, and skins began to emerge in the flickering glow of the cook fire.

Sayen drew the fur about her shoulders and whispered a greeting to White Water who had moved silently to the fire to fill a bowl with warm water.

"Wait, White Water," Sayen said, as she worked her way to the edge of the bed. "Today I will walk." She reached for a lodge pole and slowly pulled herself to a standing position. She stood still until the room stopped swimming around her.

White Water poised over the basin, holding back her words of caution, and watched. Slowly, Sayen let go of the lodge pole and took two timorous steps that brought her to White Water's side. They embraced and White Water walked with her back to the bed.

White Water delivered the basin of water and said, "Keme is not here."

"I know. I did not see him leave. He is troubled. Yesterday he told me more about his time with Hawk and asked me why his father does not fight the English strangers. He is tormented by those who say his father is friend of our enemies, the English."

"He may be at the creek. He spends a lot of time there. I think it is because that is where you and he fought the Iroquois, where he was captured and you were wounded—a bad thing for one of his age to deal with," White Water said. "He will come back when he is hungry."

Keme did not come back.

About noon on the third day of Keme's absence, the young sentry set to watch the trailhead ran across the maize field toward the Saponi town shouting, "Kadomico comes, Kadomico and Tree Son and someone come."

Relieved and excited to have Kadomico and Tree Son back, White Water set out to meet them, but she walked slowly with her head slightly bowed, still favoring her wounded arm. Kadomico sensed trouble as soon as he saw her slow movement. He had never known his sister to move slowly. Even when she stalked game, the rhythm of her moves suggested fluid movement—never so slow as now. He doubled his pace, and Tree Son and Kanti slowed to give him time alone with White Water. They met among the freshly planted mounds of maize, beans, and squash.

"I come," Kadomico said, as he reached out to his sister and touched her shoulder. White Water fought back tears of relief.

"Kadomico, Keme is missing—three suns now. We think he has gone back to Hawk."

Kadomico swallowed against the pain in his chest. *Keme missing, three suns,* the words exploded in his mind like thunder and mixed with the realization that he had lost his son even though he may be safe with Hawk. He had neglected Keme. Always, his mind and heart had been consumed by the well-being of his people: the attack on Saponi town, Sayen's sickness, his work with the governor, Fort Christanna, and the North Carolina-Tuscarora war. Even after Keme's return from captivity, it had always been something else—never Keme.

At the moment, it was more than he could deal with. He set it aside and asked, "And Sayen and our father?"

"Good. Father walks now and Sayen has started sitting up. She longs for Keme. Your return will help."

"White Water, if Keme has found Hawk, he is safe and Hawk will let us know. We will wait." Then stepping aside he motioned Tree Son and Kanti forward and said, "My sister, now you will meet Tree Son's wife, Kanti." Kadomico watched White Water's face change from sadness to surprise to confusion. "She is the daughter of Sam Layton and Starlight. She and Tree Son married in the Shawnee town we visited. We have been on the trail for many suns, and slowed by storms."

White Water recovered her composure and stepped forward to the beautiful Kanti. Ten days of dusty, and often muddy, trail conditions could not hide the warmth in Kanti's friendly smile.

"I am White Water, sister of Kadomico. You are welcome here, Kanti."

Kanti said, "I am sorry for your great loss. Tree Son has told me. I hope I can help the Saponi."

Tree Son stood by her side. "And what am I, White Water? Have you forgotten the only one you cannot outrun in a fair footrace? Shame, shame, and after all I have done for you," Tree Son shook his head.

White Water ignored the teasing, smiled at him, and said simply, "Welcome home, Tree Son." She took Kanti by the hand and they started toward the town.

As they came to the entrance to the town, Kadomico and White Water stepped aside to let Kanti and Tree Son continue toward the roundhouse of his parents. Fires throughout what was left of the town while the villagers disassembled and disposed of the charred structures of half-houses, cleaned the living areas, and rebuilt as best they could. Tree Son proudly led Kanti past the silent, staring workers. They were accustomed to seeing Tree Son return with a deer or a brace of turkeys across his shoulders, not this beautiful woman. Kanti felt their awkward silence.

"Tree Son, why do you not greet your people," she said. "It is as though you are a stranger."

Before Tree Son could answer, an old woman, smeared black from handling the charred wood, turned away from a smoldering fire, pointed a broken pole at them, and cackled. "Aeeeahya, Tree Son, you are back, and instead of food you bring us another mouth to feed. Eeeeya, Eeeeya." She shook the stick, turned her back, and shook her bony hips in contempt.

The old woman's cries brought people drifting hesitantly toward Tree Son and Kanti. Tree Son stopped and turned to face them, but Kanti stepped over to the old woman who had returned to tending the fire.

"I am Kanti of the Shawnee. I come not to eat your food but to provide you with more, not to slow the work on your houses but to help you rebuild them. If necessary, my people will join me to make the Saponi strong and safe again. Tree Son is my husband, and he has told me what we must do."

Tears formed and slipped across wrinkled cheeks of the old woman as she sat down mumbling words of the attack and her losses. Kanti began to collect debris and feed the fire.

Tree Son summoned a young boy. "Tell them the woman is my wife. We go first to my father and mother, then we will come and work with them."

As Tree Son approached Kanti, the old woman rose and took the wood from Kanti. "Go with Tree Son," she said. "This is my work. Come back and we will work together."

Kanti yielded the load of wood and walked away with Tree son."It will not be easy to be accepted here, Tree Son," Kanti said. "They see that I have taken a most revered warrior from them. They cannot yet understand that you have brought a badly needed, willing, and able member to the Saponi."

Sayen rose on her elbow and squinted when the skin covering the doorway sprang back and Kadomico entered.

He went directly to her bedside and knelt so that their heads were close enough that Kadomico could understand Sayen's softly spoken words.

"I come," he said. "White Water told me that Keme is missing." He took her hand in his as she lay back.

"It is so, Kadomico, and Keme is deeply troubled. It is why he left us." The words came with great effort, softly but clearly. She continued. "Others call him coward and speak badly of you because you work with the English." Startled, he moved to respond, but she raised an open hand. Her eyes spoke clearly. "Wait. Listen."

Sayen took a deep breath. "Before I was attacked, I told Keme to run, and I turned to face the enemy to give Keme time to escape. Then, I blacked out under their attack. The day before he left, Keme told me he had disobeyed me. Instead of running away, he ran back and leaped onto the back of the warrior who was beating me. He thought they had killed me. The last thing he remembered was crashing into the rocks on his head and falling unconscious. He did not know that he had actually stopped the beating. They grabbed and pulled him until he let go, and they all fell backwards onto one another. When Keme came to he was hanging over the shoulders of one the attackers like a dead animal. He could not see me, but I lay unconscious in the shallow stream, bleeding but still alive and breathing."

She paused before continuing. "Keme saved my life, Kadomico. He told me what he remembered the day before he left because he was ashamed of his disobedience and he somehow held himself accountable for what happened to me. He just wanted to confess before he left. I have not yet told the story. Keme is brave. He fought impossible odds to save me at the risk of his own life. I have told him so, but he is still confused because they call him a coward and the son of a coward. We must tell the council. His story must be danced before a ceremonial fire the same as our warriors have done for all time. He has earned the feather of bravery. You must see to it."

Kadomico rose, held Sayen's hand, and fought back the shame he felt for failing his son. Instead, he let Sayen see the pride brimming in his eyes. He smiled down at her and said, "I will see to it. The council meets now. I go there, and we will talk more later."

Later that same day, a messenger from Hawk arrived. He was an old Tuscarora warrior with his white hair held in place under a colorful headband decorated with porcupine quills holding three turkey tail feathers. His black eyes set in a deeply tanned face of wrinkled leather, were sharp, alert.

He was waiting outside the roundhouse when Kadomico and Tree Son returned from the council meeting.

They stopped as the old warrior rose to speak. His message was in Algonquian and short. "I am Mingan. I speak for Hawk. We have Keme. He will not return to you. If you come for him, he will run away again. He wants to stay with Hawk and fight the white man. We will keep him and explain that for now his place is with you, his people. When Hawk speaks, Keme will listen. It is best you wait for him to come back to you. Until then, we will protect him as our own."

Kadomico translated Mingan's Algonquian name as "Grey Wolf" and wondered what tribe this one might have abandoned to fight with Hawk against the strangers.

"Mingan, we are grateful for this news. Thank you for coming. I will return with you and speak to Keme. "

"You cannot return with me. If you do, I will leave you when we reach the Meherrin River. I will deliver your message and obey Hawk's command. If I do not return in two suns, the answer is no."

"And if I follow you?"

"I will lead you, but never to the place of Hawk." Mingan was clear. He would die before he betrayed Hawk.

"I will do as you say. Will you rest here in my lodge tonight?"

"I must leave at first light."

"I will be ready. Come, Mingan, and meet my family."

Four days later on the bank of the Meherrin, Kadomico stirred a small bed of coals under a roasting squirrel. This was the second day of waiting for Mingan to return with Keme. If they did not come by the next sun, he would begin a search for Hawk. He put two more squirrels on green hickory sticks, leaned them over the bed of coals, and settled back. The two days of waiting alone for Mingan had given him time to think about his work with the English, his family, Keme, and his people, and he was saddened by the visions of failure and rejections that came to him. In all his years of work, it had made no difference for the Saponi. Now they are about to be forced from their homes again. He had been absent when his people were raided and nearly destroyed. His son had run away from his family. It had gotten so that his people saw so little of him that they had forgotten him. And still, the English continued to take the land.

It was almost dark on the second day when the small canoe of elm bark slipped ashore at Kadomico's campsite. Keme knelt in the bow guiding the canoe ashore while Mingan held it against the slow current.

Mingan spoke quietly, "We come."

Kadomico stepped down to one side of the canoe and steadied it while they disembarked. Together they lifted it up the bank and turned it over to drain.

Mingan and Keme settled near the fire. Mingan sprinkled something from his pouch on the coals in acknowledgment of Okeus. They ate both squirrels in silence before Mingan spoke. "Hawk says it is a family matter to be settled between you and your son. Keme is welcome to stay with us until he is ready to return to the Saponi. If not, Hawk wishes you both great strength and happiness, and I wish you understanding. Now I go to a place downstream where I have seen deer. I will take a small one for tomorrow's food. Maybe I will stay there the night."

Keme and Kadomico sat by the tiny fire opposite each other. Kadomico let the silence linger long enough to dismiss any thoughts of demands, urgency, or haste. At this point, he felt he had lost his son simply by omitting him from his life. In addition, he had failed to explain his work with the English, often thought of as the enemy by some of the Saponi people. Nor did he explain why he did not fight them like Hawk, or why he left his people unprotected to fight with the white man in North Carolina. Now he realized how obsessed he had been to gain the support of the Virginia governor for the Saponi, to secure land and rights to land protected by Virginia law. His people did not understand that or the reasons for his personal involvement. Finally, he realized how it must have looked to Keme. Even after the attack on Keme and his mother, Kadomico had left them alone and unprotected. Kadomico groaned.

He looked at Keme sitting quietly, staring into the fire, surrounded by darkness, waiting respectfully. His shoulder-length hair reflected the flickering light of the flames. Kadomico searched the boy's face but found no evidence of feeling there, no sadness or fear, no confusion or curiosity, nothing. The expression on Keme's face was unchanging, a stoic calm. This I know, thought Kadomico, there is nothing I can say this night to give him the understanding that he must eventually find. And as for his opinion of me, he will only believe what he sees me do from now on, not what I say. The healing will be a long time coming, if at all. I have much to repay my son and his mother.

"Your mother is healing and needs you," Kadomico said. "I came to be with you on the trail home, if you wish to go."

"I wish to become a warrior." Keme spoke softly. His eyes remained locked on the dying embers.

"It is a fine thing to become a warrior. Your people will be proud."

"My people say I am weak and will not fight."

"Yes, I know. They probably say the same of me. I also know they are wrong. And when you are older you will understand why I do what I do. For now, you are strong and have already proven your bravery. Your mother told me of your attack on the Iroquois. You saved your mother's life, Keme."

"I disobeyed her. I wanted them to stop beating her."

"And they did. You did the right thing. I am proud of you and thankful that you fought them."

"Did she say that? Did she say I did the right thing?"

"She did. Only four suns ago, she told me the whole story."

"I thought I might be punished for disobeying and getting captured."

"Keme, there is no greater deed than to save the life of another at the risk of your own."

Keme fell silent at his father's words. His disobedience had weighed heavily on him, and he had believed that he was somehow responsible for the near-death beating she had taken. It would take time for this new account of that horrible day to replace the guilt he had been living with, but it was already beginning to work. He wanted to think about it.

"Hawk says I must go through the huskanaw with my people," Keme said.

"It is so. The *huskanaw* is a long-standing way of the Saponi to prove young men. It will build your strength, endurance, and resolve. It is hard in every way, physically, mentally, and spiritually, and you will need the support of your family. But it will strengthen you." A long silence followed. Keme kept staring at the fire to avoid looking at his father.

Finally, he said, "Can we sleep now?"

"Yes. When the sun returns, we will cook the deer."

Kadomico despaired at the huge gap between them, but he did not press Keme. Father and son made separate beds. Kadomico looked for a long time at Keme who had fallen asleep almost as soon as he lay down on the soft pine boughs; his head rested on his folded arm.

Now, his son safely returned to him, Kadomico crossed his legs, breathed deeply, and relaxed. The reality of being here with Keme surrounded by forest and stream under a starred sky gave him pause to think. It had been a long time since his mind had been free of the constant struggle to act as a fair-minded go-between in the differences faced by the white man and the Indian. Much to the chagrin and misunderstanding of his people, he had often made excuses for certain European differences, many of which were wasteful and destructive to nature's gifts held so reverently by the Saponi. Also, unlike Hawk and many members of his own tribe, he had come to see the futility of war with the English, and he was committed to finding a means of peaceful coexistence—not the way of the Saponi if it meant yielding yet more of their land, which it certainly meant. Because he felt that with more education he could better understand the English way and represent his people, he had harbored a relentless determination for more schooling. His work as a go-between and the constant pursuit of more knowledge had often conflicted with his responsibilities as a father and a Saponi warrior. But now, looking at Keme, he saw clearly what he must do.

At this moment, he was satisfied to be here with Keme, alone and with only Keme's well-being on his mind. Everything else faded and he reveled in the present, unburdened by anything that had been or might be.

Kadomico rose and walked over to a great outcropping of flat limestone extending into the river. The full moon hung just above the trees downstream laying down a path of silver on the calm, dark water with small glints of white where the water splashed over limestone and reflected the moonlight. He faced the rising moon and moving water and prayed to Okeus, the Saponi god of all creation, for strength and guidance.

For now, there was Keme's story to be told and the huskanaw. At the council meeting, the shaman had stood, arms folded, and announced that Keme was protected by Okeus. Rarely was a warrior singled out to receive their personal care. The shaman said that he would tell the story and commit it to the long history of the Saponi. Tree Son would dance Keme's story at the ceremony.

The huskanaw required a great deal of preparation of mind as well as body. He would guide him through it, but unless Keme showed interest, he would set aside the plan for him to learn to read, write, and speak English. There was much to make up to his son, and now it would begin.

Mingan made a great noise approaching the camp in the dim first light of dawn.

"Not a stick of firewood here yet these great warriors snore away the best part of the day," said Mingan, as he threw the deer onto a large flat limestone and began skinning. Birds, startled off their roosts, flew about fussing at the intruding noise.

Keme leaped out of his bed of pine boughs and ran for the river. The air was still and warm for so early in the day. The clear, shallow water at the bank rested calmly over a bed of pebbles that had served as a nest for a swarm of young perch. Keme sat for a moment on a bare sun-bleached trunk of driftwood with his feet dangling in the cool water. Holding to a great limb by his side, he leaned until his head was just above the surface, and splashed his face and neck vigorously, sipping the cool rivulets streaming across his lips.

He gathered an armload of dried drift wood and returned to the camp where Mingan was preparing strips of venison for roasting. Keme laid the firewood down and waited for Mingan's orders.

"Go," Mingan said. "Put more wood on the coals. We need a great bed of cooking coals." He continued carving and laying out venison. "And lay these cuts on those stones while the fire blazes. When it dies down, we'll roast them over the coals."

Kadomico had a second fire blazing away, soon to be ready for roasting the remaining venison. He was now sewing a sack from the skin of the deer to hold the excess meat for the day's journey. Keme gathered more firewood and found a young hickory with abundant limbs just right for roasting the strips of meat.

As they sat down to eat, Mingan sprinkled tobacco from his pouch on the fire as a sacrifice to Okeus.

They ate in silence. When they were finished Mingan stood. "I go now," he said. "The others wait for me." He looked at Keme.

"My mother needs me. I must return to my people. Hawk has spoken," Keme said.

"It is good that you return to your people. Hawk will be pleased."

"When I am cleansed and prepared by the huskanaw, I will come to join Hawk."

"You will be welcome," Mingan said.

Mingan and Kadomico lifted the canoe and slipped it into shallow water. Kneeling in the canoe, Mingan looked at Kadomico and offered his forearm in friendship. "You look different, Kadomico. Last night the gods gave you understanding. I am glad I did not have to kill you."

"Your orders from Hawk?" Kadomico smiled.

"Only that Keme was not to be forced to return. You were wise, and I think worthy of that fine young warrior. Go with him now." Mingan slipped his canoe through the quiet shallow water overhung with large trees leaning from the bank and was soon out of sight.

Kadomico turned back toward the camp and smiled at the realization that Mingan had kept him under observation most of the night. Back at the campsite he saw that Keme had smothered the fire and collected the deerskin pack and the remaining meat ready for packing. Together they filled the pack and strapped it to Kadomico's shoulders. One more night on the trail and they would be home.

At dark, a small, lively stream crossed the trail. Kadomico stopped and kindled a small fire. While Keme collected enough firewood for the night and morning cook fire, Kadomico broke branches of nearby pine saplings for bedding. Knowing the scent of the meat would bring bear, wolf, or cougar before dawn, Kadomico suspended the pack from a high limb on an old oak. Satisfied that it was visible in the firelight, he positioned himself so that he could keep an eye on the pack as he dozed off and on throughout the night. Only once did a pair of red eyes approach them. It probably had been a wolf following the scent, but seeing the fire and a man nearby, it had turned away.

As they prepared to continue in the morning, Kadomico approached his son. "Keme, you kept a good pace on the trail. Ability to walk and run the trail for so long a time is one of the first tasks you will do during the huskanaw. You will have no trouble. You can be proud of that."

Keme was surprised that Kadomico had noticed. He had been sure to stay within two or three steps of his father all day, and just before they stopped, it had started to be difficult to hold that pace.

"I am strong, father, and I can jump high and swim a long distance. White Water taught me, but I have not been allowed in the hunting grounds."

"We will hunt together soon, Keme. There is much to be done to store food for the winter."

Keme wanted to ask more questions and talk about hunting, but he was still uneasy being alone with his father. He wondered why his father had not been angry with him for running away. He chose to leave it there and remain silent.

They recovered the pack of meat and struck the trail to the Yadkin River.

That evening they were greeted by White Water in the maize field near the trailhead. Her first words came breathlessly. "The day you left, a trader came here from Williamsburg with a message for you to meet a party of men at the Fort Christanna site as soon as you can. Tree Son and Kanti left with him for the site the same day."

"Good," Kadomico said. "Tree Son knows what to do."

"But you must go there. They expect you."

"Tree Son will handle it. I am proud of him. Keme and I will hunt two days, less if we can kill a bear or big deer. Now let us go to Sayen and Custoga."

White Water saw the change in Kadomico immediately. It warmed her deeply to have him back. "Yes, my brother, we go there now. Keme is training to shoot birds in flight. We will show you." She motioned to Keme and they trotted toward their roundhouse.

22

Ripken was working a group of slaves clearing land, opening new ground. Dozens of stumps littered the field of dead trees. Three years ago, the tree trunks had been girdled with deep cuts through the bark and life-giving cambium and left to die standing. The work of felling and clearing the huge trunks and branches was saved for days between planting, hoeing, and harvesting. Making new ground from forest was slow, hard work, hard in any season and murderous in the June heat. Ripken had separated Zack from the rest and set him to pulling stumps alone on the opposite side of the field.

Zack had been at it without rest or water since first light—dig, chop, pull; dig, chop, pull. As the sun climbed toward its zenith, the work site sizzled in its heat. Still Ripken offered no water and no break. Zack began to back off as much as he dared as the day wore on, but it was not enough. Ripken cracked his whip and watched him try to catch his breath. Finally, Zack adjusted the chain that he would normally use to couple the load to a horse or ox. He put the chain over his shoulder and dug in to loosen the great root. Unable to budge it, he staggered back toward the stump with a shovel and collapsed.

Al Ripken saw Zack fall. He turned his mount and reached for his whip. He was heading for Zack when he saw Seth Jackson approaching. Ripken rode to the shaded edge of the field and waited.

Al removed his broad sun hat and wiped the sweat draining over his face. "And what might you be up to, Mr.

Seth, out here where slaves work? Such a rare thing for you gentlemen of the manor." Ripken's words dripped with hate and sarcasm.

Not far ahead of him, Seth saw a slave on the ground. If he were not dead, this heat would surely kill him. Seth ignored Ripken's sarcasm. "Looks like a man down over there. I have extra water." Seth turned his horse across Ripken's path just as the whip cracked near the head of his mount, startling him to rear and shy away. Seth brought his horse under control, but his temper flared, overcoming his caution to avoid trouble before his indentured service expired. Fighting to control the rage within him, he dismounted, dropped the reins to the ground to steady his horse, and looked up at Ripken.

"I'm down here beneath you, Ripken, so you'll feel a little more comfortable trying that whip out on me. Your last chance to punish me." Seth knew every horse on the property, and he knew that the stallion Ripken was riding was one of the most intelligent. He grasped the bridle of Ripken's horse at the bit, faced him, and moved his other hand to signal it to rear. The horse went up, and Ripken went over backwards. He came up with an eight-inch hunting knife held out in front of him, cutting edge up. Seth had learned street fighting the hard way in Glasgow, London, and in Newgate prison. He disarmed Ripken and sent him to the ground again with a right cross to his jaw propelled by the weight of his body and the speed it had generated. Ripken lay still. Seth led both horses toward the slave.

The workers on the opposite side of the field had stopped and were looking Seth's way—silently. They had seen what happened and it frightened them, but at the same time, it was like manna from heaven to see Al Ripken taken down. They just dared not say so. Seth stopped and faced them. They turned as if a marching signal had been given, backs bending to the work.

Seth took the skin of water from his horse and approached the body lying still where it had fallen, clothed only in a pair of cutoff breeches. He was lying face down and his head turned away from Seth. It took Seth a moment to recognize the broad shoulders, muscular legs and whip-scarred back of Zack. With recognition came nausea, fury, and fear at once. Seth soaked his kerchief from the saddle canteen, rolled Zack over, and began to bath his face. Zack's eyes opened but did not focus. Seth drenched the kerchief again and placed a tip of it on Zack's lips. The dripping kerchief flooded the lips, and a tiny bit of water fell into his mouth, enough to awaken him. His tongue began to search for more. Seth let him sip a little from the canteen, and then dragged him into the shade. After several sips, Zack regained full consciousness, still shaking from the experience.

"Can you get on this horse, Zack?

"Let me stand a lil bit, Mr. Seth. Mebbe from that stump over there." He nodded toward a nearby stump and leaned on Seth, took a step, paused, then another, and so on until he reached the stump.

Finally, Zack was astride the horse. Seth stepped into the saddle of the other horse, and they walked the horses back to the place where Ripken had lain. He was not there.

Seth and Zack had not gone far when they saw Ripken walking back to the plantation. Seth sent Zack on to the barn and turned toward Ripken. He pulled up in Ripken's way and stopped.

"Best you listen, Ripken. I'm here because the Colonel sent me to tell you to turn Zack and two more good ax men over to me. The rest of this summer and fall, they will work for me. We leave tomorrow morning for the staging area down south. I'll pick the men I want. The Colonel himself will lead us out in about two weeks.

"Now, we can leave it there, and I'll send Jason back with your mount in a little while, and that can be the end of it. Or, maybe you want to take this up with the Colonel. We can do that and see how he feels about all the trouble you've been making. I'm talking about your interfering with his use of Green Spring men and equipment, and your treatment of Zack this day. You'll need that little bottle of rum you carry around with you for courage when you find yourself fired or demoted."

Ripken stepped around Seth's horse and kept walking.

Seth caught up with Zack and continued directly to Gladys' house. She was not there. He got Zack into bed and gave him more water. Seth found bread and a bowl of cold stew in the little cupboard.

"There's stew and bread under the cloth on the table, Zack. Take what you can when you can. You need something in your belly to get your strength back and lots of water from that skin right here by the bed."

Zack murmured understanding and reached for the skin. Seth poured a gourd dipper full for him.

"I'll be back when the stock is put up. We need to talk. The sooner we leave here the better."

Seth was returning to the barn with the horses when he saw young Jason walking toward the manor house with an armload of firewood. He called to him to come back when he had delivered the wood. Jason smiled and nodded and kept going with his heavy load. He returned shortly and went directly to the stall where Seth was working.

"Afternoon, Mr. Seth."

"Hello, Jason. I want you to take this mount to Mr. Ripken. He'll be on the path to the new ground, maybe a half hour ride. Better take my horse and lead his. His is acting kind of skittish. Don't give him any slack in the lead rope and he'll give you no trouble. "

"Yes sir, Mr. Seth. I can go now." Jason loved working with Seth and the horses, and he welcomed every chance to ride them. This would be the first time he would ride alone, out of sight of Seth. It meant Seth trusted him.

"Just tether my horse in the shade outside. I'll put both of them up about dark."

Seth reflected on what had happened. His anger had abated enough that he could finally reason. He doubted that this would reach Ludwell, but if it did, he also felt that Ludwell would see his side of it. He hoped he had heard the last of Ripken. Even so, it remained for him to get Zack off the property as soon as possible. He would work on that. Right now, it was time to start staging materials, supplies, and men for the trip back to Fort Christanna.

He was oiling harness and other tack when Ripken came into the barn leading his horse, threw the reins over a hitching post, and walked out without speaking. No telling what Ripken might do, but it was too late to worry about it. Seth stopped working the harness, stripped the saddle from Ripken's mount, and led him out to the watering trough just as Jason rode in. Jason stood in the left stirrup, brought his right leg slowly over the back of his horse, and eased himself down. Seth shouldered the saddle and saddle blanket and handed the reins of both horses to Jason.

"Better water them before we shut them up for the night, Jason. I'll go fix their feed; any problems?"

"No, sir, both horses 'uz quiet all the way. Mr. Ripken, he didn't say nuthin'."

Darkness was settling over Green Spring when Seth returned to Zack's quarters. Gladys motioned him in and shut the door. She was glad to see he was not riding. A horse tied to the fence was too strong a curiosity for neighbors, never mind the danger of someone from the manor house noticing.

Zack was finishing a hot meal at the table and relishing a mug of cold milk, fresh from the spring.

Seth pulled up a half-log bench and sat across from Zack.

"You're looking better."

"I'm better, suh. I thank you, Mr. Seth, I do, I do. I guess I jus' passed out. I 'member seein' Mr. Ripken walkin'. I don know whut happened, but it seem like trouble for you—me ridin' and him walkin'."

Seth thought it best not to go into the details of what happened. "You passed out from the heat and lack of water. We used Ripken's mount to get you here. I sent Jason to return his horse."

"Massa Ripken ain gon have that, Mr. Seth. Jus' ain't. He been after Zack ever since he come back from that trip with you," Gladys said.

"I know. Zack and me, we both need to get clear of him as soon as possible. So we're leaving tomorrow morning."

Seth told them about the staging operation on Hogg Island and how the Colonel had put him in charge of it. Zack could help him with the livestock and other camp chores. On this trip, Allen was to get the first part of the surveys done and clearing for the fort and the Indian town would be started. They would be gone the best part of July and there would likely be another trip in August.

"The point is," Seth continued, "we'll be off the plantation, and it is best we get clear before anyone is up. Do you think you can be ready to leave two hours before sunup? I can return later to answer questions and face Ripken if it is necessary. I'm hoping it won't be."

"I'll be ready," Zack said.

They arrived at the James River ferry landing long before the ferryman but not before the late June sun disposed of the cool, dark night. They dismounted and used the time to discuss the work ahead. Zack was astonished at all the people, packhorses, and militia Seth expected. It would all start arriving in a day or so, and they would leave in about two weeks, early July, hot. Zack would be caretaker of the staging site in Seth's absence. Seth had to arrange for the ox and cart from Green Spring, packhorses from wherever he could find them, and a long list of things not yet known.

Ludwell had told Seth of Governor Spotswood's trip to the southern border country with a large militia force to secure peace treaties with those tribes that had survived the disruption and destruction of the Tuscarora war. Previous scouts had reported many small groups adrift in the forest, starving and without warrior or hunter among them. All were willing to do anything for food and shelter, but they were so scattered it was impossible to set up a meaningful alliance with them. Still, Spotswood wanted a firsthand view of the situation to strengthen his reports to London and his case for Fort Christanna. Seth was concerned about the threat of attack on the caravan before they reached the site. This time, no one mentioned the Saponi guides and interpreters who'd been with them before. He would remind Ludwell of that and stress the increased risk without them.

They ferried over the James River and scouted out a place to begin staging the caravan. Seth showed Zack where to clear the ground for a tent and temporary livestock pens before he returned to Green Spring to let Ludwell know they were ready to receive cargo at the Hogg Island site.

Kajika's scouts, led by Nadie, watched the growing activity in the staging area at Hogg Island. By mid June, the whites were in motion. It was now clear that the supplies building up on Hogg Island were destined for the fort site. It was time for action. He dispatched a messenger to Kajika.

On hearing this, Kajika went to the trail looking for a place to intercept the caravan. He liked the small opening in the place where the trail split. It would be a late afternoon strike with the promise of darkness for a safe retreat in case they needed it, but he wanted to see if the ferry landing at the Nottoway River might offer a better option for the ambush he had in mind, and he kept going.

When Nadie learned that Kajika was scouting the trail, he set out to find him. He tracked him to a thicket of reeds and young saplings near the Nottoway River. One call of the mourning dove produced an answer, and Nadie approached his chief silently.

"Ho, Nadie." Kajika spoke softly as Nadie passed him..

"I grow old and careless," Nadie responded, dismayed that he been taken by surprise.

Kajika was nestled against the upturned roots of a small ash tree that had yielded to the relentless current and had fallen into the Nottoway River. Tall reeds and the crown of the tree shielded him from the river. The steep riverbank behind the roots hid him from passersby—well-chosen cover.

Kajika grinned through missing teeth and disheveled hair partly covering his face. "Maybe not," he said. "I see you found me. I hope not so easy as it appears."

"I found only occasional grass still bent a little where you passed, sometimes a place where a little dust had moved about on hard ground. You move true to the meaning of your name, 'Walks Without Sound', but no man or beast can rest his weight on Mother Earth without leaving sign." Nadia joined Kajika at the roots of the ash so that their heads were close and voices low.

"Perhaps we can attack the caravan when it crosses the river there?" Kajika pointed downstream where a small ferry operated. In this area the river was narrow, perhaps seventy paces, but it was too deep to ford.

"Take the first arrivals on the other side? Yes, but even that is within killing range of their firesticks. My scouts have now counted twenty militiamen, but there are that many more men with the caravan, many muskets, horses, and long-knives."

"What else?"

"Packhorses, a cart with wheels, ox, possibly more."

As he listened to Nadie, Kajika realized the caravan was too well-protected for an all-out assault on the trail. It would require more men than he had, and it was much too late to find and include Hawk's band of raiders. He abandoned the hope of an outright attack on the caravan.

"When will they begin?"

"Soon, maybe one or two suns."

"Send five warriors to follow them. Kill any that separate from the caravan—quietly, ambush only. Take what they have. Leave their bodies for the wolves and vultures. Disappear. No prisoners. "

"Done, Kajika."

"Place an arrowhead under the stone. I will meet with Hawk next full moon."

23

Angus McHale walked off the ferry leading a big horse and joined Seth and Zack at the staging area. They had collected enough provisions to load three packhorses. Militiamen, armed and mounted, started arriving the day before the trip began and kept coming until they were twenty in all. Among them were Philip Ludwell and a Powhatan Indian guide. John Allen, the surveyor, and his assistant Paul Chandler had also camped in the staging area and were ready to travel.

On the last Friday of June, the sun rose on men packing and loading cargo on horses while others saddled their mounts for the trip. They had reserved the cart for the animal feed, powder, and ball. Every man carried his own provisions, but Jock and Seth provided an ample supply of coffee and tea from their campfire. Seth's packing and saddling was done. He watched the others forming up. Tomorrow there would be another race in Williamsburg. Ann would be there. He caught his breath and hesitated as a vivid image of her flashed across his mind. He turned quickly to Zack who held the reins of his mount and had noticed the hesitation.

"You all right, Mr. Seth?"

"Just fine, Zack. Mount up," Seth replied, still distracted

By mid-morning, the caravan was ready; twenty militiamen, Philip Ludwell, the Indian guide, Seth, Zack, Angus McHale, John Allen, and Paul Chandler, all mounted.

Three packhorses and the ox and cart completed the caravan.

Ludwell climbed onto the cart and called for attention. He explained the order of guards, point men, outriders and trail-clearing work parties, and he made it clear that no one was to leave those positions without militia escort. They would rest at noon and camp at sundown, at least three nights on the trail, maybe four depending on how much trail work would be required for the passage of the cart.

"We're on our way to the southern frontier," Ludwell said. "Most of the Indian threat disappeared with the defeat of the Tuscarora last March, but bands of renegades roam the wilderness now, and ye can be sure they'll be watching for the first sign of weakness—like somebody wandering away from the caravan. No hunting, no firing of a musket unless attacked. Stay close up, stay in position." Ludwell stepped down from the cart, swung into his saddle, and waved the line forward. He sent five militiamen out front with the Indian guide, followed by Zack and Seth with their saws and axes, then the ox cart, more outriders, and packhorses. Five militia sentries anchored the line, taking turns in pairs at backtracking and sweeping the trail to be sure they were not followed. Ludwell backed his mount off the trail and inspected each element of the train of men and horses until they all had passed, then took his position behind the advance guard.

High on a hill, hidden in the upper limbs of a great white oak, a Kajika scout watched the staging area activity through the dense forest foliage. Four companion warriors remained concealed.

Ludwell ordered Seth, Zack, and three militiamen forward to clear the trail for the passage of the cart. Seth wondered how necessary the ox and cart were. It meant at least another day, probably two more days, on the trail. He was glad to see Luther Kingston of Middle Plantation with Ludwell's militia. Luther managed operations, overseers, and workers for the Pages, owners of Middle Plantation. He had made the first trip with them to the fort site and had proved to be a knowledgeable woodsman and helpful trail companion. Seth considered Luther a man to follow, to listen to on the trail or on the plantation matters. He learned to trust Luther immediately, but he would learn much more from him before that fort was finished.

The ox set a pace about half the normal pace of horses. Seth was glad that here in the first part of the trail they had very little clearing work to do. At the end of the day, he figured they had made eighteen miles—it would be four or five days on the trail, he thought.

The attack came on the third day just before they reached the Nottoway River. Riding two hundred yards ahead of the caravan, the clearing team approached three small trees blocking the trail. Riding point and still about thirty yards from the obstruction, Luther raised his hand and stopped. The trees were not blow-downs. He could see their white stumps and the green leaves of the crowns. They had been chopped down. It was a trap. He drew his pistol, fired a shot to warn the caravan, and reined his mount about to face the others.

Seth also turned to join the others now in fast retreat back to the cart. But Zack, seeing five warriors suddenly appear in scattered positions, spurred his mount toward them, passed Luther, and reined in between the enemy and the trail party. It would have been a trap if the cart had reached the downed trees.

The first enemy warrior to show himself was Black Spirit, Kajika's favorite renegade, as mean as the devil himself, answering to no man, including Kajika, and eager to kill. His entire face, painted black and marked with three broad white stripes fingered from forehead to chin, was calm. Ignoring Kajika's orders, he had grown impatient following the caravan and planned to disrupt it, kill as many as he could, and fight the pursuers in the forest where the militia was no match against the wilderness skills of the Indians. Ignoring the five-against-thirty odds, his eyes locked on to the back of the retreating Luther, still fifty yards from him.

Infuriated at the escaping quarry, Black Spirit drew his long bow and nocked an arrow just as Zack appeared riding hard straight at him.

Seeing Luther targeted, Zack skidded his horse to a stop, reined him hard around to follow Luther, and dug his spurs into the horse's belly. He grabbed the mane, and leaned forward as close to the horse's neck as he could get, yelling, "Go, go, go."

Now between the enemy and the retreating Luther, he took Black Spirit's arrow in the massive back muscles of his left shoulder. His horse surged on toward Luther in a dead run just as ten militiamen from the caravan charged past him toward the enemy. Zack slowed his horse and looked back. The attackers had melted into the forest. The militia was milling about but there was no enemy to be seen.

Seth met Zack and helped him dismount not far from where the cart and packhorses had stopped. He unsaddled Zack's horse and spread the blanket on the ground.

Zack knelt on the blanket, opened the front of his long shirt, and slipped his right arm out of the sleeve to allow Seth to lengthen the tear and gently cut the shirt away from the arrow that had entered the back above Zack's waist. It had traveled under the skin to the shoulder before it stopped just before reaching the the deltoid muscle.

"Go belly-down here, Zack," Seth said, pointing to the blanket. "Let's see what can be done about this."

Ludwell and Luther rode up to where Zack lay.

"How does it look, Seth," Ludwell asked.

"Not as bad as I thought, sir. It looks like a glancing shot in the muscle only. I think I can see where the point is located. Good thing he was hugging that horse."

"I've seen it before, Colonel," said Luther as he dismounted for a closer look. "Might be less damage if we cut through the skin and pull the arrow on through."

"Then get it done, Luther. Seth, make a place on the cart for Zack. We need to move on."

"Don't need no place onna cart, marse, sir. Jus' cut it out 'n I be good."

"Be quick," Ludwell said to Luther, and wheeled his mount to rejoin the militiamen waiting down the trail.

Luther produced a bottle of strong brandy, poured a generous amount on the wound, knelt by Zack, and took a long pull on the bottle before he corked it, drew a pocketknife from his boot, and turned to Seth. "Build a fire and heat this blade. Keep it searing hot in case the blood gets out of hand. Such as this takes time. The colonel will just have to wait." Then looking up at three mounted militiamen slumped in their saddles watching him, Luther ground out his words between clenched teeth. "Ye gods! Gentlemen, can't ye see we need help here. We're not movin' until this arrow is out and the wound is bandaged. Now go get some bandages and a bone saw, and don't ask me where. There's bound to be a medical kit somewhere. Just go."

"There is one on the cart," Seth volunteered as he fed the fire. "Right on top, if I remember correct."

"Sit up, Zack. I need a closer look," Luther said. "The arrowhead might be flint and bees-waxed or pressure fitted to the shaft. If it is, it'll let go if I try to move the shaft by pulling it away from the arrow head. But I can see where the point is pushin' the skin up a little. Best not chance more damage trying to back it out. We'll saw as much of the shaft off as we can, then I'll cut through the shoulder right down to the head, open the way, and work it on through."

A militiaman brought him bandages and a surgeon's kit. "Oughtn't take much of a cut to reach it, but it'll bleed, and

I don't know how much. Take a long pull on this brandy, Zack. It's all I got but it'll help."

"Don' t need no likker, Mr. Luther. jus' go ahead and do what you gotta do. But did you say you goin' to saw my bones?"

"No, not atall, Zack. I need a fine saw to cut that arrow off close to the wound so we can pull and push it on through once we get a grip on it behind the arrowhead."

Allen and Seth clamped the arrow shaft below the fletching and strapped the clamps to Zack's back so the shaft could not move when they began to saw. The tiny razor-sharp saw made quick work of removing the fletched end of the arrow, and Seth removed the straps and clamps leaving only an inch of shaft visible.

Luther took another long pull on the brandy, handed Zack a roll of clean bandage, and said, "All right, Seth. Let's have the knife."

"Bite hard on that cloth, Zack. It will be over pretty quick," Luther said, as his blade went directly to the chert arrowhead and stopped. Blood flowed freely into the compress bandages that Seth kept applying. Luther probed and found the shaft, opened the way a little and tugged the arrowhead carefully to avoid separating it from the shaft. Immediately, he felt the shaft come free. Zack grimaced and bit down on the cloth. One more cut to make way for the arrowhead to exit and the whole assembly slipped out. It was over in minutes, and Zack was bandaged, standing, and asking for help to mount his horse.

Seth shook his head. "Colonel says you ride the cart, and here it is ready for you. Load up. I'll bring your horse. We'll see how you feel tomorrow morning."

"I thank 'ee, Mr. Luther," Zack said, and headed for the seat on the cart.

Luther nodded to Zack and turned to Seth. "Looks like the colonel is rarin' to go, Seth. I won't forget that your man took the arrow intended for me."

"He's a good man, sir. I'll tell him."

Ludwell abandoned the advance clearing team, and now kept the caravan closed up tight against another attack. They were two more days on the trail. Angus McHale took Zack's place on the clearing team, and between him and Seth, they kept the caravan moving at a steady but slow pace. They arrived on the site to find a partially assembled shelter, cook fire, and a beaver pelt on a stretcher frame located exactly where surveyor John Allen had previously marked the Indian town shown on Spotswood's map. Tree Son and Kanti were working on a shelter.

Allen rode over, and without dismounting greeted Tree Son. "Glad you're here. For the rest of the day, we'll be settling in farther up where the fort will be."

Tree Son returned the greeting and said, "Good. My people have spoken. Some will come, camp here, work the fort."

"Fine. We can use all the help we can get. Follow me and we'll lay out what's to be done." Allen glanced at Kanti who was still at work on the shelter. "Didn't expect to find a woman here, Tree Son. Friend of yours?"

"My wife. We work together."

Allen decided to leave it there, tipped his hat, and rode away, climbing through the thick forest to the crest of the hill above the river where he had marked the first boundary of the pentagonal fort. Ludwell was organizing the militia for sentry duties and camp work. Seth directed the cart toward a level piece of high ground immediately claimed by John Allen for his tent and surveyor's table. Angus McHale, oblivious to the sentries, arrivals, and the milling about by horses and men, leaned against a huge pine tree honing the blade of his ax, eager to get to work. There was still a little sun left in the day.

Tree Son and Kanti reached the edge of the activity and hesitated until Allen motioned them forward. As they passed a group of men unsaddling their mounts, a young man among them looked up, wiped his sleeve across his mouth and said, "Now there's the first reason I seen 'f bein' here. Hey there, sister. Hold up. I got some really nice stuff yor're gonna like."

Tree Son turned in time to see McHale's ax slam into the tree next to the boy, barely missing him and blocking his path. The militiamen were laughing at the boy who had stopped cold.

Aside from his great height and massive frame, Angus had made an impression on everyone in the caravan with his ax handling expertise. Back on the trail, they would gather just to watch his ax pass through thick limbs in a single swing. The blade flew to the mark without fail, and Angus let it go there with little effort on his part. He seemed to know before he swung whether to prepare for another strike or move on to the next branch. Such a throw as they had just seen was something new. It was going to make a good tale, embellished with each telling, for a long time to come.

Angus watched a moment after the ax struck. When the boy realized what had happened he reached for the ax, fury in his face. Angus shook his head of auburn hair and rich beard. It was all that was needed for the boy to change his mind.

Angus turned his back on the scene and approached Tree Son with his hand out. Both Tree Son and Kanti were smiling.

"McHale, me lad and lassie, Angus McHale. You'd be Tree Son. We've not met, but Governor Spotswood has spoken of you, sir, and your friend, Kadomico. I'm honored 't meet you, I am."

Neither Kanti nor Tree Son was sure about exactly what had happened. Only part of what had been said reached their ears, but Tree Son was sure that it had something to do with Kanti. Both, however, had seen the ax buried in the tree and the men laughing and pointing at someone.

Tree Son took McHale's offered hand. "I am Tree Son, Senior Warrior of the Saponi." Tree Son took Kanti's hand and drew her forward. "My wife, Kanti, Shawnee daughter of Sam Layton, of the Shenandoah Shawnee, friend of Governor Spotswood."

"Aye, Aye. Governor Spotswood has spoken of this Layton. 'Twould pleasure me 't walk wi' ye, Tree Son, it surely would." He looked up toward the cart. "I see Allen is about to speak now."

Tree Son glanced at the ax still embedded in the tree.

Angus noticed and said, "Twill be all right, lad, 'twill be all right." Kanti returned his smile and they walked over to the cart where John Allen was speaking.

"We are here to survey land parcels and clear as much as possible while we complete the surveys. I expect no more than fourteen days to do the planned surveys. The site of the fort will be the first to be marked, and that is where the clearing will begin. No one may leave this site without permission and escort, except the Indians who will be camped on the site marked for them. Tree Son and Kanti of the Saponi are already here. More Indians are expected. Treat them with respect. They are guests of Governor Spotswood. Hold your questions. There is not much daylight left. Colonel Ludwell will speak to you now about immediate fortifications. Then, Mr. Angus McHale will explain the work." Allen held up his hand for quiet and turned to Ludwell. "Colonel."

Ludwell waited for the murmuring to stop. "We have twenty armed and mounted men with us, and you can expect the woods to be full of curious, possibly hostile, and maybe friendly, Indians. Make no contact. Notify me immediately if you see strangers. The camp will be posted tonight with sentries placed within sight of each other. Tomorrow all militiamen will rotate between sentry duty and working on Angus McHale's saw and ax teams. When the temporary fortifications are done, ten militiamen will return to their homes. The rest of us will stay here until the surveys are done.

"Lt. Kingston, take five men and reconnoiter a circle about a musket shot from where I stand. Take paper and note the springs, hills, marshes, grazing ground, cliffs, everything of use to us or an enemy. Now, Mr. McHale."

Angus mounted the cart and faced the group. "'Tis a beautiful woodland we 'ave here, lads, beautiful I say, 'n it breaks me 'art to tell you that by this time tomorra a lot of it will be gone, thanks to your axes and saws. The job is simple: fell 'n buck every tree to fifteen feet and sharpen the small ends to a point. Work inside the fort markin's first, then start outside clearin' approaches. We'll work in four-man teams, wide apart. Seth here has the tools. Fell y' tree, trim 'n buck it. Rest y' pales clear of the ground and move on. Seth and Zack will be along with the cart to clear y' leavins. Keep y' blades sharp, lads. It eases the work and makes it safer."

Angus stepped down and spoke to Seth, "We'll keep the cuttin' areas clear. Trimmins'll build up fast. They won't burn easily, 'n we don't want 'em piled up to make cover for enemies. Choose a ravine to dump and fill. Once located, I'll cut a roadway for y' cart."

By nightfall, a large clearing littered with trimmed tree trunks emerged in the flickering light of three fires tended by Zack. Being mostly long, clear pine trees, there was little trimming needed. Most of them had been bucked. Seth and Luther removed the tops and limbs by throwing grappling hooks into them and snaking them off to a deep ravine.

Tree Son and Kanti returned to Zack's fires and began roasting venison and turkey parts from yesterday's hunt. They spread the cooked meat on the upturned halves of one of the large red oak logs. The aromas of the roasting meat signaled the men, and they lined up to serve themselves.

Before the evening was over, it was clear that Zack, Tree Son, and Kanti would work the kitchen for this party. Angus McHale smiled at the development. A perfect fit, he thought—frees the other men to work. He'd speak to Seth.

Shortly thereafter, Seth approached Zack with two cooking pots. "Zack, here are the pots for tea and coffee." Seth said as he set them down near the fires. "You reckon you could see to the coffee and any cookin' that's needed 'til this is over?"

"I can, Mr. Seth. 'deed I can. Tree Son and Kanti say they'll hunt tomorrow. Coffee and tea'll be ready first light, 'n the meat'll be ready come quittin' time."

"Good," Seth said. "How's the wound? Looks like you're favoring that side some."

"I be, but no more'n no less'n yesterday. Kanti and Tree Son say for me to sleep over there tonight, 'n Kanti will fix it good. Tree Son say she got the medcin' with her to make sure it don get no worse. I'd like to do that 'f you don mind."

"'Sure. It's a good thing. I'll speak to Mr. Allen 'n let him know about his. He'll be pleased. Only thing is, the camp is patrolled by sentries. Might be he will send an escort for you at day break. If not, you be loud and careful approaching the camp at first light."

"I be fine, Mr. Seth."

Seth turned away to find John Allen. It looked like they were off to a good start. This land looked so promising that the prospect of owning fifty acres of it dominated his thoughts and kept him awake until he finally yielded to the weariness of the day. That night Seth dreamed of a tobacco field, a team of fine horses, and Ann.

Tree Son, Kanti, and Zack banked the fires, stacked the morning firewood nearby, and filed out of the camp past

211

the sentries. Tree Son and Kanti each pulled a large bundle of pine tops collected from the day's cuttings.

On arrival at their shelter, Kanti made a soft bed of pine boughs for Zack, removed the bandage, and bathed the wound with warm water from their fireside. She redressed it with a poultice saturated with her own remedy of crushed yarrow and wintergreen. Zack didn't question it for he had seen Gladys apply such poultices many times.

While Kanti worked, Tree Son watched with pride. She seemed to know exactly what to do and *not* do in every situation. He knelt beside Zack and asked, "Are you Seth's slave?"

"I'm Colonel Ludwell's slave, but Mr. Seth, he mos' a free man now."

"He will be free but not you?"

Zack explained as best he could about indentured servants and slaves, then added, "Some say a black slave can buy his own self 'f he got sterlin' silver money, but it be a awful big lot of money 'n I never know a slave what bought his own self."

Kanti, curious to know about Zack's family life, joined in. "Zack, your father and mother . . . slaves?"

Zack told them about Gladys, and the three of them talked well into the night learning about each other's families. Just past midnight, Zack fell asleep in the light of a half moon hanging high in a clear sky while Tree Son was explaining the plight of the Saponi people. Kanti smiled at Tree Son and motioned to Zack's closed eyes.

"He is a good man, Tree Son."

"Yes, and he is our friend now."

24

Almost a month after his visit with Sam Layton Kadomico returned from a hunt with Keme to find Sam waiting for them. White Water had made him welcome and explained to him where Tree Son and Kanti were. Now, after the town cooking fires had turned to ashes, the sounds of night brought reassurance of the day's end. Kadomico sat opposite Sam over a small fire outside the roundhouse.

"Starlight is not with you," he observed.

"It is so. She prepares to leave. When I return we will go west to the great Ohio Valley and rejoin our Shawnee family. It is no longer possible to trap the Shenandoah and hunt the valley. Surveyors, traders, and explorers are everywhere. Soon the land will be fenced, the forest will be turned into farmland, and the game will be gone."

"It is the same here. You are fortunate. We have no great father nation in the west to receive us. Instead we must join the English or perish."

"Your people are welcome to join the Shawnee."

"My people will not give up their independence—at least, not yet."

"But they are willing to accept the land on the Meherrin? Is that it?"

"Yes, along with the protection of the English fort and cannon. As you can see, the Iroquois, Tuscarora, and other northern tribes continue to make war against us only because we are few and weak, and they take our young for their families to strengthen their numbers."

"And you believe that this time the English will keep their word, that the land they promise will be Saponi land forever more?"

"No, but it is what they say. It is what the governor himself promises. It looks possible now, but I do not believe that in the coming years it will be any better for the Saponi than it has been for the few surviving Powhatan people who are on reservations now surrounded by settler fences and plowed fields. No, I do not believe it will be forever, but for now, it is safer and offers the promise of good hunting grounds and streams."

"And eventually when they send their messenger to tell you that the land is British Crown land and you must move somewhere else?"

"Yes, eventually, it will be so, and I cannot stop it. I have been wrong to think so. By working closely with the white man, I have lost my way with my family, my people, and myself."

Sam stirred the ashes with a long stem. Kadomico was deeply troubled, and Sam felt partly responsible. Years ago, he had escorted Kadomico, then fourteen, to his first day at the grammar school in Williamsburg. He had encouraged and helped him to embrace English education and to learn to work with the white strangers. There was more hope then than now, he thought.

"And what now, Kadomico?"

"As long as our council wishes, I will work only for my people, represent them, and interpret the English intentions in the courts, the market place, and on the battlefield." Kadomico hesitated, then continued as though in deep thought.

"Sam, the English live by their laws. In the past, they show proof of their ownership with their land patents and survey markers to justify their actions. Only then does the governor act. Do you think that Saponi land ownership can be established within their laws and land patents."

214

"No, it has been tried before. Ordinarily, only Christians who are subjects of the crown and are granted the liberties and privileges of the colony and patents of land ownership. The closest we have come to that is to become a tributary tribe: swear allegiance and obedience to the crown, accept the terms of their treaties, and pay an annual tribute to Virginia."

"And when it suits them, they simply convene a session of law makers and change the law or make a new treaty," Kadomico added. "I have seen it with the Chickahominy and many of the Powhatan tribes. Still, it takes time to change laws, and the Virginia officials will not act until the law *is* changed. I have wondered if it is possible to stop them by contesting them relentlessly in their courts."

"Well, there is this," Sam said. "There has never before been a Kadomico, an educated, determined, fair minded, logical thinking tribe member like you for them to deal with. On the other hand, that strategy is work for barristers, students of the law, and I know of no one here in our land or among our people with such qualifications."

"Could it be me? Could I attend a law school?"

"Would you? The schools of law are far away in England, costly, and could take years."

Kadomico dropped his head. He knew he would not.

"On the other hand," Sam continued. "Many colonists read, even practice law, to better represent their interests; there is no reason why you could not do that. The books are in the college library. Surely, you have privileges there?"

"Yes, it is a possibility, Sam, but I'll not leave my people again, not until they are safely settled and that may never be."

"I understand," Sam said and paused, questioning his encouragement and advice to Kadomico thirteen years ago when he escorted him to the college at Williamsburg. Back then, land that was safe for settlement was more plentiful, and no one expected the vast numbers of settlers. In just these few years, European arrivals had continued to multiply almost as fast as the number of Indians declined with their losses to war and the white man's diseases. Now the harsh reality was plain enough: native hunting grounds were fast becoming the farmlands of European settlements.

Sam continued. "Still, you say the Virginia governor speaks of protection and a parcel of land measuring six miles by six miles near the Meherrin. That's encouraging—a strong case for uniting the surviving tribes. Is that not so?"

"It is. The Saponi, Occhaneechi, Stukarox and Tutelo are Siouan speakers, less than three hundred people each. All have treaties with Virginia to live in peace. The Meherrin and Nottoway speak Algonquian. They will be more difficult to work with, but they are suffering just as much as others. Still, they consider Siouan speakers their enemy. You know their language and they know you. They will listen to you."

"Who are these people and where are they located?"

"All the tribes are on or near the rivers: Roanoke, Meherrin, Nottoway, and others north of these," Kadomico said. "It will be more difficult finding, contacting, and convincing the roving bands of Tuscarora and other recently defeated North Carolina tribes."

Sam Layton considered the prospects of a piece of land six miles long and six miles wide and marked for Virginia Indians. Could it work? He knew of other such projects in the past up north as well as in Virginia, Maryland, and Pennsylvania that had failed the Indians in disastrous ways. Yet, thirty-six square miles was a lot of protected land, and it was located in the midst of the vigorous Indian fur trade. In addition, Kadomico may just be on to something. If the Virginia General Assembly would strengthen the wording of Indian rights to their property and make the treaty and other such papers instruments of law, could they not be used to defend Indian rights to the land for many years? Are there even such words, Sam wondered, words strong enough to stop or stall white man's actions to reclaim the land? Can the land be surveyed and clearly marked against squatters?

Sam could imagine ten years from now what it would be like—farms, fences, barns, livestock, and fields of money crops flowing south from the James River, splitting at the northern Indian border of the six square mile segment and continuing on down and around the sides of what would have become an intensely valuable property. Would the settlers respect those boundaries? No. Would their magistrates? Not likely, he thought, not against the settlers—too easy to look the other way. It was one thing for Spotswood to "set aside" thirty-six square miles—easy to say, even allow. It was altogether a different matter to mark, claim, and defend the boundaries against the will of the swarming settlers.

Even so, Sam thought, this offer by Spotswood has a chance of assuring the Saponi and others life in a protected land of their own. He thought of his daughter, Kanti. Now married to a Saponi warrior, she would be a part of that. Should Starlight and he join the Saponi movement—at least until they were settled?

He needed to know more. He would visit the Christanna site, the main Virginia tribes, talk to the people, then visit Williamsburg. It would be good to see his boyhood friend Jock Adams, and possibly, speak with Spotswood. All this would take time. He and Starlight would have to postpone the return to their people in the Ohio Valley.

Sam leaned back, shifted his sitting position, and spoke to his friend. "Kadomico, before we go to Williamsburg, we need to have the word of those tribes that they will join you at Fort Christanna, and their assurance that you or I can speak for them. It is also plain to see how much the Saponi need you. Perhaps I can take the first steps with the tribes while you prepare your people to move. Then, the two of us can appear before Spotswood as representatives of the tribes."

"Yes, Sam," Kadomico said. It was a relief to know that Sam had read his concern so well and was willing to take the lead. "I have a warrior who will travel with you, if you like. His name is Waya, and he is well known among most of the tribes. He speaks only Siouan, but he is a good man on the trail and in battle."

"Good, two are better than one for this work. We leave when the sun returns. Can you also send a messenger to Starlight? This will take longer than I thought. For the time being, we will have to set aside our plans to leave the valley."

"Easily done, Sam."

Sam removed a pendant of polished white crystal hanging from his neck. Within the crystal was a flame-shaped flair of red and green. Long ago, when the militia had come for him, his Shawnee mother had hung it around his neck and said, "Never forget." Sam was eight years old then.

"Give this to Starlight. She will know that the messenger is true, and she will come."

Sam's thoughts turned to the settlers who were poised to enter the Shenandoah Valley. That great hunting ground would surely yield. When Kadomico had visited them, Sam and Starlight were preparing to return to their people in the Ohio Valley. They had agreed to set aside those plans while Sam made one last visit to Williamsburg to assist Kadomico. However, the more he learned the more promising the six-mile-square tract of land and the protection of the fort appealed to him. Might this idea lead finally to a peaceful coexistence? With those thoughts came the realization that this work would take months rather than weeks, even years if he stayed through the building and settlement of the fort and Indian town.

Sam Layton felt the stirring of renewed hope, and a strange attraction to know more about all this. He could visit his old friend Jock Adams and renew other friendships in the colony capital. He and Starlight could easily postpone the return to their people, and they would see Kanti again. He thought the outlook was good, but he had no idea of the trials, rewards, and life-changing events that awaited him.

25

Fifteen-foot logs covered the ground at the building site and gave it the look of devastation rather than the orderly progress it actually represented. Most of the trees had been barked, exposing the wet, white, sapwood of their skin. A few were small enough to use without splitting, but others would be split into halves or quarters to make the pales. All were to have sharp points chopped at the small end of the twelve-foot palisade walls. John Allen had laid out and marked the pentagonal walls. Each of the five walls were to be about one hundred yards long. Instead of bastions, a log house would be built at each of the five corners so that each house could defend the other as well as its adjoining walls. At the top of the high ground, the clearing stretched a little over a hundred yards east to west. The south wall of the fort would lie in that plane. The other four sides positioned the fort on high ground, which sloped gently downward, and north toward the river.

Over at the site of the Indian town, some two hundred yards northeast of the fort, Kanti gathered the last of the summer blackberries. Tree Son worked nearby covering their roundhouse with the abundant bark left at the building site. Kanti suddenly stopped, eyes wide in surprise.

"Tree Son, listen," she said. There it was again, the call of the mourning dove. Kanti's puzzled face slowly turned into a smile. She motioned to Tree Son to come to her, and then returned the call twice in succession.

"My father is here," she said to Tree Son and began to run toward the sound. Seeing Kanti rush into the forest, two perimeter sentries shouldered their muskets and started moving to investigate. No one was to cross the site perimeter without permission and escort. Tree Son saw them coming as he followed Kanti. Walking to avoid more suspicion, he found her in a small clearing in the arms of Sam Layton, tears of joy streaming down her cheeks.

Tree Son took Layton's forearm in friendship. "The sentries come," he said.

"Father, there are sentries everywhere," Kanti said, "and you and your friend are armed strangers in breech clouts. The only thing missing is war paint. We must find the militia and bring you to Colonel Ludwell."

"That would be Ludwell of Green Spring?"

"Yes, do you know him?"

"I knew his father when Colonel Ludwell was just a boy. Yes, I know him. I visited Green Spring. Something about horses, as I recall," Sam said, then turning to Waya, "This is Waya, Saponi warrior. He travels with me."

At that point, the two militiamen emerged, their muskets pointed at the group. Before Tree Son could explain, the first one fired a pistol into the air. Tree Son began to explain. Sam added his own explanation in flawless English, but the sentries didn't like the odds. Although they knew Tree Son and Kanti, to them, it was four armed savages. Two of them were strangers that had somehow crossed their sentry line unseen. They kept their distance, muskets leveled, and waited for the reinforcements they could hear approaching. Six mounted Rangers rode in and formed a small half circle around the group.

Tree Son waited for the riders to settle into their positions, then said, "These are my guests. They are friends of Governor Spotswood. John Allen spoke of them, now they are here. We go to Allen now." Tree Son walked straight toward the first two sentries with their muskets still pointed at him, Kanti at his side. The sentries stepped aside, the riders formed up on each side of them, and the procession started toward the building site.

Ludwell had heard the shot and had seen the riders gallop away to investigate. When he saw the procession approaching he stepped out to meet them, complimented the work of the militiamen in charge, and dismissed them.

"Well, Tree Son, what have we here?" Ludwell said.

"This is our friend Sam Layton of the Shawnee, and Waya, Saponi warrior. They come in peace."

Ludwell knew Sam by reputation and had a dim memory of his Green Spring visit several years ago.

"Welcome, Sam Layton of the Shawnee. You may have noticed we're a bit testy about unheralded strangers. What brings you here?" Ludwell asked, extending his hand.

"Visiting my daughter, Kanti," Sam said, nodding toward Kanti and taking Ludwell's hand, "then to meet with the tribes and visit the governor. I wanted to see the fort layout before I meet Governor Spotswood to discuss his interest in locating the tributary tribes here—Saponi, Tutelo, and Occaneechi in particular." Sam spoke softly but clearly. The fluent English and polite mannerisms from this breech-clouted savage surprised and, for an instant, confused Ludwell. Sam had seen it before and continued, careful to put Ludwell at ease.

"However, I am at your service, if you have need of it."

"We are within a few days of departing, but the work is off to a good beginning. I am the militia commander and, Mr. John Allen is our surveyor and the governor's personal representative. We can go and meet Mr. Allen now. He may, indeed, have need of your services."

Ludwell introduced Sam to John Allen and left them to get acquainted. Sam repeated his reason for this visit and explained that Kadomico was preparing the Saponi for the move as soon as they received the word.

"Well, it is no longer a secret what we are up to. I am surprised we have not been attacked since arriving. I see no reason why the Saponi could not set up over there when they are ready and stand guard, so to speak. There may be working parties in and out throughout the winter getting ready to begin building with the first days of warm weather next spring."

"Then after you leave," Sam said, "there will be no militia left here?"

"That's right. Nor will there be anything else left here to defend other than these bare pales and temporary fortifications you see lying about, but to have an Indian presence here seems to be right along the lines of the governor's thinking. Of course, only he can say."

"Makes sense, Mr. Allen. I will see that it comes to the table for consideration."

"Good. You are welcome to travel with us. The survey work we had planned is finished. As soon as Angus McHale, our builder, gets the pales stacked in position for the palisade work, we can leave, may be another day, two at most."

"I thank you, sir, but Waya and I have several tribes to visit before we are ready go to Williamsburg and speak with the governor."

"I see. Well, Angus McHale will show you what we're about here. He is working the timber presently. Perhaps Tree Son will find him and bring him here. In the meantime, I can offer you coffee or tea while we wait? I count it a privilege to meet you, and I am eager to hear your opinion of this project."

Tree Son motioned to Kanti and Waya to follow him and said, "I go to McHale."

Sam and John Allen filled two mugs of coffee from the campfire coffee pot and walked toward the crest of the hill.

There in the deep shade of a massive oak tree, they found seats on two logs conveniently located opposite each other. A gentle breeze drifting over the crest of the hill brought relief from the midday heat, as they settled down with their coffee.

Kanti returned with slices of cold roast turkey, venison, and bread.

Allen smiled at the attention and said, "Already your visit is rewarding, Mr. Layton. I assure you, I am unaccustomed to such service as this. Thank you, Kanti."

"You are welcome," Kanti replied, pleased to show the English skills she had learned from her father.

When they were alone, Allen said, "I'm uncertain how to address you, sir. You are obviously a well-educated and respected descendent of our people but living the life of a Shawnee. So is it to be Mr. Layton, or do you have a Shawnee name by which I should call you?

"I am known as Sam Layton among my people and yours. I favor that name and hope you will use it without titles and such."

"Let it be Sam, then," Allen said, now fully at ease with this stranger.

"Sam it is," said Layton, then changed the subject. "Yesterday we crossed fresh trail sign indicating that three warriors had moved roughly in the same direction we were going. We stopped several times looking for more sign, but there was none. Their tracks were too carefully covered for them to have been hunters or traders. I suspect they knew we were there. It is more likely that their destination was the same as ours. If so, there will be others."

"Not surprised, but I'll let the colonel know and we'll tighten up. Any idea who they might be?"

"They might be northern Iroquois, or they could be one of the bands roving about in these parts, throw-offs from the recent Tuscarora war," Sam said. "You can be sure they are not friendly. Not likely they will attack since you have so many muskets, powder and ball, but keeping close together is a good tactic. If they are one of the roving bands, it will be hit and run. Tree Sun, Waya, and I will check beyond the sentry lines before supper.

Angus McHale walked up to them carrying a wide brim leather hat in one hand and wiping sweat from his face and neck with the other. If not for the huge freckled forearms and biceps flexing and relaxing in their task to dry him, his green eyes set behind rich dark lashes and brows would have been the most noticeable feature of this thirty-two-year-old, auburn-haired Scot.

" 'Pon me soul, Mr. Allen, 'ye do 'ave your share o' sun in Virginia," Angus said, laughing and reaching for the gourd dipper in a convenient cedar bucket of spring water left by Kanti.

"We do indeed, Mr. McHale. Our friend here is Sam Layton, Shawnee, interpreter, friend of Governor Spotswood, and I believe, much more than that if you get to know him. You can call him Sam."

McHale returned the dipper and turned to face Layton with his hand outstretched. "Me 'and is a mite damp, Sam. Ye'd be right to take that for honest sweat in a worthy cause."

"Done," Sam replied, "and a privilege as well." Here was a man Sam liked immediately, this big frame with rolled sleeves emanating power, a man of barely harnessed mirth and merriment straining to be free. Sam suppressed an approving chuckle as he looked straight into Angus' smiling green eyes that had just the faintest suggestion of a mischievous twinkle.

"Sit, and take some rest, if you care to," Allen said. "I have to see to the packing of the survey equipment. Sam wants to see the layout and work we are doing. Could you show him around?"

"Aye, and a pleasure 'twill be," Angus said. "Let's be about it. Time enough for rest at supper, and a grand supper 'twill be, Sam. Wait'll y' meet the bonnie lass who fixes the vittles here. Indian she is, heaven sent to the palate of every man jack amongst us. Belongs to Tree Son here, she does. Kanti's her name."

"Know her well, Angus," Sam said, thinking there was nothing to be gained by softening the news for Angus. "Kanti is my daughter."

"Loose tongue, blitherin' idjit I be," exclaimed the big Scot, not the least bit embarrassed, just amused at his own innocent impetuousness. " 'n to that I say 'well done,' Sam. Kanti is surely among your greatest blessings."

"Thank you, Angus. I will let her know of your kind words."

"Let's be off, then," said Angus, "so Mr. Allen here can get on with his work."

That night at supper, Sam took his food and walked over to where Angus and Luther King of Middle Plantation sat together on split logs with their meal. As he approached, Angus motioned him to join them.

"Sam, this is Luther King of Middle Plantation, militia officer, he is, and a good one. Sit ye self down."

Sam nodded a greeting to Luther and said, "Yes, I believe all the land now known as Williamsburg came from Middle Plantation. Good to know you, sir."

"We were just goin' over our defenses and wonderin' if we'll need 'em," Angus said, placing a half-eaten roasted turkey leg on a huge mayapple leaf that served as a plate by his side. "Tell us what ye think."

"As I said earlier, Angus, your armed men and all these ramparts you have assembled will stand off a large force of attackers. More likely, the enemy will wait until you are back on the trail, and even then they will pay a high price if they take you on. On the other hand, we know you are being watched. No man is safe outside the sentry line."

Later that evening Ludwell had a mount brought up for Sam, and they rode the sentry line together. The posts were set up about twenty paces inside the cleared area and within view of the sentry post on either side. During the past days, each sentry had fashioned a rampart with peeled pales and debris from the felled trees so that they were protected from attack within the forest and could safely guard their own and each other's flanks. On two occasions, they had taken arrows from the forest in the twilight hours, the intent being to draw them into the forest. It didn't work in either case, and there had been no more incidents.

The tree line was dark against the starry sky. Mounds of limbs appeared black in the cutting area which was still littered with debris of felled trees. Their horses had no trouble finding their way among the peeled logs lying about like a graveyard of prostrate ghosts clad in white, lighted by a near full moon.

Sam and Philip spoke loudly as they rode along discussing various matters, calling to, and occasionally stopping, to chat with a sentry. Something about Sam Layton had aroused Ludwell's interest, something elusive. Yes, he was a white-man-gone-Indian, and yes, he had managed a fair English education as well, but more than that, Ludwell sensed something unspoken about Sam. Why was he giving so much time to Spotswood's plans for Fort Christanna? He was a well-known successful fur trader from the frontier and with a brilliant record as an interpreter and go-between for the colonies. Then, Ludwell remembered his own growing interest and optimism about the trading and land patent opportunities. Could it be that Layton had seen personal property opportunities? If so, what—land? Surely not land patents were for Virginia citizens. It could be the trading business. Ludwell decided to try to draw him out.

"Sam, you are a long way from the Shawnee nation. What brings you here?"

Sam was immediately wary. The question was abrupt and borderline rude to begin with. On the other hand, it was a good one. He realized he needed, but did not have, a well thought-out answer, and while visiting-his-daughter was a good reason, it did not answer the question, especially given his intention to visit Williamsburg. Aware that his hesitation would only raise more curiosity in Ludwell's mind, he would try the veiled truth.

"Kadomico, Senior War Chief of the Saponi, is my friend. I interpreted for him at the college when he was barely fourteen, stood by him at a time when his introduction to the white man, school, and English disciplines were most difficult. I encouraged him to try to understand the way of the white man. We became close friends. When we parted, he asked, and I promised, to help him if he ever needed me. Now he is the governor's choice to coordinate the tribes and to populate the Indian town at the fort. He has asked for my help, and I am here to do what I can." Sam hoped his answer would put the matter to rest.

Ludwell seemed to accept Sam's explanation. With the picket inspection over, Sam thanked Ludwell for including him and they parted. Sam started walking back to Tree Son's and Kanti's roundhouse.

At the roundhouse, Kanti and Zack had just finished making ready the cooking equipment and food they would need over at the fort campsite for the breakfast meal. Waya and Tree Son had bedded down early and both were asleep inside. Kanti settled down with a bundle of willow withes and began working on a half-finished basket. Zack stirred and fed the little fire nearby where hot water simmered.

Although Kanti could understand the English language, her speech was more limited. After all, she had had very little opportunity to practice it. Now she addressed Zack with her best effort to be understood in English.

"Zack, . . . you. . .slave?" she asked, smiling to put him at ease.

Zack stood, bare to the waist, arms and shoulders bulging with muscle moving under black skin, his linen breeches cut off just below the knees above bare feet. His left shoulder still carried Kanti's poultice and bandage. He felt very easy in Kanti's company. They had worked side-by-side for several days now. He had learned to trust her, and he had answered her questions to the best of his ability, repeating himself often to get his thoughts across. After a while, silence fell between them. Kanti made no move to continue the conversation or to go inside. Zack squirmed about in his seat at the fire and finally looked up at Kanti and said, "I 'spect it don make no sense to you why I stay, do it?"

"Indians . . . have . . . slaves," said Kanti, hesitating between clearly spoken words. "Not many . . . some. Fix feet to stop runaway . . . or slave go away."

"Where?" Zack asked.

"Back to their tribe." The more Kanti spoke, the easier it became.

"Jus it, Miz Kanti. Ain' no tribe for black slaves 't go home to. 'ats jus' it. See? I once seen a Indian man, I think it wuz Sam Layton. Come to Green Spring after a horse when I wuz jus' a boy. I ax him 'f there's any black people in his Indian place. He hadn't seen none, he said, but color didn' matter 'f the man wuz strong and honest and loyal to the tribe."

"You thought of running away?"

Another time, another place, and that question would have been enough to send the wrath of white men down on him in lashes, starvation, and imprisonment. Right now Zack's trust and commitment to the friendship of this

Shawnee woman and her husband, Tree Son, made it natural to speak freely to her.

"I guess I did, but later on, no . . ." Zack hesitated, thinking. He realized he hadn't thought of running away in a long time. Why, he wondered. Then his feelings erupted, pouring forth words never before spoken, words of fear for Gladys back at Green Spring and for his recently developed friendship with the indentured servant Seth Jackson. He told Kanti how good it was to be working on Fort Christanna, but he kept choking back what he wanted to say about his Ella, the black slave of Middle Plantation who was never far from his thoughts. At the thought of Ella, he stopped talking, but Kanti knew there was more. She nodded silent understanding while Zack talked, and when he stopped, she waited and watched his troubled face as a single tear formed and caught the light of the tiny flame. She let the silence linger while Zack composed himself.

"Zack," she said, "speak to me. I am your friend."

"I know, Miz Kanti. I know, but I bes' not say no more. I'm powerful sleepy now 'n need t' lay me down."

Zack had no sooner found his bed than Sam stepped out of the darkness.

"It is good to have my daughter wait up for me, but the sun is not far away. Your work is heavy. The men here are grateful for your, Tree Son, and Zack's services. Off to your bed with you, young one."

"Father, Zack is sad. Must he always be a slave?"

The question caught Sam by surprise. "It is the way of the white man," Sam said, hoping that would be the end of it and knowing it would not.

"It is more than being a slave, I think," replied Kanti as she gathered her basket and withes and stood up.

Sam watched her find her way beside Tree Son and shook his head. Whatever was making Zack sad, Kanti would eventually know.

26

Hawk found Kajika sitting on bare ground leaning against the trunk of a rotting tree, head bowed, eyes closed. He had drawn his good leg up and left his bad leg stretched out to ease the pain. His hands were relaxed in his lap but he was not asleep. He wore buckskin trousers, laced leggings, and moccasins, and Hawk remembered how careful he was to keep the scars of his bad leg covered lest his enemy think him crippled and weak. The great knife was strapped to his waist in a colorful sheath of leather and quills.

"You are not well," Hawk said instead of a greeting.

"Well enough." The words were snapped back, but Kajika hadn't moved. After awhile he raised his head and squinted at Hawk through his good bloodshot eye. "We strike them at the Meherrin River crossing with the next sun. Let most of them cross over, then kill the rest. Same thing at the Nottoway. After that, we attack what is left of them on the trail. Kill the white devils and their horses."

"And the Indians left behind at the fort?" Hawk asked.

"They will be with the caravan until it is crosses the Meherrin. Strike when half the caravan is on the other side. Withdraw and leave the long knives, muskets, powder, and ball until they reach the Nottoway. There will be fewer men in the caravan at the Nottoway and fewer still after the Nottoway—plenty of time to retrieve the weapons and anything else after the Nottoway."

Hawk was not satisfied with the plan, but it had possibilities. Between them, he and Kajika had about twenty-five warriors, all wanted, all desperate, and all eager to destroy the white man. There were not, however, enough muskets, powder, and ball to arm them, nor could they successfully wage war in the open against mounted and armed militia. A stealth attack at the Meherrin River crossing would work if they could get within the killing range of their bows. Yes, the possibilities looked good. Every man in his band was a master at stalking, be it game or enemy.

The men had been on site seven days working from sun-to-sun. Allen's survey team had a good start on marking the location of the fort, Indian town, and several parcels of prime land adjacent to the fort. Ludwell had released half the militia as soon as they had defenses and clearings enough to give the remaining group of Indians, militia, and surveyors a strong advantage against attack. Provisions were running low. It was a job well done and time to leave.

The mid-July morning of departure dawned late under a clouded sky and a drizzling rain. Men wrapped in oilcloth rain gear were saddling up and loading packhorses. The kitchen crew tended cook fires surrounded with roasted meat and boiling coffee and tea water. Ludwell walked his horse toward the river crossing followed by five of his ten militiamen. The crossing, about a quarter mile below the work site, was now visible. Instead of going to the crossing, the riders broke away in two groups of three and began a sweep of the forest bordering the clearing east and west.

Ludwell's group kept moving east until they turned north toward the river and emerged from the forest near the riverbank. He raised his hand to signal a stop. There was too much cover at the bank to spot an enemy. Sitting in their saddles quietly, they waited, watching for movement or other sign of the enemy. Then, they saw it. At one place where the long wands of willow branches hung among a thicket of reeds the water moved in noticeable circles concealing something solid and large. It could be a man. They knew if there was one, there would be others. Philip raised his hand and backed his horse into the denser forest to the protection of trees. He sent a Ranger to recall the group working upstream and returned to the staging area.

"They are along the bank," Ludwell said to the assembled militia and others. "Some are actually in the water. On a day like this, it is not likely they will have powder dry enough to fire on us, but you can be sure of bows and arrows. Half way down that slope, place three Rangers on either side of the path, each with a spare loaded musket, backed up by three men: John, Luther, and Paul take the right side, Seth, Zack, and Angus, the left. Make every shot count. Two Rangers, one right, one left to guard the forest. Everyone else, keep the muskets loaded and ready to fire."

Ludwell watched the men take kneeling positions. The horses had been corralled high up on the work site, safely beyond the firing and hand-to-hand battle, if that were to be the case. Ludwell rode to the firing line.

"Aim for their hiding positions in the brush at the bank, count about five steps between your targets. Commence firing on my command. After the first volley, fire only at an enemy. If none, hold your fire and watch carefully." The Rangers picked their targets and shouldered their muskets. The men behind them held muskets ready to fire. Ludwell looked his Rangers over, first right, then left. Satisfied all six were prepared, he gave the ready command and time to settle on a target, then, "Fire at will."

Sam Layton carried two loaded pistols in a haversack. He had spent the night secluded in a thick patch of undergrowth on a forested hilltop on the north side of the river crossing. With a clear view of the crossing and probable battlefields, he had observed the enemy canoes arriving from upstream at first light. He'd watched them take positions. As he watched, a lone figure had limped toward his hill, disappeared in the undergrowth, and had eventually reappeared only a few paces from him. The disfigured cripple turned to observe the attack, but instead of the expected caravan crossing the river, he saw riders entering the forest. There was no evidence at all of a caravan. It was a trap. He moved cupped hands toward his mouth to recall his warriors, but a voice from behind stopped him.

"Don't do it, Kajika," Layton said in fluent Tuscarora language. "And don't turn around. Two pistols point at your back. Hard to miss at this range."

Kajika froze, hands half way to his mouth. "Ahhh, Sam Layton, my old friend, we meet again. If you fire the pistols, Sam, it will warn my warriors. It is just as well."

"And you will be dead from the white man's guns. Why don't we watch the fight? Your warriors will use the river to escape, then you and I can settle old scores." Sam could see Ludwell's musket line forming up. He needed to keep Kajika talking only a minute.

"Fair enough, Sam. I am old now, and my arms are tired. I will just rest them while we wait."

"Put your hands behind your back—one at a time, slowly, and keep in mind I see you clearly, but you couldn't see me even if you were facing me. So forget your famous knife throw." Ludwell's men were kneeling and shouldering their rifles. Kajika's hands began a slow descent.

"One at a time, Kajika."

"Ahhh, Sam. So careful."

Huge puffs of white smoke rose into the misty morning. On the first volley, two of Kajika's warriors rose and fell back into the water. On both sides of the crossing, water splashed and bushes moved as the attackers retreated.

In an instant, the Rangers exchanged muskets with their backup men and fired at the movements. Ludwell and two other mounted Rangers charged the banks and fired, but the enemy had vanished. Two bodies lay lodged in the river brush.

Kajika saw the white puffs from the musket fire rise on the hillside and waited for the shattering noise to follow. He timed his movements to the sound of the musket fire. The fingers of his right hand reached the knife in his waist strap exactly as the explosion reached them. In a single motion, Kajika sent his blade into the thicket where he had mentally measured the location of Sam's voice.

Sam triggered both pistols. The two balls slammed into Kajika's chest, knocking him backward over the steep slope of the hill. He landed on his back, sliding over the wet ground, tumbled on to his belly, turned crosswise to the slope, and rolled to a stop face down in the grass and leaves of the forest floor. Sam noticed that the enemy attackers were making good their escape. He returned the smoking pistols to the haversack and drew his tomahawk as he approached the dying Kajika.

"How did you know?" Kajika gasped.

"I didn't. It just looked like the weakest moment of the caravan would be at the crossings, and it was easy to check before they actually left. We made sure your scouts knew we would move out this morning, and you know the rest."

"I missed."

"Not exactly. The tree between us took your blade."

"Such things cannot be helped," Kajika murmured with his last breath and lay still, his eyes open. At the same time, Sam heard a tree limb crack behind him. It was near, loud, and not accidental, an invitation to turn around. Whoever it was could have killed him. He started his turn slowly.

"Without the tomahawk," said a faintly familiar voice.

Sam dropped the tomahawk and completed his turn. Ten paces above him stood Hawk with a piece of broken limb in each hand, a sign that he had spared Sam's life. Sam knew his pistol fire could have brought one of the fleeing warriors to the scene, but Hawk's appearance was too soon for that to be the case. Had he unknowingly shared that hill with Hawk all night? It had been thirteen years since he had seen him, but there was no mistaking the smiling eyes, set deep under rich full brows and lashes—the same eyes that, driven by his trigger-quick temper, could radiate a murderous hatred.

Sam remembered Hawk vividly. Back then, the boy was fresh from the southern frontier, a sincere, friendly young son of an Occaneechi chief in training to be a warrior, a hunter. He had been sent to Williamsburg with Kadomico to attend the grammar school. Even then, his passion to become a warrior left no room for the white man's classrooms, clothes, or church. It all simply fed the flames of a developing hatred of the white strangers. But at the same time, Hawk knew a growing loyalty and devotion to his tribe and to his friends, especially Kadomico and Sam Layton. Those were the days of his youth, and the struggle between those loyalties had taken its toll.

Now, thirteen years later and unmistakably an enemy to the colonists, he had just spared Sam's life and was challenging his old friend to make the first move. Sam's recollection shifted between the young boy he had befriended and this notorious, wanted outlaw in breechclout and war paint, more muscular, taller, and battle experienced. This was no time for sentiment. Shock, surprise, elation, fear and caution all flashed through his mind. Intuitively, he bid for time.

"Hawk," he said quietly. "It's been a while." Neither man moved.

"I am your enemy, Sam Layton. We will meet again," Hawk said, then opened his hands and released the broken limbs. Before they hit the ground, he had vanished into the forest.

Sam filled his lungs with the misty morning air as he stared at the place where Hawk had stood. It was a moment of relief and sadness. Strong and likeable young Hawk, quick to test his strength against others, devoted to his tribe, and committed to war against the white strangers had not softened his view in these thirteen years. However, Sam sensed something else. Hawk had just said goodbye. He had finally seen the impossibility of winning a war against the white strangers, and that realization had strengthened rather than diminished his will to war against them. As for the struggle between his hatred of the white man and his love for friends and family who now paid tribute to the colony governor, he had made the final decision. He would rather die in battle than concede the land of his people to the white man.

Sam picked up his tomahawk and walked away.

The skirmish was over. The caravan formed up and prepared to return to Williamsburg.

After another trip to the fort site, Zack was now back in Williamsburg, and much to Gladys' dismay and deep concern for his safety, he had spent the first three nights meeting Ella. It was a five-mile walk on foot, but he avoided discovery and reveled in Ella's love and admiration. For the first time in his life, he knew the joy and responsibility of being a man, to love and to protect someone, and to make her as happy as she made him. Each time they parted Zack swelled with pride to be so loved by such a woman. As he made his way among the plantation corn and tobacco fields and the swamp land of Powhatan Creek, thoughts of Ella strengthened him. He moved with rhythm, a black form in a black night, no step too long or too high, no water too deep. He moved, over, around, or through every obstacle as though it didn't exist, silently, with only Ella on his mind.

Zack had no idea how, but he and Ella were going to be together. No matter what it took, it would be so, he had friends now who were not slaves, folks who could help him, folks who *would* help him: Kanti and Tree Son and Mr. Seth, maybe even Mr. Sam. There was something new about these thoughts.

They were strongly supported by hope, but Zack had never known hope for a better life. He didn't understand it, but he welcomed it. It made him feel good, able.

Ella had not told him that she was pregnant.

27

September brought the first day of Seth's freedom and the promise of cooler weather. Sunlight gathered among the shadows of the great oaks and pines that stood near the naked lots and new building sites of Williamsburg. Out on the plantations, corn and tobacco harvests were in full swing. On this morning at Green Spring, Seth visited every stable, inspected the animals, and forked in fresh hay. His term expired without ceremony. He just faced his work at Green Spring in the usual way, but today he thought about the fifty acres of Virginia land that would be his and the small wages he was now earning. He inspected his arms and hands and his clothes—nothing different there, not visible anyhow. "Well, Chance, old son," he said, as he brushed away dry mud from the horse's withers, "be a little more respectful. You're being tended to by a free man, a landlord even."

For the first time in his life, Seth had choices of promising options. He could leave Green Spring, seek work elsewhere, go to sea, or sign on with the fur traders, and surely, there were other opportunities not yet known to him. However, Col. Ludwell had created a paying job for him if he would stay. This new relationship with Ludwell, and the possibility of owning land in the south and becoming a grower, fit exactly with what he most wanted—to be a landowner in Virginia. So he had accepted Col. Ludwell's offer.

Now he would have the responsibility for all the livestock, and that included the stables and tack: saddles, stirrups, bridles, halters, reins, bits, harnesses, and martingales. It also included the carriages and other wheeled conveyances. In addition, the Colonel expected him to continue following the Fort Christanna development. Unknown to Seth, Ludwell had made a written request to the patent office for a large tract of land for himself and a fifty-acre patent for Seth on the Meherrin near the fort as soon as patents became available. Seth's land would be adjacent to Ludwell's and would have a small stretch of riverfront.

Seth had saved a little from the rare occasions he had been allowed to hire himself out to other plantations. He held tight to the few shillings he earned. It was all he had to get started when he got his land patent. Ludwell had assured him that Virginia would grant him fifty acres. In addition, there was the Virginia Indian Company at the new fort. When formed, Ludwell was sure to be an investor. Word was going around that participating Indians would get a share if they accepted Spotswood's trade policies and practices at the new fort. Maybe he, Seth, could even be a shareholder. So it was just a matter of time. His next trip to Christanna would be soon now, mid-September probably.

The Colonel had cautioned him to be silent about his interest in a fifty-acre patent. Seth wasn't sure why, but it probably had something to do with treating some people with partiality. Whatever the reason, Seth did not want to risk jeopardizing the possibility of his fifty-acre allocation there. He told no one, not even Ann Stilson.

Now with only a few days left before his next trip to Fort Christanna building site, Seth touched Chance's front leg and gripped the ankle. The leg relaxed and he brought the hoof up for inspection of the shoe and the health of an old wound, but his mind was on Ann. What would she think if she knew he planned to move to the frontier and become a grower and marketer of tobacco and corn *for the market;* a life in the wilderness? Probably, she would have very little interest in such a life, Seth thought. He would talk to her about the frontier when he returned from this trip down there. Then a better idea occurred to him. He set Chance's healthy hoof down gently, went to his quarters in the barn, gathered his best clothes, and headed for Gladys' cabin.

Gladys answered his knock on her door.

"Why Mr. Seth. Zack, he ain here jus' yet. Anythin I kin do?" Gladys asked.

"Yes, Gladys. I plan to go to church in Williamsburg the first Sunday I can, and I don't have any clothes fit to wear, leastways not for church. These are the best I own, and they need some attention. Would you see what you can do with them?"

"Come on in. We'll see." Gladys took the bundle and shook out a pair of brown breeches, stockings, shoes with ties, no buckles, a neckerchief, a brown waistcoat of plain linen with missing buttons: it was typical poor farmer attire. Gladys held up the breeches and waistcoat and looked at Seth shaking her head.

"True enough, Gladys, I see they might ought to be let out some, although I thought they might stretch."

Gladys turned the waistcoat, put two fingers through a hole, and fingered the position of the missing buttons. She pushed the shoes over alongside one of Seth's feet.

"Mr. Seth, you leave 'em with me. I'll do the bes I kin, but if all this dressin' has anything to do with courtin' you need to see a tailor and a shoemaker."

Seth's face flamed and Gladys knew she had guessed right.

"You a free man now, Mr. Seth, important, 'n important folks need proper clothes. Wha'cha you got here is for po' farmers, not middlefolks like you. Now you go on, and while you lookin', find a proper gen'lmen's hat, one turned up on three sides like you see alla time now. If you cain't find buckle shoes, bring me two buckles and we'll fix these."

Still embarrassed by the courting allegation and now confused by her calling him "middlefolk," Seth backed slowly to the door. "Well, I just thought to go to church, and I thought these would do all right. I'll come back Saturday morning," he said, as he hastened his steps.

Gladys let him go without further words and closed the door. She was pleased that Mr. Seth had come to her, and she and her friend, who could do wonders with needles and thread, were going to make him proud to wear those rags. Why, he didn't even bring a cravat or tie, she thought, many times as I mended, washed, and ironed Master Ludwell's clothes, I oughta know whatta white man wears. Lotta work to be done, she mused, as she gathered up Seth's clothes.

Seth walked by the deep spring of cold water and on past the kitchen garden where neatly kept rows of pumpkin, squash, corn, and other fall vegetables were in various stages of maturity. Gladys was right about the clothes, but he wasn't so sure about being called a middleman. He knew well enough where he stood as an indentured servant, but a freeman could be anything from a starving ne're-do-well to a successful craftsman like Ann's father, and to be called "important" and "middle-folk" exaggerated his status in the community.

Was Gladys predicting? Some slaves could "see" the future. He wasn't sure. Did it matter? Virginia was not England where titles of peerage and non-peerage were rigorously imposed. Here a free man could start with his fifty acres and rise to any level, just by his hard work. It would not be easy, and he had to have at least three acres under cultivation within three years to keep his land, but he could do that. Thoughts of injury and sickness never entered his mind. Colonel Ludwell had shown him where Mr. Allen had marked his fifty acres. Since then Seth's mind could see only waving leaves of healthy green tobacco and corn. He just needed a little time.

His mind snapped back to the church on Sunday. The best he could hope for was to be seen there by Ann's family and Ann. By custom, he ought not to greet her in public unless she spoke to him first, but if she did acknowledge him in the churchyard after services with a customary curtsey, he could join her and they could walk together and converse but only in sight of the churchyard.

Seth knew that Gladys was right. If he was going to meet Ann, he'd best have the right shoes, hat, vest, and coat. He refused to spend any of his savings on such nonsense as clothes. That was start-up money for his land, and even so it was not nearly enough for seed, tools, and Queen's annual quick rents (taxes). On the other hand, he'd seen the dandy young men in the churchyard with their three-cornered, decorated hats and splendid coats sporting bright buttons and sparkling trim. He decided to speak to the tailor, but if he could not work something out, he would go with what he had— a straw hat, no coat, and no-buckle shoes. He thought of his tie-on shoes and straw hat. The vision gave him pause but not much.

Monday morning came on bright, warm, and clear. The autumn leaves of the locusts and sycamores led a promising parade of fall foliage. The gentle movement of air in the passage between the stables stirred up the scent of old leather and oil as he worked the various pieces of harness and riding tack into a black sheen and polished the brass studs on the reins and bridles. Chloe, a young slave girl from the manor house, found Seth at the stables.

"Miz Hannah, she say for you to come and she mean right now," Chloe said.

Seth swallowed. Lord, don't let this be trouble, he prayed. He had no idea why Hannah Ludwell, mistress of Green Spring, would call him. He looked at his breeches and work boots and began to untie the leather apron. "All right, Chloe, I'll just wash up a little at the watering trough yonder," Seth said, as he rose and hung the bridle he was oiling on a wooden peg.

"Miz Hannah, she didn't say nuthin' bout washin' up. She just sed 'right now' and then sed it agin."

Seth could see the girl was excited and worried that something would go wrong. He ignored her, dusted off his boots, and went to the trough. He quickly splashed the refreshing water on his face, turned about, and dried his face with a large handkerchief from his pocket as he followed the nervous young messenger, past the ox house, sheep pen, carriage house, and kitchen garden to the manor house. Both were worried and anxious as they entered through the back door. Seth pulled his wide- brim straw hat away from thick waves of sun-bleached blond hair brushing his shoulders. He was holding his hat with both hands when a woman's voice came from the room just ahead.

"In here, girl. Make haste."

"Yes'm. Here he is, mam, jus' like you say."

"That'll be all, Chloe. Leave us."

In his seven years as an indentured servant at Green Spring, Seth had never spoken to Hannah Ludwell. Although he often drove the carriage teams on her trips to Williamsburg and visits to other plantations, someone else always gave him orders. Now he stood in the doorway of a small room furnished with a table and four rush chairs. Additional straight back chairs with rush woven seats and cushions were stationed conveniently about the walls near small tables. She sat on the opposite side of the paneled room near the window out of the direct light, primly upright, back arched, hands resting in her lap. The expression on her face was as severe as her combed hair, parted in the middle, drawn back tightly, and knotted into a bun and partially hidden by the massive collar of her dark green silk gown.

"Seth Jackson, come to that table and be seated," Hannah said without moving. Seth thought of his boots again and wished he had done a better job of cleaning them as he made his way to a chair at the table.

"You are here because I have learned that you intend to appear at the church in Williamsburg Sunday, and I must remind you that you are still employed by and a part of Green Spring. You are well known by your previous work here as an indentured servant. Now, you are a free man, and my husband has given you greater responsibilities. You work with important people of this community. You now occupy a higher rank in this household, and your appearance must reflect that. How those people see you reflects on Green Spring.

"Beyond that, I suspect that your intent at church next Sunday has more to do with a young lady than with your religion or your Green Spring work. Do you understand what I am saying?"

"Yes, madam, I think so," Seth said, shocked that she knew so much and totally unprepared to explain himself if it came back to his real reason for going to church in Williamsburg.

"Fine. I have given Gladys several pieces of proper dress. If she needs more time to fit them to you, you will not go to church or any other public place where people gather until they do fit. Do you understand?"

"Yes, Madam, I do clearly understand, and I thank you. However, I am sure I cannot pay you the fair value of this generosity, but I can pay a little along until you are completely paid if that is acceptable."

"There is no charge. The clothing is part of Green Spring properties and yours as long as you remain employed here. Now do you wish to tell me anything more about this?"

He continued to look at her, stunned to silence.

245

"Well, fair enough. Keep in mind if you feel you should need my help in the future, you may ask. That is all."

Seth stood and faced the mistress of Green Spring. "I thank you, madam and I will not forget your kindness." He turned and walked out relieved and without the least thought of his dusty boots. Gladys would know what to do now, and he headed there walking quickly, past the yard and kitchen gardens, the greenhouse, stables, and finally into the slave quarters.

The door opened before he reached it. "Seein' that grin, I guess you heard," Gladys said. "Come on in."

Sunday morning, at the church, Seth waited for the dismissal amen, left his seat in the back near the entrance, and waited outside not far from where the congregation gathered in the churchyard in the warm September sun to visit and exchange news of the day. Ann appeared on her father's arm, dressed in a fine gown of yellow silk. The instant their eyes met she withdrew her arm and stepped aside from her parents. Her smile was enough to demolish any doubts in Seth's mind. He slipped past the few people moving between them, approached her, and bowed the way he had observed other men greeting ladies there.

"Miss Ann, could I have a word?" Seth said.

"Of course, let us walk. I am surprised to see you," Ann said, and they turned toward a less crowded area. As they walked away from the churchyard toward the carriages and teams, she paused for a second look at Seth. He was resplendent in his caramel coat sweeping down and away from his thighs, his black three-cornered hat and black buckled shoes below brown breeches and knee-length white stockings.

"I have been away until just recently," Seth said. "I may be leaving again soon, and I wanted to see you and tell you how much I have missed our visits after the races, but I

246

wasn't sure what you would think of that, so I came today hoping to see you and maybe find out."

Ann stopped and faced Seth. "I missed our visits as well. Yes, call on me, if that is what you wish." She wanted to throw her arms around him and never let go, but she managed to stay calm though her eyes betrayed her excitement and desire. People passed on either side of them, nodded greetings and continued on to their carriages.

"I will call," he said. "So much has been happening. I am a free man now, about to receive fifty acres of land on the southern frontier. I work for Colonel Ludwell, continue to see to the livestock at Green Spring, and manage the pack caravans to the building site of the new fort on the Meherrin River. I think I will help build the fort." Seth hesitated, then continued. "I will call. I will for sure, Miss Ann. I need to talk to you more, and this is not the best place or time."

"I hope you will. I want to hear about the fort. It is getting a lot of attention here in Williamsburg. I'd like you to meet my father and mother—just there," Ann said, gesturing toward her parents just a few steps ahead.

Seth's hope soared at her expression of interest in the fort, only to be overcome by uncertainty again and the anxiety of meeting the Stilsons so unexpectedly. He'd intended to speak to Mr. Stilson about calling on his daughter but hadn't come up with the words. Ann made it easy.

"Father, this is my friend, Mr. Seth Jackson, recently caretaker of Green Spring and a leader of the governor's wilderness expedition to build the new fort we hear so much about."

Seth barely suppressed an open mouth at the shock of Ann's exaggeration of his position. He recovered just in time to respond to her next words. "Mr. Jackson, this is my mother and father."

Seth didn't know whether to bow, remove his hat in the presence of Mrs. Stilson, offer to shake hands, speak, or remain silent. Ann again made it easy for him. Suddenly he felt her hand touch his back ever so lightly. He bowed to the Stilsons and was about to say that he was honored when Ann continued. "Mr. Jackson has much to tell us of his wilderness adventures. At the moment, however, I have promised to excuse him so that he can be about the governor's business."

Ray Stilson hadn't missed any of this. He knew Jackson as Philip Ludwell's indentured servant, coachman, and jockey of Green Spring's big, black racehorse named Chance, a favorite at the Williamsburg races. And of course, he knew his eighteen-year-old daughter's wit and amazing ability to make a remote possibility a reality simply by refusing to consider anything other than what she envisioned. Mary Stilson, an auburn-haired beauty in her own right, who matched her daughter's will and determination with her own, also knew Seth Jackson but as the Green Spring servant and stable hand, the one her daughter had been seeing at the races this past summer. She did not approve of it then and nothing since had changed her mind. It was time to face Ann and set her straight about the choice she was about to make. She reserved her usual radiant smile and simply nodded acknowledgment of Seth's bow. Ann knew the missing smile meant confrontation and probably soon. She was going to need her father's support.

Ann stepped aside to make way for Seth to leave. Instead of leaving, however, Seth faced Mary Stilson and said, "Mrs. Stilson, I worked with you and Miss Ann last spring when you organized the charity for the Saponi Indians who had been attacked. It was there I met the Saponi brave, Tree Son, and helped him load your packhorses. I was glad to be a part of it."

"Thank you, I remember, Mr. Jackson. You were very helpful," Mary said. She had forgotten that. He had found the horses, pack harnesses, and much more. Still, with the bigger issue of Ann's obvious interest in this man, she refused to smile.

Seth turned to Ann's father. "Mr. Stilson, we will have need of timber and carpentry tools at the building site by next spring. Might I stop by the shop to discuss this?"

Ray Stilson noticed Ann's impatience at momentary loss of control and smiled. "Always welcome new business, Mr. Jackson. Any time," he said, and touched the tip of his silver trimmed, three-cornered hat in a gesture of dismissal. Seth bowed to Mary and Ann, and walked away. Ann smothered a sigh of relief.

Hidden within a curtained carriage watching Seth's encounter with the Stilsons, Hannah Ludwell nodded satisfaction to herself, released the curtain, and tapped the signal for the driver to leave.

One morning the following week, Seth arrived at the blacksmith shop and found Ray Stilson in a tiny room in the forefront of the shop poring over ledgers. He rose when Seth approached the door and motioned him forward to a chair. "Good as your word, Mr. Jackson." Stilson chose a bench next to a small upturned barrel serving as a table and settled down opposite Seth with a pipe in one hand while the other searched for tobacco. "I am anxious to know more about the building site you mentioned."

"I discussed the need for your services with Colonel Ludwell," Seth replied. "He will command the militia when we go to the building site. As you know, I am employed by him. He would like you to meet Angus McHale, the governor's builder, and others to discuss the cost and availability of tools and supplies for the timber men next spring. The Colonel is willing to host the meeting at Green Spring if the governor approves. Does that sound agreeable to you?"

"Certainly, I'd be honored to sit down with them." Stilson's pipe gave off a pleasant, fresh aroma as he laid it in a shallow dish on the upturned barrel. "Now is the right time. I doubt I have the stock and smiths to provide such a big order and that means ordering from England. If so, there is still time, but none to spare. Just let me know where and when, and I'll be there."

"I will certainly let you know, sir."

Determined now, Seth eased himself upright out of his chair, swallowed, looked away, then back. Now he was facing Ann's father who was leaning forward on edge of the upturned barrel on one elbow, returning his pipe to the shallow dish.

"Is there something else, Mr. Jackson?"

"Well, yes, sir, there is. I have enjoyed the company of your daughter, Miss Ann, every time we have met. We have never intentionally met," he hastily added, "but sometimes we find ourselves in each other's company." Seth stopped there. The next well-rehearsed words suddenly seemed all wrong, weak, and blunt. Still, the silence seemed even more threatening to his cause. "I wish to call on Miss Ann, sir— that is, with your permission, sir."

Ray Stilson wasn't surprised. He had witnessed the exchange between Ann and Mary during the walk home from church: the penniless, uneducated, indentured servant had become the young, intelligent, courageous, ambitious, and capable freeman who had won the respect and confidence of Colonel Ludwell himself. Ray knew that the matter was far from resolved in his house, but he also knew that Mary's argument was not nearly as strong as he had expected.

"Sit down, Seth," Stilson said softly, switching to the first name to signal his respect and intent to be open and direct. Here was a young man who had won his daughter's admiration and her mother's suspicion. He picked up his pipe and continued. "You have my permission to call on

Ann. In fact, I'm instructed to invite you to sup with us tomorrow evening. That said, let me also be clear about my reservations, never mind her mother's outright objections. We live in a fairly safe and secure area of a dangerous wilderness. Even here there are limits to our safety, and the safety of my family is first in my mind at all times. Do you understand?"

"I do, sir. I do understand," Seth said."I can only say Miss Ann is very special and I share your concern for her safety."

Stilson picked up his pipe, stood, and walked toward the door. "Fine, we'll see you tomorrow evening, then?"

With his hat in hand, Seth stood with Stilson and shook hands. "Yes, thank you for the invitation," Seth smiled. He liked Ann's doting father. "My respects to Mrs. Stilson," he said and stepped out into the sunlight of what appeared to him to be an unusually beautiful day.

28

Kadomico and Keme stood at the hilltop looking down on their town. Below them, the few freshly built roundhouses stood out from the remains of what once was a thriving village. The mid-morning September sun spread its generous beams of light and warmth over the cool of the previous night bringing every part of the land to life. Birds sang and called to each other. A mourning dove spoke from within the forest. Nuts from the hickory, chestnut, and chinquapin trees would soon be ready to gather.

A young rabbit, more interested in grazing than safety, emerged from the thick cover beside the trail, nibbling away and moving forward at the same time, as though sampling the quality of the grass before settling down to some serious feeding. When it finally saw the two motionless strangers, it sat still for a moment, observing. Then, instead of scampering away, it simply changed directions and continued searching for the perfect grass, oblivious that it was in the company of hunters. The rabbit seemed not so much careless as just young, confident in its speed if needed, and perhaps for the first time, enjoying the feast and beauty of the day without an over cautious parent.

Neither Kadomico nor Keme drew their bow. They had taken game in the first four hours of daylight and had enough meat in the skin bags on their shoulders and on the game straps around their waists: quail, partridge, rabbit, and squirrel. In addition, Kadomico carried a large gobbler.

Below them, the maize fields were beginning to lose their rich green color, each stalk bearing three or four ears of shuck-filled maize still tender enough for roasting. The longer the maize stayed in the field the more difficult it would be to keep the forest animals away from it. Bean and squash vines covered the floor of the field. It would take several days to gather and store the food against winter. Yet, every healthy woman left in the town had her hands full caring for the children, the wounded, and sick while the few able men prepared for the fall hunts.

Over the past weeks, Kadomico and Keme traveled and worked together: rebuilding, hunting, mending weapons, training in the forest and on the streams. They had worked silently for a while, but the awkwardness of being together had faded. Keme relished being included, and Kadomico began to depend on having such a good listener. By keeping his thoughts understandable for Keme, they became clearer to himself. They now spoke their minds freely.

As they walked toward home, he thought about the on-coming winter and the need to occupy the land on the Meherrin. The scene before him reminded Kadomico that the devastating attack on their town this spring had prevented the annual Festival of the Green Maize at which they celebrated and gave thanks for their crops. Why couldn't they combine the delayed festival with the lesser but important harvest festival? The idea exploded with possibilities. A plan began to take shape in his mind.

"Keme," he said, shortening his steps so Keme would be by his side, "there is more maize than we need, and it must not be left to rot, and we need help with the harvest. We might celebrate the harvest with the Occaneechi, Tutelo, and others."

He began describing the usual festival activities to Keme who became excited and had questions at every pause in his father's words. Would there be games, shooting contests, and foot races? They reached their roundhouse and continued talking about it while skinning and butchering the game. Kadomico answered each of Keme's questions, treating them as matters of major importance, which they were. It helped him work out the skeleton of a plan. By the time they finished, they were counting on a festival. Keme could hardly wait to tell White Water and start practicing for the contests.

That night Kadomico met with his father, Custoga, and a few of the other elders who served as a temporary council. He proposed combining the two festivals at the next full moon and making it a three-day celebration. They would notify neighboring tribes and let guests gather the abundant Saponi maize crop for themselves, all they could carry. They would prepare the grounds for the grandfather fire, a huge ceremonial fire to be regarded with great respect and reverence. There would be offerings, prayers, war dances, and dances of thanksgiving. They'd have setups for trading, feasting, storytelling, contests, and award speeches by priests from other tribes. Tree Son would give them news of the fort over on the Meherrin River. Sam Layton would tell them about their meeting with Governor Spotswood and talk to them about treaties, housing, and hunting grounds. He would assure them that there would be a place for them there if they were interested.

The next day, Saponi messengers carried the word to the tribes and to Tree Son and Kanti at the fort site.

By Kadomico's calculations, the next full moon would be second day of November on the English calendar. That gave them time to prepare extra roundhouses for over-night guests, great piles of firewood to light the ceremonial fires, dancers, and storytellers, and the huge collections of food for the feasts. He scanned the ruins; they were slowly yielding as the wounded healed and the healthy redoubled their determination. The beginning of a new life for the Saponi was emerging.

To be sure, it was a sad sight—missing family members, sickness, and weakness in every lodge. They fought fever, exposure, and exhaustion as they cleared away debris, gathered green replacements for roundhouse frames, assembled the grids of the shelters, and tended the wounded. There was little time for badly needed hunting and gathering. Progress was slow, but driven by necessity and supported by a reassuring awareness of the gifts of the surrounding forest, they were moving forward, slowly but unerringly forward. As Kadomico's eyes scanned the town, he was reminded that his people needed help to prepare for the fall festival and eventually for the relocation to the Fort Christanna building site. They could not do it by themselves. He called Keme.

"Go and bring White Water and your grandfather here."

Kadomico laid out the work. White Water would speak to every woman who was still on her feet to enlist their help, however small, to collect, prepare, and store the vegetables and meat. His father Custoga agreed to assemble the surviving elders and set up the games and judges. They would also deploy the few hunters left in the town. Kadomico and Keme would use the tools sent by their Williamsburg friends to work the forest for housing poles and bark. Very soon now, Starlight and the Saponi messenger who had been sent to her would join them, and they knew that Sam Layton would come

As they planned and worked with the people they had at hand, their spirits sagged with the huge amount of work still undone.

Notified in advance by the trail sentry, White Water met Tree Son and Kanti at the trailhead. Wiping tears of joy, she embraced Kanti.

"We didn't expect you so soon," White Water said.

"Only I can stay. Tree Son must return to the fort site. He left a Williamsburg white man named Seth there to see after the weapons and some tribe member who have moved there. He will need Tree Son's help."

"It is so, White Water. I am needed for the manly work of the fort. These things you are about here are best fitted for women," Tree Son said, his eyes barely able to conceal the mischief he had in mind with such a remark.

Kanti was about to admonish him when White Water turned upon him, her head barely reaching his chin. On tiptoe, she nevertheless faced him and said, "Thank Okeus for finding another place for you, Tree Son. The only two things you can do that are useful are: *stay out of the way and bring someone else to do the work.*" She smiled sweetly and took Kanti's hand before Tree Son recovered from the scolding although scolding was exactly what he had expected.

Kanti smiled at the tussle between these two. There would no doubt be more. "White Water, we are here to help. Tell us where to begin. My father said we can expect my mother, Starlight. It is near time for her to come here where she will meet my father."

White Water's heart soared. With Starlight and Sam Layton here they were sure to be ready for the November full moon and beginning of the festival. This festival would not only be a healing event for the Saponi but also a step forward to set the stage for the eventual relocation.

Starlight and her Saponi escort arrived in the second week of October. The Saponi people acknowledged the mother/daughter reunion in a welcoming feast and ceremonial fire. The two of them proved to be tireless workers of uncommon skills. The Saponi women quickly accepted them as treasured members of the Saponi. Starlight was glad to be busy helping Kanti while she waited for Sam to return. She and Kanti worked the maize field, roundhouse structures, and dressed the game brought in by the hunters. The Saponi would soon be ready to receive guests.

Keme had followed his father night and day, hunting, gathering, building, and responding to those who needed help. It seemed that his father could do almost anything. He fashioned beds for the sick and wounded, brought game to them, found medicine, blankets, and fur coverlets for them, and listened for long periods sometimes to their stories of losses of their loved ones. It seemed to Keme that anyone with a problem went directly to Kadomico for the solution. Many times Kadomico responded with white-man solutions: medicine, muskets, kettles, blankets, and much more. A growing pride and understanding was becoming a part of Keme's image of his father.

The first day of the festival came forth in a sea of gentle breezes, clear skies, and cool temperatures. As dawn gave way to the first sunbeams, the Saponi town by the Yadkin River came quickly to life. Tiny cook fires danced over twigs of tinder in every roundhouse. Three boys were busy laying the grandfather fire to be lighted at sundown. Pit fires for cooking large animals here and there. Women and children fashioned spits for the meat and skinned and stretched hides of game that had been brought in late the day before. By daylight, several visiting warriors were deep in the forest stalking game for the festival. Two women stood at the entrance of the town to greet and recruit arrivals for trips into the forest for gathering nuts and the last of the wild grapes. Sayen, Kanti, and Starlight recruited guests to set up places for trading and marketing.

Lighted by the first rays of sunlight, Kadomico, Tree Son, and Keme stood waist deep in a bend of the Yadkin River. Partially submerged and nestled up close to the bank in the dark water, a huge sycamore lay anchored firmly to the bottom where the unrelenting current had driven two huge limbs into the sandy bottom. Stripped of their bark and branches, two others reached upward beyond the surface like banisters over stair steps.

Kadomico motioned Tree Son upstream near the partially exposed root system. He gestured to Keme to stand fast downstream in the shallow water, then eased down to his knees, leaned forward until only his head was above the surface, and without a sound, his long body faded into the depth toward the submerged trunk.

Keme knew a moment of anxiety for there was nothing to indicate that his father was there. It seemed a long time to him before Kadomico's head rose above the surface. The water was so deep he was barely able to stand with his head clear. He faced Tree Son and motioned a sign of readiness, then slipped quietly back beneath the surface again. This time he placed his hand on the belly of the big catfish and searched gently forward until he found the gills. By the time the fish sensed danger, Kadomico's hand had closed in a death grip. Man and fish started to move up and away from the tree as Kadomico's free hand gripped the other gill.

Keme and Tree Son saw the water roiled by the disturbance and moved forward to help but too late to join the fray. The fish found plenty of resistance for his great tail fin and threw his long body upward and over Kadomico so that he was between Kadomico and the surface. In a desperate attempt to free himself, the fish cleared the surface in a mighty splash. Kadomico lost his grip on gills just as Tree Son dived for the big tail, missed it, and took a strong slap by the thrashing fish.

The water was at its greatest depth in the bend where the sycamore lay. At the opposite bank it shallowed out to knee-deep. Disoriented and wounded by the loss of most of its gills, the fish thrashed into the shallow water. Keme scrambled up the bank, found his bow and arrows, and sent two arrows into the fish just before Tree Son and Kadomico reached it. The fish struggled weakly once more and settled in the shallow water. With Tree Son and Kadomico between the fish and the deep water, it was not likely that the fish could escape. They stopped and watched

Keme wading out toward them. The fish lay still, floating quietly between them and the shallow bank, and although it showed no sign of life, Tree Son and Kadomico knew better. Tempted to intervene, they looked at each other and then at Keme, now in waist deep water wading toward them. .

Kadomico watched with pride as Keme approached. When their eyes met, he nodded approval and Keme, now nearly chest deep in the water, swam silently over to shallow water and the wounded fish, approaching from behind. With firmer footing now, he drew his knife. He had mercifully killed many catfish before skinning them by stabbing their heads through the eye. Not one of them, however, had been longer than his arm. This fish was three quarters Keme's length and much stronger.

He had seen how easily the fish had thrown his father. There would be only one chance. He kept his eye on the point of his knife as he slowly moved it toward the eye. When the point reached the back edge of the eye, Keme struck, driving the point deep into the fish's head.

Tree Son grabbed the tail. Kadomico stood behind Keme ready to draw him out of the way if needed. The thrust was clean, deep, and fatal. The fish rolled slightly and settled on one side, exposing a gill and part of his white belly. Keme gripped the gill and followed Kadomico toward the shallows of the near bank.

Tree Son, wading along behind, stopped and watched as Keme drew the fish onto dry ground. Tonight he was to dance the story of Keme and the Iroquois attack. Now he had something to add to that war dance.

Keme saw his father waiting quietly and knew that he must give credit to the spirit of this fish for his fight and for the food from its body. He positioned it well clear of the water and came to Kadomico who again silently nodded his approval, turned toward the morning sun, and raised his arms. "You can say, 'Father of All Things, receive the spirit of this great fish that has fought well. I will keep a part close to me to remind me of his sacrifice'," Kadomico said. They remained facing the morning sun while Keme repeated the prayer.

Keme cut the dorsal fin out of the backbone and put it in a pouch in his breechclout for safekeeping. Then to lighten the load, he began to remove the insides of the fish.

On the opening day of the festival, the sun was approaching its zenith as they arrived with their prize. Keme gasped at all the people tending fires, fashioning shelters, playing games, cooking, skinning game, and visiting with each other. There were more on the trail walking toward the town, Sam Layton and Waya among them.

Four Saponi warriors in feathered costumes came to Chief Custoga's roundhouse to escort him to the center of the town for his opening speech. Drums began a slow beat, a crowd gathered.

White Water and Sayen had spent a good part of the morning preparing Chief Custoga. They had combed his grey hair straight back and bound it with a band of leather interwoven with tiny threads of green willow. Sayen brought new moccasins decorated with red and white porcupine quills and colorful threads and lacing. They dressed him in a knee-length deerskin mantle fringed with soft white fur, decorated with tiny white seashells, and intricately woven designs of brightly colored quills and feathers. Finally, Sayen lifted a skin cap adorned with horns and feathers. She placed the cap on Custoga and adjusted the adornments. Barely recovered from wounds he had suffered in the attack, Custoga straightened to his full height, and carrying a long lance of straight grain hickory tipped with twelve inches of glistening steel, stepped out to meet his escorts. Keme's mouth dropped open at the sight. Kadomico and Tree Son stopped and stood respectfully by as Custoga took his place with two warrior escorts on each side.

At the center of the ceremonial ground stood the huge stump of a chestnut tree covered with fall wildflowers and green pine boughs. Two smaller rounds of tree trunks made steps up to the chestnut stump. Four shamans sat two on either side of the place reserved for Chief Custoga. When Custoga was seated, the Occaneechi shaman with painted face and elbows and knees took the stand, released twelve beautiful passenger pigeons, and gave the first prayer of thanksgiving for the maize, squash, and bean harvest. Next came the Tutelo shaman and a young warrior who carried a turtle shell of red-hot fire coals. At the stump, the shaman sprinkled a black powder onto the coals sending great blossoms of white smoke skyward, drawing murmurs of amazement from the crowd, before giving thanks for their life-sustaining gifts from the forest and mother Earth.

Custoga stood and motioned for Sayen. "Bring Kadomico here," he said and took the stand. He raised his hands to the cheering crowd and waited for silence. "Many of you have come a long way. You grace this humble place with your friendship to help us celebrate the year of harvests. You have heard our prayers of thanksgiving, but now we give thanks for your friendship, perhaps the greatest of all gifts in these troubled times. The Saponi welcome you. While you are here, you are our brothers and sisters. What we have is yours. On the third sun, after you have learned all we can tell you about a new land on the Meherrin River that has been set aside for us by the Virginia governor, we will meet to consider moving there. Join us then and let us be as one before the white man."

Kadomico and Keme arrived just as Custoga continued. "Tonight we will light the grandfather fire and you will hear the stories the shamans have to tell you and see the dances of war and great deeds of our people. Tomorrow your councilmen will judge the games and shooting contests. On the third day, the festival will close but you are all welcome to stay with us, join our family, and live with us in the new land on the Meherrin."

Although his strength was failing, Custoga's voice did not waver. He raised his hands upward and outward toward the chanting crowd in appreciation of their enthusiasm and support, then raised a hand for silence. "This new land is not yet ready for us. There is still much to be said about it, and there is only one among us to lead us through these closing talks with the English leaders; only one among us who has spent thirteen winters learning and dealing with Virginia leaders, their laws, and their religion; only one Saponi who is respected and trusted by both the English and our people. Last night our Saponi counsel met and chose the one who will lead us to our new home. He is Kadomico, Senior War Chief of the Saponi, now our Chief of All Saponi." The drums began a steady beat as he turned and motioned Kadomico to join him.

Kadomico was shocked and unprepared. He turned to Sayen first. Her eyes were smiling and brimming with tears at the same time. He looked down at Keme's upturned face filled with love and admiration. Kadomico swallowed and moved toward his father. White Water followed him. They both mounted the stump. White Water stepped in front of Kadomico and began untying and removing Custoga's mantle as though it had all been rehearsed. She removed the horned cap and handed both to Custoga. All the while, the drums kept up the steady beat and the crowd fell silent.

Kadomico's mind had been racing to avoid more surprises. He now realized that his father, Chief of the Saponi, had thought all this through and summoned the council and had disclosed it only to White Water who would help him spring the surprise on the gathering and on Kadomico. He looked at White Water now standing behind Custoga, smiling. This was no time to return her smile, but clearly, White Water was one up on him.

Kadomico stepped forward and turned his back to his father who placed the mantle on his shoulders and the cap on his head. When he turned around to face Custoga, the crowd stood stamping the ground to the beat of the drums to show their approval of the new chief. White Water, ever in control of matters, straightened Kadomico's new headpiece and retied the mantle. Everyone was standing, even the shamans. Sayen was openly crying and Keme was doing his best to comfort her and deal with his own proud feelings for his father. To Sam Layton, standing with Starlight apart from the crowd, it was like having his own son recognized. This would bode well for the forthcoming talks with the English. Tree Son heard all the commotion but dismissed it, turning his attention to dressing the fish for Kanti to cook and serve later. He grumbled to himself at being left alone with the task.

Custoga, standing tall but moving slowly, started down the steps with Kadomico on one side and White Water on the other. He motioned Kadomico to take his seat among the shamans. With each step, his grip on the lance tightened and took some of his weight. Sayen replaced Kadomico at the side of Custoga. She and White Water steered him toward their roundhouse. Four escorts scurried to resume their positions around their new leader.

Left alone, Keme quietly watched the escorts surround his father and heard him dismiss them before turning to him.

"Keme, you will guard the Chief of the Saponi at all times. You begin by standing behind him at his place there." Kadomico pointed to the vacant seat between the shamans, and beaming with pride, Keme took his place.

The drums continued. Storytellers and songsters entertained with accounts of bravery and war victories. Trading became hectic. Many of the women tended the cook fires, preparing vegetables and the hunter's game.

Competitions began—races, shooting, tomahawk throws, and team games among various tribes.

At nightfall, Chief Kadomico ordered the grandfather fire lighted with great ceremony. Everyone made sacrifices of bits of tobacco, maize, or other valuable possessions to give credibility to their prayers, then gathered around the fire leaving a large open space for the big event of the evening: the dancers.

Shamans appeared in head masks of buffalo, wolf, deer, and elk, which had been in their tribes for decades. Now with buffalo nearing extinction in Virginia, the buffalo head masks gave the most fearsome effect of all. In the flickering light of the grandfather fire, the shamans dipped their heads and, without missing a single beat of the drums, charged the warriors dancing among them. They stomped the ground in rhythmic footfalls, twisting, turning, bowing, and raised their pipes, weapons, and staffs to the stars.

From far in the background came a single voice, haunting, melodic, and spellbinding. The dancers slowed to its rhythm and assumed a uniform step to the singer's cadence, the drums followed suit and faded in strength to let the focus be on the wonderful voice from deep in the forest. When the singing stopped, the drummers sounded an exit beat for the dancers to parade off the scene leaving the circle empty. Wearing robes of white buckskin, heavily fringed and decorated in beads, seashells, and quillwork and a headdress of the bald eagle positioned between elk horns, the Saponi shaman took the stump. The drumbeats faded slowly to silence and the shaman began to speak.

"When the cowardly Iroquois raided our town, many of our people were killed. They took captives and left many to die with deep wounds. They burned our houses, destroyed or carried away our food supplies. Our warriors were away on hunts or at war against the enemy Tuscarora. The cowardly killers of women and children chased our new chief's wife and son of eleven winters down that trail." He pointed to the trail leading to the creek that fed the Yadkin River.

The drums resumed a low, slow beat. The grandfather fire flamed anew and the handsome, chiseled face of Tree Son appeared, a warlock flashing three eagle feathers in his braided black hair. His huge shoulders bent nearly to the ground, his feet moving in perfect time with the drums.

The Shaman continued with the story in rhythm with the dancer and the drums. "The mother ran but she was overtaken at the creek." To the delight of the audience, Tree Son made all the moves of one trying to escape. "She sent her son onward while she turned and faced the three killers of women and children. She threw her tomahawk into the first one, but the other two struck her down and were beating her to death when her son, Keme, turned, saw his mother under attack, drew his own knife, and raced back to attack the killers."

The crowd applauded and cheered. Tree Son rose up, arms spread and raised, and with his feet still moving with the drums, drew his huge knife. He lunged, slashed, gripped an imaginary enemy around the throat, and stabbed fiercely.

The shaman continued. "Two of the killers pulled Keme from the back of the enemy that was beating his mother. They flung him onto a great rock where he fell unconscious." The crowd groaned. "The killers left his mother for dead and carried him away into captivity, but his mother was not dead. Keme had stopped the beating and she lives today. Keme saved his mother's life." The crowd clapped and cheered. Tree Son began the dance of the victorious Keme in unison with the crowd's adulation and applause. He circled the fire once more, and disappeared.

"Now Keme is promoted to Warrior of the Saponi and will wear the Feather of Bravery for his war deeds," the shaman said.

Kadomico signaled Keme forward to receive the Feather. The crowd cheered and some joined in the dance at the grandfather fire, but as darkness settled, the scattered cook fires and food grew cold, and the very old and young, wrapped in blankets, found their beds and rested from a long and joyous day. Keme yawned and rubbed his eyes. He had been up since long before daybreak. When he looked up, Kadomico was standing before him.

"Follow your grandfather and see if you can be of use to your mother. I will come soon."

Sam Layton and Starlight walked toward their guest quarters next to the river on the edge of the Saponi town. A full moon bathed the gently flowing river and the town in pale light. Drums beat with varying rhythms and strengths among the occasional chants and noise makers of the revelers. Sam and Starlight felt perfectly at ease here among the Saponi as they approached an old tulip poplar deposited there by the last flood and bleached white by the summer suns.

Starlight found a comfortable seat on its trunk and leaned back on a huge limb to face the stars. Sam propped himself up beside her so that he could see the calm features of her face framed in coal black hair spilling over her shoulders. After all this time, he thought, I have the same feeling I knew all those years ago when I looked up from loading my canoe and saw her standing against a summer sky. He moved the strands of hair reflecting moonlight away from her neck and touched her cheek. She reached out, drew him to her, and whispered, "Sam, I am so happy." They remained locked in each other's arms, moving their bodies with the sound of the river splashing over limestone, the haunting beat of drums, and the play of wind in the nearby pines.

Sam finally broke away, raised himself on one elbow, and with a smile, said. "And am I to believe that this happiness you speak of is because of me?"

"Don't tease me, Sam. Yes, it is always because of you, but this time it is also because of our Kanti. She is different in a different way. She is happier than I have ever known her to be."

"Starlight, I have been thinking. What do you say to joining the Saponi. I believe this land on the Meherrin River may be different, may be a chance to finally coexist peacefully with the Virginians and keep our way of life."

"You mean stay and live near Kanti and Tree Son?" Starlight was incredulous. It hadn't occurred to her, but yes, why not. It might work. And if it didn't, we would be there to help Kanti and Tree Son, she thought.

"Yes, that but more," Sam said. "Depending on how the negotiations go with the Virginians, I may be of help to the Saponi beyond just being a go-between. I have landowner knowledge and experience. The Laytons taught me well. I know about farming, raising livestock, keeping workhorses and marketing crops."

These words were strange to Starlight. She knew little of such things but neither did they matter. Sam knew how to make it work, how to make it possible for her to be near Kanti for a few more years. That was what mattered. The Ohio Valley and her Shawnee people could wait. She reached for him again and embraced him to hide the tears of joy.

"But I must return to the Shenandoah once more for the canoe and the silver and gold," Sam said.

"The canoe is as you left it, well hidden and protected. I did not visit the place in the cave where you left the beaver skin of silver and gold coins. I doubt I alone could move the great stone covering it, and I did not want to reveal the place by taking a warrior with me. There is no need to hurry," she answered and snuggled closer.

Tree Son finished his dance and found Kanti. "What has happened? Kadomico sits among the shamans and wears the mantle and headdress of the chief. Keme stands behind him. You and Sayen and White Water just disappeared. The fish is ready, but there is no one to cook."

Kanti brought Tree Son a gourd of spring water, warmed over the fire to his liking. She stirred the seasoned hardwood coals to make a glowing heat under a green hickory grill. "Sit down, and drink this. I will prepare the fish. Your dance was beautiful."

"Kadomico and I planned that dance, and I practiced several times. Keme deserves it. But why is Kadomico sitting with the shamans? Is he standing in for Chief Custoga?

"No. The council made him Chief of the Saponi last night while we slept. It was Chief Custoga's doing. White Water helped him, but no one else knew, not even Kadomico." Kanti filled a huge turtle shell with oil and a drink made from fermenting berries steeped in herbs from the forest. She immersed all but four of the big fish steaks in the oil and set them aside.

"These will be ready for cooking tomorrow, and these four are for us and maybe Sayen and White Water," Kanti said.

"And where is Chief Kadomico now?" Tree Son barely concealed his annoyance with the turn of events.

"I am here, Tree Son," Kadomico said as he approached. "You have done well. These fish look very good. We didn't mean to walk away from all the work. We just didn't know what my father had done." Kadomico sat down by Tree Son and took a sip from the gourd. Inside, Keme had stretched out ready to relive the evening, but sleep came upon him the instant his head touched the raised bearskin. Sayen spoke with White Water for a moment and followed her outside to join Tree Son, Kanti, and Kadomico.

"Here come Sayen and White Water. I suppose you have much to talk about. They will help me with the fish so go on with your man talk," Kanti said, then returned to her cook fire.

Left alone, Kadomico and Tree Son looked at each other for a long while before they broke into laughter.

The next day, Sam Layton, Starlight, Kanti, Tree Son, Kadomico, and Keme moved single file through the dense November forest carrying four muskets and as much powder and ball as they could collect. Frost-killed annuals drooped preparing to drop their leaves into a winter's sleep. Fall leaves covered the trail and the cool air touched their bare skin, filled their waiting lungs, and left them invigorated, grateful to be together. Were it not for the long, heavy muskets, they would be running, enjoying the brisk season. The group traveled quietly but at a steady pace where the trail permitted. When they arrived at the Meherrin River, they stopped to wait while Sam and Tree Son moved ahead to check out the partially burned roundhouse of Tree Son and Kanti. It had been left standing—sloppy work by someone in a hurry. Tree Son continued exploring the site. Sam returned for the others.

That night the men met for a final discussion of the forthcoming negotiations for enduring sovereignty and enforced boundaries of the land to be allotted to them. Six miles square, with a town only a musket shot from the fort, it had been said, and the outlook was promising. They noticed Kanti walk toward the woods to relieve herself before bedding down for the night, but they did not hear her muffled scream just before she fell unconscious.

When she did not return, Tree Son rose and walked toward the woods. Kadomico watched. Tree Son stopped at the cleared edge of the forest undergrowth and called softly. Nothing. The tree trunks and their fall leaves stood black in

269

the starlit night before moonrise. Tree Son called again, then stepped boldly into the forest. Kanti was not there.

Kadomico spoke from the edge, "Could she be in a different place, Tree Son?"

"No, I saw her enter here. They have taken her."

"We will search the rest of the area," Kadomico said. He could see the pain Tree Son was suffering, but by now her captors would be too far beyond and moving fast. In daylight, they would be easy to track, but until then it would be impossible to follow them.

"She'll not be there," Tree Son said. "I go. There may be sign."

"Tree Son, listen," Kadomico said. "This is the work of a renegade Tuscarora band. Probably the remains of the Kajika band, but it might even be Hawk's people or some other. Kanti is safe. They wanted a captive, someone to trade. They will be here soon ready to trade her back."

"Wait! Look here!" Tree Son removed a thong strap hanging on a limb. On it was a white bone carved in the shape of a fish. He showed it to Kadomico.

"It is a sign, Tree Son. I think I know this."

"What sign?"

"When Sayen and her brother were captured by the Kajika raiders many years ago, Sayen's father, Chief Tonawanda of the Nyhassans, took such a carving from Kajika's neck and used it to prove to the Tuscaroras that he held Kajika captive. Kajika was the price for her brother's return," Kadomico said.

"Then this is a sign from the remains of the Kajika band?" Tree Son reasoned.

"It is. Let's tell Sam Layton."

The men assembled, set up an all night vigil, and waited.

By first light, Starlight was tending a pot of boiling water outside the roundhouse and appeared to be alone.

Just as the sun cleared the eastern tree line, the first enemy stepped out of the forest, three eagle feathers fastened to his warlock, a lance in one hand, a tomahawk in the other. His face and body were smeared with black and white war paint. Two other attackers, similarly painted, followed him with lances, bows, and arrows. The three walked to within two steps of Starlight. The first savage was about to speak when Kanti, blindfolded and hands tied together, stumbled out of the forest into full view. A warrior on either side guided her forward. Starlight paid no attention to Kanti. Instead, she busied herself filling the gourd dipper with boiling water.

Two shots broke the silence, and the two warriors guarding Kanti fell, instantly dead from shots to their heads. Kanti removed the mask and ran toward Starlight. The warrior facing Starlight turned toward the sound of the musket shots, then back to Starlight but too late to avoid the boiling water splashing into his face.

Only one step behind him, the other two warriors rushed Starlight, as she crashed through the hanging hide doorway. Stripping away the hide, she dived to one side. The two warriors chasing her saw too late the scene before them change from the fleeing Starlight to Tree Son standing with a pistol in each hand leveled at their torsos. The explosions caught them point blank in mid-stride, and they crumpled into the roundhouse bleeding heavily.

Twelve more warriors crashed into the open with drawn bows and tomahawks, but there were no targets. Sam lay hidden behind a log rampart stationed opposite a similar rampart where Kadomico and Keme lay concealed. Between them, they could guard a large section of the tree line. There were two muskets at each position. Two of the twelve warriors fell just as Tree Son caught Kanti and threw her to the ground behind a third rampart. He primed and reloaded the two pistols, leaped back over the rampart, and almost collided with two attackers running with drawn tomahawks. Tree Son fired both pistols into the surprised attackers and drew his knife to meet the others charging him on the hillside. More shots from Kadomico and Sam reversed those charging warriors into a mad retreat to the cover of the forest.

"Find someone who is still alive and save them if you can. Otherwise, we will never know what their terms were, who sent them, or how many are still out there," Sam Layton said.

"One is definitely alive," Starlight said, "but he will never see again. He'll not even make a worthy slave, but we will keep him to see if he is willing to help us with information." The warrior she referred to was down and writhing on the ground, the skin lying in large tags and blisters on his face and shoulders. Starlight went to her daughter who stood in the arms of Tree Son, her head still oozing blood from the clubbing she took last night. Starlight separated them and took Kanti inside to begin cleansing the wound.

All the other attackers who had not escaped were dead. Four died from headshots, four from upper torso shots, and two were taking a longer time to die because they caught Tree Son's pistol shots in the gut.

"We can't leave Tree Son, Kanti, and Starlight here alone. That is clear now. The only way Kadomico and I can be about the business of meeting the governor," Sam said, "is if we find about twenty warriors willing to move in here now. If we can get twenty families in here soon, it just might give the governor what he needs to support the idea of getting started now. At least it is worth a try."

"The Occaneechi are closest. I can get enough here by tomorrow night to get started. Then we can send one or two of them out for others," Tree Son said.

Sam turned to Kadomico. "Would you be willing to stay until Tree Son has enough people here to protect the place? If you will, I'll go on to Williamsburg, get some muskets and ammunition started this way, and will be ready to meet with the governor when you arrive. I'll be staying with Jock and Rebecca."

"Yes, I will stay and join you in Williamsburg as soon as Tree Son is set up. Even if the enemy wants to try again, it will take them some time to find replacements and reform."

"Good," Sam said, as he tied the hands of the warrior. "Starlight, I wouldn't be surprised if this one is blinded, but be sure he is bound securely before you treat his burns." Then turning back to Kadomico and Tree Son, he said, "Give me a hand and we'll drag these bodies to the edge of the woods. My guess is they'll be gone by morning. The sooner I get started for Williamsburg, the better."

29

S am Layton, dressed in buckskins and moccasins, his
shoulder-length brown hair now showing the first
strands of gray, sat before a two-log fire in the high-
ceilinged living room of his boyhood friend Jock Adams.
Jock and Rebecca had seated themselves on either side of
him in straight ladder-back chairs. The fire flickered lightly
and stayed the chill of the mid-November darkness so that
the candles cast soft light and shadows outlining a table of
refreshments and several smaller side tables and chairs
around the walls of the room.

Rebecca had served tea, biscuits, jam, and butter, and
they had been talking for the best part of two hours,
updating each other on their families and current situations.
The contrasting updates were remarkable, but easily
understood by Sam and Jock, given their similar
backgrounds—born to English parents, both captured and
each raised by Shawnee and Iroquois respectively, then
recaptured by militia and adopted by Virginia farm families,
Sam by the Laytons and Jock by the Adams. Rebecca
understood the strong bond between them less, but having
known them both from school days and come to love one
and admire the other, she was thrilled to have Sam in her
living room again.

"Our three boys are scattered about shamelessly," she
told Sam. "Matthew and Mark, both officers in the militia,
are somewhere on the frontier, we know not where, and
Luke is in London studying to join Jock's business when he

returns. Shamelessly scattered, but we are so proud of them, Sam."

Sam replied with the news that their only daughter had married recently and left them facing that same emptiness and what they had done about it, smiling as he suddenly realized how much that very loss of Kanti had to do with his decision to join the Saponi. Sometimes, a man does not know himself so well as he thinks he does.

"Well, Sam, I am so glad you are with us now. Your room is ready when you are. It is long past my bedtime, and I expect you two have much more to talk about. Please breakfast with us before you start your day tomorrow."

"Oh, that is settled, Becky. He is going to the docks with me tomorrow. We'll breakfast here and be back for your excellent noon meal."

The two men rose as Rebecca left the room. Jock placed another small log on the fire and relit his pipe. "Now tell me, Sam, how can I help you on this visit to Williamsburg. I know something important has brought you away from your wife and daughter, and I know a little about the proposed Fort Christanna."

When they were seated, Sam explained that Kadomico had enlisted his help to coordinate the tribe's move to land near the proposed Fort Christanna. He had been traveling among the tribes for most of the late summer and fall seasons, had attended the Saponi festival, and now he and Kadomico were ready to report to the governor. He would wait for Kadomico and they would request an audience to discuss settling the tribes at Fort Christanna.

"Good. You will stay here with us, I hope."

"It will always be my first choice, Jock, and I thank you. There is, however, another more urgent matter." Sam explained the threat of more attacks on Tree Son and Kanti and the few families already occupying the land marked for the Indians. "Tree Son needs muskets and ammunition as soon as we can get them there. I think eight muskets and ammunition for fifty or sixty shots each will secure the place until the rangers return to man the fort."

"Sounds reasonable, Sam. We can start with a visit to Colonel Ludwell over at Green Spring. I'll set that up for this afternoon, or as soon as possible."

"There is something else, Jock, two matters actually. The first and easier of the two is that this whole business of populating the land at Fort Christanna with the tribes is a risky prospect for our people, given the history of colony agreements and treaties. I know the governors have good intentions to enforce boundaries and sustain sovereignty of the tribes, but in reality the governors can't or won't hold the settlers to the letter of their own laws. When it comes to a fight, the governors always come down on the side of the white man. We need some safeguards this time."

"That's fair, and as you already know, our magistrates will be amenable in that regard, but *keeping* the tribes and the settlers at peace where land is at stake is another matter. How do you propose to deal with the squatters, and the blatant partiality of the courts of law to the white man and to which the tribes have no recourse at all?"

"That brings me to the second matter. I intend to buy land and become a Virginia settler."

Jock couldn't conceal the shock. "Sam! Indians can't own Virginia land! Only Christians, British subjects can own land in Virginia, Sam—not tribes and not members of tribes. I know about treaties and reservations, but I don't think there is a precedent of any Indian filing for a land patent. Surely, you know that."

"That is so, but am I not as qualified as you?"

Jock's mind reeled. "But, Sam. . . . ."

"Think on it, Jock. I am the registered son of the Laytons. I was baptized into the Anglican church same as you and at the same time, if you recall. All of that is on record. I left home to become a fur trapper like many another Virginian. And I became a good one, well known at every trading post in Virginia and many others all the way to the Great Lakes. And, in all my years, I have lived only in Virginia."

Jock fought the first traces of reason. My God! he thought. Dress Sam in the finery of a Virginia gentleman, and with his command of the English language he would be a force to be reckoned with, especially if he claimed his rights as a British subject, a white man, and a Christian. He fiddled with his pipe and dropped his head to hide a slowly forming smile. He leaned forward to the fire and found a small coal, which he carefully transferred to the bowl and drew deeply.

Sam watched Jock wrestling with the outrageous suggestion of his making a switch back from Shawnee to settler. This idea had been formulating in his mind for days. He still didn't know how or exactly what he would do, but as he talked to Jock, it became clear that owning a piece of Virginia land was possible as a British subject and impossible as a Shawnee or Saponi.

Beyond that, the idea clouded. Did he really want to switch? If no, then why? Help the Saponi? Sure, but he could do that as Sam Layton, the white Shawnee. It is why he came to Williamsburg. He could help the Saponi without all this business of claiming his rights as a British subject. No, there was more to it. Still the notion of becoming a Virginia landowner was intriguing, and by not making an argument, Jock was confirming the possibility.

Sam continued in an exploratory way. "As you know, Jock, I did pretty well as a farmer during the years with the Laytons. My adopted father and family will confirm that."

"And so will I," said Jock, still smiling at the thought of the ruckus this could cause if it came to a fight among the burgesses or other landowners. "Forgive me, Sam, but I'm trying to come to grips with you as a settler. You will recall thirteen years ago that I offered you a full partnership in my business—generous if I do say so. You turned it down without giving it a single thought. 'I am Shawnee,' you said with resolute finality."

"Times change," Sam said softly, well aware that he owed Jock a better explanation. Truth was, however, Sam had not thought it through and simply could not yet explain it. One thing was clear. He was now convinced that he could do more for the tribes of Virginia as a white subject of the crown than as a white Shawnee.

"There is no need to announce it just yet, not until I have spent some time here discussing land issues, frontier security, tobacco prices and other matters of commerce, shipping, labor, and piracy. You are the expert in such matters. Perhaps you will help me convince those I meet of my ability and wish to work with them. It will ease the shock when I apply for land patents."

"Right," Jock said. "No need to announce your downstream intentions yet—first things first. We need to get the guns, ammunition, and tools to Tree Son. The expense alone is going to be a problem."

"I will pay the expenses if necessary," Sam said. "Seems to me our problem is getting it authorized."

"Ludwell can handle that. The expense could be considerable and probably ought to come from colony coffers," Jock said, obviously concerned that Sam should not bear the burden even if he could.

"Just let it not be a problem or delay us for this first move, Jock. I will pay in gold."

Jock's eyes blinked in shock again after an evening of such shocks. "I didn't doubt for an instant that you could pay, Sam, but in gold? Pardon my surprise, but that is a rarity in Virginia. As you know, we are denied the right to coin our own money, and therefore we do business with tobacco vouchers. Good enough, but not like having coin for trading."

"Jock, for thirteen years I and the Shawnee trapped and traded fur, much of it with the French of the north. When I could I made attractive offers for my furs if they could be paid for in gold or silver. It is a marketing idea I learned from my adopted father. Thirteen years of tossing the coins into a beaver skin bag has made it nearly impossible to lift." Sam watched the expression on Jock's face change again to awe.

"And of course, you never had need of coin in all those years. Lord be with us! Sam, if you collected only a few pounds of sterling, Spanish doubloons, or French coins each season, after thirteen years you must have . . . "

"Much more than that, Jock. I will pay."

"Well, Sam, it has been a night of surprises, more than I can arrange and account for this night, which by the way is almost past. Let us sleep on these matters and deal only with tomorrow."

"Fair enough. It has been an exciting evening, but my eyes are losing the battle fast."

They stood for a moment facing each other. Jock began to shake his head, then locked eyes with Sam, and they both began to laugh. "Your bed is in here, Sam. Rest well."

Sam rinsed his face at the washstand, lay down on the huge bearskin rug beside the bed, and, before he could review the events of the evening, he fell fast asleep.

Somewhere on the Roanoke River, two days travel southwest of the Fort Christanna site, Hawk eased himself out of the rushing mid-stream white-water up onto a great limestone complex of boulders, slabs, and gravel. Two large poplar tree trunks, shorn of all but their main limbs, were wedged among the rocks, thrown there by the spring runoff and unlikely to be free again until they decayed or the Roanoke rose to unprecedented heights and floated them upward.

Hawk found the sheltered crevice well known to him and floored with sand warmed by the morning November sun. He scanned the shorelines quickly before he shook himself free of the cold Roanoke droplets and moved into the narrow crevice. He stepped over to a wall and began to climb vertically, sure of every familiar foothold until he reached the top. From there, with only his head showing, he could reconnoiter a great expanse of ground in every direction. He found a shelf and rested there for a long time drinking in the view of faded yellows, reds and greens lining the banks, then shifting to watch a school of young smallmouth bass chasing minnows, but mostly just frolicking in the way of youth, unaware of the predators lurking nearby. Shifting his view to the downstream splashes of white water over rocks, he thought how the invasion of his homeland was very like the water. No matter how strong the rock, it was destined to lose the battle to the endless, unrelenting wear of the stream.

Hawk returned to the floor of the crevice, found a comfortable position in the warm sand, and slept. When he woke, he checked the downstream bend of the river, and as expected, saw a lone warrior sitting on the bank. That would be Mingan, right on time. He slipped into the quiet backwater formed on the downstream side of his little island and pushed himself into the cold depths of the still pool. Hawk opened his eyes and watched the disturbance he made lift and fan his long black hair. For a moment, he wondered what it would be like to stay there forever. His lungs drove him back to the surface, and he struck out for the shore noticing that Mingan had moved.

The sun was near down when they met. The evening air moved ever so silently. They sat by each other on the lee side of a tiny near-smokeless fire. Mingan had produced two pipes and tobacco. They made a gift of tobacco to their god and lit up to wait out the roasting of the two pigeons Mingan had brought.

"What news, my friend?" Hawk asked, as he smeared his arms and shoulders with bear grease against the falling evening temperatures.

"Not good, Hawk. Kajika's warriors, and maybe some Iroquois, made a clumsy effort to attack the fort. They lost several warriors, got away with nothing, not even a scalp."

"Many militia?"

"No, the man I talked with didn't know what happened. He said he saw no militia, no horses and no warriors, only a woman tending a fire, but musket fire was everywhere, many dead."

"And what do you think? Kajika's warriors are seasoned fighters."

"Bad judgment, Hawk, they took a woman captive the night before and intended to trade her back the next morning, but the instant she appeared the musket fire started, no talk, no warning, just killing everywhere, I was told."

"Nothing like what they expected," Hawk mused. "It looks like the fort people knew exactly what was going to happen and were ready with muskets, powder, ball and were well concealed. It is the kind of thing Sam Layton would do."

"Who is Sam Layton?"

"Someone I knew long ago. He killed Kijika, a master of stealth and ambush, and Kijika means *Moves Without Sound.* One of the best ever."

" I see," Mingan said. "I went there before I came here and watched unseen. I don't think I saw this Sam Layton, but they have places built where they can hide and fire muskets. The roundhouse faces open fields of fire in all directions. Now other roundhouses are being built and many people from the tribes are there. I saw no English, no horses, just roundhouses and many places to fire weapons," Mingan said, then started to speak again and hesitated.

"What else, Mingan?"

Mingan's face showed agony. "I think the birds are ready, Hawk,"

"What else, Mingan?"

"Hawk, I saw Kadomico and Keme."

"No surprise. We both know that Kadomico is a leader there, an ally of the Virginia governor, a friend of the men who will guard the fort when it is built," Hawk said, hesitated, then continued. "Kadomico is the enemy and so is Keme. We will stop that fort, but we can't do it in open fields of fire. It has to be done on their supply trail little by little by stealth, ambush, and retreat, like water over stone until the stone becomes sand. No one who travels with them will be spared, including Kadomico and Keme. The English will make some progress, but it will be forever slow and costly."

"Not Keme," Mingan challenged, wide-eyed in disbelief.

"Yes, Keme. Perhaps you will capture and train him." Hawk looked away, unwilling to face the piercing look of the old warrior.

"The bird is ready now," Hawk said. "Eat. We have much traveling to do in the next sun."

30

The messenger found Jock and Sam at the College Landing dock trading news with the crew of a shallop, a large heavy boat equipped with oars and used for ferrying cargo between ships and College Landing. The dock was busy with men rolling barrel-like shipping containers called hogsheads from the warehouse to dockside where the shallops waited for loading. With the right tide, the shallops could travel the creek even when loaded. Anchored just beyond the mouth of College Creek in the James River, the Discovery, small sea-going ship of the a British East India Company, was taking on a cargo of tobacco and fur bound for England.

"Tide ought to soon be high enough for these shallops to start running the creek out to the ship," Jock said.

The young messenger approached Jock. "Mr. Adams, the Colonel says he can meet you at Page's Ordinary at mid-afternoon today."

"Fine," Jock replied, rewarding the messenger with a tuppence. "We'll be there."

Turning back to Sam, Jock said, "We'd best get started, Sam. Rebecca will have a hot meal waiting." They mounted their horses and headed back.

Sam and Jock sat opposite each other in Page's Ordinary, the only public place on Duke of Gloucester Street where food, drink and a night's lodging was available.

Now, fourteen years since Williamsburg became the capital, the street had progressed from being an occasional horse-path to a wide and busy, mile-long carriage and wagon road but still crossed in three places by deep ravines.

Jock tasted the ale, found it to his liking, raised his glass to Sam, and drank. "You know, Sam, Rebecca and I just can't imagine Tree Son married. You must bring him and Kanti to visit. We remember him as a carefree spirit more disposed to laughing and living than anything so serious as marriage. Young Luke idolized him, and by his letters from London, I suspect he still does."

"I recalled that same spirited youngster you speak of when my strong-minded daughter named him her fiancé after only an afternoon of knowing him. When I saw what was happening so quickly and to the exclusion of everything else around them, my first impulse was to object, but, Jock, it was so unusual and so real—their being together, I mean." Sam paused to let his conviction register with Jock. "Well, watching them, I still hesitated until I saw that they moved, spoke, smiled, and behaved as one. It was as if they had known each other all their lives. They didn't seem excited as I would have expected, but sure as bark on trees, they were committed to each other from the start."

"It is a great story, Sam, Rebecca will be pleased. She will also enjoy the prospect, as will I, of having the Laytons as neighbors or frontier settlers. After all, the Christanna site is only an overnight trek, and when the trail is developed, even less by horseback. I can see where the well-being of these two will weigh heavily on your mind until they are settled."

"It does, Jock, but it gets clearer every time I come back to it, and Starlight agrees, for different reasons, but definitely agrees."

"Look, I have watched the collapse of treaties and land grants for years, faithfully followed by raids and wars among and between the colonies and the tribes. It is why I now believe that the key to peaceful coexistence is the establishment of clearly defined and enforced boundaries. Only when the boundaries are enforced by law and honored by settlers and land speculators will we see improvements in peaceful coexistence."

"Under the circumstances, it is hard to imagine, Sam."

"True and it will take generations to happen, but I want to try with this generous allocation of land that has been promised to the tribes. The boundaries are key. That is what I want from the governor and the burgesses—well-marked, publicized, and enforced boundaries."

"Well, Sam, marking off a perimeter of six square miles is a lot of marking, 'specially in a wilderness. If a land-hungry settler comes across a cleared spot like a river savanna or interior feeding ground for big animals that looks unused to him , how do you keep him from squatting and planting his tobacco?"

"You can't—unless the land is already planted and tended. If it is, they are more likely to respect that and move on, just as they would expect others to do if the crops were theirs. On the other hand, it doesn't make sense to an Englishman to see vast areas of forest and wilderness unused—lying fallow, as they say—when there is such a great demand for the potential harvest it can provide. It rarely occurs to them that what appears to them as a waste of rich farm land is the very source of the tribes food supply."

"I see your point, Sam." Jock shifted his weight searching for the right words to express his skepticism, "but while I know you to be a truly extraordinary and capable man, you are but one, and six miles by six miles is a staggering area." Skeptical as he was, he was enjoying Sam's argument—no telling what a rich Shawnee living as a Virginia farmer might do. He leaned forward, eager to hear Sam's reply just as Colonel Ludwell approached.

"Gentlemen, please forgive me—not my custom to be late. My horse threw a shoe crossing Powhatan Creek swamp land and it slowed us."

"Not at all, Colonel, you may remember Sam Layton. Your first meeting was back in 1700," Jock said, rising and signaling for service.

Sam rose, exchanged greetings, and said, "We are pleased that you can meet with us on such short notice."

Jock motioned the waiter forward, recommended the ale, and asked Ludwell if he could have his horse attended to.

"Thank you for your offer, Mr. Adams. The proprietor here sent the horse over to Stilwell's smithy. I expect it will be back shortly."

Ludwell took a seat and Sam related the current situation at Christanna: Occaneechi and Saponi families arriving in unexpected numbers, Tree Son managing defenses, and the threat of more attacks by roving bands of Tuscarora and Iroquois.

"A very interesting development, Mr. Layton. The governor will be glad to hear about this. I am seeing him tomorrow on another matter. What is it you need of me?"

"As I said, renegade bands of Tuscarora and Iroquois are all about in that area and further south in North Carolina. Tree Son needs muskets, powder, and ball. He has four muskets on site. I'd say eight more and enough powder and ball for about sixty rounds each will get them through the winter. Then they'll have the site ready for building by the first warm days."

"I am so sure that the governor will authorize this that I encourage you to continue planning. Allow me three days to have the cargo packed and ready to travel. Six mounted Rangers are all I can provide for protection."

"The Rangers won't be necessary, Colonel, if you will permit me to use the warriors that will meet us at the trail head on the other side of the James River," Sam said.

"Done, and that makes it much easier." Ludwell rose, shook hands, took a final sip of the ale, and left.

"Well, *that* was easy," Sam said, surprised at how fast things were moving. "Jock, can you spare me a mount for a few days? I'll fetch Tree Son and the escorts for the arms and ammunition."

"They come in pairs. I'll be riding the other one."

"First light?"

"First light. Maybe I'll eventually be able to make heads or tails of what you are planning."

"My friend, I wish it were as orderly as a plan. Right now I'm just taking it day by day. Supporting Tree Son and the others at Christanna is first. I want to take a close look at nearby plantations, see the crops, livestock, and barns. It has been a long time since you and I were boys working the Laytons and the Adams farms "

"It has indeed," Jock said. "Well then, fine. Tomorrow we will ride down to the mouth of College Creek on the James River. We'll be passing through Green Spring and Middle plantations. Both are good examples of raising crops and livestock."

"And if there is time, I'd like to look closer at the processes: growing and preparing tobacco for shipment, corn shocks, and other methods of storage, and livestock maintenance. I'm sure there's not enough time for all of that, but I have to start learning somewhere, and anything at all will be helpful."

Jock could hardly believe his ears, but there it was: Shawnee Sam looking seriously at becoming a farmer.

The next evening, just before nightfall, Sam and Jock pulled up at the Nottoway River ferry, staked their horses, and made a roaring campfire against the cool November night.

As they rustled through their packs for Rebecca's generous supply of bread, meat, and apples, Jock leaned back against a stately oak, satisfied that the heat from the fire had started to subside.

"Yesterday, when Colonel Ludwell arrived, I think I was about to learn how one man can work a six-by-six mile farm," Jock said.

"Not exactly one man, Jock, I'm thinking more like a whole nation of families."

"It is hard to imagine, Indian farmers."

"They already are farmers, Jock. Think about it. They are great growers of the so-called three sisters, maize, beans, and squash."

"But only your women are farmers."

"True, but if I show them how easy it is to grow tobacco and exchange it for cloth, kettles, beads, mirrors and cooking pots, I can see them as tobacco planters. And when the warriors see that tobacco can be exchanged for guns and ammunition, steel knives, tomahawks and, I'm sorry to say, rum, I can see them farming as well—not all but many. I'm sure of it."

"And you see them in their new land farming the savannas and land cleared by grazing elk, deer, and what's left of the buffalo ?"

"Yes, not only the cleared land but the forest as well. Look at Virginia's great plantations. The English have adopted the tribe's method of farming: girdle the trees, hill, seed, and harvest—not pretty but proven."

Jock scratched his head and began to smile. "You mean we actually learned something from these so-called savages?"

Sam caught the mixed derision and enlightenment in Jock's reply.

"Yes. Truth is, the English observed our way to avoid the backbreaking work of the clearing and plowing they remember back in England. Here, we simply girdle trees for new ground. The trees die, the leaves fall, and the sun strikes the ground. All that is left is to hill, seed, and harvest.

When the land is worn out, we girdle another tract, set up new planting hills, and let the former land return to replenish the forest. Look at the great plantations we visited yesterday. Ugly as they are, their new ground is almost labor free, and continually available. Unlike England, there are millions of acres of forest here, and as you know, tobacco wears out the land in only a few crops."

"Sam, it looks so good it's a wonder the tribes had not turned to commercial farming long ago." Jock stirred the fire without adding fuel. The radiating coals lighted his face and hands against the darkness and warmed him before he settled back.

"It is not our way," Sam said. "From your days with the Iroquois, you will remember, we live by the gifts of the forest and the earth. We farm the three sisters to survive. The English farm for profit and tobacco farming is very profitable." Sam spread his saddle blanket over the grass-covered soft ground and stretched out. His buckskins were good protection against the cold air moving gently but persistently over them.

Jock took the hint and prepared his own bed for the night, but he was not nearly through talking. If Sam did have a beaver skin full of gold and silver, there was not much that Virginia could offer that he couldn't buy. He didn't feel easy thinking about his friend's fortune, but he couldn't help wondering where it was, how much there was, and how Sam would use it. In addition, they needed to talk about the audience with the governor. What would they ask for? What would be the terms of occupying the allotted land? There must be abundant opportunities: the fur trade, shares in the new company, the school for the children of the tribes, shipping on the Meherrin River, new land patents.

He was about to speak when Sam interrupted his thoughts. "That's a good warm fire you got there. A man could get a good night's sleep if you keep up the good work." Sam smiled, turned on his side, and buried his face in the soft buckskins covering his arms.

31

Ella lay on her back with her hand over her stomach. She could feel the difference now. She'd be showing soon, and then she'd have to answer questions. When did this happen? Who was the father? No, no. She'd not say Zack, not ever. They'd whip him bad. No, she would never tell that it was Zack's child. She would not do that—no, never. When the time came, she would just not speak, not even if they whipped her. A tear formed and she moved her hand slightly as though to comfort the child, but instead she was comforted by the thought of Zack's child. No, she would never speak his name, and he must not either. She would tell him that tonight. She wiped the tear and smiled at the thought of Zack beside her soon.

Zack was late. A fence had broken, and they'd had to chase hogs out of the kitchen garden and make repairs before things settled down enough for him to slip away. Only Gladys saw him go, watched him ease out the door. She remained silent on her little bed and watched, knowing the risk he took, knowing how slow he would be in the field the next day, and knowing that nothing could stop him. She stroked the bag of potions she kept close by and prayed for his safety.

He moved cautiously until he was clear of the mansion house and slave quarters, then ran through the moonlit night keeping to the edge of the trail in the shadows as much as possible. He crossed a small brook, climbed a sloping patch of hardwoods, and checked the wind as he neared the flatland on the outskirts of the Middle Plantation slave quarters. He was relieved to feel the air moving lightly over his face downwind from the penned up hunting hounds. One whiff of his scent and they would make enough noise to raise the dead. He squatted low and was about to whisper his call to Ella when she stepped out the back door of the one-room cabin and motioned him forward.

They embraced, knowing the warmth and ecstasy of each other's touch, and it drew them even closer, turning to passion, and finally, undeniable passion before either spoke. Ella guided them to the bed where they lay in each other's arms, yielding to each other. Zack's passion outlasted Ella's, and the thing she had to tell Zack finally overcame her own passion and she pushed him away.

"Now you jus' stop and be still, Zack. I got somethin' to say, somethin' to tell you. Now you lissen," she said, holding Zack at arm's length.

Zack's left foot found the floor by the side of the narrow bed just in time for him to avoid being pushed over the edge. He gripped Ella's wrist and pulled himself back a little, laughing at his predicament.

"Woman, you nearly pushed me out. Now what's got into you? I do somethin' wrong?"

"Well, you surely *did* do *somethin'*, and that's a fact. I'm goin' to have your baby, Zack. 'ats what I been tryin' 't tell you ever since you got here, but you. . ."

"What!" Zack dropped her wrist and half rose from the bed. "What you say, Ella? A baby! My baby?" Zack fell silent. He had not counted on a baby, hadn't even thought of it. An avalanche of questions flooded his mind, leaving him speechless while he groped for the one to ask first.

Not sure what his reaction might be, Ella's eyes had never left his, and seeing his confusion, she said, "Ain't nuthin' for you to be concerned about, Zack. Babies is born ever' day, 'cept we don tell nobody cuz there ain't no tellin' how Massa Page will take you being the father, so we jus'

292

won't tell him. He cain't have no trouble with gettin' another slave."

Zack was calmed by her words. That put the whole matter in a practical light, beyond the mysteries of birth and fatherhood. "Well what about you? Us? All this rompin' we been doin'? What about that and the baby?"

Ella was pleased that he was thinking of her and the baby. "Like I sed, Zack, it ain't nuthin to be concerned about. The baby's fine 'n I'm fine. You gonna be a father, Zack. That's all."

They loved and talked and dozed until, without warning, the night was spent.

Finally, speaking firmly, Ella roused Zack to get him on his way. Now he ran against the first light of dawn, thrilled with the thought of her with his child. The baby would come in early spring, she'd said, a good time for birthin' and that was all Zack knew. When he'd asked what she needed, she'd told him she'd be fine—'birthin and raisin babies' were womanly matters, nothing for him to be concerned about. It was not exactly a none-of-your-business reply, but it did close the subject.

True enough, men in general and slave men in particular had no part in birthing and raising babies. Nor did they see any connection between their women and their experiences with plantation livestock or emerging plants in the kitchen garden. The whole business of babies was an unchallenged, unspoken, mystery to the men. So Zack ran on, freely oblivious to the risk and expense of birthing and follow-on care and how Middle Plantation owners might react. If Ella had the least concern, Zack knew nothing of it.

The strong predawn light dismissed his cover of darkness and exposed his arrival as he headed for his little cabin. He tried to make it look like he was just coming back from an early morning visit to the woods to relieve himself. He pretended, but he was sure that many inquisitive eyes would be on him. If he were lucky, they would be slave eyes only.

Gladys met him at the door, her face drawn with worry. "You hear that?" she said, facing him and pointing over her shoulder. "It's the field wagon," she scolded, pushing a slice of corn pone into his shirt. "He done been here, that Massa Al, done been here lookin' for you. I tole him you sick and gone to the woods. He's a mean one, that overseer. Now you git on out there 'n ketch 'at wagon." She shoved him on through the one-room cabin and out the other door toward the wagon road. "He sed he gonna look for you in the field. You be there."

Zack glanced at the slow-moving wagon and turned to speak to Gladys. "I been seein' Ella . . . "

"I knows where you been, Zack. Jus' you git on out there. You be in that field workin' when he come there. You be there." She shoved him again. "I'll bring you somthin' to eat at noon time. We can talk 'bout Ella then." Gladys rolled her eyes and said, "Lord knows you'n that Ella woman's bound to make trouble, bad trouble. I tole you and tole you. Now go."

Zack met the wagon just in time and slipped onto the flatbed, his feet dangling over the side. Even the bumping and grinding of the rutted road could not keep him from dropping off to sleep. Late November work meant gleaning the fields and cleaning the grounds for spring hilling and planting. Residues of tobacco, corn, and hay lay among hundreds of acres at Green Spring and its five outlying farms. With harvesting done, there was little but girdling trees and clearing new planting areas to keep the slaves busy, and idleness bred the kind of trouble owners feared most: insurrection, rebellion, and runaways.

No sooner had Zack joined the others than he saw Ripken riding in from the west road, keeping his horse in a steady trot. Zack bent to the work of gleaning corn, but in a way that he could keep the overseer in his peripheral vision.

When Ripken was within a few paces, Zack saw him unroll his long whip and let it trail on the ground behind him. As the distance to Zack closed, Ripken drew the black leather snake forward past his horse's vision alerting Zack to what was about to happen. Zack watched him drag the lash, draw it up, over, and back so that the whip and plaited tip stretched out full length above and behind him.

Zack braced for it. Ripken's timing was perfect. He reversed the direction of the flying whip and started it rolling toward Zack. The ear-splitting crack shattered the morning silence. On the opposite side of the field, men working the corn jumped even though they were watching and knew it was about to happen.

The whip didn't touch him, and Zack did his best not to flinch. He managed that so well that Ripken took it as insolence, grounds for a whipping.

He was about to strike again when the thunder of a running horse caused him to hesitate. Seth stopped his mount a whip-length away and behind Ripken.

"Don't know what all the noise is about, Mr. Ripken, but I hope it has nothing to do with Zack yonder because the Colonel has sent for him."

"Yer day's coming, free-boy," Ripken said, as he turned the stallion to face Seth and coiled the whip. "I'll tend to that insolent bastard later." And both Seth and Zack knew that he would.

It was just a matter of time and the right circumstances before Al Ripken would maim or kill Zack. It would not happen while Seth was around, but that was the problem. Seth could not *be* around at all times. Only last evening Ludwell had given him orders to collect muskets and ammunition at the colony armory and take them to the trailhead on the other side of the James River. Seth had asked for and got permission to use Zack, but when he called this morning, Gladys had told him Zack was in the field working and stressed her concern that the overseer was bound to hurt Zack. Getting there in time to stop Ripken was just a stroke of luck. Something had to be done, but what?

"Zack, you look like something the cat dragged in," Seth said, referring to Zack's sagging shoulders and red eyes. "You work all night?"

"In a way, I guess so, Mr. Seth, but there's enuff left 'o me to thank you for comin'."

"Well, get on behind me. We have work to do. I'll drop you at the stables. Get a cart rigged to pick up a load of muskets and ammunition. And I don't have to tell you, stay clear of Ripken. He's madder'n a stepped-on rattlesnake. We'll be gone maybe two, three weeks."

Seth walked his horse to a tree stump to ease the way for Zack to climb on behind him. Riding back, he tried to see a way to keep Al Ripken from beating Zack to death or just outright killing him. If it happened, there wasn't a white man in Virginia that would notice and the law was clear. A master could not be prosecuted if a slave died from a whipping. Whipping was the only way to keep the slaves in line and the only reason they worked was to avoid it. Slaves were property and no one would intentionally destroy their own property. Still, accidents happen. Clearly, Ripken could inflict as much punishment as he cared to. The law and the planters would side with him no matter the circumstances.

Three days later, Sam Layton and Jock Adams rode out of the trailhead into the open area beyond the ferry landing. They found Seth and Zack camped a safe distance from the cart where the black powder was stored. Jock recognized them immediately and spoke a greeting as they dismounted and led their horses forward.

"Kadomico and his son Keme are just a little while behind us with a few braves from the fort site. We're here for the guns and ammunition, Seth."

"Right there on the cart, Mr. Adams, eight muskets, trade guns they be with smooth bores," Seth replied, then added. "Coffee's hot and fairly fresh. Zack's not perfect, but making camp coffee is not one of his failings."

Sam poured two mugs half-full of the steaming coffee and handed one to Jock who was passing the reins of both horses to Zack.

"Smooth bore guns will do just fine," Sam said. "Faster loading and firing than the new rifles."

Taking their coffee to the lee side of the smoldering coals, they began updating each other.

"In addition to Kadomico and his son Keme, there are ten warriors in the party," Sam said, "enough to carry the muskets. But what about the powder and ball?"

"We have it divided in ten skins, four for the powder and six for the balls. They'll ride safely on that little bay yonder. She's packed before," Seth said. "She can pull, tow, carry the pack, and is a saddle mount as well, good company on the trail. Zack and me, we'll be staying with the weapons until they are delivered to Tree Son."

"Excellent," Sam said. "Then I can go on to Williamsburg with Kadomico and Jock."

"You can, sir," Seth replied. "Could you take the other horse and the cart back to Green Spring?"

"Sure," said Jock. "We'll need to report to Colonel Ludwell anyhow."

The second-floor meeting room was in one of the south-facing semi-circular apses in the eight-year-old capitol building. It was walled with splendid clear, stained oak panels, separated by three long round windows. Eight high-back, padded armchairs surrounded the table leaving only a narrow passage on either side. Diffused light filtered by huge pines and a tall, dense white oak filled the small room illuminating a colored tablecloth with intricately woven designs that matched the color of the panels. At night, fire being an ever-present danger, the great candle chandelier above the table was rarely used. In addition, the architects had omitted fireplaces throughout the building and smoking inside the building was strictly prohibited.

Consequently, although the cold of the late November night had given way to a morning of sunlight, the room was still cool as Sam Layton, Kadomico, Jock Adams, and Colonel Phillip Ludwell filed in and took seats near the semi-circle end of the room on either side of the end chair reserved for the governor. They had barely taken their seats when Governor Alexander Spotswood walked in. They all rose to acknowledge his arrival. Spotswood greeted each of them, shaking hands and expressing his pleasure to have them there on the business of Fort Christanna.

To set up this meeting Jock Adams and Phillip Ludwell had briefed Spotswood informally the day before. Nevertheless, the governor had a clerk present, and after congratulating Kadomico on his recent selection as Chief of the Saponi, he asked for a brief statement from each of them. By the time all had spoken, the group was well prepared to hear Sam and Kadomico state their cases.

Spotswood leaned forward over his teacup. He squinted for emphasis, rested his elbows on the table, interlocked his fingers, and began. "Before we get to specifics, let me make it clear." He waited for the clerk to catch up with his notes. "The purpose of Fort Christanna is to make the southern frontier safe for our people, to open the land for settlement, and to provide a single market place for all southern and western frontier trade, the fur trade in particular. Now, let us be guided accordingly. Sam, what say the tribes?"

Sam's unchanged expression hid a burning disappointment in Spotswood's list of principal purposes. He'd expected "homes and hunting grounds for the Saponi." Should have known, he thought, same as always.

He paused until Spotswood looked at him, then said, "Four tribes can guarantee a hundred families, including the ones currently there, ready to move onto the land that has been set aside for them. However, the chiefs are hesitant. They look at the reservations of the Powhatan tribes and how they have been moved from time to time to accommodate settler growth. What they have seen causes them to be reluctant to abandon the land they currently occupy."

"Well, when the surveying is complete much of the land they currently occupy will be included within that six miles-by-six miles and there will be a lot more in addition," the governor said. "They can do whatever they please with it." No mention of ownership of any kind: patent, grant, posted boundary.

Sam was dismayed. Spotswood merely wanted to repeat the process of getting the tribes out of the way of the settlers: make a treaty, collect the diminished tribes separately into unused areas, and move them again later if it served Virginia's purposes.

"Chief Kadomico and I have worked closely with these four tribes," Sam said," and we're convinced that agreements will be strengthened to the benefit of both parties if it contains wording that assures the tribes of their sovereignty and the integrity of the borders around their allotted 23,049 acres."

Spotswood winced at the word sovereignty. "I will personally support the integrity of the borders that we survey. But you know as well as I, that in a distant wilderness of unmarked lines where honest families are carving out a living, border disputes will always be a problem."

Sam looked at Kadomico for support.

"It is true, Governor, and we will work to ease those disputes from the beginning by setting up productive farms at intervals along the borders," Kadomico said.

"Indian farmers? Preposterous, Chief. We have no such thing in Virginia." As incredulous as such a notion was, Spotswood sensed a glimmer of logic and some interesting possibilities there.

"It will take time, Governor," Sam added, "but there are many mutual benefits. It is sure to work. I will be the first."

Spotswood's eyes opened wide again in surprise. "Sam Layton, the well-known Shawnee fur trader and colony go-between, to take up farming and become a Saponi?" Spotswood's expression slowly changed from surprise to a dubious frown

"It is so, Governor," Sam said. "I believe this is an opportunity to prove that there can be peaceful, productive coexistence among the settlers and our people, and I will be pleased to help if I can. For example, the Nottoway and the Meherrin are Algonquian speakers. They refuse to join the Siouan speaking tribes at Fort Christanna. However, they're eager to have the protection of the fort and willing to look at other ways they can meet your terms and still avoid uniting with the Siouans. I believe I can help work this out. Their concerns can be met by positioning them on the opposite side of the river." Sam left it there. No point in complicating matters by disclosing his intentions to buy land himself as a Virginian.

"Your help is welcomed as always, Sam." The governor hesitated, smiled, and leaned forward again, this time appearing to be reassured. "And while you are planning and moving among the tribes, keep in mind that there will be an Indian school and a place for them to trade and be assured of fair treatment.

"You are on the right track, gentlemen. Yes, let us encourage the tribes to join us on the Meherrin. We will look to Chief Kadomico for their distribution and locations, and as for peaceful coexistence, that is assured. I have made treaties with some of the tribes this past fall, and just this morning Colonel Ludwell sent militia and rangers to take the last of the resistance leaders, the renegade Hawk and his band. We have one of his warriors, a deserter from his band. He will lead us to Hawk's camp. With any luck, we will remove the last of organized resistance in that area.

Kadomico's head snapped up with the mention of Hawk. He managed to keep his composure, but the knowledge of Hawk's impending capture flooded his mind against all efforts to follow the discussion here.

They continued with the details and planning of the next steps until Spotswood had plenty of upbeat news and progress to report to the Bishop of London. Such news would not be ignored. The Bishop was passionately investing resources and applying his influence to convert the children of the savages to Christianity. In addition, he wanted that Indian school established at Fort Christanna. The London Board of Trade would also be pleased to know that Sam Layton and Chief Kadomico would be coordinating the settlement of the tribes. With the support of those two governing forces, he reasoned, Fort Christanna was a certainty. Pleased with the progress these men had made, he adjourned the meeting.

Sam, Kadomico, and Jock stepped up into the carriage that Jock had provided from his stables. Jock took the reins and said, "Gentlemen, I think you made a good impression on the governor. It sure looks like the fort and your people are in for some exciting times, a new beginning in the south. Congratulations."

"Jock, we are indebted to you and Colonel Ludwell for your parts," Kadomico said.

"Yes, the Chief speaks for both of us, Jock," Sam said. "Your intervention on our behalf turned an uncertain situation into a smooth roadway. However, there is much to be negotiated, and we have heard nothing of negotiations, nothing of ownership within Virginia law. The Saponi have much work to do.

"By the way, I think you can expect commerce expansion if the governor is successful in locking in all the trade with the tribes through the fort. In addition, tobacco shipping on the Meherrin River will develop."

"Right you are, Sam. I'm watching it closely. I want to be a part of that expansion. So you see, I might be a little bit self-serving with all this intervention you speak of." Jock smiled at his mild confession and turned into the lane in front of his house.

They stood at the hitching rail. Shadows had lengthened in the late afternoon November sun. Jock fastened a halter lead while Sam explained to him that he would be leaving early the next morning with Kadomico and Keme to bring Tree Son up to date and to get started on settling the tribes.

Keme waited respectfully at the gate. He had seen their approach and had alerted Rebecca, who now stood on the porch brushing a bit of flour residue from her apron.

Kadomico joined Keme. There would be much to tell him, but later, on the trail. Somehow they must warn Hawk, but how?

The next morning Sam, Kadomico, and Keme said their thanks and goodbyes to the Adams and struck the trail for the ferry and on south to the fort. They camped one night near the Nottoway River. The next day about noon, they arrived at the building site of the fort. After greetings, they exchanged news and updates with Tree Son.

"I'll be leaving as soon as you can spare me, Tree Son," Sam said. "I have to go back to the Shenandoah for my canoe and a few belongings. It will take some time, maybe two full moons, maybe more, depending on weather and trouble. Waya is a valuable traveling companion. I hope you can spare him."

"Yes, Waya will go with you. Right now, we need you to show us how to train the warriors on the muskets and the care of powder and ball—maybe one or two suns."

"Done," Sam replied. "Let's start right away with locating protected storage for the powder."

Kadomico motioned to Tree Son and said, "Keme and I must continue on, Tree Son. We will prepare our people for the move here. They will be ready when the leaves return. Remember that we have plenty of food in storage if you need it this winter,".

Seth cleaned and oiled muskets, checked powder horns for flawed or leaky parts, and sorted the lead ammunition. Tree Son now had a total of twelve muskets and Sam Layton's two pistols racked up on the walls of his roundhouse. He and Seth were ready to demonstrate care and use of their small armory to selected warriors who, when qualified, could check out guns to practice loading and cleaning but not firing. To conserve the precious powder and shot for actual defense against marauding bands of raiders, highly competitive and well-attended firing practices would be limited and controlled.

Zack had made himself so useful to both Kanti and Tree Son that they had come to rely on him. He was first up in the morning kindling a fire and heating water. He worked with Tree Son, gathering poles and bark and building roundhouses. Fifteen of them now stood in a circle on a plain near the river and the slope leading up to another small cluster of roundhouses at the top. Here, Tree Son and Kanti, Sam and Starlight, and Seth and Zack had set up their houses. Tree Son had expanded his to serve as a longhouse for council meetings, the armory, and extra food storage.

Kanti and Zack were skinning and cutting rabbit, squirrel, and raccoon into roasting sizes. A large gobbler, plucked clean, hung from a tree nearby with other small game carcasses yet to be dressed. The generous supply of hardwood limbs that Zack had gathered from the forest were slowly turning to a bed of cooking coals. Grids of small, straight second-growth hickory limbs were stacked nearby to use for the small game bits and pieces. The turkey and a shoulder of venison were ready for roasting on a spit over the other fire pit.

"Zack," Kanti said, as she cut and skewered the bits of meat for roasting, "we are happy you come back. My English is not so good. Do you understand?"

"I do, Miss Kanti, and your English is jus' fine. I like workin' here. Mr. Seth says he gone try to keep me here as much as he can."

"When we talked before you seemed unhappy," Kanti said, "but now you are not. I think something good has happened."

Zack jumped at the chance to share his good news. "My Ella is goin t' have a baby come early spring."

"Why, Zack, I didn't know you were married."

"No mam, don't nobody else know either 'cept Gladys back on the plantation. Gladys, she raised me jus' like a mother. Ella, she a slave on Mr. Page's plantation. Me 'n Ella, we same as married last summer, not proper married by a preacher but married jus' the same." Zack couldn't stop talking about it, so eager he was to tell someone. Kanti would understand. And although Kanti did not understand every word from Zack, it was impossible to miss the joy in his face and the tone of his voice.

"Slaves can't marry 'les the master say so, Miss Kanti, and Marse Ludwell and Marse Page don't know, least ways not yet," Zack continued. Then the thought struck him that it might be bad for him and Ella when they found out. He just didn't know what might happen. His face turned to gloom as the dark thoughts descended on him. "I jus' don't know what'll happen if they find out."

"Zack, they will know soon, even if they are not told."

Zack was silent. It was more than he could bear. The only thing he could do was talk to Gladys. He and Mr. Seth would be leaving soon. Maybe Marse Ludwell would let him work for Marse Page at night or on Sundays to pay the keep of the baby. Maybe Mr. Seth could talk for him.

"If I ax him, I think Mr. Seth might talk to Marse Ludwell." Zack mumbled the words, unsure whether that was possible and having no idea at all what Seth might say.

Kanti did not hear exactly what he said, but she saw the stress on his black face as he struggled with his thoughts. Saddened by his trouble, she rinsed her hands and stepped over to dry them at the fire, wondering how to comfort him, what to say. Finally, she walked back to where Zack had finished skinning and cutting the small game. He was bent over the waste at his worksite, cleaning and scrubbing away the residue of the butchering, his huge black shoulders moving smoothly under the torn shirt that only partially covered his scarred back.

"Zack," she said, and then waited for him to straighten up and turn to her. She looked up at him, smiling. "It is—." She searched for the English word she wanted, and then continued."Wonderful, you will be a father. I am glad for you and Ella. You will tell me more of this Ella. She must be wonderful too. Do not worry. It will be only good for you and Ella."

It worked. Zack's face made the shift back to pride and love for Ella and the baby. Miss Kanti was right. It was going to be good for Ella. That there was very little to support that notion did not occur to him. Miss Kanti understood just like he knew she would, and she'd said it would be a good thing for him and Ella. That was all he needed to hear.

That night after all others had retired, Kanti came to Sam's and Starlight's bedside. "Father, I know you will leave again early tomorrow, and I must tell you something."

Sam stirred under the blankets and got up on one elbow. "You sure this can't wait until morning, Kanti?"

"No father, it cannot, and it is for your ears only."

Sam patted Starlight. "Might as well hear this. The child gets her determination from you. There'll be no peace until it is said."

"Kanti is troubled, Sam. We will listen," Starlight said.

"All right, Kanti, what is this all about?"

"Father, Zack is in trouble. I am afraid they will hurt him when they find out."

"Go on," Sam said.

Kanti told him all she knew. Sam was relieved that it was no more than that.

"We will help him all we can, Kanti, but I honestly don't believe this will cause him or his woman trouble. I will look into it. Let's get some sleep now."

"Thank you, father, I knew you would help," Kanti said, then slipped back to her own bed.

Sam lay on his back resting his head in his hands, thinking. "Starlight, when I return, you will become the wife of a farmer. What do you think of that?"

"Better that than a widow. Just be safe, Sam Layton."

"No, seriously now. I will buy land, plant tobacco and raise cattle, hogs, chickens, maybe even sheep. What do you think of that?"

"I just wonder why. It seems a lot of work and you are not getting younger."

Sam went defensive. "I am as strong, even stronger than ever before, woman. What do you mean?"

"I know that, but what you speak of sounds like many winters of work. I know you as a hunter and a warrior. These other things you know about, I know nothing."

"Yes, it is true, but you also know more about planting and harvesting than anyone I know. Remember your maize field and the squash and beans. You are a farmer. You will show me how." Then, Sam told her of his plan to build

306

farms on the land of the tribes and teach them how to grow tobacco, market it, and buy blankets, bright cloth, dishes, pots, pans, and kettles. "Women are eager to have these things," he continued.

He had been talking for a long while, much of it just thinking out loud, when noticing Starlight's silent, even breathing, he paused to assure himself that she had not fallen asleep and said, "What would you say to buying Zack and Ella?" Sam chuckled at the notion of buying a slave. It had just popped into his mind as he talked. "They are young and strong, and as you said, we are growing old."

"Yes, Sam, not exactly what I said, but I am here for whatever you say. We sleep now."

Sam pulled her to him. "Not now," he said, as she took her favorite place in his arms.

Kadomico and Keme left the Christanna site after a short visit with Tree Son and Kanti. They reached the Roanoke River about nightfall on a cold day in late November.

"We'll camp here, Keme, and cross over when there is light again." Kadomico pointed out a deep impression in the high rising bank a short way from the river's edge. Made almost invisible by a shield of young cedars, it would offer good protection from wind and rain or snow.

Keme kindled a small fire while Kadomico walked to the river's edge looking for sign of other travelers. Night had not yet settled in. The sleeping animals were just bedding down or roosting, the nocturnal prowlers and feeders not yet moving. Only the fall of the Roanoke waters over occasional limestone outcroppings broke the silence. Kadomico stood on the bank listening, his head cocked toward Keme. Not a sound. Neither was his fire visible, but the air was not still, and though it moved gently and intermittently, anyone downwind would get the scent.

Kadomico returned to the campsite and found a place to sit with his back to the steep rise. A flicker of the small flame fell across Keme's face as he tended the fire and warming water. Leaning against the wall, Kadomico's pride swelled. Keme moved silently and kept the little fire burning brightly and almost smokeless with tiny, dry, hardwood twigs.

"Father, we eat." Keme placed the gourd container of warm water within reach of Kadomico and smothered the fire. He moved back next to Kadomico. They settled down, shared the warm water, and searched their food pouches for parched corn, dried venison, fresh chinquapins and hickory nuts.

"Keme, we must try to find Hawk. Virginia Rangers are riding toward his camp, two days now. We must warn him. Even now, we may be too late, but we must try. Can you remember the way to his camp?"

"Oh no, Father!" Keme exclaimed. "They cannot take Hawk. I think he will die first."

"It is so, Keme, but if he is warned he can escape. It was about here that Mingan brought you to me. Do you recall?"

"Yes, I remember that. Hawk's place is on the other side, downstream, not far, but a long way inland after you leave the river. His camp is on a high hill in the middle of a swamp."

Good, Kadomico thought, they'll not surprise him and no matter their strength, his high ground advantage will be costly to the attackers.

"The Rangers will be mounted, but that will do them no good in a big swamp," Kadomico said.

"The swamp is deep in most places," Keme replied, "but there is one shallow way to the hill. It is hidden underwater."

"We will go there."

Ben Matthews, captain of the militia, was a wilderness wise, hardened Indian fighter and fur trapper, chosen by Colonel Ludwell for this mission. With him were the Indian guide that had betrayed Hawk, five paid Virginia Rangers, and eleven volunteers anxious for the reward money and the small stipend to be paid for their services. They had been camped five days a half mile from the swamp while they collected canoes from the tribes of the Roanoke River.

Matthews had used this time to explore the condition of the swamp. It was a vast area of shallow black water and huge cypress trees, broken occasionally by small islands covered with brush and vines. It would be easy traveling in a canoe but also easy to become lost--no clearings were visible from where he explored. They would have to mark their passage for a safe return.

According to the guide, Hawk's swamp-island hide-out was about a half mile from where they were camped. Shaped like a teardrop, it was about a quarter mile long and half that wide. They would arrive at the point of the tear-drop. From there it sloped upward to a rock outcropping then dropped steeply back to the water's edge. According to his guide, Hawk's band would be camped near the rock. By the end of this day, he would have the six canoes he needed, enough to surround the island and wait until he had some idea of how many of the armed enemy were there. They would break camp the next morning.

Hawk rested near the top of a rocky pinnacle, among stunted, wind-twisted scrub oak and pine saplings. From that position forty feet above the surrounding swamp, he could watch all approaches. Out there beyond a small

309

clearing of water around his island, the cypress trees and occasional tiny islands of brush, briar, and vines shared the black, chest-deep water of the swamp. Fifteen feet below him, his camp occupied a plateau of level ground with two roundhouses and a large pit of smoldering cook fires.

Scouting the teardrop close to the water's edge, Mingan paused to watch two wood ducks rise nosily and navigate expertly through the trees to open space. When the noise receded, the birdcalls and usual sounds of the swamp did not resume.

Mingan strung a bow, shouldered a quiver of arrows, and moved toward the entrance trail.

"Visitors," Mingan shouted up to Hawk, motioning toward the submerged swamp trail.

Hawk rested the long barrel of a musket on a limb of scrub oak and aimed at the trail.

"It is Keme and Kadomico," Mingan said.

Standing in knee-deep water, Kadomico said, "Ho, Mingan. We are here to warn you. The militia comes."

"Stop. We know. Go back now." Mingan's words came low but vehement, followed by Hawk's musket fire, a splash, and excited voices from the dense swamp.

Kadomico pulled Keme with him and stepped off the path into deeper water.

"Mingan, go with Kadomico and Keme. Now!" Hawk's command rang with finality.

He fired again but there were no more voices, no return fire.

Mingan pulled Keme up the bank and motioned Kadomico to follow. Covered by the brush and reeds, they made their way around to the steep end of the island to a canoe hidden among the bank willows.

"No," said Kadomico. "Wait here. I will bring Hawk."

"There is no time. They have canoes. They're moving to surround the island. Hawk will not come,"

Mingan said. He eased Keme over the gunwale and motioned him to lie still while he freed the canoe from the bank. Knowing the agony that Kadomico felt, Mingan turned, faced him up close, and whispered. "There is no time. We go."

A hail of musket shots broke the silence. Hawk returned fire and reloaded his three muskets. Kadomico looked upward toward Hawk and froze. His debt to Hawk penetrated his very soul. His respect and admiration for the dedicated defender of their native land was boundless. He wanted to stand with Hawk just as Hawk had stood with him. But, there also stood Mingan, whose loyalty and allegiance to Hawk and their cause was absolute. Mingan clearly intended to obey his last order from Hawk, take them to safety. Moreover, there was Keme, raised on one elbow looking at him. Kadomico saw Mingan's knowing look. Words could not have been plainer. He must go with them.

"It is as he wishes," Mingan said, and eased down into the water so that only his head was visible alongside the bow. He gripped the gunwale and moved the canoe outward.

Kadomico followed Mingan's lead but turned his head and locked his eyes on the pinnacle. His heart sank, not even a glimpse of Hawk. He murmured, no, no, not this way. The inevitability of it swelled in his throat and dimmed his eyes. They glided away silently into the dark density of trees and swamp.

Hawk watched the six canoes, each with three armed musket men, moving to surround the island. He fired on the ones moving toward the path Mingan had taken. His shots gave the enemy a better notion of his position but interrupted their progress and forced them to cover. There was no return fire. They clearly intended to surround the tiny island, beach the boats, and take him from all sides.

Hawk reloaded the three muskets for the last time. By now, they knew where he was and that he was alone. He moved to the backside of the pinnacle, fired all three muskets into the air, and threw them aside in plain sight. He glanced toward Mingan's canoe, saw that it had safely disappeared, and returned to the other side of the pinnacle.

Six enemy canoes were out there with three musket men in each, widely separated and still well back from the island. He watched them advance cautiously, converging a little but still widely separated. They finally split into two groups and advanced toward opposite sides of the island. He checked the movements of both groups, went belly down in the hillside brush, and worked his way slowly down to the water's edge.

Hawk waited, allowing enough time for the canoes to land and the men to disembark. He chose the nearest canoe, worked his way along the bank among reeds and brush until he reached its stern. Slipping it backward into the water, he gave it a gentle push outward. Moving on, he set the second canoe adrift. He was searching for the third canoe when he heard shouting from the pinnacle. Some of the attackers had reached the pinnacle and had sighted the two drifting canoes They shouted the alert and started crashing down through the brush firing their muskets. But they found no trace of Hawk. He had crossed to the opposite side and now lay hidden.

Meanwhile six of Matthews' group responded to the musket fire by abandoning their search, reversing their direction, and heading back past where they had left their canoes. They filed by within inches of Hawk. When they had passed he rose, soundlessly tomahawked the last man, and eased him down into the marsh.

Hawk returned to the water and set two more canoes adrift. There were now four adrift in the dark waters of the swamp.

On discovering that one of his men was missing, Ben Matthews stopped near the water's edge and sounded recall. Two of his riflemen scrambled down from the camp at the pinnacle carrying Hawk's three muskets.

The first man to arrive reported. "We burned what bows and arrows we found at his camp. There is no evidence of more than two, probably just one man, Cap'n,".

"Nice piece of work, men. Not likely he'll be shootin', but from here on we'll be chasin' an invisible man. You'll not see him until he wants you to. Keep it in mind. "

Mathews stood alongside his canoe. His men, edgy now, made a semi-circle about him and scanned in every direction.

"He's there," shouted one militiaman, as he shouldered his weapon and fired into the brush where the last canoe had been set adrift. The others followed suit, saturating the suspected launch area with musket fire.

"Hold your fire, boys," Matthews ordered. "He's either dead or gone. Either way more shootin' won't help.

"Charlie, you and Jake take this canoe and round up those four driftin' out there. Watch your backsides. It don't look like he'll be shootin' at ye, but he could rise outta that water easy as he could from the brush. For the rest 'o ye, stay together, within two arm lengths of someone. Lonnie is missing. Let's not make it more. We'll camp right here and wait him out."

"And what's 't keep him from escaping on t'other side while we wait? I'm fer scour'n this brush until we flush him out, Cap'n," said Alvin, an impatient young militiaman.

"If he wanted to escape," Matthews replied, "he would have done so when he had the chance with that first canoe. He wants to fight. Let him come to us. He knows every blade of grass on this island. You can't find him if he doesn't want you to. If it's a fight you want, Alvie, you can have the first go at him when he appears, and appear he will."

Charlie and Jake placed loaded pistols within easy reach and paddled out to start gathering canoes. They quickly overtook the four, fastened their bowlines to a towing line, and returned to the island.

When Charlie and Jake had completed their retrieval task, Jake pointed toward the other side of the island and spoke to Matthews. "Cap'n, we spotted the other canoe just out of sight yonder, hidden in grass and brush."

With all canoes and men accounted for, Matthews said, "Charlie, you and Jake go get that canoe, but give me time to get there first. I'll cover you from the bank. You won't see me or I you, so keep talking and talk loud. I'll want to know, and I want him to know, where you are at all times. The canoe is our bait. Everyone else, stay here." Matthews strapped two pistols tucked in a skin pouch onto his back and disappeared into the brush. Although his men watched and listened carefully, neither they nor Hawk could detect his movements as he made his way through the dense foliage.

Hawk had also found that canoe and had taken a place in the water among the offshore cypress trees. Many cypress knees rose several inches above the water and made a convenient cover. From his vantage point, Hawk could see the beached canoe. He watched as Charlie and Jake approached the area.

Nearing the place of the hidden canoe, Matthews found a bayberry thicket from where he could scan the lay of the land, unseen. He finally spotted the canoe high on the bank where the cover thinned a little. The brush and grass were thickest beyond it. Matthews was still too far away to risk exposing himself, but he could probably make it safely to the cover of an old rotting tree trunk there on his side of the canoe. He could not see Charlie or Jake but he could hear bits of their chatter as they moved in. Certain that Hawk would attack there, he retrieved both pistols from his back, and listened to Charlie and Jake's voices.

"Thar she is, Jake. Just ease me in and I'll fetch 'er quick like." Charlie put his paddle alongside his knees and leaned forward over the bow. Kneeling and paddling from the stern, Jake eased their canoe forward. Hawk slipped under the shallow water and moved toward them.

Charlie stretched out over the bow to grasp a reed and guide the bow toward a narrow inverted U-shaped inlet of water at the beach. As he leaned and reached forward, something grabbed his wrist and pulled him overboard. Jake immediately shifted his weight to counter the over-turning canoe, but with Charlie in the water, there was nothing to counter and the canoe upset, spilling Jake into waist-deep water with the flooded canoe between him and Hawk.

Hawk shifted his grip on Charlie to a headlock and pulled him to the bottom. There, he struck the deathblow with his knife. Then, he pulled himself under the canoe, and exploded through the surface, sucking air around the knife clenched in his teeth. He reached for the sputtering Jake with both hands, his bare back to Matthews, who stood legs-apart with both pistols at the ready.

Hawk felt no pain, just a blinding flash of light that seemed to numb his arms and legs, and he crumpled onto the flooded canoe, one ball in his heart, the other in his collapsed right lung.

Across the swamp, the shots were barely audible, but Kadomico had been reading the sounds from the battle site. Something told him the pistol shots were final. He choked back the tears and turned away from Keme and Mingan.

32

In early January, 1714, two fur-clad men turned their beautiful birch bark canoe away from the rough waters of the York River into the mouth of Queens Creek. They were about to put a welcomed end to a cold nine-week journey from the Shenandoah River. Although it was well past noon, dark skies laden with moisture hid the sun and showered the bleak land below with sleet and rain mixed with snow, and a gusty wind attacked their bearded faces with punishing force. They would have stopped and taken cover under the canoe, except they were so close to Capitol Landing, their destination at Williamsburg that they pushed on.

The tide was running with them and the brush-covered creek banks gave them occasional protection from the vicious wind. Waya, the Saponi warrior, rode the bow position, Sam Layton the stern. Between them lay a beaver-skin sack bulging with silver and gold coins. They had been traveling nine weeks: north on the Shenandoah River to its confluence with the Potomac, then east, portaging around Great Falls and Little Falls and on to the Chesapeake Bay before turning south. They followed the Chesapeake shoreline southward to the York River and Queens Creek, the final leg of their journey.

The Capitol Landing dock was vacant. Beyond dockside was an open shelter. They unloaded the cargo and lifted it onto the dock and over to the shelter. Sam left Waya there while he made his way about a mile to get help from Jock Adams. Sam's legs stretched into long strides, relieved to be free of the hours of restricted kneeling position in the canoe.

Just before twilight turned to darkness, Sam's knock on the door surprised Jock. He declined Jock's insistence for him to warm by the fire and requested a team and a carriage or cart.

"We have cargo we best not leave unattended overnight," Sam said.

"But you and your man will stay the night, surely," Jock said.

"Of course they will, Jock. No need to ask that," Rebecca gently scolded. Her concern was obvious. The dark shape before her was covered with buffalo hide, hooded in soft fur with a nine-week beard leaving only the whites of the eyes discernible. "Sam, your room will be ready when you return." Rebecca had seen enough wilderness men emerging from long journeys on hunting and trapping trips to recognize the single-minded focus possessing Sam.

Jock pulled on a pair of boots, a heavy fur coat, and stepped out, striding toward the gate. Sam followed like a ghostly shadow. Not much longer, was the only thought he permitted himself. He had still to make the stable, harness a team, and collect Waya and the beaver skin of money. The snow had stopped but the wind was picking up and the sleet and rain continued. The road would be filled with deep mud-filled ruts and washouts. His debt to Jock was growing. But his legs responded to the exercise and stretched into the walk, and in spite of his determination to keep his mind on the freezing tasks before him, he warmed to the thought of ending the journey when his tasks were done.

Later, the three men sat by a four-log, seasoned-oak fire, blazing brightly while they sipped the neat brandy and hot tea Rebecca served. The beaver skin of gold and silver coin sat on the floor near them.

"I really don't know how much is in that skin, Jock." Sam swallowed the burning brandy. "I never counted it. It has been in the making for nearly fourteen years. I traded a lot on the St. Lawrence River. There the French seemed to have the gold francs but also Spanish doubloons, pieces-of-eight and lesser coins in silver. Here in Virginia, gold and silver was less likely to be available, but sometimes it was, especially from ship's crews.

"I guess it depends on how much is gold and how much is silver. But if you collected just £40 a year, it could easily come to £500."

"It could be twice that, Jock, even more. We had some good years and there were several Shawnee trapping beaver. I often took their catches to market as well as my own."

They agreed to sort the coins by country, mostly Spanish, French, and English, and make a preliminary count the next day. Jock would see to the safekeeping.

"I won't need the money until the patent office is ready to disperse land except for one matter, and on that I need your help," Sam said.

"All right, how can I help?"

"Can you make arrangements for me to buy Zack from Phillip Ludwell? Zack Hunter is his name, I have been told."

The idea caught Jock by surprise, but he saw the benefits of it immediately and responded likewise. "I'll work on it, Sam. An excellent idea, but Zack is a valuable asset. It could be costly, the market is strong this time of the year with the planters preparing for the growing season. The property transfer papers will take some time."

"Good. You can tell Ludwell the offer is dependent on Zack's willingness and that Zack will continue working the Christanna site with Seth Jackson and me until it is finished. After that, he will work my land as long as he wishes and just leave it at that. In addition, will you please also draw up confidential papers that will make Zack a free man and keep it confidential until we see how all this is going to work out?"

Jock assured Sam that his offer looked reasonable, and he would meet with Ludwell as soon as possible. He would bring in an accountant the next day to divide and weigh the coins, and to secure them safely with Sam's approval.

"Jock, there is more for me to do tomorrow, and if for a fair fee you will represent me, I will not be needed here. I do insist, however, on paying for your services—and I am deeply grateful to have them and all the other support you have given."

"A fee is not necessary, except for the accountant's expense."

"It is a condition of our arrangement, Jock. If you refuse, I will find other quarters. That has to be final. I need you to act for me, and I need to pay you for your help since I cannot be here for all that has to be done."

"As you wish, Sam, I'll draw up the papers. You will be off tomorrow, then?"

"Yes, I am going to Middle Plantation to find Luther Kingston and let him know that Zack is the father of one of the plantation's unborn slaves. Zack considers himself married to the mother, Ella. I don't know what Kingston can do about it, but the least he can do is see after the mother and child and make it allowable for Zack to visit."

Jock took a deep breath. Is there no end to the Sam Layton surprises? Does he really plan to abandon his Shawnee heritage, become a Saponi, a Virginia citizen, a slave owner, a matchmaker and a landowner? Jock glanced at the unbelievable beaver skin bag of gold and silver and shook his head.

"I see," he said. "No doubt Kingston will help. He has been very vocal about Zack saving his life on the trail." Jock hesitated, thinking. "Sam, you overwhelm me with these surprises, but I am glad to be working for you."

"*With* me, I hope, Jock. It will take both of us for me to come out of all this without making enemies on both sides. I am counting on the help of many: you, Zack, Kadomico

319

and Tree Son, Spotswood, Kingston, and Ludwell, to mention a few. So you see, it is a lot to ask, and some of it is without precedent."

Given their similar backgrounds as white Indian captives, rescued, and adopted by different Virginia farm families, Jock knew Sam as no other knew him and had deep confidence in his ability. In addition, he could see the extraordinary business opportunities—untested and without precedent, yes, but entirely possible.

"I'm with you, Sam. Make my house your headquarters in Williamsburg."

Sam smiled as he replied. "Seems I have already done that, but I do appreciate the spoken invitation."

"You're family, Sam. Say no more about it."

"Done," Sam replied. He took the last sip of the brandy and stood. "We leave for Christanna as soon as I have seen Kingston and we find storage for the canoe. We'll come back for it when the weather warms."

"I see you've still a lot of traveling ahead of you. It is a couple of miles to where you'll find Kingston. Take a mount from my stable and feel free to do that any time. I'll see about Ludwell tomorrow, may even be able to meet with him before you leave," Jock replied. Then pointing to Waya, who was sound asleep, he smiled and continued, "In spite of our exciting and lofty business talk, it looks like your companion has found more important matters to attend to."

"Good judgment." Sam extended his open hand. Jock took his forearm in the Indian fashion of trust and friendship.

Luther Kingston, nearing sixty years of age, walked the partially frozen ground of what had been a cornfield the previous year. He wrapped the three-quarter length coat lined with sheepskin closer about him and turned up the generous collar against the steady January wind. It was actually a bit early to be out in the weather, but Luther could stand the four walls of a house just so long. The outdoors suited him, awaited him, no matter the weather, but he had to admit this was stretching it. However, planting time was not far off. He shuffled inside the coat and squinted past the downturned hat brim into the afternoon sun. He did not recognize the rider approaching him, also wrapped in a heavy coat with upturned collar, but he did recognize the fine Arabian stallion from the Williamsburg races.

Sam rode up alongside Luther and dismounted. "Sam Layton, Mr. Kingston, from Williamsburg," Sam said. "We met at Fort Christanna last summer."

"Luther'll do, Sam. I recognized the horse. Runs a respectable race for Jock Adams on our summer Saturdays." The two men shook hands now on common ground, immediately at ease with each other, and began exchanging news and opinions on the fort as they made their way back toward the Middle Plantation barn. At one point, their discussion reached the Indian attack where Luther, thanks to Zack Hunter, had narrowly escaped with his life. That had happened on his first expedition to the building site. It was the perfect time for Sam to mention the reason for his visit. They came to the barn and stepped inside. While Luther forked fodder for Sam's horse, Sam walked over to the horse stalls, admiring the animals and farm equipment. It had been several years since he had been inside such a barn and he recognized the hanging plow lines, harnesses, cart, slides on wooden runners and stockpiles of feed. He returned to the doorway and propped up on the cart just as Luther hung the hayfork on a wall peg and turned to Sam with a small bottle of brandy.

"Thank you, Luther. A taste of brandy on a day like today couldn't be more welcome."

"Well put, Sam." Luther passed the tiny bottle of amber liquid just as the two found seats, Luther on a huge tool box, and Sam on the end gate of the cart.

"Luther, reason I'm here is to tell you about the slave Zack, the one you just mentioned as taking that arrow for you out on the trail. I am making an offer to buy him. If it goes through, Zack will leave Green Spring to work the fort, maybe for me eventually. Problem is, Zack is the father of a baby about to be born to a slave girl name of Ella here on Middle Plantation."

"Well, yes we all know about Ella being pregnant, but not that Zack is the father. That's hard to believe. We haven't seen anything of him around here at all."

"I just learned of it recently. No doubt Zack visited Ella at night."

"That doesn't say much for our dogs. Generally speakin', I wouldn't expect man nor beast to get anywhere near our buildings without us knowin' it day or night. Good dogs, if I do say so."

"Could be Zack knows about staying downwind from dogs. He's done a lot of hunting with the Ludwell men. Whatever the case, it is true. I just wanted to let you know that I will help with expenses or any other way I can."

"I'll take your word for it, Sam. You can tell Zack he can visit Ella and the child any time he wants. Just let me know in advance, and no more of those night shenanigans. Ella is pretty far along. We'll take good care of her."

"It is more than I could ask, Luther, and I do appreciate it. Here is about ten pounds in silver for expenses they're bound to have, medical help or other. You have only to notify me when more is needed. I'll be at the fort from now until it is finished, but Jock Adams represents me and he will reimburse you as needed."

"I'll be down at the fort from time to time myself. We're providing some of the labor. I will work with Adams as needed and keep an account for you."

The two men shook hands, and Luther opened the barn door as Sam swung into the saddle and reined his horse toward the outside.

33

Having just returned from one of his trips to Christanna in late February of the new year, Seth was sitting at the Stilson's oblong dining room table. Even though it seemed right that he fill that vacant space across from Ann with Ray Stilson at the head and Mary opposite him, he could not relax there. He had learned to seat Ann, and now he had the proper clothes for visiting and dining, but there seemed an insurmountable collection of manners and behavior in Mary Stilson's dining room. Each one was a challenge to Seth.

Ann raised smiling eyes to meet Seth's as she leaned forward to taste the delicate turtle soup. Being the perfect hostess and aware of Seth's dining shortcomings, Mary Stilson made sure that he was not embarrassed. Tonight their only servant, Amanda, brought dishes to the table for diners to serve themselves. One was a roasted hen. Mary saw to it that Ray carved enough for Seth before he passed it. Seth managed the peas by watching Ann, was glad that Mary served him bread, and remembered that the main purpose here was conversation.

"Mrs. Stilson, it is a pleasure to be at your table again. Thank you for having me." Seth raised his glass of Madeira to Mary and said exactly the words he had practiced from a previous conversation with Ann. Mary beamed. Still a long way to go but the fellow was learning, Mary thought, as she nodded in response to the compliment.

Seth gave them an account of his trip. He made it sound safe and exciting: extraordinary forests, soil-rich savannas, and a navigable river to the Carolina sounds and the markets in Norfolk and Charleston. Ray followed up with questions about progress on the fort and shipping on the river. Mary asked about the nearest English settlement, church, and school. Ann finally interrupted the questions, rose and excused herself. Mary joined her and they retired upstairs not only to give the men some time alone with their brandy and man-talk, but to refresh themselves and to test each other with their opposing viewpoints of Seth, the frontier, and Ann's future.

Ray lit his pipe and led Seth to the drawing room. The lad knew his business and his limits, eager to learn, trustworthy, young, strong, and bound for the adventures of the frontier. Ray admired Seth, actually envied him in many ways, but he refrained from considering outright approval of him as a family member until Ann declared her intentions.

In about half an hour, the chatter of Mary and Ann on the stairway preceded them in the drawing room. On hearing it, Ray interrupted a description of fashioning tools at the forge and looked toward the doorway.

"More about this later, Seth," Ray said. "We're about to be rewarded for our patience. We may even learn what those two have been talking about all this time." He rose when mother and daughter entered; their brightly colored silk gowns flowed past tiny waists to conceal their ankles but not the black leather shoes. Seth was awestruck by their beauty. He had been with them all evening but had not seen them like this: together, smiling, beauty beyond description. It did not occur to him that they had spent the last half hour freshening make-up, combing and resetting each other's hair, selecting colorful handkerchiefs and bright shawls as they prepared for this entrance.

Ray seated the women and poured cordials while Mary explained that just a small one would be enough. She had a few things to do and would say goodnight shortly. Ray read the signal, measured the remaining brandy in his snifter, and prepared to leave with her.

When the door closed behind her parents, Seth and Ann were left standing side-by-side at the fire, two tall, young adults, bathed in the flickering lights of the fire and a standing candelabrum. She turned slowly to face him, closer than they had ever been. She lacked only a hand's width matching his height. So close was she that he had to tilt his head to see her upturned face. There he saw the flames of desire moisten her eyes. Seth's rational thinking dissolved into oblivion. Gone were all thoughts of his low life in Newgate prison, indentured service and his obsession with a life on the frontier, his poverty, her family's wealth, his illiteracy, her education—all of them vanished. He touched her waist and she came to him, her head resting on his shoulder. They stood there holding each other without speaking for a long time. Finally, Ann stepped back laughing with tears forming on her eyelids.

"I have long wanted that," she said, as she led him to a chaise longue.

Seth's head was still spinning with the realization of what had happened, unplanned, actually undreamed of. He had hoped to have a long conversation with Ann, tell her how much he liked being with her even though with all his faults he could not expect more than friendship, but that he would someday be a successful planter. That was as far as he could see, as far as he could confidently go. This embrace turned all that upside down. His mind could not begin to sort out all the implications.

Ann had no such misgivings.

"Seth," she said, as they seated themselves close to each other, holding hands, "I am proud of you. You are the future of Virginia. I am excited that you are involved in development of the frontier, a man on his own with the new world before him. I have spent so much time away in London, I had forgotten what a wonderful place Virginia is, and here you are making it more so."

Reason was slowly returning to Seth, and these words from Ann eased his confusion about the previous moment. "It is true, Ann. Many wonderful things are about to happen in Virginia. Many of the men and women I work with now depend only on the forest, streams, and earth and know how to live within those limits. Others learn from them and add their knowledge of taking more from the land and fur trade. Virginia offers unlimited opportunity to anyone willing to work and to learn."

Seth had never put all those notions into words and Ann was hanging on to every syllable. There was more and Seth was holding forth as never before when Ann interrupted.

"Don't you see, Seth. We are young. We will see all this happen, the very things you speak of." Her enthusiasm encouraged him. Her questions gave him cause to think more deeply.

"True," Seth replied, "but there is much to learn. I often go to the patent office to see the papers they post outside and listen to others talk about them. Sam Layton talks a lot about books and such, and he sets a lot of store by them."

Reluctant to admit that he could not read very well, Seth continued. "I can cipher pretty good, but it takes me a while to read most anything. Sometimes I wish I was a better reader."

"And you shall be, Seth. I will read all your papers to you, and I will teach you to read and write. You come here every day you can and we will work together. You'll see."

They talked on and on until they heard the door slam.

"That will be my brother, Nathan," Ann said, "in from a night out with his rowdy friends. Expect him to come in with some silly remarks. If he does, I'll kill him."

No sooner were the words out than the door opened, and Nathan leaned through the doorway and said, "Oops, sorry for the interruption, sister. Evenin' to you, Mr. Jackson."

The message from Ann's straight-arm and pointing finger was clear enough for Nathan. Smiling with satisfaction and feigned innocence, he quietly closed the door.

Ann heard the reassuring footfalls carry Nathan and his mischief safely away. Turning back to Seth she said, "Brothers!"

"Well, it is obvious also that he cares about you. Maybe he doesn't like the idea of me calling on you."

"More like he just wants to devil me."

Seth looked down searching for the right words but there were none. "I had better be on my way, Ann." He started to rise, but Ann put a staying hand on his forearm and leaned toward him.

Ann wanted to keep talking. This evening was a beginning. She would be with Seth every chance she had, in church, at the races, fairs, wherever and whenever she could. She might even become a frontier wife someday, but for now it was enough to be with Seth, to be seen with him, and to help him achieve whatever he chose to do. He was an unusual man with enormous potential to succeed. She knew she wanted to be part of his life in any way she could. She took his hand and looked longingly into his eyes.

"Seth, you will do all the things you have set out to do. Colonel Ludwell is lucky to have you handling so much of his interests. He also knows you will succeed. I want to help in any way I can, and I want you to take me to the building site as soon as you can. I must see this place you speak of.

Until then, I will help you do what you need to do here to make things possible there."

Seth stood and pulled her to him. "Beats me, how you know exactly what to say, and the best I can do is mumble." He kissed her gently and drew back, alarmed at the tears in her eyes.

"Wha. . .? You are crying."

"Never mind. It is enough for you to know that I am happy."

Seth wasn't sure. She had returned his kiss, and now she was crying and saying she was happy. He didn't know much about kissing and courting—hadn't been a part of his life at all, except when other boys or men talked, teased, or bragged about it. He knew that this was special and expected to happen privately between couples, but tears and happiness mixed?

Ann found her handkerchief, dabbed at her tears, and led Seth to the foyer for his coat and hat.

"I'll meet you at church Sunday," he said, reaching for her waist again.

"Yes, we will sit together, and you will come home with us for dinner."

That was the beginning of a weekly event when Seth was not away. Mary's objections to Seth diminished with time, guardedly but noticeably. Ray's approval grew. Seth often appeared in the Stilson's home for supper, evening games, and for reading and writing sessions with Ann. He sometimes rode into Williamsburg leading a side-saddled mount from the Green Spring stables for Ann. It fit right in with his job to keep the horses exercised and ready for Green Spring riders. He and Ann rode the local trails, visited friends, and Seth delivered packages and messages and conducted Green Spring business. And, when Seth had to travel to the ferry or to one of the James River plantations, he rode Chance and led a chestnut mare named Katie. The mistress of Green Spring, Hannah Ludwell, often observed these occasions, always with approval and a knowing smile.

Reluctant at first, Ludwell had Seth look into the prospect of selling Zack to Sam Layton who made it clear that Zack must be willing. In the meantime, Ludwell checked the local market for slaves and learned that Zack would bring a high price, maybe £50. The going price in Annapolis of fresh arrivals on the slave ships was £30 to £35 a head. Ludwell was as good a businessman as any, but in the matter of Green Spring slaves, he insisted on humane treatment within the limits of the despicable circumstances of slave law and labor. Ask Zack what he thinks, he had told Seth.

What Zack thought was, no, he'd best not leave Green Spring. Seth couldn't change his mind so he took the matter to Gladys, who called Zack in and scolded him unmercifully in the presence of Seth. Didn't he see it was one chance he would never have again—a way to get shut of fieldwork and Al Ripken and the other overseers?

"And don't tell me that Ella gal over Middle Plantation ain't the cause," she had said. "And if Zack had a lick a sense, he'd see he could do more for that gal if he belonged to Marse Layton than here on Green Spring plantation."

Seth had not known about Ella. Hearing all this, he told Zack he would see after her as best he could, visit her, and give her news of Zack. And Zack couldn't help anyone if Al Ripken killed him. Zack should agree to this sale and leave Green Spring.

Zack finally agreed. Adams and Ludwell made the transfer papers a matter of confidential business. As instructed by Sam, Adams also drew up confidential papers making Zack Hunter a free man and sent the unmarked package to Sam by Seth on his next trip.

Zack and Seth continued to work together delivering supplies and escorting travelers to the site. No one knew when the ownership of Zack actually changed hands. Nothing changed except that Zack spent very little time at Green Spring now. Sometimes he stayed at the fort between trips. He worked timber under Sam's supervision and Seth had told him that Sam would become his master soon, but neither Seth nor Zack knew that the papers they delivered to Sam were Zack's freedom papers.

To Sam Layton, the whole idea of buying and selling slaves was disgusting. To force an enemy into slave labor for the tribe was one thing, but to practice owning, buying and selling, often indiscriminately splitting up families, was abhorrent. Sam was willing to let Virginia do what it felt it had to do with slavery, but he wanted no part of it except in this one case, and he would rid himself of that soon enough. For the time being, he would work to get the Saponi and his own family settled. As promised, Seth visited Ella who was now huge with child. He explained about the sale of Zack and his long absences. He assured her that he and Gladys would do everything they could for her and the baby when it came.

The baby came in February 1714, but it was a month later before Zack returned from Christanna, learned of the birth, and was able to visit mother and child. Arriving at the little cabin, he hesitated at the door. Ella was inside standing with the baby in her arms.

"Our baby?" he said as though stunned.

"His name is John, after John the Baptist."

"His name is John the Baptist?"

"No, just John Hunter."

Ella moved to the doorway so Zack could see the baby. As he gazed at the child, he suddenly felt he was the protector, provider, and guardian of these two before him, as impossible as that was. "It's going to be all right from now on, Ella. Marse Luther says I can visit any time I want, and I will."

Ella motioned Zack in and they talked most of the night away. Zack had to leave the next day, but now for the first time he had someone to look after, a responsibility, someone to love. And, it was going to be all right. Ella would see.

By the summer of 1714, there had been no violence at the site in several months. The treaties that Spotswood had made with the tribes in the spring seemed to be working, and the Saponi, Occaneechi, and Tutelo were slowly migrating to Fort Christanna.

One warm morning in late July at Stilson's blacksmith shop, Seth and Zack were staging a supply of tools and materials for transport to the Christanna site when a family of newly arrived English settlers, the Burkes, stopped and talked with him about settling near Fort Christanna. He explained the trail travel and that they would be among the first white people to take land on the Meherrin River. Tom Burke visited Seth often with questions about farming, Indians, and land management. Finally, they arranged to go with him on the next trip to the building site of the fort. They and Seth had received their patents for land there about the same time.

It was the perfect opportunity to take Ann to the frontier. With his patent in hand, Ann to help him read it, and with the surveyor team present, they would find the markers and walk the boundaries of Seth's fifty acres.

Later, camped on the Nottoway River at the ferry landing, the Burkes were busy settling the family for the night when Ann spread Seth's patent papers over her riding skirt. Seth squatted next to her looking over her shoulder, proudly watching her finger follow the words. She leaned a little to catch the full benefit of the firelight and said, "It says here if the land does not have three acres under cultivation and a habitable building on it within three years, it reverts back to the crown." She spoke softly to avoid attracting attention.

Seth was proud to watch her read the lines, and it was just like her to worry the details. He told her he had heard something like that at the patent office, but no one seemed concerned. "They say it don't mean anything," Seth said, "just in there to keep wealthy land speculators from buyin' up the whole frontier."

Ann kept her voice low but couldn't hide being miffed at the audacity of the condition and Seth's casual response. "Surprises me," she said and decided to leave it there.

Seth reacted to her demeanor more than her words. "Yes, and it could take a lot of work to get all that done, 'specially for a man with a job takin' most of his time— definitely somethin' to keep in mind."

The next day near noon, they ferried over the Meherrin under clear skies. Tree Son, Kanti, and Angus McHale awaited them on the south bank, waving their welcome. Seth and Zack could hardly believe their eyes. There were dozens of men erecting the fort palisade; others were hewing timbers for the buildings at each corner of the pentagon. Teams of oxen snaked great logs to the site where ax men and sawyers converted them to building materials. On that warm summer day the gently moving air was filled with the sounds of biting axes, the swish of planes, and drawknives, and the rasping sound of saws mixing with the fragrance of fresh white shavings, chips, and sawdust.

Seth delivered the package of papers to Sam while Zack brought the packhorses up for unloading within the partially finished palisades. Kanti motioned for Zack to follow her. She and Starlight received the Burkes and offered to show them a roundhouse they could use until they settled on their own property.

As the Burkes followed Starlight with their mounts and pack horses, Tom Burke glanced at Indians all around him. Some were walking with them. He placed his hand on his wife, Elaine's shoulder. "It don't look like we're goin' to be short on help, ma. You goin' to be all right here?"

"Well, we sure can't camp among the workmen. We'd be in the way. And I don't see any other shelter, so I have to say let's be grateful and get on with it."

Elaine always was a practical-minded woman, thought Tom, but he could not help being nervous among so many half-naked men and women. However, it turned out to be a good example of two cultures mixing in a situation where needs overshadowed differences in attitude, language, opinion, and beliefs.

The men at the fort with their steel tools paced themselves and struck a rhythm sustained by the vision of the rising palisade, growing toward house foundations at each corner of the pentagonal wall. Native women replenished firewood, dressed game, repaired and expanded their roundhouses, sewed and stitched leather clothing and moccasins and still found time to offer help to new comers like the Burkes.

Kanti motioned for Zack. Seth nodded his agreement and Zack left the packhorses.

"Zack, someone waits to speak with you . . . in my house. Go."

Zack looked back at the work he had just left. "Miss Kanti, I'm s'posed . . ."

"Don't argue, Zack. Go," Kanti said, pointing. Zack walked up the hill, glancing uncertainly back to where men unloaded packhorses and stored supplies while others continued barking, hewing, and building. He walked on and stepped through the skin-covered doorway into the arms of Ella. His son, John, lay sound asleep behind her on a pole-and-rope bed of furs built into a wall. The surprise so consumed him that he could not grasp the meaning.

Speechless, he alternately embraced Ella and pushed her away at arm's length to see her. Finally, he said, "They didn't tell me."

"I know," Ella said, "They wanted to surprise you. I'm cookin' and washin' for the workmen. Marse Luther fixed it. He tole me I'm hired out to the guvnor.."

Luther Kingston and Sam Layton watched Zack enter the doorway.

"Looks like you did a good thing, Luther."

Luther lit a pipe of tobacco. "Well, at least for the time being, Sam."

"For the time being," Sam repeated thoughtfully. "Yes, true enough, and their next separation will be the hardest yet".

Luther looked up at Sam over the first puff of tobacco smoke, winked, and said, "Unless we fix it."

"Agreed. There's plenty of time yet to work on that," Sam replied.

34

Four years later, in the early fall of 1718, Fort Christanna was a beehive of activity; Indian trade was booming, the Indian school was a rousing success, new farms were coming up all along the Meherrin River, and peace had settled over the area. The Virginia Indian Company was in full swing and paying for fort operations and security.

Two riders made an impressive sight as they approached the stately log home designed and built by Angus McHale for the Laytons. Sam Layton, dressed in buckskins open at the throat and exposing a still massive chest, rode a black Arabian. By his side, Mr. Charles Griffin, the tall, thin schoolmaster of the fort sat, ramrod straight on a bay mare marked with white stockings. As they pulled up to the hitching rail, Griffin brushed aside a shock of unruly blond hair worrying his brow and started to dismount.

"Thanks for a splendid ride, Sam. Not often do I get the chance to leave the classroom. I can walk the short distance to the fort."

"No need, Mr. Griffin. When you get to the fort, just free that bridle and hang it on the saddle. She knows the way home and she knows it's feeding time."

"Never known you to exaggerate, Sam, so I'll give it a try, but I can't help having a little doubt about that."

"Don't give it a thought. I want you to know we are all very proud of what you have done with the Indian school. Virginia, Maryland, nor any other colony, I suspect, can boast a class of seventy Indian students and one hundred percent approval among their families. That French fellow that visited with Governor Spotswood last year, John Fontaine, as I recall, was right when he said the tribes would make you their king if you would permit it."

"I really have to give the credit to the Lord, Sam. I just follow His word and the Book of Common Prayer. It's easy for me. Besides, Governor Spotswood pays me regular, right out of his own pocket. As for Mr. Fontaine, he was impressed that all the children could recite the Lord's Prayer."

"Won't you come in for some refreshment?" Sam said as he dismounted and laid the reins over the rail.

"No, I best be getting on. You have done wonders yourself, Sam. It's now been years since there was any kind of violence around here. The tobacco crops we saw today prove what the natives can do, and your own spread is a beacon for new settlers. And, yes, I am proud of these children of the tribes."

"It does seem to be working, school master, but we have yet a long way to go. I worry about the rumors from London's Parliament and those people speaking against the Virginia Indian Company. The Company provides most of the funds from their profits to run the fort, and there is talk of ruling it a monopoly and closing them down. To lose the support of the Company could lead to abandonment of the fort."

"Be a shame, Sam. Let us pray for the Lord's attention and abide by whatever he divines." Charles Griffin removed his hat, wiped his brow clear of the wayward locks, and backed his mare away from the rail. He shifted in the saddle, pulled the brim of the huge leather hat down against the mid-afternoon sun, and tipped the brim to salute Sam.

"God's blessings on your family, Sam, and my kindest respects to Miss Starlight." He turned the mare onto the carriage road and walked her downhill through the tall pines.

Sam climbed the three steps to his porch. Kanti stepped out to meet him. "Wasn't that Mr. Griffin, father?"

"Yes, I believe so, Kanti. We rode the crop lands together today."

"Wonderful! What did he tell you about the Seth Jackson and Ann Stilson wedding?"

"Well, we didn't discuss that, Kanti."

"How could you not discuss that, father? That is the biggest news in Virginia. And it is rumored that they will visit Fort Christanna. Mr. Griffin is our lay reader here and he would surely know about that. Now he must have mentioned it."

"No, not to my hearing, child. Sorry." Sam looked for but didn't see any way to get past Kanti. Starlight rescued him.

"This way, Kanti. Sorry to say, your father is nearly insensitive to anything but farm tools, horses, and crops these days," Starlight said.

"And young warriors," Sam said, as he picked up Kanti's first-born and accepted a mug of water from Starlight.

Late evening that same day Sam sat on the porch steps. One thing he had never learned was being easy in a chair. His back rested on a banister end-post as he carved a dancing warrior. His grandson stood in the soft pine shavings, arm resting on Sam's drawn- up knee watching him work the piece.

"It's bedtime for that baby, father." Kanti spoke through the open door behind Sam. At the sound of his mother's voice and confident that his grandfather could set the bedtime business aside, the child leaned closer and asked, "Gramda, will you tell me a story?"

Sam laid his pipe and carving down. "Mother, just a few more minutes," he said over his shoulder to Kanti.

When he heard her retreating footsteps, he gathered the boy into his lap, shifted to a comfortable position and looked up. An evening mist was rising on the river beyond. A crewmember steered a raft packed with furs toward the downstream markets.

Zack, followed by little John half running and half skipping to keep up, was crossing just beyond the fenced yard. Zack shifted the ax on his shoulder and waved. They were on their way to their cabin near the back of Sam's property. Ella would be along after managing supper for the fort workers. Sam remembered Zack's answer when he had given him his freedom papers and asked him why he wanted to be a free man.

"Cause, Marse Sam, 'f anything happened to you, no tellin' who I might get sold to. Me 'n Ella, we want to stay with you and Miss Starlight no matter what, and these freedom papers don't make no difference 'bout that. 'Cept now you payin' me jus' like a regular tradesman, 'n I'll be payin' you back for them papers a little along 'til it's right, then I be savin' hard as I can to buy John and Ella's freedom."

Starlight came out, sat down opposite him and the boy, and began decorating a moccasin with brightly colored porcupine quills. Her moccasins brought a good price at the fort trade store.

"So what story shall I tell this young warrior, Gramma?" Sam teased.

It worked. "Oh! Tell me about Hawk, Gramda. Tell me *that* story."

"Well, let me see now, Little Hawk, I'll do my best to remember it." Sam held his grandson close and began the story once again. Starlight paused her stitching and looked at them with eyes as misty as the air closing about them. Little Hawk snuggled, closed his eyes, and saw the great warrior he would become, just like Hawk.

EPILOGUE

Spotswood's vision for Fort Christanna became a reality in 1714 when the palisade walls of the fort were raised and occupation began with the Saponi, several other tribes, settlers, five fourteen-hundred-pound cannon and a well-armed garrison of twelve men. At last, Virginia's southern frontier was secure and safe. Settlers came with families and set up farms. Charles Griffin opened the first successful Indian school of seventy-seven young, willing, and successful students. Indian trade soared, border violence ceased, and the Virginia Indian Company began paying the way of the fort. Then things began to fall apart.

Only three years later on May 24, 1717, Spotswood lost a hard-fought battle with William Byrd II and other fur traders who had yielded the lucrative fur business to the Virginia Indian Company. They argued to the British Board or Trade that the Company was a monopoly. They also charged Spotswood with misconduct, misappropriation of funds, and actions to personally profit from the Christanna project such as the "handsome house" he was building near the fort.

In spite of all Spotswood's brilliant rebuttals, the Board of Trade was convinced. They dissolved the Virginia Indian Company in 1717 thereby losing the funding for fort operations, and a year later, the burgesses voted to abandon the fort. The Saponi moved into the fort and remained there until 1740 when they (and allied tribes) moved north and were absorbed by the Cayuga.

Of the fictional characters in *CHRISTANNA*, Tree Son and Kanti continued as leaders of the Saponi and allied tribes, raised their children in the ways of the Saponi and Shawnee, and eventually migrated west to the Ohio Valley and joined the Shawnee nation.

Sam Layton and Kadomico became prosperous farmers, traders, and trusted go-betweens among settler and tribal issues. Between them, they expanded their land holdings within the six-by-six mile land allocation near the fort and became valuable landowners. Although Sam was the owner of record, he and Kadomico divided the land and the business fifty-fifty. Keme followed his father's example.

Zack and his family were satisfied to live under the protection of Sam Layton and work toward buying the freedom of young John and Ella.

Seth and Ann married and moved into a small house on Green Spring Plantation prepared for them under Mistress Ludwell's direction. They managed a small profit from their fifty acres on the Meherrin River, and Seth's firsthand knowledge of trade and transport on the southern frontier drew him into light business transactions there: guiding, advising, running supplies. Jock Adams mentored him and the business grew. He remained an employee of Green Spring under Colonel Ludwell. The educated Ann Stilson became a valuable business asset to Seth and, like her mother, a leader in the community.

AUTHOR'S NOTE

CHRISTANNA is a sequel to *DANGEROUS DIF-FERENCES, 2010.* It is set in the southern wilderness frontier of the Virginia colony and in Williamsburg in the year 1713-1718. Fourteen years earlier, the capital of the Virginia colony had been relocated six miles west from the site of the original capital, Jamestown, to the more favorable terrain and climate of Middle Plantation. There the town was established and named Williamsburg in 1699.

During the time of this novel, Alexander Spotswood was Lt. Governor of Virginia, and William Byrd II was a member of the colony council and maintained one of the largest plantations in Virginia. The events, dialogue, and behavior appearing with these names, however, are entirely the products of my imagination as are all other names, characters, and events.

Although sachem, werowance, emperor, king, and other words denoting leadership actually appeared in the speech and writing of the times, the title "Chief" is simpler, widely understood, and I use it throughout to denote "leader." The word "Indian" actually encompasses the people of two continents and dozens, if not hundreds of cultures, but I use it in this book to denote only the collective indigenous people of Southeastern America.

Over a period of three and a half years, I have relied on the Virginia Department of Historical Resources, the John D. Rockefeller, Jr. Library, Williamsburg Regional Library, Virginia Historical Society, Colonial Williamsburg Foundation, and Earl Greg Swem Library of the College of William and Mary for the answers to so many questions. In doing so, I have been privileged to meet local historian Martha McCartney and to have by my side at every writing session, *Fort Christanna Archeological Reconnaissance Survey,* 1979 by McCartney and Hazzard. I am indebted to the many people of these organizations who were ever willing and able to guide me through their vast resources to answers and solutions.

The story developed over three and a half years during which time I received the help of a group of successful authors to whom I am deeply grateful. Sally Stiles (*PLUNGE!*), writer, teacher, and editor, organized and led the monthly reviews and edits. Authors Katharine Fournier, *The Reality Series*, Patricia Gray, *Petra*, and John Conlee, Professor of English Literature at the College of William and Mary (novels of ancient Britain), spent hours reading, marking, questioning, and commenting on strengths and weaknesses of the text

Along the way other experts in their own field made valuable contributions. Col. George Pollin, retired U.S. Army, patiently walked with me among the restored fort at Jamestown, pointing out the features of palisades, positions and make of cannon, and checked my interpretations of tactical warfare among the colonists and the tribes. My son, Jeffrey Laird, Certified Mapping Scientist, brought clarity and understanding to the locations and relationships of the tribes, trails, and settlers with maps and diagrams. And I thank B.J. Pryor, a career interpreter with the Colonial Williamsburg Foundation, for the many hours spent reading and pointing out ways to improve the manuscript by bringing it closer to circumstance and life in the Virginia of the first quarter of the 18th century. Finally, throughout the time during which the story developed and after each change, my wife, Johnnie, continued to read, re-read, and read again the manuscript and make suggestions.

When I look back at all the people who have given to this book, I shudder at the debt I bear and smile at my good fortune to know them and to have worked with them. But let the reader be assured, any errors that have survived all this help are certainly mine and mine alone.

ML
Williamsburg, 2013

BIBLIOGRAPHICAL NOTE

During the research and writing of this novel, I found the following works to be rich with examples and descriptions of life in the Virginia and North Carolina colonies. I am particularly grateful to these writers, historians, and archeologists.

Robert Beverly, *The History and Present State of Virginia, 1705*; Edited by Louis B. Wright, 1947

Edmund Morgan, *American Slavery, American Freedom,* 1975

John Lawson, *History of North Carolina, 1709*; Edited by Frances Latham Harriss, 1937

John Fontaine, *The Journal of John Fontaine, 1710-1719*

Gen. LeLouterel, *Military Reconnaissances,Temporary Fortification,and Partisan Warfare for Officers of Infantry and Calvary, 1862.* Translated by John Richardson, Professor of Mathematics, Georgia Military Institute, Marietta GA formerly Major of the 21st Reg't H. C. Troops, C. S. A.

James Axtell, *The Invasion Within*, 1985

Martha W. McCartney, *A History of Green Spring Plantation*, 1998

CHRISTANNA

David E. Hazzard and Martha W. McCartney, *Fort Christanna: An Archeological Reconnaissance Survey,* 1979

Helen Roundtree, The *Powhatan Indians of Virginia,* 1989

John Swanton, *The Indians of Southeastern United States,* 1946

Jamestown Narratives, The First Decade, 1607-1617; Edited with commentary by Edward Wright Haile, 1998

The Virginia Indian Heritage Trail, 2007; Edited by Karenne Wood

John W. Reps, *Tidewater Towns: City Planning in Colonial Virginia and Maryland,* 1972

William Byrd II, *Histories of the Dividing Line betwixt Virginia and North Carolina,* with Introduction and Notes by William K. Boyd, 1967

Sarah S. Hughes, *Surveyors and Statesmen,* 1979

Silvio A. Bedini, *With Compass and Chain,* 2001

William M. Kelso, *Jamestown Rediscovery, 1994-2004*

William M. Kelso, *Jamestown The Buried Truth,* 2006

Margaret Connell Szasz, *Indian Education in the American Colonies, 1607-1783, 1988*

Gay Neal, *Brunswick County,* 1975

MAC LAIRD

OTHER BOOKS By

THIS AUTHOR

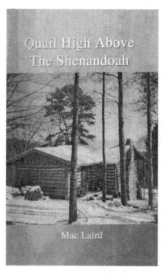

Quail High Above The Shenandoah

Mac Laird

Here is a chronicle of one man's life- changing experiences as he immerses himself in a decades-long labor of love constructing a unique cabin from natural materials in Virginia's Blue Ridge Mountains. The book introduces us to a fascinating array of characters, including greenwood craftsmen, colorful mountain folk—one of whom is a practicing water witch—as well as to skillful (and not so skillful) fishermen and poker players. This book informs us that " *If you build it . . . it will be immensely satisfying, whether they come or not.*"But they came, in great numbers. Who could not? After all it is a cabin of logs on a friendly mountain in the heart of the beautiful Shenandoah Valley

Quail High Books, 154 pages, Paperback
Distributed by Ingram, Inc.
Print-on-Demand by Lightning Source
ISBN   978-0-9825443-1-0
Available at mwww.quailhigh.com, Barnes & Noble, Amazon.com, mslaird1@cox.net,

NOMINATED BY LIBRARY OF VIRGINIA FOR 14TH ANNUAL LITERARY FICTION AWARDS

Recommended & reviewed in "Mindquest Review of Books" by Lightword Publishing"

The masterful, historically accurate account (1700) about cultural differences between Virginia's European settlers and the area's Native Americans, depicts how the indigenous tribes try to adjust to different people and their expansion. The fast-paced literary account includes riveting events and vivid descriptions of the awe-inspiring territory. NOTEWORTHY: The book is suitable for readers of all ages. Woven into the in-depth accounts of Native American cultures is edge-of-your-seat action: canoe river travels, a Nahyssan woman warrior, trading deals, vivid attack accounts, and close combat. Readers will easily visualize the beautiful depictions of the pristine splendor of the Eastern Woodlands.

Published by: Quail High Books, 374 pages,
Distributed by Ingram, Inc.
Print-on-Demand by Lightning Sources
ISBN 978-0-982544303 Paperback,
ISBN 978-0-982544-327 Hardback
Available at www.quailhigh.com, Barnes & Noble, Amazon.com, mslaird1@cox.net

CPSIA information can be obtained at www.ICGtesting.com
Printed in the USA
BVOW08*2317301013

334514BV00001BA/2/P

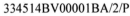

9 780982 544341